Bestow
On Us
Your Grace

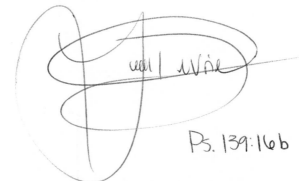

To Mrs. McDowell ☺

Ps. 139:16b

Bestow On Us Your Grace

Jean De Vries

ISBN: 978-0-9974659-7-6

Published and printed in the United States of America by the Write
Place, Inc. For more information, please contact:

the Write Place, Inc.
809 W. 8th Street, Suite 2
Pella, Iowa 50219
www.thewriteplace.biz

Cover and interior design by Michelle Stam, the Write Place, Inc.
Hands woodworking: thinkstock.com – Zoran Zeremski
Heart carved: thinkstock.com – CarlosAndreSantos

Copies of this book may be ordered online at Amazon and
BarnesandNoble.com.

— Prologue —

Kirsten stood in the doorway of her mother's room, barely able to make out the shape of her body huddled beneath the blankets. Despite the dark, it was only 6:30 in the evening, the winter sun having gone down an hour ago. Kirsten listened and was relieved to hear only the sound of her mother's quiet breathing. Last night her mother had woken her with her sobbing, and Kirsten had crawled into her parents' bed, wrapping her eight-year-old arms around her mother. Suddenly, strangely, their roles had been reversed.

She turned from the door and went to the dark living room, picking up an overdue library book and flicking on the lamp beside the couch. She grabbed a box of cereal out of the cupboard and sat down, crunching through the Fruit Loops as she slowly turned the illustrated pages. Turning on the television was out of the question. Nothing was worth waking her mother. Even worse was the pain of watching commercials and sitcoms full of happy children with their fathers.

A strange clattering outside brought Kirsten to the living room window. No headlights or sound of an engine. Only the black form of a horse shifting slightly, a shadowy buggy behind it. The doorbell's piercing chime startled her, even though she was expecting it. Ever since that police officer rang the doorbell just days ago, the sound had become an ominous source of fear. Kirsten's mother shuffled around the corner and turned robotically to the door, her face void of expression. It was either all emotion or none the past few days.

"Hello, Mary." Her mom's voice sounded hollow and wooden as she stood in the doorway, one hand still clutching the doorknob for support. Kirsten silently stepped beside her and wrapped her arm around her mother's leg, staring wide-eyed at a woman in a long dress who was standing on their front step holding a covered basket.

"Elizabeth," the bonnet-headed woman said, blinking slowly. "We are so very sorry for yer loss."

Her mother nodded. Why was she nodding? Daddy wasn't lost. Kirsten knew precisely where he was. In a hole in the ground at the cemetery in town.

Kirsten's mother accepted the basket from the woman. She'd seen others dressed like her before, of course. They lived all around. In fact, it was Kirsten and her family who were the oddity in this particular area of the county.

The woman turned to look for a long moment at Kirsten, who stared back up at her. Kirsten saw there the same expression all the grown-ups gave her lately. No one smiled at her anymore.

"May you find comfort and strength in the Lord," the woman said, turning her attention slowly back to Kirsten's mother.

"Thank you," Elizabeth mumbled. Kirsten could feel her mother's leg tremble and gripped tighter. Slowly, Elizabeth shut the door and turned to stumble back toward her room, pulling away from Kirsten's grasp. She carelessly dropped the basket in the middle of the living room floor. Kirsten went to watch out the window as the woman climbed back into the buggy. The horse started forward in a slow circle and left the yard.

"Mom?" she said, turning to see that Elizabeth had nearly reached the doorway to her room. "Why don't they drive a car?"

Her mother stopped and spoke over her shoulder. "They don't have one."

"Why not?"

"They're Amish."

— CHAPTER ONE —

Ten years later

Mary leaned far over the table, stretching to place the bowl of steaming mashed potatoes in the center. Footsteps sounded on the wraparound porch just moments before the screen door screeched its own announcement, then slammed shut. Following closely behind, louder thudding footsteps sounded against the floor boards and the door screeched open again. Her young daughters quickly finished setting the silverware on the dining room table and sat down, looking so small in the high-backed chairs. The sound of boots being peeled off and thumping to the floor was soon followed by water splashing down over what she knew would be dirty hands and forearms.

She stood upright when Daniel came in the room, his face already smiling above his beard, his eyes glancing from the table to her and meeting her gaze. Even after all these years, she found it impossible not to smile back into his dancing eyes, crinkled at the corners. Caleb slipped quietly behind his father and sat eagerly in his place between the wide window and the table that stretched along it. Mary was giving Caleb a disapproving look as he pulled the platter of fried chicken close to him when she saw a shadow fall across the table. Silas walked around behind her, his silhouette stretching far across the kitchen and into the living room.

She watched him lower into the ladder-back chair across from Caleb and shook her head in wonder. It never ceased to amaze her how one day they went from looking so small, as four-year-old Anna Mae did now, to growing up so quickly that they towered over their parents. All of her sons had passed her up. Three of them now stood every bit as tall as or taller than their father's six feet. Only Caleb still looked up to speak to Daniel, though it wouldn't be long before even that would change. At the age of fourteen, he was following in his brothers' large footsteps.

Mary turned to Amy, her eldest daughter, as she set the plate of freshly sliced bread on the table and took her place next to Caleb. Mary quickly sat and looked across the table to where Daniel was waiting. With a nod, they dropped their heads simultaneously in silent prayer. At her husband's intake of breath, their heads raised and Caleb began eagerly filling his plate.

She'd heard of some Amish families who ate in silence, spending their mealtime eating instead of talking. But she'd always been thankful for Daniel's love of storytelling and conversation. The chatter around their table whenever they were gathered was boisterous and lively. Though there were many times she had to remind the little ones to keep eating, she'd never minded much. The reward was hearing about their day and getting a window into their minds and hearts.

Tonight, the discussion was about the frogs Caleb had discovered down at the creek that afternoon. It wasn't long before he had his three sisters excited about a trip to the creek after supper. Silas, ever the quiet one, listened and smiled at their excitement but said little. Nothing unusual there. His older brothers, David and Michael, had been and were still so unlike him. Silas was an ocean of perfectly still water while they were bubbling brooks.

Anna Mae and Shelby Jo were bouncing in their chairs while Caleb quickly shoveled mouthfuls of sour cream chocolate cake into his mouth. With a smile and a nod from Daniel, their chairs scraped back across the floor and four of her children went racing outside. Even seventeen-year-old Amy followed, the bottoms of her bare feet flashing white beneath her dark blue skirt as she ran.

Silas calmly sat and slowly ate his dessert.

"Joseph King was asking me why you haven't been at the Singings lately," Daniel said to Silas, who was seated close to him.

Mary stood and quietly worked at clearing off the table and doing the dishes. Her ears were carefully tuned to listen for Silas's response. They needn't have been. He gave none.

"Yer brothers were building houses and planning weddings by your age," Daniel said with a smile. It could have been taken as a cruel statement, but Daniel's easy way and gentle smile showed his lighthearted intention.

Silas simply stared at the patterns in the wood grain of the handmade table in front of him and shrugged.

David and Michael had both taken wives at the age of twenty. Silas would be twenty-one within the week. Certainly not a cause for concern but for the fact that he did not seem at all interested in such an endeavor. For the past several months he hadn't even been going to Singings on Sunday nights, as was typical for single boys his age. It was how the Amish young people socialized and found marriage partners. That Silas wouldn't go was…a puzzle to her.

Daniel was undeterred by Silas's lack of conversation. "Joseph's daughter, Emily, seems a nice young woman. She's about your age, isn't she?"

Silas only nodded. Though now, Mary observed, he looked visibly uncomfortable. Mary knew Emily King. And though she was nearly twenty years old, she was still unattached and a sweet girl. Emily was a fine baker, famous for her coffee cakes, and Mary had noticed at several quilting frolics how fine her stitching was. She had a quiet, gentle, and shy way about her, much like Silas. She'd make a *gut* Amish wife.

"Oh well, perhaps she'll wait for our Caleb," Daniel teased and smiled at Mary. She watched as Silas's mouth tried to grin, but he gave up. Silas caught her watching him and quickly averted his gaze out the window.

"Perhaps Silas has his sights set on someone else," Mary lightly reminded Daniel.

Daniel turned his gaze back to Silas, his brow raised in a question.

"No," Silas answered.

"Amy would appreciate yer going to Singings again. She doesn't like to drive herself, especially when it's a long ways," Mary encouraged.

Silas was again silent, staring out the window with a determined set to his face.

"Speaking of Amy, I should go down to the creek and fetch her and the children back. They and their muddy, frog-filled pockets." Daniel winked at Mary. His boots made loud, slow stomping sounds down the front porch steps. Silas stood to follow him.

"You'd like being married, Silas," Mary called to him, stopping him at the door. "Someone to help ya with yer work. Someone to talk to, raise a family with."

She watched his shoulders rise and fall in a silent sigh. "Yes, Mama," he said without turning to face her. Mary watched Silas walk slowly away to the refuge of his workshop.

.ₒ◖ ◗ₒ.

Silas crunched across the gravel driveway that ran through the farmyard and tugged open the door of the workshop. The light was dim despite the abundant presence of windows. He'd installed those just a few years ago, hoping to be able to work longer hours in the shop. Of course, in a woodworker's shop, the windows were perpetually covered in a layer of sawdust. He could see it floating even now in the sun-streaked air. Deciding against working on the rocker he had started that afternoon, he walked back out and passed the house on his way to the garden that stretched for two full acres between the barn and the road. The earliest sprouts were just peeking through the perfectly straight rows.

It wasn't that the idea of a wife wasn't appealing to him. It was. More than he could say. He simply had never found anyone who was...right. He'd driven a few girls home from Singing. But after years of attending, it was getting old. He was tired of the same old song-and-dance—the jockeying for position and the hopeful glances of girls he had once considered friends but who clearly wanted more. Most of his friends had sought baptism and gotten married in the last year. It confused him a little every time he sat amongst the congregation and watched his buddies marry girls they had known all their lives. He had often wondered, but never asked, what had changed—how they had come to see a certain girl as a potential wife rather than an old classmate or neighbor.

He didn't mean to worry his mother. His father's questions were as much for her benefit as his own. David and Michael had been so eager and determined when it came to socializing. But it wasn't Silas's way. And compared to them, he imagined he looked reserved, shy, and withdrawn. For years his mother had needlessly worried that he was a fence-jumper—that he might one day leave the People. His *Rumspringa* had caused her near constant stress, though Silas's running-around years were extraordinarily tame compared to those of other young people. When he'd bent the knee and received baptism, he could almost hear her audible sigh of relief. Silas had never been tempted to leave his family, his way of life, or his faith. But neither did he always feel that their well-worn paths would be his.

The cool spring air sifted through his shirt, and he turned to watch the sun sink slowly behind the tree-covered hills to the north and west. The Miller farm stretched north of the gravel road that ran east and west. A few miles south, just across the highway, was their family store—the Amish Country Market. His mother and father worked there six days a week along with their hired staff, who were other Amish from the area. Silas, Amy, and Caleb worked at home. Amy watched their little sisters, kept house, and cooked meals. Silas managed the few cows, the horses, the garden, and the small orchard. But his primary interest and occupation was that of furniture making. As Caleb had gotten older and was able to help around the home more, Silas had been freed up to spend more time in his woodshop. Together, the whole family worked to supply produce and goods to the market. Even Silas's brothers and their wives supplied whatever they could to the inventory of the store. Spring and summer months were busy with gardening and took hours away from his woodworking. But the long, cold winter months were an oddly welcome excuse to spend his time doing what he truly loved.

Silas surveyed the garden, making a list of things he needed to tend to in the morning, as the sound of a car grinding across the gravel road stole his attention away from the plants. He watched as a beat-up car sped by in a cloud of dust. It was a familiar vehicle. Almost no one traveled east of their driveway except for their English neighbors, the Walkers. He'd seen the car and an old van parked near their trailer, though the car was a more recent addition to the sparse yard.

The sounds of his siblings returning from their frogging adventure turned his attention back to the house. With a sigh and a smile, he turned and made his way to meet them in the yard.

.୭ହ ୨ୡ.

Kirsten's stomach roiled as her car tumbled over the loose gravel. The plastic bag on the passenger seat was practically screaming at her. She checked the clock on the dash—7:30. Her mom wouldn't be home from her job at the gas station for several hours. It was plenty of time, but Kirsten slammed on the brakes in front of the old trailer, snatched the sack off the seat, and ran inside.

Her hands shook badly as she tore open the box and dropped the contents onto the vanity. The tremors were so bad she could barely read the instructions. She knew what the results would show her. Of course she did.

Seconds later, two little lines intersected, forming a plus sign in the tiny plastic window. Kirsten stared at it, blinking rapidly, breathing only shallow gasps of air. Her hand gripped the vanity and the room spun around her. She felt herself shaking violently long before the first sob tore through her chest. Slowly, she slid down the wall to the worn linoleum floor, her slim body quaking as silent sobs heaved through her. Tightly, she hugged her knees to her chest and buried her face in her arms as she cried, one hand still clutching the small plastic stick.

"No," she moaned quietly. "Just...no."

It had been a stupid mistake. Why she'd ever gone to that party, she didn't know. She'd regretted it almost as soon as she had gotten there. Out in the middle of nowhere there had been dozens and dozens of teens, a huge bonfire, and lots of alcohol. She'd carried around a cup just to fit in, but she'd never tasted a drop. She had sat way back in the shadows, bundled in her winter coat. Which is where Logan Webb had found her. Everyone knew Logan. He was the quintessential senior football jock, and Kirsten had been in shock when he sat down next to her and started talking to her. Then he'd offered to let her warm up a bit in his car. How obvious. How stupidly obvious. And she'd fallen for it. She hadn't realized just how much he'd been drinking until he started to kiss her. The euphoria of having a boy, and a cute one, pay attention to her had intoxicated her more than any drink could have. In that cold backseat, she had agreed to way too much, had lost her innocence, and had had a nagging suspicion the entire time that she'd regret it.

The whole experience had been quick and aggressive. Logan hadn't wasted any time being gentle. But the physical pain of that night had paled in comparison to the injury of the following morning.

She'd been standing at her locker when he quickly approached. Her smile had faded at the fierce look on his face.

"Hey..." she'd started, but he didn't even let her get a greeting out. She could still remember the way her face had burned at that moment. He wasn't the first boy she had kissed, though there hadn't been any since junior high. But she'd never given herself to anyone. The memory of the intimacy they had shared made her pulse race.

"Last night never happened!" he'd furiously hissed as he cast worried glances around. He hadn't even looked at her. He'd simply slung his bag over his shoulder and swiftly walked away. It was later that she'd found out he had reunited with his ex-girlfriend, Deb Duncan. It had stung bitterly, but Kirsten had valiantly resolved to do just what he'd said—forget that night had ever happened.

Now, it did not look like that would be possible. Not that it had been in the first place.

Pregnant at eighteen. She knew what they would all say. It was because of her fatherless upbringing, making it acceptable to pity her all over again. She'd had about as much pity as she could handle over the last ten years since her dad had died in a car accident on his way home from work. As far as Kirsten could see, pity came with no offers of help or extra care. Just people feeling superior and relieved because they didn't have to suffer the way she did.

Only one person had ever really stepped out of her comfort zone to lend a hand connected to a heart. Mary Miller, their Amish neighbor. She'd brought countless meals those first few weeks. Ever since then, Kirsten and her mother had done their grocery shopping at the Amish Country Market, where Mary would smile and inquire about their lives.

Kirsten slowly got up and stumbled through the dark trailer to the kitchen. She filled a glass and quickly drained it. There was no point in eating right now. She'd only end up losing it, what with her nerves. She rested her hand on her stomach in disbelief. It didn't seem real. It just couldn't be real.

She was sitting at the small kitchen table when Elizabeth Walker got home from work.

"Hey, pumpkin. How was your day?" her mom asked, draping an old jacket over the back of the other kitchen chair.

There was a long pause and Kirsten slowly lifted her face to look in her mom's weary eyes. Elizabeth worked so hard and got so little in return. Kirsten hated how unfair and cruel life had been to both of them. But they were all each other had.

"I'm pregnant," Kirsten whispered as tears fell in her lap.

— CHAPTER TWO —

If there was any silver lining in this awful storm cloud, it was that in a little more than a month, Kirsten would graduate high school and never have to spend another minute, much less countless hours, in the presence of the blissfully happy Logan and Deb.

Elizabeth had taken the news hard, but she had remained calm. For a long while, there had been no words and Kirsten had just watched the emotions, intense as they were, flash across her mom's face. Confusion. Anger. Frustration. Hopelessness. Pain. She'd landed on pain. Finally, the words had started choking out and Kirsten answered how, when, where, and who. It was a hard lesson to learn at such a young age, Elizabeth had said to Kirsten. But she had promised to help in whatever way she could.

Logan, on the other hand, had not been so compassionate or sympathetic.

"Are you saying it's mine?" his voice had buzzed over the phone.

"Yes, of course it's yours."

"Well, I guess you'll have to get rid of it," he'd snapped.

"Get rid of it?"

"Abort it, give it away, I don't care what you do. Just get rid of it!"

"I might keep it."

"Why would you?" he'd asked with disgust.

"Because…it's mine."

"Yeah, well, it's mine too and I say give the kid away if you can't handle the abortion. Just get rid of it!"

"So you're saying you'd waive your...parental rights or something?"

"God, yes. Couldn't want it less."

"Oh."

"Look, I'll pay for the abortion. It would be easier."

Kirsten doubted that anything would be easy in the next several years. But at least she was free to make her own decisions about her baby. It was hers, after all. Logan certainly didn't want any part of it. He wasn't ready to be a father, which was not all that surprising. Kirsten didn't feel ready to be a mother, either, but she didn't have the luxury of escaping her part in this.

She'd lived for ten years without a father. It wasn't fun or easy, but it was...doable. At least she'd have something in common with her child. She knew firsthand what it was to be raised by a single mother. Of course, there were a few things she'd do differently.

Kirsten pulled into the Amish Country Market on her way home from school. The market was located on the busy highway not far from Kristen's home. Rather than dozens of roadside stands, most of the local Amish sold their homespun, homegrown, and homemade goods at the market. Kirsten opened her wallet and counted exactly $24.73 to spend on a week's worth of breakfast and supper for her and her mom. It wasn't much, but they were good at making money stretch far enough for food. They would buy the few things they couldn't get at the market at the grocery store in town. They were too proud, too stubborn, to accept any government aid. So they scraped by on next to nothing.

Kirsten stepped into the large wooden building and picked up a woven shopping basket. She wandered the produce aisles and the baked goods, making careful selections as she went. Satisfied she had enough for the week but not eager to go home to an empty house, she wandered the handmade goods. Racks of unspeakably beautiful quilts. Rows of rocking chairs. Tables laden with bolts of fabric. A small rack of baby clothes caught her attention, and she was unable to do anything other than walk toward it. She stared at the long baby dresses—so simple, but so perfectly beautiful. Shyly, she touched a hem and ran her fingers across the buttons.

She dropped her hand. Of its own volition, it moved to touch her stomach. Could there really be a baby in there? A person who would look at her with love and affection? Someone who would need her and want her?

Suddenly, she remembered herself and started, quickly looking around to see if anyone was watching. The other customers, tourists mostly, seemed to be engaged in their own activities and unaware of her curious condition.

Kirsten marched determinedly to the front counter where Mary Miller stood, folding embroidered towels.

"Good afternoon, Kirsten," she said as she smiled warmly.

"Hello, Mary," Kirsten answered.

"How is yer mother doing?"

"Oh…okay." Kirsten nodded, dropping her eyes.

Mary smiled as she wrote the purchases on a ledger and totaled it all without using a cash register or calculator. Out of pure curiosity, Kirsten always checked Mary's math. She had never made an error.

"Needing a baby gift?" Mary asked, the warm smile still firmly in place. So she had seen her then.

"N-no," Kirsten stammered uneasily. "I was just…admiring it." She could feel her face flaming. Surely Mary had seen her hand pressed to her stomach. She wasn't showing yet, but her actions were making the announcement much earlier than necessary.

"Did ya see the fresh loaves of cinnamon bread?" Mary asked her with twinkling eyes. She knew, somehow, that they were Kirsten's favorite.

Kirsten nodded and gave a small, tight-lipped grimace. "I did." She didn't have enough money, though she'd dearly love to swap out the bag of green beans for just one small loaf. "Maybe next time," Kirsten said with a shrug. No need to tell someone just how broke they were, even though that someone was the kindest person she'd ever known.

Mary only nodded in return and slipped Kirsten's groceries into the canvas shopping bags Kirsten had brought in. Despite spending only $23.27, she had shopped carefully and had two very full bags. Mary pushed them across the counter one at a time. Kirsten was surprised at how heavy they were as she looped her arms through the handles and slid them off the counter.

"Thank you, Mary," Kirsten said as she smiled shyly at her.

Mary smiled in return and said, "Yer welcome, as usual. *Gott segen eich.*" Mary was never shy, it seemed. Kirsten thought the other Amish people were downright bashful compared to Mary's warm and engaging personality. Kirsten couldn't imagine Mary would treat her any better if Kirsten was Amish.

Kirsten's flip-flops slapped loudly as she made her way across the wooden deck to the stairs that led down to the parking lot. Arms full with her bags, Kirsten slid her foot onto the step without gripping the railing. It was almost too late when she felt the front piece of her shoe catch on the step, making her wobble and grab the railing. She clutched the wooden beam and spent several long moments trying to regain her balance. She was staring down at the stairs, trying to slow her pulse when she suddenly found herself cast in shadow.

"Here," a voice drawled behind her, "let me help ya with those." She wanted to turn to see the face behind the voice, but given her wobbly state, she decided against it and waited until he was standing in front of her to lift her eyes from the stairs and inspect the kind stranger.

He was younger than she had expected, but older than she was. And he was Amish—that much had been obvious simply from his accent. His clothes, suspenders included, were only confirmation. And, of course, the wide-brimmed straw hat. But beneath the brim she could see his eyes were the most startling shade of sky blue. Despite the early spring weather, he was tan. And strikingly handsome.

Kirsten knew she was staring at him. It was hard not to. She handed her bags into his large, leanly muscled hands and grabbed the rail for the rest of her trip down the stairs.

"Are ya all right?" he asked, staring straight into her eyes. Why had she ever thought the Amish were bashful? Non-Amish men never made eye contact like this.

"I'm fine, thank you," she said, dropping her eyes shyly again to the plank boards beneath her feet. "Perhaps I should wear more sensible shoes," she laughed, staring down at her dusty black flip-flops. She peeked up at him and was rewarded with a blinding smile. She could just make out a few curls of dark blond hair beneath his hat. It wasn't until she had followed him down the stairs and into the parking lot that she realized just how tall he was. She was five feet and ten inches, something that made most high school boys uncomfortable. But he was well over six feet. She led the way to her dusty silver Camry and opened the back door. He carefully placed the bags on the floor where they couldn't tip over.

"I get better service here than anywhere in town," she laughed. "Once, I went to Fareway and they stuffed the plastic sack so full that it busted open in the parking lot. I was chasing groceries all over the place, trying to pick them up before anyone drove over them. That's part of the reason I got these bags." She was rambling. She knew she was rambling. She shielded her eyes and looked up, squinting to see his eyes. He was smiling.

"It's a *gut* idea," he replied sincerely. The words came out slowly, quietly, and smoothly. It was almost as if something in her vibrated at the sound. Maybe he was older than she thought.

"Can I ask you something?" she prefaced, waiting for his reply. He visibly stiffened, paused, and then cautiously nodded.

"What does '*Gott segen eich*' mean?"

He flashed a grin. "'*Gott segen eich*' means 'God bless you.'"

"Oh! Mary always says that and I'm always too shy to ask her what it means," Kirsten laughed. "Is it German?"

He cocked his head in acknowledgement, but said, "Pennsylvania Dutch."

Kirsten nodded.

"How do you say 'thank you' in Pennsylvania Dutch?" she asked as she smiled up at him.

"*Denki.*"

"*Denki,*" she tried it out herself. "Well, thank you—*denki*—for your help."

He lowered his head so that she couldn't see his eyes, but she could still see his smile.

"Yer welcome."

She made herself move then, climbing quickly and carefully into the driver's seat. He made his way past her car and back up the stairs to the store, but she could see him in her rearview mirror as he stopped to watch her drive away.

✒⟐✒

"That was nice of ya," Mary said to her son when he walked in the store. Silas glanced at her, nodded, and cast his eyes back to the produce tables. Mary turned to watch out the window as the silver Camry crunched down the gravel frontage road and waited to cross the highway. Silas looked back at her and noticed the curious pinch of his mother's eyes.

"What's wrong?" he asked her quietly, stepping closer to follow her gaze.

She shook her head. "I don't know," she said so softly he could hardly hear her. "When you get home, tell Amy to start another batch of cinnamon bread," she said, abruptly swinging to face the aisle of shelves. Silas nodded once and walked back out to the parking lot. He hoisted himself into the old truck that he had backed up to the loading dock, started the engine, and pulled out onto the road.

Not for the first time, he thanked God for the blessing of a vehicle to transport goods from home to the market. They traveled almost exclusively by horse and buggy, but the ministers had given special approval for the purchase of a vehicle to transport goods to the store. There were many freedoms in their church district that he knew other districts would not allow.

He slowly made his way down the gravel road, spotting a silver car some distance ahead of him. Of course it was her, the girl from the store. He slowed to watch her turn into the Walker place just down the road. He recognized the car now. For years he had assumed it was Elizabeth Walker driving by.

Silas's mind drifted back to that night ten years ago when he had driven his mother up the road and onto the small yard with the trailer and one falling-down outbuilding. He'd been only eleven at the time, so he'd sat in the buggy minding the horse. He'd seen her then—the small girl clinging to Mrs. Walker's legs as she accepted the basket of baked goods from his mother. All these years, he'd known that Mrs. Walker and her daughter lived at the trailer just up the road. Obviously, Mrs. Walker's daughter was no longer a little girl.

Silas's mouth twitched with a smile as he remembered her awkward German phrases and her flimsy shoes. He would never understand why people wore those things. It would be easier to just go barefoot, as Amy and his little sisters did all summer long. Even some English men wore them, which confounded him further. How did they do any work with shoes like that? Locals and tourists alike always traipsed into the market wearing the oddest clothes. What was most amusing was that Englishers thought his clothes were so curious. He was always comfortable, which is something he doubted outsiders could say, judging by how revealing some of their outfits were. How could anyone ever be comfortable showing the world so much of their body?

He parked the truck in the shed, next to the buggies. Amy was hanging laundry on the line behind the house.

"Mom wants more cinnamon bread for the market," he called out to her.

"Already? I made that batch yesterday afternoon!"

Silas shrugged, then smiled. "Must have been *gut*."

— CHAPTER THREE —

Just two more weeks and so much misery would be behind her. In two weeks, she'd graduate and leave the gossipy halls of Bradford High School behind. Even this paled in comparison to the promised respite from the morning sickness that Kirsten could not control.

Several times each morning she would rush out of class to be sick in the bathroom. She'd tried every home remedy she could find on the internet in the library. None of them worked well, and now the rumor mill was starting.

It was just after first period when Kirsten emerged from the restroom, her face flushed and her hands clammy. She shuffled to her locker and fumbled with the combination. By the time she got it open, the hallway was nearly empty. Her next class was advanced calculus—an easy class for Kirsten.

She tried to slip quietly into the noisy room, but too many eyes fell on her and it grew eerily silent for a classroom with a missing teacher. She looked up to see Logan staring at her with pure disgust. Kirsten knew by the expressions on her classmates' faces that they all knew. And if looks could kill, Logan's would have her six feet under in a cheap casket next to her dad.

"Get yourself knocked up?" one of the boys laughed. A chorus of giggles and not-so-quiet snickers echoed around her.

Kirsten said nothing as she slid into a seat near the door—her new favorite place to be.

"You responsible for this, Webb?" one of Logan's friends sneered. Obviously Logan had told their little secret to someone. Kirsten certainly hadn't. In fact, she was planning on taking that secret to the grave, precisely where Logan probably wished she was.

"Who would sleep with that ugly bitch?" Logan said bitingly, his lip curling in disgust. Again the laughter.

"Bet they don't have a graduation gown big enough. You'll just have to wear a garbage bag," said one of Deb's friends.

Kirsten zipped her sweatshirt up further, concealing most of her stomach. She was, always had been, slim. In the past week or so, she'd noticed that she had the smallest of bumps, making some of her clothes feel just the tiniest bit tight. She could still button her size-four jeans, but it wouldn't be long before she couldn't.

Still, she was a long way from being too big for a graduation gown. But the words stung. Fiercely, she kept her head up and her eyes focused straight ahead, refusing to acknowledge anyone.

No sane person would have begrudged her leaving school early. But Kirsten had to use the computer lab to type yet another paper for Advanced English. Of course, the other kids would all type theirs at home on their own personal laptops, something she couldn't dream of having any time soon.

The teacher abruptly entered the room, and Kirsten soon lost herself in a series of numbers and calculations. She'd always liked the predictability of math. The logic appealed to her. She had taken and aced every math class her high school had to offer. With her grades and an impressive score on the SAT, she was in position to get into a good college. Of course, all those plans and hopes were now very much in jeopardy.

When the final bell rang, she escaped to the computer lab while the others made plans for the evening. She typed quickly and quietly in a corner of the lab, eventually leaving the school to find a nearly empty parking lot. She started her Camry and pulled onto the highway.

She slowed as she passed the market. How her empty stomach craved some of Mary Miller's cinnamon bread. She'd found several loaves of it in her bag that afternoon when she'd nearly tumbled down the stairs at the market. Mary had somehow slipped them in without Kirsten knowing. But today she didn't have enough money for cinnamon bread, much less gas to get to and from school, so she turned toward home.

Home. An empty, run-down trailer. Her parents had purchased the land just a few years before her father's accident. They'd always intended to build a modest home, but after her father's death, Elizabeth struggled to make the mortgage payments on the property, let alone look at building a new house. The trailer was never intended to be a permanent home. But for the past ten years, that is exactly what it had been. With every passing year, its condition deteriorated and became less livable. Elizabeth and Kirsten had stayed for the first several years because it hurt too much to leave. And now…they stayed simply because they were used to it.

But it wasn't a good home. No. It was ugly. Beat-up. Unwanted. Broken. Like her.

The tear scalded Kirsten's cheek as her pain finally broke free and ran down her face. The hours of scorn and rejection poured out of her, and sobs racked her thin body as she clutched the steering wheel with both hands. She was almost home when her tires caught a patch of loose gravel.

The wheels lost their traction and her car slid sideways one way, then the other before coming to a lurching stop in the shallow ditch. Kirsten sat, both hands still clutching the steering wheel, for a few minutes trying to evaluate her physical condition. Other than being terrified, she felt okay. She flung the car door open and looked to see if there was a way to climb out safely. She was just sliding from the car when she heard gravel-crunching footsteps running toward her.

"Are ya all right?" he called. That voice. It was him. His shadow loomed over her and she squinted up at him again. In one lithe leap, he was down the embankment and at her side.

"Are ya all right?" he repeated, his words coming out fast despite his drawl, and his concerned eyes searched her face.

"Y-y-yeah. I think so," Kirsten stuttered. "Just shaken up, I think."

"Let me help ya out," he spoke slower, quieter this time—the panic gone, but the concern still pinching his eyes.

Kirsten grabbed his arm while he pulled her away from the car. She wobbled and felt his other arm wrap around her waist. Wordlessly, he hauled her up out of the ditch, one cautious step at a time, until they were standing on the road, looking down at her car.

"I can pull it out for ya," he said calmly, as though this were an everyday event. Kirsten tried to absorb some of his calm and found her heart slowing. She couldn't speak, but she managed to nod, blinking rapidly. She watched him walk down the road and turn in the Millers' driveway.

So he was one of Mary's sons. Kirsten didn't know how many children Mary had, but she knew there were several.

Minutes later, he was back with a truck. He climbed out, a heavy chain dangling from a tanned, muscled forearm. She watched as he attached it to her car and then his truck. Silently, she prayed her car would not tear in two as he climbed in his truck and slipped it into gear. Slowly, so slowly, he pulled the car onto the road. Clumps of grass were wedged in the bumper and wheel wells. He bent down and plucked them forcefully away, revealing a flat front tire.

Kirsten willed herself not to cry.

"Do ya have a spare?" he asked as he unhooked the chain.

"Um…I think so." She peered in the trunk as he peeled back the carpet to find a spare. Effortlessly, he pulled the tire and jack from her car and set to work changing the tire. She watched silently as he worked. For a member of a people who did not normally own or drive vehicles, he was surprisingly capable and soon had the donut in place.

"Let's see if it runs," he suggested, dusting his hands off on his trousers.

Kirsten climbed in and started the engine. She left it running as she stood by her car and watched him easily put the damaged tire in her trunk.

"Thank you for your help," she breathed.

"Yer welcome." He was studying her again.

"I'm sorry…I don't even know your name."

"Silas."

"Silas," she repeated, smiling for the first time all day. "I'm Kirsten, by the way."

He nodded. She couldn't tell if he already knew that or if he was just acknowledging that he had heard her.

"You keep showing up right when I need you," she said, smiling shyly.

A slow grin spread across his face. "Neighbors should help each other," he answered with a shrug.

"Well, I'm glad you're mine. My neighbor, that is," she said. Blushing, she climbed into her car before she could say anything else embarrassing and drove down the road, waving at Silas as she passed him where he stood with his hands on his hips.

— Chapter Four —

It was early when Elizabeth pulled her old Caravan into the parking lot at the market. Mary watched her through the window of the glass double doors as she unlocked them, throwing them open for Elizabeth. "Good morning, Mary. I'm sorry I'm so early." Elizabeth smiled tiredly at her.

"Yer always welcome, Elizabeth," Mary said, smiling at her. "Are ya on yer way home from work?"

"Yes," Kirsten's mom sighed. "I'm working extra shifts lately at the station. I'm afraid it's running me ragged. But we need the money." Elizabeth paused and drew a deep breath before continuing. "I guess I'm here mostly to thank you—your son—for his kindness to my daughter yesterday."

"Oh? What kindness would that be?" Mary's mind raced as she tried to remember any mention from any one of her sons about Kirsten Walker, but none came to mind.

"Kirsten had a little accident between your place and ours on her way home from school. Lost control of her car and ended up in the ditch. Your boy was good enough to pull her car out and change her flat tire."

"Is she all right?" Mary managed to ask, though her mind was suddenly fixed on Silas.

Elizabeth's lip visibly quivered, and her hand went to her mouth. Mary was so moved by the expression she saw that she touched the younger woman's arm in concern.

"Kirsten is…pregnant," Elizabeth choked. "It was a horrible mistake." She took a deep, shuddering breath. "She plans to keep the baby, even though the father wants nothing to do with her and told her to get rid of it."

Mary's grip tightened on Elizabeth's arm, and her chest constricted painfully as she remembered Kirsten's expression in the market a few weeks ago. The pieces of the puzzle now made sense, revealing a sad picture.

"I know how this seems…" Elizabeth sniffled. "She is a good girl who just…made a bad choice."

"I'm so very sorry," Mary said quietly. These types of things were not unheard of, even in the strictest of Amish circles. But still, she could not imagine the pain of watching your own daughter go through such a trial.

Elizabeth smiled sadly. "Please tell your son how much I appreciate his helping Kirsten."

Mary nodded.

"And if you have any, I'd like to buy a loaf of your cinnamon bread for Kirsten. It's her favorite and about the only thing she can eat without getting sick."

Mary nodded while she moved quickly, grabbed the biggest loaf she could find, and handed it to Kirsten's mom, waving away the crumpled money she tried to pay her.

"You go home and take care of yerself and yer Kirsten now," Mary gently instructed.

Elizabeth only nodded and moved wearily to the door. Mary held it open for her and watched her drive away. She let the door swing shut and turned her gaze to Silas, who was unloading crates of vegetables onto the loading dock. He had not mentioned the accident, which was unusual in a way and unsurprising in another. He was so quiet. Mary stared out the window at Silas. What she wouldn't do to see inside his heart. She wasn't surprised by his kindness to Kirsten. That was his way. That was the Amish way. But that he hadn't spoken about the incident at all was puzzling.

.⊙ 9⊙.

Silas worked steadily through the morning, and it was nearly ten o'clock when he sat back on his haunches to feel the cool spring breeze on his face. He rolled his shoulders back and felt his shirt stick against the sweat running down his neck and spine. Sweeping the hat off his head, he closed his eyes as the breeze ruffled his sandy hair. He opened his eyes just in time to see a silver car pull into the long driveway next to the garden.

Kirsten got out and began making her way toward him. The handkerchief in his pocket did a poor job of cleaning his hands, but it was all he had. He placed his hat on his head and halfheartedly slapped at the dirt on his trousers. He moved to the end of the row and met her on the strip of grass between the lane and the rows and rows of vegetables.

"Hi, Silas," Kirsten said with a smile.

"Hullo, Kirsten," he replied.

"It's a beautiful day, isn't it?" she said, craning her head up to see the bright blue sky of spring.

"It is," he answered, watching her and not following her gaze.

"I was just on my way to the library and I wanted to give you this," Kirsten said as she thrust a small white envelope across the distance between them. He took it without speaking, his brow furrowed in confusion.

"A thank-you note," she explained.

"Oh," he said finally, looking down at the pristine white envelope in his dirty fingers.

It had been a while since a girl had given him a note. In fact, he couldn't remember ever having received one. He'd seen his brothers pass notes to girls before. And he knew some of his friends did it. But it had never happened to him and certainly not in the middle of the day. He somehow knew that this was both the least and the most she could do to thank him.

"Is this your garden?" she asked, laughing lightly at her question. "I mean, it's obviously a garden. But is it yours?"

"We all work in it," he said, shrugging.

"It's, well…it's gigantic," she said with wide eyes. "Is this your…job…then?"

"Part of it," he said with a grin. She smiled up at him just as the breeze caught her auburn hair, sending it waving past her face. He was mesmerized as she swept it back behind her ear.

"You must spend a lot of time out here," she observed, taking in again the acres of produce in front of her.

He swallowed hard and merely nodded in response. Usually, he made a conscious choice to be quiet. But at the moment, words simply failed him.

"Well, I should get going," Kirsten said after a pause. "Have a good rest of your day." She smiled shyly and backed slowly away before turning and walking back to her car. He watched her, not saying anything in reply. As she drove down the road toward the highway, he cast a quick glance around to see if any of his siblings had witnessed Kirsten's surprise visit. Quickly, he tucked the envelope in his pocket and went back to work. He'd read it later, somewhere far away from curious eyes.

There was no chance to read it before supper, so Silas spent most of the meal completely distracted by the note practically burning a hole in his pocket. He ate so fast he beat Caleb, which won him a raised eyebrow from his mother. The conversation was as plentiful as the food, but it came to a screeching halt when Mary told the family about Elizabeth's early morning visit in regards to the accident. Silas froze as the eyes of his family swung to his face.

"Accident? What's this about, Silas?" Daniel said quietly in the hush that had fallen over the table.

"Kirsten's car slid off the road. I used the truck to pull it out." Silas shrugged. Inwardly, he cringed. If it wasn't a big deal, he would have had no reason to stay silent about it yesterday at suppertime. But he'd kept it to himself for reasons he could hardly understand, and now he looked like he was hiding something.

"And ya changed a flat tire," Mary reminded him. Silas only nodded.

"Was Kirsten hurt?" his father inquired.

"No. Shaken up a little maybe," he answered.

There was a long silence before Mary prompted the children to finish their supper. Minutes later, Caleb, Anna, and Shelby were excused outside to play in the lingering hours of daylight.

"Why didn't ya tell us?" Daniel asked, his hand smoothing his beard as he considered Silas with wondering eyes.

Silas shrugged and shook his head.

"It's good ya were there, Silas," Mary said, turning away from the sink. "Elizabeth told me that Kirsten is expecting a baby. The accident had upset her poor mother."

Silas felt the room wobble. Kirsten was expecting a baby?

"She never would have been able to change a flat tire, much less get out of the ditch," Mary continued as she dried the plate in her hands.

"Is she getting married, then?" Amy asked from her place at the sink. It was no secret Amy had a fascination with weddings, Amish and English.

Mary's eyes fell. "No," she said quietly. "The young man doesn't want Kirsten or the baby."

Silas's pulse thrummed loudly in his ears as he remembered her tear-streaked face. He'd thought she was upset by the accident. Now he wondered if the reason had been something else entirely.

Daniel shook his head, concern furrowing his brow. Running the market meant more interaction with English in one day than most Amish have in a lifetime. His parents were no strangers to life on the outside, having observed it on a daily basis for nearly thirty-five years. Still, Silas knew it was hard for them to understand why anyone would ever want to live that way.

Daniel pushed his chair back and Silas rose to follow him out. Daniel drifted toward the barn, but Silas walked briskly toward the orchard that stretched behind the house and all the way to the creek at the northern edge of their property. The branches were heavy with fruit, but the sun still glittered through the leaves and heavy foliage. It was a glorious evening, one that made it hard to believe there was anything wrong in the world. But there was. Oh, how there was. Kirsten was pregnant. He didn't understand why it bothered him so. But it did. It ate at him.

He scanned the grove quickly, making sure he was indeed as alone as it seemed. Then he pulled the note from his pocket, found a seat beneath an apple tree, and stared past his dirty fingerprints at his name printed on the envelope in her handwriting. *Silas.* Even the way she wrote his name in her small but neat script did funny things to him.

He turned the envelope over and slid a calloused finger beneath the sealed flap. This was for him alone. He liked that too. He flipped open the embossed card and read her words.

Silas,

Thank you so much for your help yesterday with my car. I had a terrible day at school, but your kindness was an unexpected gift. Thank you for helping me.

Sincerely,

Kirsten

He read the note three times before carefully folding it, sliding it back in the dirty envelope, and slipping it all back into his pocket.

He hung his head in his hands, running his fingers through his hair. She didn't look pregnant—obviously it was still very early in her pregnancy. Kirsten was so slim, a fact not hidden by her jeans and t-shirt, and pleasantly shaped. Her auburn hair hung in a perfectly straightened cascade down to her shoulder blades. And her eyes matched her hair almost perfectly. Kirsten's skin was smooth and pale. And though it was mostly flawless, he could see a trace of freckles just across the bridge of her nose and her cheeks. He had seen her sad, and it was heartbreaking. But when she smiled, he had trouble breathing normally. She was beautiful by any standard—Amish or English.

But it was more than that. Kirsten was the only woman who had ever looked him in the eye and smiled out of genuine friendliness. Most of the outsiders who looked at him and smiled bore an unmistakable expression of curiosity or ridicule. He rarely had the desire to meet their eyes. Kirsten, on the other hand, had been friendly and warm and not at all condescending. She wasn't afraid to smile at him or talk to him. She wasn't bashful, but she wasn't pushy either. In fact, she seemed like a wonderful girl.

How anyone could disrespect her, disgrace her, and abandon her and her baby, he just did not comprehend. If it was him, he certainly wouldn't be walking away.

⋅⊱⋅⊰⋅

Mary watched from a distance. She could only see his back, but she knew from the set of his shoulders that something was bothering her son. And because it was Silas, she doubted very much if she would ever truly know what it was. He wasn't a talker. It was almost as if David and Michael had used up all the words, so Silas was left to simply sit and take in all that happened around him.

His reluctance to pair up with any of the eligible young women in their community was disconcerting, but not shocking. Mary could hardly imagine him talking to a girl. And in her heart, she was afraid. If Silas couldn't get past this introverted behavior, he'd almost surely never find himself a wife.

Still, she hoped he'd find happiness, fulfillment, and companionship. It wasn't that she was worried about him being alone. That was nearly impossible in a family such as theirs. No, she worried about him being lonely. And right now, he looked lonelier than he ever had before.

◦◌◌◦

Kirsten walked across the stage with her head held high and honor cords dangling around her neck when her name was called. She took her diploma, shook the principal's hand, and went back to her seat. She kept her eyes down in her lap while Logan accepted his diploma to a chorus of cheers and shouts from his friends and family.

It was at that moment she felt it—movement—like a ripple or a series of bubbles tickling her from within. As inconspicuously as possible, she touched the small bulge beneath her graduation gown. It was as if they were the only two people in the world. Now, from this moment forward, everything she did would be for her baby—the same way Elizabeth had given up all her dreams and plans when Kirsten's father died. All that seemed to matter now was protecting her baby—from Logan, from Deb, from the whole nasty, unfair world.

The next day, an early Monday morning, she lay on the table and winced as the radiologist squirted a blob of cold gel on her abdomen. The technician slid the wand over Kirsten's stomach as Kirsten and her mom watched the blurry images flicker across the monitor.

Then the technician spoke the words Kirsten already knew she would hear.

"It's a girl."

— CHAPTER FIVE —

Silas pulled the buggy up to the front porch where his sisters waited, their skirts swirling around their legs and their bonnet strings flittering in the breeze. He helped the little ones in, then climbed in front next to Amy, grabbed the reins, and flicked them lightly.

Trips into town were special occasions. His sisters chattered excitedly about the day's planned activities, which included a stop at the library. Several minutes later, they had made their way into town. There were a few other buggies clattering down the streets. The citizens of Bradford knew and accepted their Amish neighbors with moderate warmth and accommodation. Even so, the goal of the Amish was not to fit in. Silas carefully guided the buggy into the library parking lot, tying his horse to a lamppost.

Inside, he leaned on a low bookshelf and shivered in the air conditioning. Anna and Shelby scurried silently, but excitedly, around the children's section.

He casually scanned the library patrons and jumped when he saw Kirsten walking toward the checkout desk with her arms wrapped around a stack of books.

She looked up, caught his gaze, and smiled at him. Silas found himself unable to do anything other than smile warmly back at her. She walked past the checkout desk and stopped just a few feet from his perch at the end of the children's section.

"Hi, Silas," she said in a noisy whisper.

He smiled and looked down at his boots, "How are ya, Kirsten?"

Her face flushed slightly, but she shrugged. "Good."

Her attention was abruptly caught by a group of three girls who walked in. They noticed her and made a beeline past the checkout desk, moving closely behind Kirsten. One of them brazenly flipped Kirsten's own hair to hit her in the face. Silas watched her stand statue-still, not shrinking away but not engaging in their game.

"Apparently, you missed the book about safe sex," one of them sneered.

"Is there a book about how not to get fat when pregnant?" another mocked.

"Is this your boyfriend? He's cute!" the last one said, turning her attention to Silas. Her sarcasm dripped off every word, but Silas looked calmly back at her as though she'd just commented about the weather. His calm exterior belied the turmoil he felt within.

The girls laughed loudly despite library etiquette. Kirsten closed her eyes and blushed furiously until they finally walked away.

"I'm sorry, Silas," she whispered, not meeting his gaze.

He shook off Kirsten's apology and looked intently at her. "Are ya okay?"

She shrugged and smiled sadly. "I'm kinda used to it."

Silas stared at her, unsure how anyone could treat someone so badly, or how she could be used to such treatment.

Kirsten's eyes fell suddenly and lit with surprise. Silas felt Anna press against his leg and saw her peeking shyly up at Kirsten.

"Hello." Kirsten smiled down at her. Soon Shelby's serious face appeared next to Anna.

"Are these your sisters?" Kirsten said as she smiled at Silas.

"Two of them," he drawled. "This is Anna Mae. She's four. And this is Shelby Jo and she is six."

"It's nice to meet you." She beamed down at the two tiny, bonneted girls nearly hiding behind him. "Do you like the library?"

Both girls stared up at Kirsten, casting nervous glances up at Silas.

"Oh, I'm sorry. Are they not allowed to talk to me?" Kirsten quickly apologized, a worried frown creasing her forehead. Silas could hardly breathe for the way she earnestly looked up into his face.

He smiled broadly at her worry and then looked down at his shy sisters. "They're allowed. Just shy." Gently, he laid his hand on Anna's bonneted head and smiled into her eyes. On cue, she smiled widely at Kirsten, ducking her head bashfully. Shelby hid further behind him.

Amy suddenly appeared next to Silas, looking first at him and then turning her attention to Kirsten.

"This is Amy. She's seventeen," Silas introduced his sister, noticing but ignoring the look Amy gave him.

"I'm glad you were both okay after yer accident," Amy said. Silas stared at her in disbelief. When he looked back at Kirsten, she was nodding and blushing crimson. He didn't want to leave her, but neither did he want Amy to say anything further, especially not in front of Shelby and Anna.

"Are ya ready to go?" he asked the little ones still hiding behind his legs. They nodded and made their way to the checkout desk. Silas, Amy, and Kirsten followed. After checking out their books, Amy politely waved Kirsten in front of her and they all walked out together.

"Have fun reading your books," Kirsten said as she smiled down at Anna and Shelby. Silas gently helped them in before untying the horse. Kirsten was watching him and he felt strangely thrilled by it.

He came around the horse and handed the reins to Amy.

"It was good to see you, Silas," Kirsten said very quietly so only he could hear.

He paused as he looked at her. "Kirsten, what those girls said…"

"Yeah. They don't like me much," she said, grimacing. Silas looked at her, wishing he had the right words. But he didn't. He wished even more that he could erase the words they'd said. The horse shifted and his attention swung to the buggy.

"It wasn't…" Wasn't true. Wasn't right. Wasn't human. All of those fit, but he couldn't choose one.

"I know," she said, nodding.

Begrudgingly, he turned away from Kirsten and climbed in the buggy. She waved and smiled as they pulled away. Silas nodded, still ignoring the look on Amy's face. His heart felt lighter and heavier at the same time.

They finished their errands and made the thirty-minute trip home to find supper on the table. Amy rushed the girls inside to wash up for supper while Silas unhitched Titus and put him up for the night. He noted the extra horses and buggies scattered around the yard, which signaled that his brothers and their families had come over for supper, as they often did.

The table was crowded by the time Silas stepped into the kitchen. He squeezed his broad frame into the seat next to his father and across from his brother, Michael. The level of noise was at an all-time high as brothers discussed farming, horses, and weather. The children told their mothers about their adventures. Silas half listened to it all and concentrated on shoveling forkfuls of potatoes into his mouth instead.

"How was yer trip into town today?" Mary asked as she smiled at Shelby and Anna.

"Silas talked to a girl at the library!" Anna Mae announced in what was, of course, the only lull in conversation.

"Oh? Who was that, Silas?" his mother asked, clearly surprised at this news. Silas was tempted to throw a withering look at Anna Mae but thought better of it.

"Kirsten," Amy answered for him. Silas gave his withering look to her.

"Finally! A love interest!" David sighed in exasperation. Michael laughed. Silas froze.

"She's not Amish," Amy clarified.

David stopped laughing and looked sternly at Silas. Even though he wasn't much of a talker, Silas knew how to hold his own with his brothers. He met David's eyes and didn't look away.

"Kirsten Walker is our neighbor," Mary reminded David and Michael lightly. "How is she, Silas?" his mother asked, most likely nervous about the staring.

"She's fine," Silas answered. He could feel his father's eyes on him.

"Hmm...would you marry her if she was Amish?" Michael questioned, a mischievous glint in his eyes.

"She's pregnant," Amy blurted.

The table fell into total silence. Silas felt his neck growing hot. He blinked slowly and turned his head just enough to see Amy out of the corner of his eye.

"Amy Miller!" Mary whispered furiously.

Amy checked herself immediately and dropped her eyes to her lap.

Silas never answered Michael's question out loud, but he spun it over and over again in his mind.

After dinner they all gathered to see off the two families in their buggies. Shelby and Anna were herded inside and off to bed. Silas sat wearily on the front porch steps. Daniel slowly lowered himself down beside him. They were silent for a long while.

"You seem to have a friend in Kirsten Walker," Daniel commented.

Silas shrugged. Many long, quiet moments passed, the cicadas' buzzing filling the silence between them.

"Do ya have feelings for this girl, Silas?" Daniel finally asked.

Silas looked away, utterly unable to answer.

— CHAPTER SIX —

Sleep only came in short stretches for Silas that night. He rolled out of bed, trying not to disturb Caleb while he got dressed. It was still dark outside as Silas climbed the ladder into the hayloft in the barn.

He tossed a few bales down while the sun peeked over the horizon. He stopped to look out the east window in the loft. He could see Kirsten's house from here.

The sunlight streaked across the ground, streaming red, yellow, and orange in its wake. He watched as the sun carved large shadows out of the darkness and the dew began to glitter on the grass.

He noticed that the colors played strangely on Kirsten's trailer. They weren't fading or evening out as they did on the ground. Something was wrong. Silas blinked and squinted his eyes, but he couldn't make sense of the picture. Surely those weren't bright blotches on her house.

With a sinking feeling, Silas crept away from the window. He ran the length of the haymow, dropped down the ladder, and hurried out to the horse stable. He threw a bridle on Titus and swung himself up, not bothering with a saddle.

Moments later, he slid off Titus in Kirsten's yard, unable to tear his eyes off the large splotches of red paint on the side of her trailer. It was paint, but it looked like blood. It looked like massive, gaping wounds, dripping grotesquely and running in rivers over the siding. He stood next to Titus, almost unable to move. But he needed to know if she was okay. Silas crossed the yard and knocked firmly on the door, half hoping Elizabeth would answer his knock even though her van wasn't in the gravel driveway. Eventually, Kirsten's face peeked out at him through the rusty screen door.

"Silas? Is something wrong?" He'd woken her. That much was obvious by her t-shirt, flannel pajama pants, and messy ponytail.

"I'm sorry to…disturb ya so early," he apologized.

"It's fine." She shook her head. "What's wrong?"

"Yer house…" he indicated with a nod.

Kirsten came out to stand next to him. Motionlessly, she stared at the damage.

"I heard them last night, but I thought it was just eggs or something. I was too afraid to come out and check," she murmured stiffly, her eyes staring almost unseeingly at the marring. "I have to call Mom," she said, turning to go back inside. Silas stood staring until she returned.

"Mom called the police," Kirsten said robotically. "You don't have to stay."

Silas looked at her intently, but she would not meet his eyes. Her face was emotionless. Blank. He wanted to stay, but he turned away, swung up on Titus, and made for home.

.ᴏⱸ Ꮆᴀ.

It took two full days and three coats of paint, but Caleb and Silas finished painting over the splotches left by the paintball guns by Saturday noon. Neither Kirsten nor Elizabeth had asked for the help. But when Silas had knocked on their door a second time and spoken to Elizabeth, she'd gratefully accepted his offer, stating that they had no insurance and no way to pay for the necessary repainting.

It was a relief for him to finally be able to do something—to erase in some manner the hate that had been hurled at Kirsten.

He had seen her only one time since that morning. She'd come out and watched them work. He had forced himself not to turn and look at her, but he could see her reflection in the window next to him. Kirsten had held herself rigidly, her arms tightly wrapped around her chest as though she were cold. They'd said nothing to each other, but Silas had sensed that she was holding on by a mere thread.

At the end of two days, Caleb and Silas packed up the wagon and drove home in silence. It had been quiet work, but Silas was glad for Caleb's easy company.

It was mid-afternoon on Sunday when Silas finished helping Michael and David unhitch their buggies and put their horses up in the pasture. They gathered in the front lawn for a game of horseshoes. Silas bent down to show Anna how to hold the shoe for her toss.

"Looks like you have a visitor, brother," Michael said from his spot next to Silas. Silas turned to see Kirsten walking slowly down the road and turning into their lane. Part of him wanted to deny that she was there for him, but he knew she was. His long legs brought him to her quickly, long before she'd made it halfway down the driveway. She was wearing black pants, a gray University of Iowa t-shirt, and sneakers. Her hair was pulled back in a ponytail. Silas was still in his Sunday best from meeting.

"Out for a walk?" he asked her. She stood staring blankly at the garden beside them, not answering. For once he felt like the talkative one.

After a long pause, she turned her face to his and looked intently into his eyes. He noticed then the tears that were welling as she tried to blink them away. She dropped her gaze to her hands.

"Silas...what you and your brother did for me...for us..." Kirsten paused to shake her head. "There are no words." She swiped a tear off her cheek and crossed her arms tightly in front of her chest. She looked down at her tennis shoes and then squinted up into his face. "Thank you." It was barely more than a whisper, but he was close enough to hear.

"Yer welcome," he replied after a beat, his voice low and quiet.

She stared up at him, unsmiling and serious. For several long minutes, her eyes searched his face —for what he didn't know.

"You're a good man, Silas Miller," she finally said before turning to walk back down the lane. He watched her until she reached the road, then turned abruptly and strode back toward the house, his long legs taking him quickly past the games in the front yard.

"Silas..." Michael called loudly to him. Silas heard him, but his steps never slowed. He stormed through the shaded corridor of the orchard and stopped at the end, kicking a fallen apple as hard as he could. His pulse throbbed behind his eyes and in his temples. He clenched his jaw and his hands.

He could no longer stand to see Kirsten's pain. Watching her eyes well as she bit her lip had almost been his undoing. His hand trembled when he relaxed his fist. How he longed to spare her the harsh realities of her world—to shield her somehow from the people who hated her so. And here he was, completely incapable of doing any of the things he felt so compelled to do. He was limited to buying eight gallons of white paint and spending two days painting her rundown, broken trailer while she hid inside.

The visit she had just paid him was the most she'd been away from her newly painted trailer in three days. He knew that for a fact.

Silas lowered himself against a tree trunk and tilted his face up to catch the spots of sunlight peeking through the leaves. He closed his eyes and took a deep breath. He didn't know, couldn't understand, what it was that captured him so, but he was utterly captivated by her. It was sudden, but she mattered to him. Mattered way too much.

— CHAPTER SEVEN —

Kirsten took a cool shower in an effort to lower her body temperature. It figured that on the first day of June their old window unit air conditioner had decided to die. An Iowa June is no joke. An Iowa July is worse still.

Too hot to turn on her hair dryer, she gathered up her long hair in a messy, twisted bun and tucked a few loose strands behind her ears. She slipped a billowy blouse over her head and reluctantly stepped into her one pair of maternity jeans. Most of her shirts could work until cooler weather came. But the bottoms had been a dilemma. Most days she was at home in a pair of shorts. But occasionally she had to go out and about, so she had bought one pair of jeans, hoping they could serve their purpose in the summer and the winter. It was uncomfortable, but she had no extra money for an entire wardrobe of clothing with expandable tummy panels.

She stepped outside and groaned. The humidity was stifling, and she felt as though she was melting inside the thick denim. Kirsten started her car and took several moments to just bask in the air conditioning blasting through the vents. It was a piece-of-junk car, but it had a good air conditioner. That was worth something.

She glanced back at the trailer and sighed. She lived every day in fear that the red paint would come back, that it would seep through the layers and layers of white or that the culprits would return for another paintball-target torture session.

It was a small relief to see neither scenario had come true. What once was a broken-down, falling-apart, pathetic trailer was now a broken-down, falling-apart, pathetic trailer with a fresh paint job.

Silas.

She'd never asked him to paint the marks away. He'd simply shown up and offered to help. The gratitude Kirsten and Elizabeth felt was beyond expression. The red wounds would still be there if he hadn't shown up with those gallons of paint.

There was no money to spare now with the impending medical expenses and baby necessities. On Kirsten's desk was a letter from her attorney regarding the child support she could expect to receive from Logan. Since he was going to college, the funds she would receive from him would be negligible. Still, every little bit would help. Even $20 meant a pack of diapers or half a can of formula.

The local hospital was only about four miles away—not nearly enough for her to feel like she'd cooled down. She walked quickly through the automatic doors and breathed a sigh of relief as the cold breeze swept over her.

The drill was already familiar. Check in, step on the scale, give a urine sample, have blood pressure checked, etc. All routine and all things that seemed to be happening outside of her—as though it were all happening to someone else and she was just observing. At least until Dr. Burke would come in, squeeze a blob of gel on her tummy, and find the fast thrumming of another heart buried deep within her. Then it became startlingly real and intensely personal. Another life, so vibrant within her. She marveled at how it made her feel more alone than ever.

Kirsten had never been popular, save the one night Logan had coaxed her to his car. Most of her life had been quiet and removed since her father's death. Elizabeth worked countless jobs and left Kirsten home alone by necessity. There had never been a gaggle of friends inviting her over for sleepovers or birthday parties. The trend had continued into high school, where Kirsten was never invited to go shopping or to go to the movies with friends. She'd never made the effort, really. Honestly, she preferred to be home in a way. It was comforting, familiar.

Until recently, kids had not been cruel to her—only ignored her. She was tall, but very thin. Her hair was a gentle auburn. Her clothes were cheap or second-hand. Her car was borderline embarrassing. She was utterly forgettable.

Except, of course, to her enemies. Logan clearly loathed her—even more so now that he'd be held legally responsible for this child. Deb's hatred and jealousy were directed entirely at Kirsten.

After her appointment, Kirsten slowed to turn north off the highway and onto the gravel road, careful to remember the way the gravel had sucked her car around the road. She rounded the bend, and her gaze locked on the farmstead on her left.

It had been quiet when she'd driven by earlier, but now the yard was alive with activity. Anna and Shelby were sweeping off the porch. Caleb was washing a buggy near the barn. A few men were repairing a piece of machinery in the back of the yard.

And Silas was in the garden. Her heart flipped a little when she saw him, his straw hat shielding his face from the harsh sun. At the sound of her passing, his head lifted and she could see him looking at her. She smiled and waved at him. He waved back at her, his face unsmiling.

It was completely unreasonable, she knew, for her to feel about him the way she did. But three times now he had been there in a moment of pain or embarrassment. And each time he had been profoundly kind, sincere, and calm.

When the world had sucked her dry of all the hope she had, she had soaked up his goodness to her like a dry sponge. She'd never had to ask—he'd just given of his time, his help, and his concern without hesitation.

And perhaps that was all there would have been—gratitude for his neighborliness and a contentment with calling him a friend. But try as she might, Kirsten could not get past the way the sound of his voice stirred her very soul. No one had ever done that to her. It was an involuntary reaction, almost a reflexive response to his slow drawl.

He was beautiful, yes. Tall and broad, but thin. His arms were long; his hands were big with long fingers. And those eyes—the color of the sky on a bright summer morning. She'd smiled at him in the library, despite her initial nervousness. It was the first time she'd seen him without his hat on. His short blond hair curled tightly around his tan face and neck. Silas was handsome. No one could deny that, even if they made fun of him, as Deb had, for his simple clothing.

But mere beauty alone wasn't the reason for this attraction she felt every time she saw him. This was about much more than lust. She'd seen enough of lust to last her a lifetime and wanted no part of it. She felt impossibly drawn to Silas, like it was beyond anything she could really control.

In the back of her mind, Kirsten knew that Amish men did not pursue English women. And that meant even more heartache for a heart nearly overflowing with rejection and loneliness.

— CHAPTER EIGHT —

At the urging of his parents, Silas agreed to take Caleb on a trip to central Missouri where their cousin was building a house. He'd written asking for help, and Daniel felt some time away would do Silas some good. Perhaps give him room to think.

At first, Silas had resisted. But he'd soon realized that he needed the space, even if he didn't really want it. A car had been hired to take them down on Monday and bring them back on Thursday. Caleb's enthusiasm about the trip was amusing, but not necessarily contagious.

Caleb was so unlike Silas. But still, Silas felt a bond with him that he had not shared with David or Michael. Caleb had a carefree spirit about him, as if all of life was truly play, even when it was very hard work. Silas prayed fervently that Caleb would keep his lightheartedness throughout his life. Truthfully, he admired the joy Caleb got simply out of living.

Even the way they rode in the car was markedly different. Caleb sat forward in his seat, his back rarely coming in contact with the seatback. Silas, on the other hand, reclined, stretching his long legs as best he could, his head resting on the headrest and swaying with the gentle motion of the car.

As the miles rolled by, Silas stared out the window at the countryside blurring past. Though the bishop had declared driving motor vehicles to be a permissible activity when work-related, Silas still preferred to travel by horse and buggy. He didn't like going fast, nor did he particularly enjoy going very far. A fact not lost on him now as the car sped further and further away from his home.

If he was looking for distance, he'd found it. There would be no chance encounters—no accidental meetings—with Kirsten. He'd be able to work a full day and not be distracted by her car driving by, her unexpected visits, or her shopping at the market. It wasn't that he didn't want to see her. But every time he did, it both tortured and thrilled him.

But now if she drove her car off the road, it would not be his problem. Distance. Space. Freedom. It should feel better, more fulfilling, than it did. Silas was too tired from an early morning in the garden and a long car ride to think any more about why that would be. By the time they arrived at their Uncle Isaac's house where they would be staying, he was ready for a full night's sleep.

It was not yet dawn when Caleb shook Silas awake and they got dressed in their work pants and shirts. Breakfast was hardy—breakfast casserole, homemade cinnamon rolls, bacon and sausages, and hot coffee.

The crew was out, hammers swinging, when the sun's first beams spilled over the horizon. For six blessed hours, Silas's mind was full of nothing but thoughts of his work and those around him. The sun was high in the sky when the men broke for lunch, served on-site at tables tucked under trees. There were at least thirty men, and nearly as many women had pooled their efforts to prepare a good lunch.

Silas ate quickly, gulping down a slice of cherry pie that was not nearly as good as his mother's and walking a short distance away to stretch his legs beneath a small apple tree. He kicked aside a few fallen apples and lay down on his back. With a deep sigh, he let his muscles relax. He laced his fingers beneath his head, closed his eyes, and let his mind wander.

It was as if the tide had been stemmed too long. With a rush, thoughts of Kirsten came flooding into his mind. The reprieve while he was working had been welcome, in a way. For a moment, he considered fighting this overwhelming flood of thought. But he wearily gave in to the things he hardly dared allow.

One of his favorite things about being Amish was the freedom to dream. His life was untouched by television or internet or cell phones.

Growing up as he had, Silas spent a great deal of time daydreaming while he worked in the garden or the workshop. It was a part of his childhood, and it was still part of his life.

Silas sank further into his daydreams, opened his mind, and imagined a horse and buggy pulling into the lane and jostling slowly toward him as he stood on the porch steps, waiting. Three white bonnets slowly came into view as the buggy pulled closer. The buggy stopped. Anna Mae and Shelby Jo bounded out, giggling.

His heart pounded.

Kirsten's face turned to him, and she smiled at him from the driver's seat. Kirsten was in a blue dress, white bonnet, white apron, and sensible shoes, holding the reins out to him.

Silas's eyes flew open. Where had that come from? It was almost as if he were reading a book someone else was writing. These could not be his thoughts; this could hardly be his daydream. These images that would surely haunt him were completely impossible, and it was not like him to be illogical.

Kirsten was not Amish and he definitely was. It wasn't just that he preferred a simple life separate from the world, though he did. It was his faith—the place he found truth and meaning, forgiveness and grace, hope and peace. He could no sooner be non-Amish than he could cease to be a man. He could only live in the Amish world.

But how he ached for Kirsten to be part of that world—his world. How he longed for her to be at this construction site, to be one of those girls clearing tables over there.

The men were stirring now, rising to go back to work. Silas jumped to his feet and briskly walked to join them. Caleb ran to catch up, and Silas threw himself into the work. He was like a man possessed, filled with an unrestrained urgency and intensity that he barely understood. Maybe he was desperate to think of something other than her—to clear his head. Maybe he just needed to do something tangible and good. Maybe he felt guilty, as though he had strangely told God exactly what He, the Almighty, should have done. Maybe he hoped to tire himself out so entirely that tonight, when his head hit the pillow, he'd have no energy for thinking or dreaming and would be rewarded with a deep sleep.

Whatever it was, it had him spent by the day's end. Silas slept hard and woke with aching muscles. Unintentionally, he had created a new routine for himself, and again, after a good lunch, he found himself basking in the breeze of the apple tree, picking up where he had left off.

Kirsten had gone inside to help fix supper. He had tended to the horse and buggy and then gone in to wash up for the evening. His mother, Amy, Anna Mae, and Shelby Jo were all bustling around. But it was Kirsten setting the bread on the table that he noticed. She spared him another smile as she smoothed her hands over her apron. There was a quiet cry, and she turned away quickly, rushing out of the kitchen. She returned with a bundle in her arms. The look on her face as she smiled down and whispered to the infant was tender and sweet. She crossed the room to him, and as she did he could hear her murmur quietly, "Here, you go to your dad for a few minutes and he can tell you all about his day." She smiled up into his eyes and lifted the small bundle up to his waiting arms. Silas held the baby close, and it was then that something inside him—the real him lying under the apple tree in Missouri—nearly exploded and filled every place in his heart with fire. He choked for air and sat bolt upright, his eyes wide and his pulse racing.

"What's the matter with ya?" Caleb laughed from his perch nearby.

Silas blinked rapidly and shook his head, as though he could somehow shake the vision of Kirsten and the baby out of his mind.

"I...I must have fallen asleep."

"I should wonder why," Caleb smirked. "You've been working like a madman."

Silas was silent, his body nearly trembling from the force of his daydreams. It had been so very real—as if he could almost feel the weight of the baby in his arms or hear Kirsten's soft, murmuring voice.

Distance was not solving any problems; it was creating new ones. It had given Silas room to think, just as was intended, but now his mind had run away with him.

Slowly, Silas rose to his feet and followed the other men to the worksite. The house was fully framed and they were now putting up sheeting. As usual, the men knew each other fairly well and worked together smoothly. Silas spoke little, listened a lot, and communicated mostly with his actions.

At the end of the day, he escaped his uncle's storytelling in the living room and went to his room. Normally, he loved storytelling. It was something his father and uncle had grown up with and had brought into their own families. But tonight Silas had to reconcile himself to his thoughts.

What had it all meant? Perhaps nothing but harmless curiosity. Or perhaps he truly wished God could change the circumstances just a little. He knew, no matter what he hoped, that the reality was harsh compared to these wanderings of his mind. Kirsten was not Amish. And as an Amish man, he could not court her. He could not truthfully see a future for them if those basic facts were not altered. Which meant these daydreams, these fantasies, were nothing but painful illusions. Temptations.

Silas pinched his eyes shut as that realization hit him. No, he could not hope for this life that had captured his imagination so completely. The truth ripped open the gaping hole in his heart—Kirsten would never be his. Somehow, he had to wrap his heart around those words, painful barbs though they were. It wasn't complicated. It was simple, much like him. Silas would never be free to love Kirsten and he had to let the dream of a life with her die.

It was the thought he repeated to himself all the next day as he worked, making an effort to think only of that which was and not what he wished could be. He would not tell God that He had made a mistake. God's ways are higher than man's. Silas trusted and believed that deeply, not in spite of the broken condition of the world, but because of it. He had to believe there was a God who would redeem the ugliness of pain and loss for His own good and glory. Besides, Silas very much doubted that God would take orders, or even gentle instructions, from him. For whatever reason, God in His unsearchable wisdom had not put Kirsten in an Amish family. It was not His will.

Silas pounded the nails into boards as he pounded these thoughts and truths into his heart, each one piercing in its own way. At the end of the day on Wednesday, he felt physically, mentally, emotionally, and spiritually spent. It was as though God had opened some part of him that he had been hiding, even from himself.

On the car ride home late Thursday night, Silas admitted to himself that he loved an English woman whom he would never have. It was the most honest he had been with himself or his Creator in many months. The reality of it made the wound throb. There are no funeral services or graves for dead dreams, and Silas struggled to keep his mourning a secret. And as much as he wanted to ask God why, he knew the answer wouldn't matter. It wouldn't change anything and thereby wouldn't satisfy him.

.๏ඏ ඏ๑.

It was late when the car made its way back to Bradford. Caleb and Silas wearily set their bags down in the kitchen where Mary had lemonade and cookies waiting.

She smiled and welcomed them home with a hug and a light kiss on the cheek. First Caleb, then Silas. Her hands rested on his shoulders for a brief moment as she looked in his eyes. The frustration was gone, as she and Daniel had prayed it would be. But something new had taken its place. There was an emptiness in his eyes now. Something had happened to him. And though Silas looked outwardly calm, Mary sensed his pain.

Caleb revived enough to recount stories to his parents while Silas sat silently eating the monster cookies Mary had just taken out of the oven. He answered an occasional question but offered little extra. Soon the boys said goodnight and shuffled up the stairs to their room, careful not to wake their sisters.

Mary watched them go. Slowly, her gaze swung to Daniel, who was still seated at the table, watching her. Mary was normally able to read his face so well, but tonight his expression was mysterious and guarded, even in her presence.

"Did ya make it to the Walkers' today?" Mary asked, hoping to ease the worried lines on her husband's face.

"No," he visibly paused and shook his head.

Mary waited for an explanation, wondering why Daniel had not paid a visit to their neighbors as they had discussed just this morning. It wasn't like him to not hold up his end of a promise to her. Any time Mary asked him to do something for her, he usually dropped all his work to fulfill her request. It was a touching way of showing his love for her. But tonight, there was something weighing on him. He stood slowly, as though he was heavily burdened.

"I'll go in the morning," Daniel said quietly, turning to her and holding his hand out for hers. Mary stood and wove her fingers into his.

— CHAPTER NINE —

It was safest if Kirsten stayed at home, she decided. As long as she stayed within the four walls of the trailer, no one stared at her, called her names, or gave her a pitying look. Of course, the downside was that no one ever saw her, spoke to her, or smiled at her. She liked being home, but being a hermit was becoming annoying.

By Thursday, she had to get out of her house. Kirsten eased her car onto the gravel road and drove carefully. Neither her pride nor her wallet could afford to go in the ditch again. Though that would be one way to see Silas. She glanced out the passenger window as she rumbled slowly past the Miller farm. Two girls, one of them Amy, were in the garden. But there was no sign of Silas. Kirsten tried to convince herself that she wasn't disappointed.

The library was blissfully quiet and free from Debs or Logans. She took her time checking her email, surfing the internet, and loading up on books. She waited patiently at the checkout counter as a mom with two children and a baby in a car seat checked out. The woman looked over at her, met her eyes, and smiled.

"When are you due?" She seemed genuine and pleasant.

"November 10," Kirsten said shyly. She could have told the woman exactly how many days away that was, but she kept it to herself.

"Well, that's exciting!" the stranger answered. "Do you know what you're having?"

"A girl," Kirsten said, suddenly breathless.

"Ah, lots of pink," the woman said with a smile.

Kirsten could only nod. The truth was she didn't have a single thing for this baby.

"Got a name picked out yet?"

"No..." Kirsten shook her head. She'd read through a few name books, but nothing seemed quite right.

"You've got some time yet," the woman reassured her.

Kirsten nodded again, trying to calm the anxiety she felt creeping up inside her. She had no pink things. No name. No crib. No father. Nothing. She could only hope this woman wouldn't ask any more questions.

"Good luck!" The woman smiled at Kirsten as she herded her children out the door.

Kirsten heaved a sigh of relief that she had had both a perfectly pleasant conversation about her pregnancy and that it was over. She brought her books out to her car, dumping them in the backseat in a messy heap. She slumped behind the steering wheel, jammed the key in the ignition and...nothing.

Nothing aside from a sickening whirring sound. She tried slamming her fist down on the dash like they did in movies, but that didn't do anything other than hurt her hand. Of course it didn't.

Kirsten sighed again, the sweat already running down the side of her face. Maybe she could just use her non-existent cell phone to call Silas's non-existent cell phone, and he could pick her up in his horse and buggy. A giggle escaped her, followed by another and another until her whole body was shaking with laughter. She rested her forehead on the steering wheel with a *thunk* and decided to walk to the gas station where her mom worked. It was too hot to be walking around town, and Kirsten was drenched with sweat by the time she made it to the station where her mom was standing behind the register.

After a brief conversation, Kirsten got the keys to her mom's van, promising to come back and get her when her shift was done. Kirsten went back to get her books out of her car and drove home. Nearly every buggy she passed could be him, and since it was almost noon there were many rolling on the shoulder alongside the highway. But none of the straw-hatted men looked up as she went by—none of them waved. Where was Silas now? Perhaps he might be avoiding her after her emotional visit on Sunday. She hadn't seen him since.

It was ridiculous really. Silas didn't seem the hiding type. And yet he was nowhere to be found when she drove by.

ᴥᴥ

Kirsten was lying on her bed, reading *The Grapes of Wrath* while the fan blew on her legs. She figured she'd at least start the recommended reading for college preparation that her English teacher had given her, even if college classes were mostly likely not in her immediate future.

Elizabeth was home this Friday morning, preparing for a long shift at the gas station.

Above the hum of the box fan whirring away in her window, she heard something in the yard. Kirsten lifted her head off the pillow to peer through the spinning fan blades. She blinked several times, but no, she was not seeing things. There, parked in her driveway behind the van, was a black buggy. Kirsten jolted upright and the baby kicked in protest. With one hand on her stomach where the baby had kicked and one hand finger-combing her long hair, she stared out her window. He'd only shown up once before, and that had been to point out her paintball-riddled trailer. She'd been out to the mailbox this morning, so she was pretty sure this wouldn't be about vandalism. Her mind raced as she turned to her reflection in the mirror.

Whatever Silas's reason for visiting, she didn't want him to see her quite like this—hair still damp from the shower, cutoff sweats, and a white tank top. She wasn't even sure her own mother should see her like this. Kirsten snapped into action at the sound of a firm knock on the door and threw her hair in a ponytail as she listened to her mom open the door with a greeting.

"Hello, Daniel. Everything okay?" It was normal to expect bad news, it seemed.

Daniel. Not Silas. Kirsten felt a flicker of disappointment before her heart slowed a bit, but she could still feel her pulse thrumming in her ears as she swapped out the shorts for a pair of stretchy exercise pants.

"*Gut* morning, Elizabeth." Oh, that familiar lilting drawl. "Everything is fine. I just came by to invite you and Kirsten to dinner tomorrow night."

Kirsten froze, one arm through the sleeve of her t-shirt. Dinner. At Silas's house. In Silas's house. Her heart raced again at the thought.

"Oh! That would be lovely. What time?"

"My Mary will have supper ready around six o'clock or so." Kirsten could hear the similarity in Daniel and Silas's voices—the pitch was the same.

"Can I bring anything?"

"Just yerselves." She could actually hear the smile in his voice.

"Okay. We'll be there. Thank you, Daniel," Elizabeth called after him.

Kirsten sat on her bed, pulling the t-shirt back over her head and tossing it on the chair by her desk. This was new. She'd never been any farther than halfway down the Millers' driveway. It certainly wasn't unheard of for the Amish to invite their English neighbors over for supper now and then. In fact, Mary had done just that several times in the past ten years. But Kirsten had always shyly begged out of it, making up excuses like studying for a test or writing a paper.

Kirsten looked up at her mom standing in her doorway.

"You heard?"

Kirsten nodded.

"I know you don't feel like going places lately," Elizabeth allowed.

"It's okay," Kirsten said nonchalantly.

"It is?"

"Yeah mom. It's fine. Sounds...fun."

"Really?" Elizabeth questioned. "I thought you didn't like going out. You always want to just stay in."

"I like the Millers," Kirsten said with a shrug. One of them in particular.

"I didn't realize you knew they existed, much less liked them."

"I know Mary. And Silas. They've both been very nice to me," she said quietly, staring at her feet.

Elizabeth seemed to ponder that for a moment before going back to packing her lunch.

This was going to be a very interesting weekend.

— CHAPTER TEN —

Silas had just finished helping Michael with the chores when Amy came out to the barn.

"Silas, Mom says ya should come in and wash up for dinner," she announced a little too distractedly.

"Why?"

Amy shifted uncomfortably, like she was keeping a secret. "We're having company over for supper."

Silas stared at her a few moments longer, trying to decide if he wanted to know what was going on or not. It was only 5:30. Thirty minutes to clean up seemed a bit excessive.

"Trust me," Amy said quietly, "You want to go get cleaned up."

Silas's brow furrowed, one side of his mouth twitched in an almost-smile. "Am I that dirty, Amy?" he laughed, exaggeratedly examining his hands and arms.

"Just go." She smiled back, giving him a playful shove in the back. The kitchen was a bustling place, all the girls scurrying around while Mary directed them. Silas got another set of instructions to go get cleaned up and put on a clean shirt. He shuffled up the stairs, took a shower, and slipped into a clean shirt and pants. He could hear voices as he came down the stairs.

"Kirsten is hoping to find some work in town." It was Elizabeth's voice.

"What kind of work would ya like to find?" Mary asked.

"Oh…I'm open to just about anything."

Silas could hardly move, but he forced his legs to walk toward the sound of her voice. She was standing in the kitchen, just inside the door, her mother next to her. Kirsten's eyes blinked up at him when he stepped in the room, her face lighting in a smile he was powerless to not return.

"Hi, Silas."

"Hullo, Kirsten." Saying her name out loud felt good.

Daniel entered then, warmly welcoming the dinner guests and claiming their attention for a few moments. Silas flashed a look at Mary, who simply smiled. He'd not spoken of his heartache with either of his parents, not even when his father had asked. They had no way of knowing. The fact that Kirsten and Elizabeth were standing in his home was proof that they were clueless about his tormented heart. And now, he almost wished he had said something. But he hadn't expected them to invite her over for dinner either. Now it was too late, and he would have to spend one gloriously torturous meal with the one he wanted but could never have.

He lowered himself heavily into a place at the table, which was brimming with food: pot roast, mashed potatoes, green beans, fruit salad, and sweet rolls. Mary and the girls had created a feast, and she was nearly bouncing with excitement as she always was when she had a full table.

Mary directed Kirsten to the chair across from him, and Silas was relieved when Daniel directed them to bow their heads for prayer. Silas silently added his own prayer for strength and then focused as much as politely possible on the food being passed around and loaded onto plates.

He chanced a glance at Kirsten, only to find she was looking at him, a question in her eyes. He looked away nervously. She was quiet as well, allowing Elizabeth to handle most of the conversation.

As Silas knew would happen, his mother attempted to draw Kirsten out.

"Are ya having a *gut* summer so far, Kirsten?"

Kirsten visibly paused, and Silas's eyes flashed up to watch her face. An indecipherable look passed over her features before she smoothed her expression.

"It's been good in some ways," she admitted quietly. Silas could hear the other unspoken half of her answer.

"How have ya been feeling lately?" Mary persisted.

Silas struggled to contain his grimace, wishing she'd just let it go and wanting to hear Kirsten's response at the same time.

"Um, well, okay, I suppose. Just really hot," Kirsten stammered, and then blushed deeply as if she'd just shared too much. Silas stared at her dark lashes, resting gently on her pink cheeks.

Mary smiled at her, pretending not to notice Kirsten's embarrassment. "The heat has been oppressive," she agreed. "Even our garden has suffered a bit," she added, looking pointedly at Silas.

He desperately wished that she would leave him out of the conversation. To be fair, his mother thought that he and Kirsten were friends—which he supposed was partially true. And her attempts to draw him into the conversation were not meant to hurt him. Still, they were unwanted. Silas merely nodded and forked more food into his mouth.

It was a relief of sorts when dessert was served. Cherry pie. Silas's favorite. No chance of skipping dessert and escaping to the outdoors.

They finished up and the kids eagerly ran outside to play hide-and-seek at Daniel's suggestion. Silas followed and watched Amy, Shelby, and Anna scatter as Caleb counted loudly under the maple tree. The screen door quietly squeaked behind him. Silas turned and found her standing on the covered porch. He looked away momentarily, tempted to follow his sisters and find a good hiding place. But he turned back toward her instead.

"Would ya like to go for a walk?" It was as if someone else was putting words in his mouth. Every minute with her was painful. He didn't know if he could bear another second.

"Sure." Kirsten smiled and came toward him.

Oh well. He was bound to be haunted by a thousand images of this night. Kirsten sitting across from him at the table. Kirsten laughing at Caleb's goose story. Kirsten shyly smiling at him. Kirsten talking about her baby. Kirsten's hand lightly resting on her stomach. He felt as if he had been dragged into the desert to be tempted.

They slowly walked to the orchard and then through the leafy arches where Silas had gone to escape her.

"Are these all apple trees?" she asked, her head tipping back to examine the branches.

"Most of them. We have a row of peach trees over there and a few cherry trees in the front," he answered, pointing to different places.

"This is a magical place," Kirsten breathed as she slowly turned around. Indeed, it looked ethereal with the soft glow of the evening sun pouring in through the shaded canopy.

"It's my favorite," he said with a smile, looking away from her.

"You have such a beautiful home, a beautiful family," she said wistfully.

"I am...very...thankful for my life," he said slowly.

Silas looked up to see her touching an apple hanging low on a burdened branch, her fingers gently tracing it while she examined it. He waited for her to pull it from the branch. It wasn't ripe, but even Shelby couldn't resist picking the low-hanging apples. Kirsten stepped closer and lightly touched the apple to her nose, the branch bending to her inspection. And then she released it, gently allowing the fruit to swing back on the branch.

"How old are ya, Kirsten?" he asked her suddenly.

Her eyes snapped to him. "Eighteen. How old are you, Silas?"

"Twenty-one."

He gazed at her, remembering his vision of her in an Amish dress, and a smile crept across his face.

"What?" she asked warily, spying his look of chagrin.

He laughed once, shook his head, and dropped his eyes to the ground. "I wish you were...Amish."

"Oh," she said sadly. He hadn't expected the look of disappointment that shadowed her face. Truthfully, he had anticipated her laughter. But not this. Not this grief that clouded her features and made her so solemn.

"Kirsten?"

She looked up and tried to smile, but there in her eyes he saw his pain—his frustration—echoed back to him.

"I wish I were Amish, too," she said with a grimace.

Silas's heart gave a hard thud in his chest, nearly knocking the wind out of him and leaving a lump in his throat. She couldn't truly mean that. Many people claimed they wanted to be Amish, but so few were ever able to convert to the strict lifestyle. Outsiders often had idealistic visions of Amish life that were ridiculously off the mark. Even if she thought she wanted to be Amish, he doubted that she really knew what she was saying. Still, it wasn't impossible. And he needed to know how serious she was. There was a very good chance that he was digging an impossibly deep hole for himself, but he was unable to stop until he knew with absolute certainty.

"You want to live this simple life?" His eyes never left her face.

"I think you have a beautiful life," she replied.

"No cars. No electricity. No blue jeans or t-shirts." He could go on, but he stopped. What was he asking her?

"No pesky flat tires or car repairs. No punching a time clock. No ever-changing fashion trends," she countered.

"No college degree," he said finally. And for a minute he could see her consider that. But then her eyes dropped to the ground.

"That dream is gone anyway," she murmured quietly.

Silas stared at her, not at all sure she was even remotely aware of the basic principles and practices of Amish life.

"Why do you want me to be Amish?" she asked him softly.

"I...like you. I'd like to court ya." He shrugged, embarrassed, but relieved too. It was far more than he'd ever said to any other girl before. And it was honest.

"You want me like this?" she asked pointedly. Her real question was not lost on him.

"Yes," Silas answered without hesitation.

"Another man's baby growing inside me?"

"Yer more than just a soon-to-be mother," he replied, shaking his head.

"But there's no way. Is there?" The question hurt her to ask. He could hear the pain in her voice.

His heart hammered within him. Yes, there was a way. Of course there was a way. Though he didn't know if the bishop would approve. There were steps she'd have to take, one of them being to live with an Amish family for a year. She'd have to attend services, take classes, live according to the *Ordnung*. It was not designed to be an easy process—but it was a necessary one. But could he dare to believe, to trust that this was what was best for her? For them?

"Silas?"

"There's a way."

She was watching him intently now, her eyes searching his face.

"With the permission of the bishop, we could get married and you could become Amish. After a time, you could take instruction and join the church."

Kirsten was silent for several long moments.

"Marry you?" she asked quietly.

"I would provide for ya and you would be sheltered from the outside world. You would be a part of my family."

"My baby?" Kirsten's hand moved to her stomach.

"I'd raise it as my own…as I was raised," he gently reassured her.

Kirsten was quiet as the words he'd spoken sank in deeper, taking root. He waited, hardly able to breathe. So this was it then, the moment she would decide and he would know. He had asked her to carry the burden of changing her life in exchange for his offer to carry the burden of raising her child. He knew, without a doubt, that he wouldn't consider his end of the deal to be a burden.

"Is that what you want, Silas?" she asked him, squinting up into his face.

He dropped his eyes. "Yes. More than anything." It was the first time he'd admitted his feelings out loud, much less to another person. And now he'd confessed them to her.

"Me too," she finally whispered.

Silas's eyes slowly lifted to hers. She was serious. He could tell as much by the look on her face.

"It's not merely a lifestyle, Kirsten. It's our belief that this is how God would have us live and how we can best serve Him. There'll be religious instruction, and they'll expect you to join the church and agree with our teachings," he warned.

"Silas, I've sort of lost my way," she said thickly. "I see the peace and purpose your faith gives you. How could I not want that? I know I would have so much to learn…" Kirsten said with a small smile. "But I'm a fast learner."

"I need to talk to the bishop and my parents first," he said, still searching her face for a trace of uncertainty.

"And I should talk to my mom," Kirsten said with a nod.

Silas shook his head in agreement.

"Are ya sure, Kirsten?" he asked, taking her hand in his.
Kirsten's smile was tentative at first, then blinding.
"Yes, Silas. I'm sure."
Silas smiled back at her, knowing he was sure, too.

— CHAPTER ELEVEN —

Mary had been worried when Silas knocked on her and Daniel's bedroom door that evening. And his request had shocked her speechless. She had not seen this coming. Daniel, on the other hand, had sat stoically and silently until Silas had said all he had to say. His eyes had been riveted on his son, and Mary had watched as he calmly listened and rubbed his beard.

Silas had been respectful, but confident. He wanted to marry Kirsten, to help her become Amish and raise her baby as his own. To an outsider, it might sound like a reasonable and decent thing to do. But now, as she sat amongst the People on this Sunday morning, listening to the preachers, her heart churned uneasily within her.

Any of the mothers surrounding her this morning would have panicked. Surely she had never desired for any of her children to marry outside their faith. That hadn't been her intention in inviting Elizabeth and Kirsten over for supper. Silas and Kirsten were at least acquainted, and it had been some years since they had invited their neighbors over for supper. She'd thought it would cheer him up. When she'd asked Daniel to extend the invitation, he had stared at her long and hard. Had he known about Silas's affection for Kirsten? He must have.

And yet, as terrifying as this uncharted territory was, she felt a strange sense of excitement simmering just beneath her fear. Mary had always loved Kirsten and felt a strong connection with her. Silas was not leaving their faith—quite the opposite. He was bringing in someone who certainly needed the Lord. How she would love to see Kirsten bend her knee in baptism and find her joy and purpose in living for Jesus instead of desperately searching for love in all the wrong places. Could Silas lead her there? Could she?

Yes, the deep desire to see Kirsten as a sister in the Lord was aching within her. If Silas felt so strongly about her, she could only imagine how earnest his efforts would be to lead Kirsten to their Savior.

Daniel must have felt the same. He had strenuously questioned Silas's commitment to the church and to the People, only to be reassured by Silas that none of his beliefs or convictions had changed. It was apparent that their son was more committed than ever to his faith, confessing that he had actually decided to deny his feelings for Kirsten. At least until she had expressed a desire to become Amish and a hunger for their faith. That had changed everything.

During the long silence, Daniel had paced the floorboards in their bedroom, Silas and Mary's eyes following his every move.

"We would have to ask the bishop," Daniel had finally said, turning to Silas.

The look on Silas's face then was one Mary had never seen. Hope, desire, joy. His eyes had been wide as he nodded eagerly.

Daniel had looked to her for her approval, and she had nodded with wide eyes. It was as hard to believe then as it was now.

As much as David and Michael surely shared Daniel's joyful countenance, she could see now that Silas shared her heart.

They had stayed up late into the night, discussing the consequences and the meaning of what Silas was proposing. Parents were not usually involved in a couple's decision to marry, but this was a special case. Silas was asking for their help in teaching Kirsten the Amish ways. Living with an Amish family was the best way for her to learn the simple life. Mary's mind swam with all the things she would teach her—lessons she had spread out over all of Amy's seventeen years. The burden of teaching Kirsten their ways would largely fall on Mary's shoulders. The other guidance and support would fall to Silas. It was only through prayer that Mary felt the final confirmation that God would lead them on this uncharted course.

There were other things to consider as well. Normally, a young woman wishing to join the People would need to live with an Amish family for a year, studying the life and the faith. There were instructional classes and then, finally, a baptism. Only after the baptism would she be allowed to marry another baptized member of the church. But Kirsten was expecting a baby soon. And that made things far more complicated. She didn't know what the bishop would say or if the same requirements would be in place.

Mary's eyes flicked up to where the men sat across from the women at Sunday meeting. She watched Silas as he listened intently to the preacher's sermon. He seemed so unafraid, as if their meeting with the bishop was already behind him and not mere minutes away.

If for some reason Kirsten ever decided to leave them, the heartbreak on all sides would be unbearable. If Kirsten failed to seek out baptism, Silas could be shunned. Could Mary risk her son's heart this way?

Visions of Abraham faithfully offering up his own son filled her mind as Daniel quietly asked the bishop for a moment of his time while the others filed out of the benches to the lunch being prepared. Was this a test of faith? Was God asking them to sacrifice their son? Truly, He'd done no less for them. That thought alone was the only way she could make her legs move to follow Daniel, the bishop, and her sweet Silas to the quiet, secluded shade of the maple tree in the Lapps' side yard.

If God would open the doors, they would walk through them. Mary shuddered inwardly, wondering if or when one would slam in their faces.

— CHAPTER TWELVE —

Kirsten watched the buggy pull into her yard, holding her breath and hoping it would be Silas this time. In the dim evening light, she could see his tall, thin silhouette step down and stride confidently toward the trailer. She answered his knock, smiling to see him at her front door.

"I came to see if you'd like to go fer a ride," Silas said with an easy smile.

Kirsten beamed back at him and glanced down at her clothes.

"Can I have a second to change?"

He nodded once and she hurried back to her room. Several frantic minutes later, Kirsten let the screen door slam behind her and walked down the short sidewalk to where Silas stood, quietly murmuring to the horse hitched to a sleek, black buggy. Silas smiled brilliantly when he saw her and moved to help her into the buggy.

Kirsten had certainly never been in an Amish buggy before, though she'd always been curious about what it would be like to ride in one. Inside, she was surprised to see how small it was—even smaller than her compact car.

Silas lightly stepped in and sat beside her. Kirsten desperately fought to slow her racing heartbeat. She tried to convince herself that she was still winded from her whirlwind wardrobe change. Her blouse and jeans were far from "acceptable Amish attire," but it was the best (and only) thing she could do.

Silas sat so close that his leg pressed gently against hers. She watched as he guided the horse back onto the road, and she gripped the seat, trying to relax. The wind blew into the buggy, and the horse trotted at what she suspected was a relaxed pace. The rhythm was mesmerizing. Kirsten breathed deeply and felt herself relax in the seat next to Silas.

"Tell me about your horse," she said, breaking the silence.

"His name is Titus. He's about three years old," he answered easily.

"What kind of horse is he?" Kirsten asked, turning to study Silas's profile.

"A Standardbred."

Kirsten's eyes traveled the length of the reins, from the harness to where they rested lightly in Silas's large hands. He held them loosely. His calloused palms marked his days spent doing physical labor.

"Does it take a long time to learn how to...drive?" she questioned.

Silas smiled at her uncertainty, his eyes focused on the horse's back.

"No," he shook his head. "You'll learn soon enough, I 'spect."

"Oh." Kirsten hadn't expected him to say that.

"Did ya talk with yer mother, Kirsten?" he asked quietly.

Kirsten nodded, her pulse quickening again.

"What did she say?" he asked.

Kirsten realized she was being overly shy.

"She wasn't so sure at first. But as we talked, I think she was more okay. In the end, she said it was my decision and that she'd support me in whatever I chose."

Silas looked at her then. "Did she...help you think it over?"

"Yes," Kirsten said simply, remembering her mother's initial shock. The utter silence followed by the searching for words. And when the words came, they didn't stop. So many questions her mom had put to her. More than Silas had. But with each answer, Kirsten felt more and more sure that she knew what she wanted for her life.

After several long, silent minutes, Elizabeth had choked out, "Are you sure honey? It would be such a different life for you. For your baby."

"A different life might be good for us," Kirsten had answered quietly, a lump stuck in her throat as she considered all the nights she'd spent home alone while her mother worked tirelessly.

"But you're...it's not his baby," Elizabeth had stammered.

"Silas said he wants to be a father to my baby."

"Do you love him, Kirsten?"

"Silas is extremely kind. And good. And I really like him," Kirsten had said, studying the pattern in the rug. "I think I could love him."

Elizabeth had stared at her for a long time.

"The Millers are good people," Elizabeth had finally said.

"I know."

Kirsten looked at Silas to find that his eyes had been on her as she'd been reminiscing. She smiled at him, knowing he'd be a good father.

"And you, Silas? How do your parents feel about...me?"

He grinned as he spoke. "Oh, they like you. They understand and support our intentions. They're willing to help you learn how to live plain. We'll live in their house for a while—until we're ready for our own place," he explained.

Kirsten processed all this, wondering if it was as easy for Daniel and Mary as Silas made it sound. Somehow, she doubted it.

"This is my brother Michael's place," Silas said, nodding to a farmstead on the north side of the road, just a quarter mile west of Silas's home. Kirsten followed his gaze to a farm with a white two-story house and a large white barn surrounded by other white outbuildings. All of it was surrounded by a beautifully shaded yard.

"He has a dairy," Silas continued. "He's married to Deborah, and they have one son and a baby on the way."

Kirsten looked long at the quiet farm, the buildings and shaded yard nearly glowing in the early evening sun.

"So you're an uncle," Kirsten said with a grin.

"Oh, *jah*—three times over so far," he laughed. "David, my oldest brother, and his wife, Sarah, live over here," Silas pointed to a property along the south side of the road. The house was set farther back than Michael's, but it was also large and white. "He farms most of this quarter," Silas said with a wave. "They have two children. Danny is two and Maria is about six months."

Kirsten nodded and smiled, trying desperately to commit all this information to memory.

They'd only been riding for about fifteen minutes when Silas pulled the buggy into an abandoned farmyard. Only an old barn stood amongst the tall, mature trees.

It was blissfully quiet—no sounds of passing cars, no radios or TVs droning in the background. The only noise was the sound of the breeze ruffling the leaves, whooshing through the grass, and making the leather harnesses creak. Kirsten closed her eyes and inhaled deeply, the air blowing gently on her face. She smelled the leather interior and Silas—he smelled faintly of soap. She smiled to herself and opened her eyes to find him looking intently at her.

"Kirsten, being Amish isn't just a way of life—it's a life of deep faith. You'd be expected to follow the teachings and ordinances of the church. Some of it might seem very...different to ya."

She was silent as he spoke. "It will mean more than learning how to do the laundry, sew a shirt, or drive a buggy. You'll be learning, studying, and living according to the Scriptures."

"Are you trying to talk me out of it?" Kirsten asked after a time, confusion lacing her words and clouding her face.

"No!" Silas said in surprise. Then more calmly, "No."

"Do you think I can do it?" she asked then, wondering at the reason for his speech.

"*Jah*, I think ya can. Of course, we'll all help ya in whatever way we can. There are classes you can take one day that will help explain our beliefs."

Kirsten nodded, still not sure what to say.

"I just don't want ya to be...too surprised," he said as he gently smiled at her.

Kirsten looked deeply into his blue eyes, still bright in the dim light, and felt peace at his words. True to his character, he was being far more caring to her than anyone had ever been. If he had thought she couldn't do it, that she couldn't make the transition, he would never have asked her to try.

But she could see that Silas confidently believed that she could be, should be, his wife. And his judgment was most likely more sound than hers. Though right now, she had no doubt that marrying Silas Miller was the right thing to do. The very best thing to do. He clearly believed in Someone, so she felt conviction that this path to him was, for once, the very place she should be.

"I believe," she said hesitantly, reading his eyes, "that I should be with you."

He smiled again at her, his eyes dancing in the twilight.

"Will you marry me then, Kirsten?" he asked, beaming down at her.

She smiled back at him. It would be impossible not to.

"Yes, Silas. I'll marry you."

She expected him to kiss her then, but instead he grabbed the reins and snapped them, jolting the buggy forward. He urged Titus on at a faster clip, and they were soon cruising past David's and Michael's farms, the sun setting behind them. It was darker now in the buggy, much darker, but Kirsten could faintly make out Silas's face, the grin still tugging at the corner of his mouth.

"My mom would like it if ya could come over in the next day or two. She's working on yer dress and wants to do some fittin'." He turned to Kirsten abruptly, as though he remembered something he had forgotten. "I've spoken to the bishop, and since this is a special situation, he's given permission for us to marry soon. He's willing to give you some special classes after you've had some time to adjust," he explained.

"How soon will we be married?"

"In a couple weeks," he said as he watched her face.

Kirsten supposed she should feel shocked at the timing he was suggesting, but relief swept over her instead.

"Sounds like a good plan," she said with a shy smile.

Silas seemed relieved and reassured, and he swung his gaze back to the road.

"I can come by tomorrow, if that would work for your mom," Kirsten offered as he turned into her driveway.

Silas nodded. "I'll come to pick ya up around four o'clock."

"Oh, I can walk. It's no trouble," Kirsten said, shrugging.

"No. I'll pick ya up," he stated quietly, and she knew instinctively that this was something she shouldn't argue against.

"That would be nice," she agreed with a nod.

"After yer done with Mom, I thought we could go out for supper," he said as he smiled bashfully.

"Out? You go...out? Like on dates?"

Silas laughed quietly and nodded.

Okay." Kirsten doubted she would ever figure this man out.

He pulled the buggy to a stop in front of her home, jumped down, and turned to gently help her out of the buggy, his hands firm around her waist.

"Thanks for the ride," she said, suddenly breathless from his touch.

Silas leaned down and brushed his lips across her cheek. Her skin blazed beneath his lips.

"Good night, Kirsten," he murmured against her temple.

Those were the last words she wanted to hear every night for the rest of her life.

— Chapter Thirteen —

Silas sat up tall in the buggy as he drove down the lane the next afternoon with Kirsten by his side. He parked between the house and the barn and got out to help her down. She had said she was about five months along, but she was still so small. He wondered to himself if her time would come earlier than expected, and he was overcome with a sudden urge to treat her like an overripe peach.

Mary met them on the stairs with a bright, warm smile. He watched his mother embrace Kirsten tightly. Without so much as a glance his way, Mary ushered his bride into the house, seeming to have forgotten his existence for the time being.

Silas had wondered how his parents would treat Kirsten, and it was a relief to see that now that the bishop had given his approval for the marriage due to the special circumstances, his parents had completely committed themselves to helping Kirsten in her transition. There was not a hint of hesitation or fear in their dealings with her.

Having watered his horse and checked and rechecked the harnesses, Silas waited on the porch steps for the better part of an hour.

Eventually, Kirsten reappeared, Mary's arm gently guiding her around the waist.

"Silas," Mary called, "You will bring Kirsten and her mother over the night after next for supper?" She'd made it sound like a question, though Silas knew it wasn't. He nodded, his eyes fixed on Kirsten.

"*Gut.* I'll see ya day after next," Mary said to Kirsten with a glowing look. Clearly, his mother had found another daughter. Silas's heart flopped in his chest at the thought.

Almost without thinking, he reached his hand out to Kirsten and was nearly surprised to feel her much smaller hand take his. He led her to the buggy and reluctantly released her hand once she was seated comfortably.

He had not been able to forget the pleasant feeling of having her sitting close on the bench seat. But then again, he didn't want to forget.

Kirsten was quiet, staring silently out at the farms they passed on their way into town. Occasionally, a car would pass them and she'd jump in surprise. Silas remained unaffected by the traffic, but he secretly enjoyed the way she almost imperceptibly leaned into him when she was startled.

He waved at a buggy across the road, recognizing Jacob and Anna Troyer. With a mix of annoyance and satisfaction, he watched them stare in open-mouthed surprise.

"Where would ya like to eat?" he asked Kirsten when they were almost to town.

"Oh, um, doesn't matter to me. Do you have a favorite?" she asked, genuine curiosity in her eyes.

He smiled wryly and sighed. "Pizza is my favorite."

"That sounds good to me." Kirsten nodded in agreement.

Silas wordlessly guided the buggy into the parking lot of the pizza place, tied Titus to a light post, and came back to offer her a hand down, his skin tingling when she touched him.

"Will Titus be okay here?" Kirsten asked, peering worriedly back at the horse.

Silas was surprised at her concern, but he smiled to reassure her. "*Jah,* he'll be just fine."

The smell of pizza overtook his senses the moment they walked inside. He almost didn't notice that Kirsten had frozen solid. Her jaw was clenched shut—that much he could plainly see. But before he could ask her what was wrong, a waitress appeared, her eyes showing her obvious surprise. Silas knew it wasn't because he was Amish—at least not solely.

"Booth or table?" the waitress asked, making an effort to get over her surprise.

"Booth, please," Silas answered.

"Right this way."

Kirsten woodenly followed in the waitress's footsteps, and Silas slowly sauntered after them. They slid in across from one another, and Kirsten immediately glued her attention to the menu in front of her. Silas sat, relaxed, his hands folded lightly on top of the menu. The waitress left with a promise to come back in a few minutes. Kirsten followed her departure out of the corner of her eye. Her gaze swung back and she noticed Silas looking at her.

"Are ya all right?" he asked lowly, so only she could hear.

She nodded almost imperceptibly and slid back against the seat.

"How do you endure the staring?" she asked quietly.

Silas shrugged. "I don't even notice. Was someone staring?"

Kirsten slowly shook her head. "Silas, I'll bring shame to you—your family."

Her voice cracked on the words. He waited until she looked up at him, the glimmer of tears in her eyes wrenching him. Silas reached his hand across the table, palm up, and waited.

Kirsten stared at his extended hand for several long seconds before timidly placing her trembling hand in his strong, steady one. At his touch, she sighed. He watched her battle the tears away.

"Kirsten, you are my family," he said quietly but firmly. "And I will never be ashamed of you." He meant it with every fiber of his being and gripped her hand as tightly as he dared.

She smiled and squeezed his hand back.

"You haven't even opened your menu," she observed with a raised brow.

"I like it all," he said with a smile.

"Are you always this easy-going, Silas Miller?"

"No," he answered, a playful smile on his face. "I hate losing at Monopoly."

Kirsten laughed and her whole body seemed to relax. He released her hand and they decided on a simple pepperoni pizza.

"Silas?" He loved the sound of his name from her lips, her English accent free from any trace of a Pennsylvania Dutch drawl. His words must sound as different to her as hers did to him. "Your mom was talking a little about the wedding, and...I have a lot of questions," she said with a grin. "It's just that English weddings are so different from what she was describing, and I've never been to an Amish wedding before."

He shook his head. "Mom or Amy could answer yer questions. They know more about weddings than I do."

"Okay." He hated how disappointed she looked. "I have one about something else."

He looked at her, waiting while she struggled to find the words.

"Will I have to have my baby at home, or can I go to a hospital?" she finally managed.

Silas waited until she looked at him. "You may do whatever ya wish, but most Amish in this area go to the hospital."

"Oh! Good." Kirsten's relief was evident.

The pizza arrived and their attention was diverted. Silas could almost feel her tension melting away. They left the restaurant with a takeout box for Caleb. It wasn't until he had nearly driven past her on the street that Silas noticed one of the girls from the library standing on the sidewalk, watching them in total shock. Kirsten noticed her, but surprisingly she didn't react at all. Instead, she turned and looked up into his face for a long moment before smiling and breathing deeply.

They wound their way out of town, carefully but confidently navigating the busy streets. Silas breathed an audible sigh of relief when the horses turned onto the first stretch of gravel road that led home.

"The world all seems so different when you just slow down a bit," Kirsten said quietly, making eye contact with a deer that was lingering in a field as they slowly passed by.

"That's because you can actually see it and it isn't just one big blur out yer window," Silas said with a grin.

Kirsten laughed and pulled a hairband out of her pocket. She reached up and twisted her hair into a knot, fastening the band around it. It wasn't the way a plain woman would pull up her hair, but Silas's heart pounded in his chest. Loose tendrils of hair curled lightly against her neck, and he was powerless to look away.

The extra buggies parked in the yard between the house and the barn were a helpful diversion.

"Would ya like to meet my brothers?" Silas asked after clearing his throat. At Kirsten's nod, he turned into the lane and pulled up next to the barn. Caleb peeked out of the barn's side door and ran to the buggy, taking the reins from Silas while he turned to help Kirsten down.

Wordlessly, Silas handed the pizza box to Caleb and watched his little brother's eyes light up in surprise.

"*Denki,* Silas!" he said, beaming.

"David and Michael are here?" Silas asked Caleb, trying not to be distracted by Kirsten's closeness as she stood precisely where he'd put her, mere inches away from him.

"*Jah,* they're here. Deborah and Sarah, too."

"Remember to share with yer sisters," Silas reminded Caleb, ruffling his hair.

Caleb ran ahead of them into the house, taking three stairs in one leap. Silas shook his head and took Kirsten's hand in his, gently tugging her toward the house. She seemed nervous, and Silas couldn't ignore the flutter in his own stomach. His brothers, married fathers though they were, were boisterous and often mischievous. Silas wasn't sure what waited for them inside.

The family had all gathered in the living room, the supper dishes already cleaned up and put away. Conversation stopped as Silas rounded the corner and stepped into the doorway, Kirsten standing quietly in his shadow. He looked back at Kirsten, her eyes bashfully darting around the room before glancing up at him. He smiled down at her before turning back to his family.

"Hullo," he said to the room full of people. Several "hullos" echoed back at him.

"Kirsten," he said, turning slightly towards her. "This is my brother, David, and his wife, Sarah. This is their Danny and their Maria," he said, pointing. "And this is my brother, Michael, and his wife, Deborah, and their Johnny." Silas bent slightly to touch the little boy who had wrapped his arms around his leg.

"It's nice to meet all of you." Kirsten smiled at them.

Michael stood and picked up Johnny from Silas's leg.

"What's this I hear about a wedding, brother?" Michael asked loudly, throwing his loose arm around Silas's shoulders. "I got the news from Lizzie Yoder!"

Silas half smiled and half grimaced.

I got the news from a much more reliable source," David announced.

"Who?!" Michael demanded.

"Caleb," David replied with a smirk. Everyone roared with laughter; even Kirsten smiled widely.

Mary bustled into the kitchen and soon had Kirsten and Silas seated next to one another on kitchen chairs pulled into the living room, desserts in their hands. It was almost unreal to Silas to be sitting next to Kirsten, surrounded by his family. For over an hour they sat, listening to the lively conversations and stories bounce around the room the way the light from the gas lamps danced off the walls. It was dark when Silas brought the buggy near the porch and helped Kirsten up to the seat. They were quiet as they rode the short distance to Kirsten's house.

"Silas," she started, and again he felt his blood warm at the sound of his name. "I had a really nice time tonight."

"*Jah*?" he said quietly, wanting desperately to believe her.

"Yeah," she laughed.

"Me too," he said after a pause. Nice didn't come close to describing how he felt about the night.

"Thank you," Kirsten said, her voice barely about a whisper.

"Yer welcome."

"I'll see you Thursday, then?" she asked after he helped her down and walked her to her front door.

"You will," he assured her.

Again, Silas leaned down and kissed her cheek.

"Good night, Kirsten," he whispered.

"Good night, Silas," she answered.

Silas walked back to the buggy feeling like Thursday was a lifetime away.

— Chapter Fourteen —

"August 10. A Tuesday?" Elizabeth echoed Daniel.

"Tuesdays and Thursdays are the traditional wedding days in our order," Daniel explained politely.

Elizabeth nodded her understanding, still looking a bit shell-shocked.

"That's only twelve days away." She paused and turned to look at Kirsten sitting beside her. "Is that...okay with you, honey?"

Kirsten looked from her mother across the table to Silas. His arms were folded and resting on the smooth varnished surface. He smiled at her and Kirsten beamed at him.

"Yeah. Yeah, twelve days is good," Kirsten said, her eyes not leaving his face.

"Oh. Okay then." Her mom was surprised by everything lately, and Kirsten couldn't really blame her. "What types of arrangements need to be made?" Elizabeth asked, trying valiantly to overcome her shock.

Daniel explained that the people would be invited on the next Sunday, that the wedding would be at their home—perhaps in the backyard due to the heat—and that Kirsten would wear the traditional Amish wedding dress, most of which Mary had just finished sewing.

Elizabeth bobbed her head as he spoke, and Kirsten stole repeated glances at Silas, who was listening attentively to Daniel's overview.

"Three hundred people?" Elizabeth gasped.

"Thereabouts. Most of the church will be coming," Daniel confirmed.

"Even though Kirsten isn't . . ." Elizabeth left the sentence hanging.

"August 10 will mark the first day of Kirsten's Amish life. Though she will not be an official member, she has been offered a place in our community by the bishop. The people will come," Daniel said it all so confidently, and Kirsten felt comforted by his certainty.

There was a long silence as each person around the table absorbed what Daniel had said.

Finally Elizabeth spoke, breaking the spell. "Can I see the dress?"

.₀൭ඔ൭₀

Kirsten's daily routine remained largely untouched. The only difference was that her days of studying and preparing for college were now filled with the task of cleaning out her room and boxing up all the things she wouldn't need anymore. Which was nearly everything. Only her most prized possessions found a place in the "keep" pile. A few mementos from her dad were tucked into a small box that she would take with her: a photo of the two of them together when she was a young girl, his silver watch, and one of his favorite old t-shirts. There were several boxes of her favorite books stacked at the foot of her bed that she would have to ask Silas to move because they were just too heavy for her. But all of her clothes were packed away to be donated.

And every evening at precisely seven o'clock, a knock would sound on her door and she'd open it to find Silas standing on her front step with a smile and bright eyes. They would walk along the gravel road, sometimes wandering around the bend that neither of them ever traveled in their normal day-to-day activities. He was always attentive and friendly, staying with her for several hours. He liked lemonade, and Kirsten made sure to always have some in the fridge. They'd sit on her front steps after their walk, drinking slowly and talking easily until Kirsten felt her body aching. Whether he picked up on her slight shifting or felt weary himself, Kirsten didn't know. But Silas seemed to know when she was uncomfortable and would excuse himself with a promise to come back the following night. Even though she desperately wanted to get up, she still hated to see him go. In fact, she might have been tempted to beg him to sit back down if she didn't know he would lightly kiss her cheek and whisper goodnight if she stood. It was a sweet, pleasant routine. Silas was not talkative, but she gathered from the little bits he shared that he and his family were very busy with the wedding preparations. Kirsten had offered countless times to help in whatever way she could, but Silas only smiled gently and shook his head.

"You need this time with yer mom," he'd said. She knew he was right.

Daniel had gone to great lengths to assure Elizabeth that she would always be welcome and that Kirsten would most certainly be encouraged to visit or invite her over often. It had brought tears to Kirsten's eyes, the way her future father-in-law had insisted that Elizabeth was gaining an entire family instead of losing a daughter. But the truth of the matter was still that Kirsten was moving out and life was about to change for both of them.

The Monday before the wedding, Kirsten and Elizabeth went to the Millers' so that Kirsten could try on her completed wedding outfit. They'd seen pieces, but Mary had been sewing feverishly for the past several days to finish Kirsten's dress in plenty of time.

Silas was nowhere to be seen on their arrival. Kirsten stared out the dusty windshield of the van, watching dozens of men bustle around the yard, hauling benches off a wagon to the backyard for the ceremony and bringing tables inside to the basement where the meals would be served. Kirsten searched each brim-shadowed face for Silas's deep blue eyes and white smile, but she gave up after a few minutes and followed her mother inside.

The kitchen was swarming with women, but Kirsten found herself in Mary's embrace before she could even scan the unfamiliar faces. There was a hush and all activity slowed as Mary hugged her tightly. For a split second, Kirsten wanted to hide. But Mary cupped Kirsten's face in her hands and looked warmly into her eyes.

"Let's see how yer dress fits," Mary said, beaming at her. Kirsten filled her lungs with air and nodded slowly at her soon to be mother-in-law.

Mary led her upstairs to a large room that was painted a soft shade of pink. Against one wall there was a set of bunk beds, and against the other wall there was a single twin bed. Rows of little dresses lined the walls with tiny shoes lined up underneath them. A brilliant blue dress was lying upon the bed next to an assembly of other pieces.

Kirsten slipped out of her blouse and jeans and into the dress. Mary pulled the apron into place and tied it firmly, but not tightly, above Kirsten's stomach.

"It's beautiful, Mary. Thank you," Kirsten breathed. She meant it, too. The dress was, by design, purpose, and rule, plain. There were no lacey hems or beaded bodices. It came up to her neck, covered her arms up to her elbows, and fell past her knees. There was absolutely nothing fancy about it. But the simple, clean lines, the perfect tailoring, and the precision of each pleat were breathtaking.

Mary smiled brightly at her. "I imagine it's mighty simple compared to an English wedding dress."

"It's absolutely beautiful," Kirsten repeated, unable to take her eyes from her reflection in the mirror. Kirsten was surprised by how pretty she felt. She hadn't realized how unfeminine blue jeans really made her feel. But with the skirt gently swishing around her long legs and the apron cinched at her waist, she felt like the outfit flattered her. It was far more girly than anything she had ever worn before, but Kirsten liked it.

"Let me do up yer hair," Mary said, twisting Kirsten's long auburn locks into a bun and pinning it in place. She slipped the white bonnet over Kirsten's hair and stepped back. Kirsten turned in a slow circle and looked at Mary, both of them smiling.

"I'll go get yer Mom," Mary said, tears filling her eyes as she took in the transformed girl in front of her.

"Oh, Kirsten!" Elizabeth breathed, just exactly the way she would have if Kirsten had been adorned in a modern bridal gown from a boutique. Kirsten did another slow spin for her mother, still beaming. Amy joined Mary just inside the doorway.

"Amy made yer cap and apron herself," Mary said as she smiled warmly at her daughter.

Kirsten smiled her thanks.

"This will be yer Sunday dress from now on. And I think once that baby is born, I'll be able to take this in here a bit," Mary said, stepping close again and pinching a span of fabric between her fingers. The ladies were all so busy fussing over Kirsten's dress that they never heard the heavy footsteps running up the stairs behind them.

"Mom, Dad wants to know where—" Silas's voice died away as he came into the room and his eyes fell on Kirsten. He was speechless. Immovable. His eyes traveled the full length of her form, landing finally on her face. His shocked expression lingered for an instant before it gave way to a blinding, exultant smile. Kirsten, as usual, found it impossible not to return his brilliant smile. And they would have stood there all day staring at each other if Mary hadn't flapped her arms like a mad hen.

"*Ach!* Silas! Don't ya know to knock?"

"The door was open," he argued without taking his eyes from Kirsten or losing his smile.

"Out with ya!" Mary herded him out of view.

Elizabeth inspected Kirsten carefully, finally taking her by the shoulders, her face only inches away.

"Kirsten, I need to know that you're sure about this."

Kirsten looked deep into her mother's eyes, then back to the empty doorway.

"I am absolutely positive," she said with a smile. "In fact, I think this is the smartest thing I have ever done."

— CHAPTER FIFTEEN —

Sleep was illusive, and Kirsten woke with a stomach full of nervous butterflies. Breakfast was a lost cause, no matter how much Elizabeth coaxed her to eat. Kirsten had packed her small bag of belongings the night before. Silas had stopped by yesterday and effortlessly loaded up her boxes of books and the smaller boxes of keepsakes. All that remained with Kirsten was the bag containing the few things Mary had said she might want to keep, like socks, underwear, her hair brush, and a mirror. For a few moments, she and Elizabeth stood in the trailer.

"Well, we better get going," Elizabeth said quietly, almost to herself. She'd chosen a modest, long black skirt and white button-down blouse for her mother-of-the-bride outfit. It was a simple outfit, but Kirsten thought her mom looked genuinely lovely. And a little nervous. They walked slowly and silently to the van and drove away.

"I'm really glad they'll let you come visit me," Elizabeth said with a smile.

"You'll always be welcome at the Millers', too, Mom," Kirsten choked. Somehow, she wanted to tell her Mom how much she wanted her to come visit, but the lump in her throat took away all her words.

"Are you ready for all this?" Elizabeth asked as they drove down the lane where buggies were already being lined up along the length of the drive.

"Yes…and no," Kirsten said honestly with a nervous smile. "There's a lot of logistics to remember."

"That is true," her mother agreed.

They parked near the house and noticed Daniel waiting outside to greet them.

"*Gut* morning!" he boomed, his arms thrown open wide and a gleaming smile on his face. Kirsten could suddenly see the family resemblance between him and Silas. "It's a wonderful day for a wedding!" he continued as they climbed out of the van. "You go on inside. Mary's ready for ya." His smile was downright contagious.

Kirsten smiled at his exuberance and followed Elizabeth into the bustling house. The kitchen was once again full of women preparing the meals to be served later that day.

"*Gut* morning! *Gut* morning!" Mary chortled, her eyes dancing with delight. "Let's get ya on up to yer room," she said brightly as she hustled Kirsten toward the stairs.

Kirsten's stomach flipped uneasily. Her room. As in her new room that came with a roommate—her husband. Truth be told, the only thing that gave her any pause on this day was the thought of how awfully awkward her wedding night was sure to be. Her advancing pregnancy combined with the fact that Silas had yet to kiss her on the lips was a recipe for an uncomfortable situation. Not to mention her room was evidently one—two—three doors down from Silas's parents and directly next door to the pink room that housed all of his sisters.

Kirsten stepped through the doorway to find a bright, sunny room on the south side of the house, overlooking the front yard. The walls were pale yellow. Along the western wall was an antique bureau. Across from it, a gorgeous queen-size bed with an elaborately carved wooden headboard. The bed had snow-white sheets, perfectly smoothed. On top was a ribbon-bound bundle.

"This is yer wedding quilt," Mary said with a joyful reverence.

Kirsten got the distinct impression that this was a special gift, though she wasn't exactly sure why. Carefully, she untied the ribbons and unfolded the hand-stitched, embroidered quilt, revealing its intricate pattern. The fabrics were white, pale blue, and pale green. It was more beautiful than any of the gorgeous quilts she had seen hanging in the market.

"Oh, Mary. It's beautiful!" Kirsten breathed, running her fingers over the patch-worked pieces.

"*Ach*...ya better be calling me 'Mom' now."

Kirsten smiled and smoothed the quilt.

"Here. Let's put it on the bed," Mary suggested as she tugged a corner down. The quilt was unspeakably beautiful. Surely Kirsten had never owned anything so precious or lovely as this quit. Immediately, it was one of her most treasured possessions.

Mary gestured behind her to a row of hooks stretching along the wall behind the door. On one of the hooks hung Kirsten's wedding dress—one of her other most treasured possession. Next to it hung a pale blue dress, a navy dress, and a light summer nightgown.

"Can I help ya get dressed?" Mary asked, barely containing her excitement. Kirsten nodded and put her bag down by the bed. A few minutes later, Kirsten was dressed and ready for the festivities. Elizabeth came in and smiled at her.

"Well, this is it, isn't it?" she sighed as she took Kirsten's hands in hers. "There are a lot of people here already! They're all very nice," her mom chattered nervously.

A firm knock sounded on the door, and Kirsten's stomach rolled. It was Daniel, ready to escort them downstairs.

This was it.

.തെ ഇ.

Silas slipped his arms into the sleeves of his new white shirt and black vest. He combed through his hair and picked up his new, wide-brimmed black hat.

She was surely here. Just down the hall. Was she nervous? He fought the urge to seek her out.

He bowed his head and prayed silently for the day, for his bride, and for the life they would share.

Caleb stood in the doorway and waited until Silas lifted his head and opened his eyes.

"They're ready for ya, brother," he said, grinning.

He waited downstairs in the living room, his black coat and hat in place. There were slow footsteps on the stairs and quiet voices. He looked up to see her standing before him, a nervous smile flickering on her face. He held out his hand to her, and she visibly relaxed as she slipped her hand into his.

Bishop Samuel looked warmly upon Kirsten, and Silas breathed a sigh of relief that they'd met with him together the week before.

"Well, the guests are waiting outside. Are you ready?"

Kirsten's face was fixed on the bishop as she listened intently. There wasn't even a flicker of reservation in her eyes. Her grip on his hand was steady, though tight.

"Yes." Her answer sounded strong and sure.

The bishop's eyes swung to Silas. "Yes." It was an easy answer.

"Then let's be going out to the ceremony!" Bishop Samuel said jovially.

⟨ஒ௰ஓ⟩

Kirsten's fingers tightened around his, and he squeezed them in return. They slowly followed in the bishop's wake out the door to the backyard, where the benches were lined up in rows beneath the shady canopy of the trees high overhead. They walked up the aisle in silence, women on the left and men on the right.

Kirsten glanced quickly at Silas's face, shadowed by the brim of his hat. His expression was serious, but calm.

He released her hand, and she felt a flare of panic until she saw Amy smile at her and dip her head ever so slightly to the empty spot on the bench at the front. Kirsten smiled at her attendant—the Amish equivalent of a bridesmaid—and gratefully sat next to her.

As if by some unspoken signal, all the men simultaneously removed their hats. Kirsten could clearly see Silas's face now; his eyes locked on her and did not stray.

One of the ministers stood and began to speak in a lively, building manner. Though he was speaking, surprisingly, in English, his words and phrases were unfamiliar to Kirsten. She knew so little about anything spiritual, though she was sure she would receive a quick education in the coming weeks.

She looked again at Silas's serene expression and let the words fill her mind. Behind Silas, she could see David, Michael, and Daniel, their eyes focused on the minister. Only Silas was staring intently at her, his posture straight and sure.

Her back was beginning to ache when the first minister sat and another stood in his place and continued where the first one had left off. Kirsten shifted as inconspicuously as possible. She felt the familiar flutter in her abdomen, followed by a series of little kicks. Her hand gently rubbed the spot where the little foot had tapped her through her new dress.

She looked up to see that Silas's eyes had changed; they now burned with intensity and concern. She smiled shyly at him, dropping her eyes for a moment. When she looked back up, his eyes had changed yet again. Now they were smiling at her, the corners of his mouth just barely turned up in a grin.

For another hour, they sat listening to the preacher's rhythmic chant. But then the preaching ceased and the bishop stood in his place. Kirsten sensed the change in momentum and knew the long wait was over. The vows would be next.

She mirrored Silas's movements and positioning. She followed when he stood and she took his hand, his peace spreading through her. His expression was calm and sure, even when the bishop paused to hear any objections. Kirsten anchored herself next to Silas and did not look away from him as she said her vows. His echoed promise to love and cherish her reverberated in her heart as his voice, slow and deliberate and with its gentle accent, swept over and around her.

The smile that covered her face was involuntary. Being with Silas was exactly what she needed. His promise to always be there for her made her lighthearted and giddy. That he wanted her, even as she was, made all the difference in the world.

With one proclamation, she became Kirsten Miller, wife of Silas Miller, daughter of Daniel and Mary Miller, member of the Amish community. One who has forsaken the outside world.

— Chapter Sixteen —

Kirsten sat next to her new husband at the table in the corner of the basement of the Miller home. Women were bustling around, passing bowls and plates of food. Kirsten finally felt relaxed enough to eat.

She felt a hand rest lightly on her back and turned to see Deborah leaning over her to slide a platter onto the table in front of her. Deborah smiled warmly at Kirsten, her brown eyes shining.

"How are ya, sister Kirsten?" she asked quietly, with a tenderness and a caring that Kirsten had had so little of in her life.

"I'm good. Thank you." Kirsten smiled back.

"*Gut!*"

The meal was enormous, and Kirsten was surprised when the men stood up and moved out to make room for the next wave of people.

Silas was only able to take a few bites of food every once in a while as people kept coming up to him to congratulate him. He made sure to always introduce Kirsten, but she quickly gave up on memorizing names and faces. That was just too much pressure for an already full day.

Immediately after the meal, Mary claimed her and brought her around to sit with some ladies in a quiet, shady spot in the front yard. Deborah lowered herself down next to Kirsten. Kirsten felt strangely protected by her presence—almost as sheltered as she felt with Silas.

The older children played outdoors, engaging in games that were both familiar and unfamiliar to Kirsten. She tried to imagine her daughter napping on the quilt next to her, just as little Johnny was curled up against Deborah, his dark hair rustling in the breeze. Johnny looked like a little Michael—dark hair, dark brows, and dark brown eyes. David's Danny, too, looked like his father, with light brown hair that curled about his little face. Silas and Caleb were the only men with blond hair in the Miller family.

"This is a beautiful wedding day," Deborah observed.

"It is," Kirsten agreed, peering up at a bright blue summer sky.

"Our wedding was in November, and it was bitter cold," Deborah laughed lightly. "My parents' house was so full of people that we hardly needed to run the furnace."

"Where do your parents live?" Kirsten asked, longing to know more about her new sister-in-law.

"Missouri," Deborah said wistfully.

"Do you see them...ever?" Kirsten asked, her heart aching for Deborah.

"Oh, *jah*. We usually go to see them a few times a year," Deborah reassured Kirsten. "Did yer Mom go home?"

"Yeah, she had to work tonight and wanted to get some rest first."

"It will be nice fer ya to have her so close by!"

Kirsten agreed.

A shadow loomed over them, and both women craned their necks to see Michael standing tall above them. He sat on the other side of Deborah, careful not to disturb Johnny.

"Silas was on his way over to find you, but Joseph Lapp found him and is talking his ear off," Michael explained with a wry smile. "He might need to be rescued."

Kirsten could see the teasing light in his eyes, but finding Silas sounded like a good idea. She stood quickly and wobbled as she tried to find her balance. Michael moved to help her but she waved him off.

There was no sign of her husband as she made her way across the front yard and down past the house. As she passed by the clusters of people, she could feel their eyes following her. Their eyes made her nervous, and she searched for a friendly, familiar face. There were more than a hundred men—all of them in black coats or vests over white shirts, just like Silas. Further complicating her efforts were their identical black hats. She searched amongst them for someone as tall as her husband, but he was nowhere to be found. She felt a rising panic and shielded her eyes from the late afternoon sun, trying to calm herself down while searching the unfamiliar faces scattered all over the yard. If he happened to be standing with his back to her, she'd never find him.

This was taking too long. Surely everyone could see that. Surely they all knew exactly which one was her husband and were waiting to see how long it would take her to find him. Kirsten chastised herself inwardly. What kind of bride can't even find her groom at her wedding? Her pulse raced and her eyes hunted more and more frantically.

A sudden movement caught Kirsten's attention, and she instantly recognized the gait of the hat-hidden man strolling toward her. He must have spotted her. And it was probably painfully easy for him. Despite her new Amish clothes, she didn't blend in the way every single one of them did.

"Looking for somebody?" Silas asked as he smiled down at her, his eyes a darker blue in the shadow of his brim.

"I couldn't find you," she breathed heavily.

"I'm the one in the black hat," he teased, still smiling.

Kirsten still heaved for air, feeling for all the world that she had failed her first test as a wife. She swallowed hard and closed her eyes against the tide of fear.

She couldn't bring herself to smile or even look at his face; she was trying much too hard to keep from crying or running to her room. His feet stepped closer and all teasing was gone from his voice, leaving it low and serious.

"Kirsten, are ya all right?"

She drew a deep, shaky breath and tilted her head back to look up into his eyes. They were soft and focused solely on her. She gulped again and dropped her eyes to his vest.

"I think I just need a...break." She didn't know if it was an appropriate or acceptable thing to ask, but it was honest. Her mind went back to riding with him in the dark privacy of the buggy, sitting next to him down the road at the old, abandoned farm place where he'd asked her to marry him. Those were easy new things. This getting lost in big crowds was going to be a major challenge.

"Take a walk with me." His voice was soft, but insistent. He grabbed her hand and pulled her with him. They walked hand-in-hand to the orchard, past the clusters of people talking in the backyard. She grasped his hand tighter as they strolled beneath the canopy. Kirsten's legs shook with relief at the fading sound of the people behind them. Hoping to steady herself more, she reached across and grabbed his arm so that she was nearly clinging to him. She knew he was watching her, but she focused on the grass beneath her feet.

"Let's sit here," Silas said, waving his hand to a grassy spot beneath an apple tree. Kirsten sank to the ground and took her first full breath. Silas stood nearby, still watching.

"Aren't you going to sit?" she asked, squinting up at him.

"In a minute," he replied and handed her his hat.

She took it, confused, and watched as he looked up high overhead. He was scanning the branches above them, but for what she did not know. With no warning, he suddenly jumped and swung himself up onto a branch, climbing so easily and quickly that she could hardly see him.

"Silas, is this a good idea in your suit?"

His answer was a loud laugh, and in mere seconds he was back in view.

"I," he began, pausing to drop out of the tree, "am an excellent tree-climber." He handed her a perfect green apple, his eyes betraying the smile he was trying to hide.

Kirsten took the apple from him and polished it on her apron. She took a giant, crunching bite, feeling the juice run down her chin and neck. Silas sat beside her, his legs stretched out long in front of him, propping himself up on an elbow. Kirsten hadn't realized how hungry and thirsty she had gotten. The apple satisfied both perfectly.

"This is the best apple I have ever eaten," she said as she chewed. She'd eaten half of it, but offered the rest to him. He took it and she watched as he took a massive bite, his lips touching where hers had been. It felt oddly intimate.

"*Gut* things are best shared," he agreed, handing it back to her. She blushed at his comment, innocent though it had been. Combined with her thoughts of the approaching night, it seemed directly related to events yet to come.

"I know this is…different for ya," he said suddenly, not noticing the blush on her face. "But yer doing fine. It'll be over in a few hours."

Kirsten shook her head. "I'm not nervous when I'm with you," she clarified. She wondered if he understood all she was trying to say.

"Well, then I'll do my best not to lose ya again," he promised with a grin. Abruptly, Silas jumped to his feet and offered her his hand. He steadied her when she stood and took the remnant of the apple from her. She followed his lead to the horse pasture where one of the horses was grazing near the fence. He approached slowly, placed the apple core in his palm, and whistled low. A horse shyly came near and took the apple from his outstretched hand.

They walked back to the backyard where the guests were just now getting up to go to supper. Silas led her down to the basement and back to their spot at the corner table. This time, instead of shyly focusing on her food, Kirsten picked up her chin and looked around. Young men, many about Silas's age she guessed, stood in groups watching the young women dashing about. Mothers herded their children while fathers talked in groups of two or three. There was vibrancy and life humming all around her. The lanterns on the tables were lit, and the supper was served by the assigned kitchen helpers.

Slowly, the guests began to filter away, some having several hours to travel by buggy. The more people that left, the more nervous Kirsten grew. When they were gone, she'd go inside with her new family and her new husband.

To his credit, Silas never left her side. He looked so handsome in his black hat and coat, his white shirt gleaming against his tanned skin, his smile still bright in the dim light. Some of the men began loading benches and tables into large flatbed wagons when Mary suddenly appeared at her side.

"I'm sure yer tired," she murmured quietly to Kirsten. "I'll help ya get ready for bed."

Kirsten moved to follow, but she felt Silas's grip tighten on her hand. She turned back to see him anxiously looking at her. Though it defied everything she was feeling, she gave him a reassuring smile, squeezed his hand, let go, and walked up the porch steps of her new home.

Mary helped Kirsten out of her dress and slipped the nightgown over her head.

"We take our showers in the evening. This is yer towel. You just let us know if ya need anything."

Kirsten could only nod her thanks and understanding as Mary wished her a good night and left her alone in her room. Kirsten quickly gathered her towel, washcloth, and soap and made her way to the one bathroom down the hall. The warm shower felt good and should have been relaxing, but Kirsten's tense muscles only got tighter. She rushed through it and nearly sprinted down the hall to her room, her nerves making her jumpy.

Surprisingly, her room was still empty—no new husband in sight. She spent some time hanging her dress on the hook and her towel over the back of the wooden chair, eventually resorting to unpacking her small overnight bag. Still no Silas. Perhaps he was waiting for a signal that she was ready for bed. Hurriedly, she folded down the beautiful wedding quilt and climbed into the firm bed. She gently smoothed the sheets over herself and tried to calm her racing heart by taking deep breaths.

She could still hear people moving about downstairs and in their bedrooms. But as she settled in her bed, the house grew more and more quiet. Finally, a set of heavy footsteps sounded on the stairs and her pulse raced. They paused and then moved farther and farther away.

Kirsten laid still and alert. If a moth had so much as bumped against her window, she would have yelped. But soon the silence became deafening. How could a house so full of people be so quiet? Was he waiting until his family was asleep?

Kirsten scanned the room. Her brush on the antique bureau. Her dresses hanging on the hooks. Two pairs of black shoes lined up beside the bureau.

Not a single thing of her husband. No shirts, boots, trousers, suspenders, or socks. Nothing. It dawned on her then that this was not Silas's room. It was hers and hers alone. Her bureau, her row of hooks, her towel on the chair. Her bed.

Silas would not be joining her. His black coat and hat hung on a different row of hooks. His black boots filled another corner.

She turned onto her side, away from the door, and faced the open window to watch the curtains suck against the screen. She'd been so scared, looking for him and not finding him. Then, gripping his arm and feeling the hard muscle of his bicep beneath his jacket, she'd felt safe and secure. Exactly what she'd needed. And now, the absence of him filled her room. A shiver ran up her body, and the weight of the emptiness she felt pressed heavily on her. This was not what she had anticipated, and now it was much too late to clarify living arrangements.

There are already two of us in this bed. The thought screamed in her head. The pain of that statement tore through her and stuck in her throat.

She stared at the empty pillow beside her until it blurred through her tears. She'd been wrong. Wrong again, only this time she had been so sure. How could she have misunderstood his intentions? He'd asked her to be his wife and that was what she had promised to be to him. Not...this.

Perhaps all Silas Miller had really wanted was a new sister.

◦◦◦

He did not even dare to look when he reached the top of the stairs. His parents and siblings had retired to their rooms while he sat for a long time in the dark, listening. Slowly, reluctantly, he climbed the stairs and abruptly turned to the room at the opposite end of the hall.

Caleb was snoring soundly, as usual. Silas noiselessly slipped into bed next to him. He stared out the window, feeling the breeze blowing on his face.

This was his wedding night. Not precisely what he had always wanted, but exactly what he had planned. Still, his heart pounded painfully in his chest, waging a war with his body, making sleep impossible.

Visions of his bride, a thousand memories of Kirsten, flickered through his mind. The serious look on her face when they'd spoken to the bishop before the ceremony. The shy smile she'd flashed at him during the preaching. Her eyes desperately searching for him in the yard and melting in relief when she saw him. Her cap-covered head beneath him in the apple tree.

How was it possible that she haunted him even more now that she was his wife? It was his own doing, really. His parents had been confused by his requested arrangements, but they had left it as his decision. He'd made a choice and now, somehow, he had to find a way to live with it.

— CHAPTER SEVENTEEN —

The sun was up long before Kirsten. When at last she stirred and stretched, she could sense the quiet emptiness of the house. Not even a sound from Anna Mae or Shelby Jo. The day had begun and had nearly passed her by, even though it was only eight o'clock.

They had probably been up for hours. Quickly, she jumped out of bed, put the covers neatly back in place, got dressed in the light blue everyday dress, and brushed her teeth. Surely someone would be downstairs or outside somewhere.

"*Gut* morning," Amy said, wiping her flour-covered hands on her apron.

"Morning," Kirsten said sheepishly.

"Need some help with yer hair?" Amy asked as she spied the bonnet and pins in Kirsten's hands.

Kirsten nodded gratefully and watched as Amy demonstrated a proper Amish bun yet again on her own light brown hair. A few minutes later, Kirsten had twisted her hair up and pinned it, settling her cap in place.

"*Gut*," Amy said, nodding as she supervised.

Her younger sister-in-law, though not by much, sliced a few pieces of cinnamon bread and poured her a glass of orange juice.

"We do chores at five and have breakfast together at seven. Dad and Mom leave for the store just after breakfast and will be there all day. We are to bake bread, clean up the kitchen, and make the meals."

Kirsten nodded at the to-do list, wordlessly wondering where Silas had disappeared to.

"And do the everyday chores," Amy added with a smirk.

"Where do we start?" Kirsten asked as she washed her own dishes.

Amy slapped a mound of dough into a pan and handed Kirsten a small metal bucket.

"We get the eggs," she said, giving Kirsten a tight, businesslike smile. Kirsten took the pail and followed Amy to a small building with a wooden fence surrounding it. As Amy marched in, there was a flurry of feathers and clucking. Kirsten timidly followed, shrinking back when a hen approached her.

Confidently, Amy reached into each boxed nest and retrieved the eggs, often plunging her hand right underneath the hen's body and pulling out the warm eggs. Kirsten tried to suck it up and be brave, but the minute a hen's head would jerk toward her, she'd snatch her hand back.

Amy's bucket was full and Kirsten had only managed to grab three eggs—every one of them from an empty box.

There was only one box left, and it was clear that Amy was waiting for Kirsten to check it. Mustering her courage, Kirsten slowly slipped her hand inside the box, but the minute she touched the hen it let out a squawk and fluttered its wings in annoyance. Kirsten shrieked and dropped the egg she'd grabbed on the dirt floor of the coop, where it smacked open in a pool of ooze and bits of shell.

"Oh! I'm sorry!" Kirsten moaned. Amy looked like she was about to either scold her or burst into laughter. She did neither.

"Are there any more?" Amy asked, her lips pursed tightly.

The hen had vacated the box, so Kirsten retrieved the last egg, adding it to her sorry collection. Amy wordlessly led her back to the house, where they dropped off the eggs, and then suggested they get the milk for the day. In the barn, she showed Kirsten how to get the milk out of the tank. Amy filled a pail and brought it to the house, pouring it from the bucket and into a pitcher through a strainer.

"Now you try," Amy instructed with a smile.

Kirsten nodded and left Amy in the kitchen as she went out to the barn to repeat the process. She managed to fill the bucket, just as she'd been shown, but when she went to pick it up, she stumbled under its weight. Amy had carried it with one hand, but there was no way Kirsten was going to be able to match her.

With two hands on the handle, she awkwardly lifted the pail and waddled with it across the side yard to the house. Milk sloshed wildly, much of it spilling onto Kirsten's skirt and seeping into her shoes. She was not yet even halfway to the house and she could feel her arms trembling, her grip slipping. Footsteps came running toward her.

"Here, I'll take that." She dared not look at him. How many times did he have to come to her rescue? How many times could she fail at the simplest tasks and need his help? How long before he tired of her neediness and just sent her away?

Silas's long fingers grasped the handle and he lifted it easily. Kirsten stifled a sigh and nodded, still unable to look at her husband of less than twenty-four hours. She hastily wiped her hands on her apron and led the way into the house. He set the pail on the counter next to the empty pitcher.

"Thank you," Kirsten said without turning to look at him. She could feel him hesitating before he finally turned to go back to wherever it was he had come from.

Kirsten managed to pour from the bucket through the strainer and into the pitcher despite her shaking muscles and trembling hands.

Amy's next assignment was to begin preparing lunch. Hamburgers and roasted potatoes. Kirsten gratefully sat at the table and peeled while Amy prepared the patties. She'd only managed to finish a few potatoes by the time Amy was finished. Amy took over and asked her to set the table. Kirsten set out the plates and silverware, feeling a sense of satisfaction as she placed the pitcher of milk on the table. Knowing she had earned that small part of the meal gave her a new sense of appreciation for every bit of food.

Silas and Caleb filtered in after Amy rang the dinner bell on the front porch. Kirsten waited until the men were all seated and Amy signaled to her to sit down next to Silas. She knew to expect a prayer before the meal; she did not expect Silas's hand to grasp hers under the table. They ate quickly and quietly, not lingering over conversation or storytelling. When Silas finished and pushed away from the table, Caleb followed him to the small washroom where they slipped on their boots and hats and walked out the door.

Kirsten washed the dishes while Amy made up another batch of bread dough. As Kirsten dried, Amy began sweeping out the kitchen, stopping to survey the result.

"I think we'll have to scrub down the walls and the floor," Amy stated. "I'll do the walls because you shouldn't be on the ladder, and you can do the floors."

Kirsten copied Amy, filling a bucket with hot, soapy water and grabbing a brush out of the washroom cabinet. They worked silently, the only sound the *scrub, scrub, scrub* of their brushes against the wood-paneled walls and floorboards.

She could feel the beads of sweat roll down her back and around her rib cage, catching in the tight band of her apron. Her shoulders ached, and soon her arms were shaking with exertion. Still, she kept scrubbing, spending extra time by the floor in front of the stove.

After several hours of backbreaking work and awkward silence, she finished and emptied her bucket on the flowerbed by the steps.

"Here, you sweep the porch while I make supper," Amy chimed cheerfully. Kirsten swept the entire porch, which wrapped around the entire southern and eastern sides of the house. Her arms and legs felt wobbly from the scrubbing, and she could hardly make the broom move effectively against the wood planks. When she was finished, Amy suggested she go clean up before supper and Kirsten smiled her thanks.

The cold shower felt good and worked wonders in cooling her body after the heat of physical labor. She brushed through her hair and twisted it back up as Amy had shown her, finding it easier to do when wet. Her dress and apron were badly soiled from the day's work, so she pulled on the navy dress.

"Mom will be home in a minute," Amy announced as Kirsten came back in the kitchen to find an entire meal nearly ready. "Go sit in the living room for a while until supper."

Almost robotically, Kirsten walked to the living room and sank into a rocker. She closed her eyes and leaned her head back, mindlessly rubbing her stomach. The baby squirmed and thumped—the first she'd had a chance to notice movement all day. As Kirsten rocked, she heard a horse and buggy pull up, and soon after Mary entered the house.

"What *gut* work you girls did here today!" she loudly praised. Kirsten made no move to go to the kitchen, just kept rocking.

"Where are Shelby Jo and Anna Mae?" Mary asked.

"At Sarah's to help pick strawberries and make jam," Amy replied.

"Oh, that's nice!" Mary climbed the stairs and Amy rang the dinner bell. Kirsten hoisted herself up from the rocker and gingerly walked to her chair at the table, her back protesting with every step. She'd beaten everyone but Caleb. Ever so slowly, Kirsten lowered herself into her chair, making extra effort not to wince. Caleb watched her with wide eyes. Kirsten shot him a look he didn't deserve. He quickly looked down at his plate and didn't look up until Silas and Daniel strode in and sat in their places. Amy and Mary set the food on the table, and then they all bowed their heads for prayer. Kirsten prayed for only two things: strength and that she'd be able to stay awake long enough to eat.

࣭ೲ౨౧ೲ࣭

It wasn't like him to feel the need to be talkative and conversational, but he'd never spent a meal with Kirsten where she spoke as little as she had tonight. Mary had tried, almost desperately, to draw her into their discussion, finally giving up when Daniel gave her a single solitary shake of his head.

Silas spent most of the meal watching his young wife's pale face, finding it remained nearly emotionless. Of course it had to be a hard transition for her. He didn't doubt it would be any easier for her to become Amish than it would be for him to become English. Still, she seemed... hollow.

Amy asked permission to go visit the Lapps that night to see her best friend, Emily. Silas's parents had agreed, complimenting her on a solid day of work. Kirsten sat stone still.

Mary offered a choice of dessert that night, smiling broadly when Kirsten opted for a slice of leftover wedding cake.

"Silas?" his mother said, turning to him.

"It's a tough choice," he smirked playfully. She laughed and waved him off, turning to dish up his favorite. She slid the piece of cherry pie in front of him and turned to Daniel. Silas noticed Kirsten staring at the cherry pie in front of him and then back at her cake, a look he didn't know flashing in her eyes and then disappearing.

His father chose wedding cake.

"I'm not done celebrating our new daughter!"

Kirsten's eyes lifted to Daniel's warm smile, and Silas inwardly cringed at the look of gratitude that swept her features. It was the first time he'd seen her smile since she'd left him last night. The realization made his stomach churn.

Caleb meekly asked for wedding cake, which annoyed Silas. The only person who liked cherry pie more than Silas was his little brother. Out of the corner of his eye, he saw Kirsten smile gently at Caleb, who blushed fiercely.

The clattering of a buggy sounded through the screen door and little footsteps clattered across the planks of the front porch. Shelby Jo and Anna Mae bounded in, each clutching a jar of red strawberry jam—their reward for a day helping Sarah. David stomped in after them, waving a "hullo" and distracting Silas's jealous inner turmoil.

Mary invited David and his family over for a big family supper on Sunday; David promised they'd be there. He bid them all goodnight and left.

Of course both Shelby and Anna asked for a piece of wedding cake as they peeked shyly across the table at Kirsten. She smiled kindly back at them. She had yet to even look at him. Silas was vaguely uncomfortable and sensed that something was wrong.

Daniel soon lit the lanterns in the living room and everyone came to sit a while before bed.

Kirsten sank into one of the two rockers, leaving Silas and Daniel on the couch.

"Shelby Jo, I stopped in the henhouse this evening. It seems ya rushed through yer chores," Daniel chided gently, but firmly.

Shelby was silent for several long moments. "I didn't do my chores today."

Daniel's brow lifted as he considered the little girl before him. "Why not?"

"Amy said we could go early, right after breakfast, and that she'd do our chores," Shelby quietly explained.

"It was my fault," Kirsten interjected. Silas watched her face twist in guilt and shame. "I dropped the egg," she confessed. "It seems I'm a little afraid…of chickens."

If it hadn't been for the grief-stricken look on her face, all of them would have burst into laughter. Caleb fought to stifle a laugh, and Silas shot him a warning look that could freeze boiling water.

"I'm sorry." She swallowed hard, looking sadly at Daniel.

His father nodded to accept her apology.

"I expect there's a lot of things to learn around here, Kirsten. Soon you'll be bossing those old hens around." How did Daniel always know just what to say to make her smile?

It was quiet, and Silas watched Kirsten yawn.

"You may go to bed, Kirsten," he said, hoping she'd at least look at him. She did. Her eyes snapped up and she nodded, looking away quickly.

She stood very slowly, and he fought the urge to help her. She straightened up, turned, and doubled-over, her hand on her stomach. Silas jolted upright.

"No, no. I just got up too fast. I'm fine," she gasped. It was a preposterous thing to say, given how slowly she was moving, but he stayed rooted in place as she hobbled out of the room and made her way carefully up the stairs. He stared after her, and his eyes flashed to his mother, who was rocking slowly in her chair. Not until he heard Kirsten's door close did Silas ease back onto the couch.

"Shelby Jo?" Mary called quietly.

"Yes, Mama?"

"You were at Sarah's all day?"

"Yes, Mama."

Mary's brow furrowed in thought.

— CHAPTER EIGHTEEN —

Daniel's voice boomed down the hall the next morning promptly at five o'clock instead of the respectful knock of the day before. Caleb and Silas tromped into the barn for chores. It smelled of cinnamon, bacon, eggs, and coffee when they came in at seven. Mary, Amy, Shelby, and Anna were all bustling around. Kirsten was nowhere in sight.

"Shelby Jo, will you please let Kirsten know breakfast is ready," Mary instructed.

"She missed breakfast yesterday, too," Amy told her mother.

Silas added that worry to his list.

Shelby returned from her errand and whispered to her mother. Mary instantly turned from the table and hurried up the stairs.

In mere minutes, she was back, a rare angry look etched on her face.

"Amy Miller," Mary said as she snatched the plate from Kirsten's place at the table. "I want a full accounting of everything Kirsten did yesterday."

Silas's eyes bounced back and forth between them.

Amy breathed deeply and listed every activity Kirsten had engaged in from the time she woke up until supper. It was a long list. Too long a list for someone's first day as an Amish woman. Definitely too long a list for an expectant mother.

No one spoke. No one moved. Mary began wordlessly filling a plate of food, her mouth pinched in a tense line.

"She scrubbed how much of the floor?" she asked tensely as she grabbed the silverware from the table beside Silas.

"The whole thing," Amy answered meekly.

"How long did that take?"

"Three hours," Amy whispered.

Mary stared at her for a long time. Silas felt his pulse thrumming in his temples.

"Is there a problem?" Daniel asked his wife.

"Kirsten is in bed, unable to move," Mary answered matter-of-factly.

Silas's stomach dropped and his vision blurred.

"Does she need a doctor?" Daniel asked, concerned.

"I don't know yet," Mary quietly replied, sounding defeated.

Daniel nodded and Mary took the plate with a full glass of milk up the stairs. Silas slid his chair back and silently followed her. He waited in the hall as Mary went in and rounded the bed. Kirsten was on her side, her back to the door. Mary gently sat on the bed, setting the plate and glass on the small night table.

Silas watched her tenderly stroke Kirsten's long hair away from her face and neck.

"How about some breakfast?" Mary suggested softly.

Kirsten nodded.

"Oh, Kirsten, there now. Don't cry," Mary soothed, wiping away tears with the corner of her apron.

"I just feel so...stupid...and pathetic...and...weak."

Silas wanted to rip his heart out at the sound of her choking sob. Hadn't he promised to protect her? Hadn't he offered her a beautiful life? He had brought her to this life, and now she lay beaten and hurt.

"No, no," Mary quietly cooed. "You'll be just fine in a day or two. You just overdid it a bit and need some rest."

Kirsten nodded and took a shuddering breath.

"Let me help ya with yer breakfast, and then I'll make up some nice, soothing tea," Mary said in a calming voice, just as she had when Silas got sick when he was little.

Silently, he made his way down the hall and back to the kitchen. He sat heavily at the table where his family was eating. Wordlessly and without looking at anyone, he filled his plate and shoveled food into his mouth, not tasting a bite. They finished and Daniel read from the Bible. After prayer, his father laid a hand on Silas's shoulder.

"Caleb an' I will take supplies to the market today. You stay close to home."

Silas nodded, staring at his empty plate. One day. He hadn't been able to shelter her for even one day.

The rest of the family rose from the table. Shelby and Anna went out to do the rest of their chores while Amy cleared the table. She worked quietly for several minutes before turning to Silas. He gave her a long, angry glare.

"It's not an easy life, Silas," Amy said, shrugging.

Silas shot to his feet. "You made it impossible," he growled.

"I'll not have ya fighting," Mary said as she strolled into the kitchen with empty dishes. "Amy, you've done wrong to yer new sister. This may be a hard life, but she's lived a hard one already. We need to make the transition slower and easier. You best be thinking about how you'd feel in her shoes. Do unto others as you would have done to you."

"Yes, Mama."

"Silas," Mary turned to him. "I'm sorry. I shoulda been here for her first day. It's my fault. It's not yer doin'."

Silas closed his eyes and sighed.

"I'll look after her," Mary vowed.

He stuffed his feet into his boots and trudged out the door. He took out his frustrations in his work, the sweat soon running down his face, neck, and back.

Kirsten's chair was still empty at lunch. He looked from her chair to his mother, lifting an eyebrow.

"Yer wife is resting," Mary said.

It was the best he could hope to hear, he supposed. Mary fixed another plate and brought it upstairs, returning quickly to eat with the family.

The table was quiet, much as it had been yesterday. Silas remembered seeing her strain to carry the milk bucket to the house. How heavily she had panted, even after he took it from her. Her dress had been soaked all down the front. He wanted to see her and let her know how concerned he was.

After lunch, Silas left the table and went out to the flower beds that surrounded the front yard. Minutes later, he returned to the empty house. Mary was in the garden with the rest of the girls. He quietly crept up the stairs and nudged her door open.

She was asleep, her auburn hair falling loosely on the pillow beneath her. He watched her for several long seconds. He had wanted to talk to her, tell her how sorry he was that she'd had such a hard first day, explain that she didn't have to learn it all at once, tell her that they'd take things slowly. It could wait, he supposed. He could wait.

⋅ೋ⊚ 🙰ೋ⋅

Kirsten opened her eyes to the bright, sun-filled room. Gingerly, she rolled over, her muscles protesting. Her back and arms were still extremely sore, but rest, herbal tea, and Mary's tender care had made a world of difference.

Slowly, she turned and caught a flash of color out of the corner of her eye. A single, brilliant red rose sat in a tiny glass on her nightstand. It was stunning. Kirsten searched for a flaw, but she was unable to find a single imperfection. She stared at it in all of its freshly picked splendor. She was still staring at it when Mary brought her supper tray.

"Yer sitting up! You must be feeling better," Mary cried.

Kirsten nodded. "Thanks for the pretty flower," she said with a smile.

Mary's eyes snapped to the rose sitting on Kirsten's nightstand. She stared in disbelief at the bright bloom.

"That would be from yer husband, I 'spect," Mary said. "He's awful worried about ya."

Kirsten stared at the rose. If he was worried, then he at least knew she was alive. At least there was that. And Mary hadn't been the delivery person, so he must have brought it himself.

He'd been in her room. The mere thought made her heart throb painfully.

"No one's ever given me a flower," she murmured.

"I've always thought the best gifts are the ones that we've poured our time, attention, and love into," Mary said as she smiled at Kirsten.

"What do you mean?"

"That flower is from Silas's rosebushes near the front steps. He's pretty particular about them. I've never known him to cut off a bloom."

"Oh." Kirsten warmed at the meaningful act behind the seemingly simple gift. Still, he'd barely spoken to her, and all things considered, she still felt as though he had married her on paper alone.

— Chapter Nineteen —

Daniel called loudly down the hall at five o'clock again on Friday. Kirsten heard him and rolled slowly to her side. It still hurt, but at least she could move. There were footsteps in the hall, and the front door slammed shut over Caleb's laughter. It was tempting to stay in bed. Part of her wanted to hide out of sheer embarrassment over her obvious weakness.

She walked carefully down the hall to the empty bathroom. It took much longer than normal, but she showered, towel dried her hair, and brushed her teeth. After several long minutes of struggle, she managed to slip into her only clean everyday dress and tie the apron behind her. Her shoulders ached badly as she twisted her hair into a bun, fitting her cap above the damp knot.

Amy was busy frying bacon at the stove when Kirsten made her way into the kitchen.

"Morning," Kirsten greeted.

"*Gut* morning," Amy replied, surprised.

"How can I help?" Kirsten raised her hands in gesture.

Amy seemed terribly uneasy as she considered her response. "You could slice the bread?"

"Sure."

Amy got the proper knife and suggested Kirsten sit down to cut the homemade loaf.

She was in her chair at the table when the family filed into the house for breakfast, feeling very humbled by her need for a recovery after one day of work. Mary smiled brightly, and Shelby and Anna seemed delighted to have her back, making her feel a little more relaxed. Caleb dashed in soon after and wished her an overzealous "*Gut* morning!" Silas came in last and visibly stared at her. Kirsten pretended not to notice.

"Yer feeling better then, Kirsten?" Daniel inquired.

"I'm on the mend," she answered, blushing.

As she spoke, Silas's hand grazed across her shoulder blades and he moved behind her to sit in his chair.

"*Gut* morning, Kirsten." It never ceased to amaze her how low and smooth his voice was.

"Morning," she replied politely, annoyed that his touch and his voice had such an effect on her. It would be easier if he just kept his hands to himself. If he wasn't really going to be a husband, she wished he wouldn't act the part. The flower was a nice gesture of concern, but it didn't make up for the sting of rejection she still felt from their wedding night. And every night thereafter.

Breakfast was quiet and contemplative. Daniel read from the Bible and led the family in silent prayer. Kirsten didn't really know how prayer worked, but she bowed her head just the same and hoped for renewed health. She quickly rose to help with the breakfast dishes, avoiding Silas's eyes. When she turned back around, he was gone.

The morning passed quickly, with Mary giving her little jobs to do here and there, but encouraging her to just shadow her and watch what she did. By suppertime, Kirsten was feeling much better about Amish life. If this was a typical day, she was reasonably sure she could adjust. Eventually.

She'd just put away the last plate when Silas came downstairs, fresh from the shower. His hair lay in thick, dark curls and he looked dangerously handsome.

Would ya like to go fer a walk?" His voice was like maple syrup, thick and smooth and warm. Her body betrayed her, and goose bumps broke out all over her arms. She nodded once, refusing to smile.

He led the way out the door, down the steps, and to the orchard. His long legs carried him much farther and faster than hers, and she lagged behind, careful not to overexert herself.

He stopped a few strides in and reached his hand back to her. Kirsten stared at it for a long moment but made no move to accept it. Did he want her or not? She no longer knew.

Her eyes lifted to his and she couldn't stop the tears from welling. He dropped his hand and looked away in confusion. Slowly now, he walked, his hands jammed in his pockets. Kirsten followed a step or two behind.

"Are ya angry with me?" he asked, turning toward her at the end of the row.

Kirsten swallowed and answered him with a question of her own. "What am I to you, Silas?"

The pause was so long she almost gave up on getting an answer.

"Yer my wife," he said finally, firmly.

"I don't understand. You say that, but I have my own room and you won't kiss me and…I just don't understand," she stammered.

His gaze swung away from her to the fruit-laden branches. He touched an apple, examining it and releasing it, just as she had the night he'd asked her to become Amish.

"I thought it might be best to take this slowly. Not to rush it. Give ya time to adjust to living a plain life."

Their eyes met and she considered the honesty of his words.

"It's not because I'm pregnant?" she pressed. "I know it's not very attractive," she admitted, embarrassed again.

"Kirsten Miller, when I share a bed with you, it will have nothing to do with what ya look like. But I want it to be about love. Not expectation or duty or obligation." He ducked under branches to stand so close to her that his toes nearly touched hers.

"I am willing to wait," he said deliberately.

Silas's words and the intensity in his blue eyes—it all made sense now. He valued her in a way no one ever had. He saw her worth and knew it would be better for both of them to learn to love each other before they forced it. Of course Silas wouldn't rush. He'd married her so he could court her—it was the only way. But apart from the illusion that they'd rushed into marriage, he'd chosen to let the love happen naturally, freely. Then and only then would it be sweet. She got a small glimpse of herself through his eyes.

"Oh." She blinked up at him.

"I should have said something before…"

"I understand now."

"*Gut.*"

Kirsten held out her hand to him and he took it, smiling. They walked slowly back to the house, taking their time.

"I'm glad yer feeling better," he said, squeezing her hand slightly.

"I'm still pretty sore, but definitely improving."

He nodded, and his thumb rubbed against her fingers.

"Thank you for the rose, by the way," she said with a smile.

"Yer welcome." He was still shy.

"I do have one more question," she said as she curled her fingers around his.

His eyes flickered up to her face and considered her seriously.

"Will you teach me how to be mean to chickens?"

His booming laugh echoed off the barn.

— CHAPTER TWENTY —

In all her life, Kirsten had rarely gotten out of bed at five o'clock, but she was determined to at least follow the Millers' schedule. Even if she couldn't do the chores yet, she wanted to be able to observe. She had showered on Friday night, so when Daniel's voice boomed down the hall, she rose quickly and dressed.

She made it downstairs in time to see Silas putting on his boots. She met his sleepy smile and turned to Mary.

"You'll mind her condition?" Mary asked Silas, though it was more of an order. Silas nodded and stood tall, his eyes focused on Kirsten.

She understood from their exchange that she'd be her husband's charge this morning. The thought made her smile at him again expectantly. He motioned to the screen door, and Kirsten stepped out into the still night-dark morning.

"First, we feed the horses while Dad and Caleb do the milking," Silas said, stepping easily beside her. His voice was gruff from sleep, and she had to bite her lip to keep from smiling at the sound.

He pulled the door open and set out a small wooden stool for her where she would be out of the way but able to watch. All along the far side of the barn was a row of stalls. The buggies, carriages, and wagons were all stored in a separate, garage-like building near the house.

Silas moved quickly, lighting a few lanterns and hanging them from high hooks in between the stalls. Kirsten watched in the dim light as he scooped feed and gave it to each of the nine horses. She heard his voice quietly murmuring in one of the stalls, and she strained to catch the words. Whatever he was saying, it was not in English.

"What were you saying in there?" Kirsten asked when he stepped near her to grab a pitchfork.

"Just telling her *gut* morning," he said with a shrug.

Kirsten watched him finish with the horses and was surprised when he took down the lanterns and extinguished them completely. The horse barn was cast into total darkness, and she froze, unable to see even her stark white apron. Silas's warm hand on the small of her back startled her, and she jumped at his touch. Her pulse raced at his closeness.

"This way," Silas murmured to her, gently guiding her to a barely noticeable line of light where the door must be. It swung open at his touch, and she could see how much it had lightened outside in the short time they'd been tending to the horses. The sun was just peeking over the horizon, casting the sky in a warm creep of color, like a blush rising on the face of the morning.

Silas dropped his hand, and Kirsten was disappointed, but still happy to be with him. He strode into the larger barn and she followed. Daniel and Caleb were working quickly, milking their twenty cows with the help of electric milkers. It surprised Kirsten, but she was quickly learning that most of her assumptions about Amish life were wrong.

Silas stepped to the milk tank and filled two buckets nearly full. Kirsten followed him in awe and amazement as he effortlessly carried the pails to the house, not splashing or sloshing at all. This explained the muscles in his arms.

Silas came back out with two metal pails that Kirsten instantly recognized. He was fighting a smile, but losing the battle. He handed one to her without speaking. Kirsten sighed, took it from him, and led the way to the small chicken coop.

"They can't hurt ya," he said with a smile once they were inside the fenced yard. "The best way to learn is by doin'," he encouraged, while Kirsten eyed the hens, all clucking nervously. Silas's hand was gentle, but firm on her back as he pushed her toward the twitching hens.

Kirsten took a deep breath and reached under one, grasped an egg, and placed it lightly in her bucket. She was going back for a second egg when the hen jerked its head around and pecked her soundly on the wrist.

"Ouch!" she hissed, jerking her hand away. It hadn't hurt really, just startled her. She glared viciously at the bird. As her shock eased into annoyance, she could sense Silas's body shaking with laughter.

"You try that again, and I'll eat you for supper," Kirsten threatened, pointing her finger at the bird that was eyeing her.

Silas couldn't keep it in any longer and laughter burst out of him. Kirsten smiled at the sound and steeled herself for a re-approach. She knew that he'd never allow her to do anything he didn't feel she was able to do. He was deliberately guiding her and placing her in safe locations. Even now, he stood a mere foot away for her comfort.

She confidently reached in and took another egg out from under the hen. She repeated the process, making sure to glare at two more birds that saw fit to peck her. She'd gathered all the eggs, and with two full buckets in hand, she strolled through the kitchen door that Silas held open for her, a self-satisfied smile on her face.

"You go in and help Mom with breakfast while I check on the garden," he said as she passed. She watched him for several long moments while he strode away from her down the lane, the sun illuminating his tall, thin frame. This was going to be a marvelous day.

ᥒᥱ᥇᥆ᥒ

Kirsten looked with pride on the bowl of steaming scrambled eggs sitting on the table in front of her. Silas held her hand during prayer, and Kirsten smiled the whole time. Morning prayer was her favorite. The whole family recited a prayer from memory. Kirsten loved hearing their voices, loud and strong, young and old, blended together as the words were spoken in unison. She leaned slightly to her right to hear Silas's voice amongst the others. It was almost disappointing when the "Amen" came. Silas grabbed the bowl of eggs and took an extra-large helping. Kirsten knew she'd never miss those dry cereals or foil-wrapped Pop Tarts.

After breakfast, Mary shooed her out the door with Silas. He grabbed two empty five-gallon buckets, and they started off down the lane toward the garden. He pointed out rows and sections as they passed, stopping at perfectly ordered clumps of pepper plants and tomato vines. He named each variety, telling her what made it unique and different from the others. Kirsten leaned over him as he knelt beside a large tomato vine. Silas explained the signs of ripeness, pulling a few brilliant red, ripe tomatoes and handing them to her for examination.

She squatted down and set to work, carefully selecting the ones she hoped would meet with his approval. When her mother's van pulled into the lane and stopped near the garden, Kirsten rose quickly and walked to her mother's open arms.

"*Gut* morning, Mrs. Walker," Silas politely greeted her. Kirsten hadn't heard him come up behind her and nearly stumbled back into him.

"Morning, Silas," Elizabeth returned. "I was just driving by on my way home and saw you here." She smiled at Kirsten.

"We're picking a peck of peppers," Kirsten laughed. Her mom smiled but didn't laugh. Her eyes were searching Kirsten's face intently.

"How are you, honey? Not working too hard, are you?" her mom questioned.

"I'm fine, Mom," Kirsten insisted. It didn't seem like a good idea to go into detail about her previous overexertion.

"You're taking care of my girl?" Elizabeth asked, looking up at Silas.

"Yes, Mrs. Walker." Kirsten could sense Silas's hesitation, but Elizabeth didn't seem to notice. She just nodded her head.

"What's wrong, Mom?" she finally asked.

Elizabeth struggled for words and sighed.

"I've been thinking about moving," she confessed. "Not far. Just to an apartment in town. It's a decent place. Nicer than…" Her eyes drifted to the trailer down the road. Shaking her head, she continued. "It's a one bedroom. Close to work. I could save a lot of money on gas and utilities."

Kirsten listened while Elizabeth stumbled through her speech.

"It's a good idea, Mom," Kirsten said. And it was. In Kirsten's mind, the trailer was more a place of great pain than one full of happy memories.

She'd sought refuge there too many times. And on her wedding day, she'd walked out the door almost feeling like she had been released from a prison of her own making.

Elizabeth looked relieved. "I was hoping you wouldn't be upset. I didn't want you to feel like I was just selling your home."

Kirsten shook her head. She had a home now. A good one. But reminding her mom of that seemed cruel, so she just squeezed her hand.

"Would ya like some help with the move?" Silas asked.

"Oh! Well…that might be nice. It will be a week or so before I can make all the arrangements."

Silas nodded.

"Well, I better get some sleep. Take care, honey," Kirsten's mom said as she embraced her again.

Silas stood next to Kirsten, waving as Elizabeth backed out of the lane and drove away. He turned back to the garden and made his way down one of the rows.

"Silas Miller!" Kirsten called loudly, her tone stern. He froze momentarily and turned to her. Kirsten walked up to him and boldly peered up into his face, her lips pursed tightly.

"I really like you." She took a long look in his eyes and then strode past him to her bucket. There was no missing the grin he wore as he went back to work.

Yes, it was turning out to be a wonderful day.

.ஐ௧௯௨.

Mary returned home after lunch when the hired staff showed up at the market. Kirsten suspected that she was taking time off to help her adjust. She had made up her mind to be more of a help than a hindrance, and after a pleasant morning in the garden with her husband, she was in good spirits.

Mary announced her plans to wash the bedding, and Kirsten gladly offered to help. They made work of stripping the beds. Kirsten carefully folded her wedding quilt before briskly yanking the white sheets off her bed. Mary had already stripped her own bed and was busy in the girls' room. Kirsten made her way to the end of the long hallway to a room she'd never entered.

This was certainly her husband's room. The hooks lining the walls held his jackets, hats, and trousers. His good boots were lined up neatly under the window. Smaller hats and coats hung along the wall beside the door—Caleb's things.

Slowly, Kirsten walked around the bed to the wall where Silas's black suit coat hung—the one he'd worn on their wedding day. Her fingers reverently stroked the hand-stitched garment.

She turned to survey the bed and noticed his suspenders draped over the bedpost. This was where he slept. On the small table between the bed and the window was a Bible, its leather cover creased and its pages dog-eared.

Kirsten folded back the summer quilt on his bed to see the light blue sheets. Carefully, she pulled them loose, smelling his scent as it wafted from the fabric. She carefully bundled it all in her arms and clutched it close to her chest. There was something so sweetly wonderful about washing her husband's sheets. He was outside working hard all day to provide for her. The least she could do was provide a nice, clean place for him to lay his weary body down at night. He'd been so kind to her over and over again in ways she probably didn't even realize. He'd given of himself so selflessly, valuing her well-being above his own. This small act of care for him touched her in a way she couldn't possibly have expected.

She met Mary in the washroom behind the kitchen, already hard at work. She watched her fill the basin, add detergent, and scrub at the clothes before running them through the wringer. It was a repetitive task, and Kirsten soon had the steps figured out.

"May I try?" she asked as Mary reached for the light blue sheets. Mary nodded and moved aside, patiently observing as Kirsten tried to mimic her motions. Silas's words came back to her now as she plunged her hands in the water.

You learn best by doin'.

At last, she turned to Mary, hoping for a nod of approval. Her mother-in-law grinned and showed Kirsten again, commenting on how quickly she was picking it up. Kirsten's second effort won her praise.

"*Jah!* That's *gut!*" Mary cheered as she tossed the sheets into the basket full of wet, clean laundry. Kirsten followed her outside to the multiple long lines that were strung the length of the backyard.

Several minutes later, Kirsten stood back and watched the pale blue sheets billow in the wind where she had pinned them to the clothesline.

"What the modern world doesn't know," Kirsten mumbled to the long lines of clean bedding, "is how deeply satisfying it is to be Amish."

.ିଣ ଗ.

It was well after supper, and the girls were still busy in the kitchen preparing for tomorrow's Sunday-meeting picnic. Daniel led Silas and Caleb into the house after they'd completed the evening chores. Caleb's laughter preceded the slam of the screen door.

"There seems to be a lot of bedding on the line at this late hour," Daniel announced with a twinkle in his eye.

"*Ach!*" Mary exclaimed, her hands stained red from slicing strawberries.

Kirsten jumped to her feet from her observation perch and hurried to the washroom for the large wicker basket. It was nearly dark as she plucked the pins from the sheets, letting them tumble down into her arms, smelling of summer sun and soap—much the way Silas did.

Caleb emerged in the fading light to carry in the full basket for her. Kirsten winked at him as she tossed the last bundle on the heap. He carried it all the way upstairs and set it in the hallway at her request.

She started in Caleb and Silas's room, tucking the sheets carefully, precisely, smoothing them gently with her hand, and at last pulling the quilt on top.

Next she made Daniel and Mary's bed, taking time again to do her work well. She unfurled their wedding quilt over their bed and studied it for a moment. This was the quilt that had warmed their bed for their twenty-eight years of marriage. All seven of their babies had been conceived on this bed, in this house. Kirsten thought of her own wedding quilt and was momentarily saddened by the realization that she could not tell her children a similar story one day. She deeply wished that she could go back and rewrite some of her pages.

Shelby Jo and Anna Mae had begun making the beds in their room, so Kirsten pulled out the last set of sheets and spread them on her bed. Gently, she unfolded the precious quilt and tugged it even. A small sound startled her, and she turned to see Shelby Jo peeking around her door.

"You have the prettiest bed," Shelby sighed quietly.

"Thank you." Kirsten smiled. "I like it, too."

"Silas made it," Shelby said, her eyes lingering on the intricate carving on the headboard.

"My Silas made this bed?" Kirsten asked as her own eyes trailed across the vines and leaves before landing on the almost life-like blooming roses etched into the surface of the wood.

Shelby nodded and stepped closer. "He asked Dad to bring it home from the market for ya after Mama had fit ya for yer wedding dress."

Kirsten stared as Shelby's fingers trailed over the butter-smooth finish.

"It's beautiful," Kirsten breathed in agreement, remembering the rows of furniture at the market. How much of it was made by her husband's own hand?

"Did Silas make anything else in this room?" Kirsten asked Shelby as she swung her eyes to the nightstands and high-backed chair.

"No, I don't think so," Shelby said, following her gaze.

"Not even the quilt?" Kirsten asked, playfully narrowing her eyes.

"No!" Shelby giggled.

"Kirsten, Shelby, time for evening prayer," Daniel's voice called up the stairs. Kirsten followed Shelby down the stairs and into the living room where the rest of the Millers had gathered.

Kirsten sat in the rocker, staring at Silas. He had sprawled out on the couch, his head leaned back against the cushion and his legs stretched over the floor. His eyes were closed, and he looked as though he might be asleep. None of which was odd or surprising, really.

But his clothes were. He wore a t-shirt with the sleeves cut off, exposing large patches of skin on his side. And blue jeans. Actual store-bought blue jeans. She was sure that if he stood and turned around, she'd find a Levis label across his waist. His feet were bare, and he'd obviously just come from the shower as his hair was still wet. It was as if they'd switched places—she in her Amish dress and cap and he in a thoroughly modern outfit that any boy she'd ever known would wear.

Her eyes strayed again to the bare skin along his side. She doubted there was an ounce of fat on him. His bare arms, though long and lean, bore well-defined muscles. She looked to his face and saw he was watching her through barely open eyes. She blushed deeply and dropped her gaze to her lap.

She needn't be embarrassed, she supposed. He was her husband, technically speaking. Still, she felt her face flame in the dim lantern light.

Daniel cleared his throat and began reading a portion of Scripture. Kirsten forced herself to focus on his words. While he read, no one moved, except for the occasional, gentle rock in a rocking chair. There was absolute silence until he reverently closed the book and everyone stood. Silas crossed the room to Kirsten as his family knelt in a small circle. He offered his hand, and Kirsten slowly, awkwardly slid to her knees. He knelt beside her and kept her hand in his. Mary claimed the other, closing the circle. Kirsten's throat tightened, and she felt tears pricking her eyes. That she was a part of the circle now was not lost on her. The symbolism was rich and strong. They had welcomed her, not just into their home, but into their family.

All gut things are best shared. Silas had said those words on their wedding day. Kirsten couldn't agree more.

— CHAPTER TWENTY-ONE —

At the two-hour mark, Silas noticed Kirsten move uncomfortably in her spot on the bench between his mother and Deborah. He watched her bite her lip and wince as she squirmed. He tried to catch her eye, but when he did, she grimaced instead of grinning. As soon as the benediction was given, she jumped to her feet and rushed to the house. Silas watched for her, but he didn't see her again until she and Deborah were spreading a blanket on the grass. He lowered himself next to her, and they feasted on cold fried chicken that had been prepared the day before. Near the end of the meal, he felt her lean lightly against him. Her back pressed against his side and her muscles trembled wearily.

"Are ya ready to go home?" he quietly murmured to her.

Kirsten turned her head slightly and nodded. He rose to his feet and walked down the row of buggies, untying Titus and checking the harnesses. When he looked up, he saw her walking very slowly along the buggy-lined driveway, her eyes searching anxiously. He stepped around to the back of the buggy, and she spotted him immediately. Her smile was radiant as she approached him, a basket on her arm, and Silas felt as though his bones had turned to butter and were melting away.

"You found me," he said, smiling at her and taking the basket from her arm.

"You wanted to be found," she said, grinning at him.

He laughed and turned to lift her into the buggy. Sitting next to her was definitely one of his new favorite things. Always would be as far as he could tell. They rode off in silence, having an hour-long trip to make together.

"Tired?" Silas asked as she gave a huge yawn.

"A little," she said with a shy smile. He was reasonably sure he could stare at her eyelashes all day.

"How long will they stay?" Kirsten asked.

"Not long. Caleb and the girls should be home from Sunday school already."

They jostled a little further down the road, and he felt her hand on his arm. He gripped the reins in one hand and let her lace her fingers into his. Timidly at first, she leaned her head against his shoulder. As the buggy swayed, he felt her relax completely against him—sound asleep.

"Kirsten," he said quietly, gently squeezing her hand. "Kirsten, we're almost home." She stirred then and sat up, blinking awake. He pulled the buggy up to the side-porch steps and jumped out, reaching back for her.

"Go inside and get some rest," he told her gently.

The door to her room was closed when he made his way upstairs to change out of his suit. He slipped into a pair of gray trousers and a blue collarless shirt before lying down on his bed. Even now, he could feel the light weight of her against him, her head resting on his shoulder, her delicate fingers wound through his.

The next thing he knew, she was leaning over him, her fingers shyly combing through his hair. It was the most intimate moment they had ever shared, and he struggled to know whether he was asleep or having a fantastic dream.

"Silas," she whispered in a sing-song voice.

He stared up at her soft eyes, peering down into his.

"Silas, your mom said to wake you up and tell you David and Michael are here," she murmured quietly.

He nodded, wishing she would keep combing through his hair. But she stopped and stepped back. He swung his legs over the side of the bed and sat up. He looped an arm through the suspenders hanging loosely at his sides and snapped them into place.

"Did ya get some sleep?" he asked her.

"No. I tried. I just slept too well on the way home," she admitted sheepishly.

He smiled at her, noticing the light blush on her face.

The sound of Danny's laughter downstairs jolted them out of their daze. Silas followed Kirsten downstairs to find the house full and bustling, filled with voices and laughter. He gently nudged Kirsten away from the edge of the room. Caleb soon suggested a game of volleyball, and everyone went outside.

That night the supper table was crowded, much to Silas's delight. Not so long ago, he had not enjoyed having his brothers' presence at the table due to their merciless teasing. But tonight, the extra guests meant Kirsten's chair was that much closer to his.

"Yer a married man now, brother," Michael observed shortly after the meal began. "Where's yer beard?" Perhaps Kirsten's presence would only exacerbate his brothers' joshing.

"Not all married men have beards," Silas said with a shrug.

"They should," David mumbled.

"Abe Yoder doesn't have one. Or Micah Beiler," Silas stated, still not looking up from his plate.

"*Hmpf.* They have English jobs in factories that prohibit beards," Michael argued.

"Safety precautions." Silas nodded in agreement. "I don't think a beard is the safest idea around a spinning lathe, either." He looked Michael square in the eye, knowing no one could argue with him.

"It's not against the *Ordnung*. Yer brother can make his own choices," Daniel declared, settling the debate.

The conversation turned then, and it was Deborah who spoke first to Kirsten.

"How was yer first week plain, Kirsten?"

"It's a big change," Kirsten admitted, glancing at Silas, "but I really love it here." She dropped her eyes, and Silas could do nothing but stare at her.

"I'm curious what you miss the most," David quizzed.

She appeared to think seriously about the question for several long moments.

"I know what it is," Silas interjected. Out of the corner of his eye, he saw his wife's head snap up in confusion and surprise. He concentrated on gathering a forkful of pizza casserole in a deliberately slow, aloof manner. He had everyone's attention.

"What?" Kirsten finally asked.

"Yer car," he said, shoveling a bite into his mouth. It was a perfectly believable and reasonable answer. But just as he expected, laughter bubbled up within her and Kirsten laughed joyfully, her eyes dancing. He smiled wryly at their private joke. He knew she hated her hunk-of-junk car. He also knew how much she had loved every buggy ride he'd ever taken her on. Her car may well have been the easiest possession for her to leave behind.

Michael and David looked at each other, stunned that Silas had made what was apparently a joke. Their shocked expressions only broadened Silas's grin.

Amy soon started talking excitedly of the plans being made for the upcoming wedding of Rebecca Lapp, an older sister to Amy's best friend, Emily. The wedding was a week from Tuesday. Silas cringed when he heard that both his brothers and their wives were asked to be kitchen helpers. It was an honor to be asked. That Silas and Kirsten had not been included was a subtle slight. Briefly, Silas met Daniel's eyes and watched him shake his head.

At least Kirsten's ignorance shielded her from some of the offense. Daniel had warned him early on that not all of their friends and neighbors would feel so welcoming of an English girl expecting another man's baby. Still, it stung.

"It wasn't that surprising," Amy laughed. "Their garden was nearly overflowing with celery."

"Celery?" Kirsten asked.

"It's tradition to grow enough celery to feed at the wedding supper if ya have a daughter who might be gettin' married," Daniel explained.

"Oh," Kirsten paused. "There was plenty of celery at our wedding." She turned her quizzical expression to Mary.

"That's because yer husband grew enough celery to feed the county this year!" David laughed loudly. Silas flashed him a look and glanced over to find Kirsten looking thoughtfully up at him, not laughing like everyone else.

"Silas is a very smart man," she said, staring into his eyes.

Pride was a sin. Silas knew that. It was one of the reasons they lived the way they did. Living simply helped avoid falling into pride. Still, he could have floated right through the roof.

"Perhaps Joseph should learn a lesson from Silas. With all those daughters, he'll be needing a steady crop of celery for years to come," Michael said with a smirk.

"Maybe Silas will be blessed with a daughter," Deborah said as she smiled at Kirsten.

"Oh, he will," Kirsten said shyly.

"Sounds like yer hopin' fer a girl," Mary said, beaming at her daughter-in-law.

"Oh, I already know it's a…girl," Kirsten's voice trailed off and Silas froze, his fork halfway to his mouth. He looked at her and she blinked up at him, suddenly realizing this was new information to him. He stared into her eyes, searching.

"I had an ultrasound about a month ago and found out," she explained, her eyes pleading. "Only my mom and I knew."

Silas was simply unable to move.

"A daughter, then!" Daniel's voice boomed, breaking the silence. He clapped his hand on Silas's shoulder and jarred him back to life. Silas swallowed and nodded.

"Would you like to see it? The ultrasound, I mean?" Kirsten asked, her eyes alive with excitement and her hand grasping his arm.

Silas nodded and Kirsten jumped up from the table, her footsteps fast on the stairs. He'd seen an x-ray once when Michael had broken his arm. The Amish didn't take pictures, as that encouraged vanity.

But this was different.

Kirsten was back with a tiny frame in her hands before he'd sorted out his thoughts. She bit her lip and smiled up at him as she handed him the frame.

To Silas, it was a mess of black, gray, and white swirls—much less clear than Michael's x-ray had been. He squinted and held the image closer to his eyes. Kirsten leaned against him and traced the outline of the baby's face, arm, hand, belly, and legs. He blinked in surprise as the outline became suddenly clear to him.

Her daughter that they'd raise as theirs. To him, there would be no distinction. Even now, he felt a tenderness and awe that only a father could feel.

This was his daughter.

He smiled and handed the ultrasound back to Kirsten.

"Would anyone else like to see?" she waved it in the air, and Silas panicked that they'd all refuse. Deborah's face snapped up to Michael's, pleading. He nodded his consent, and she reached for the frame. They studied the image together, clearly amazed at the outline. Daniel nodded his consent, and Mary studied the picture until understanding lit her face. Amy and Caleb, too, examined the ultrasound while Amy pointed out the features to her little brother. Even Daniel took several long moments to study the image and shook his head in amazement. David and Sarah notably declined. Not at all surprising, but annoying to Silas just the same.

Kirsten placed the small silver frame in her lap and resumed eating with the rest of them.

It was late when he helped his brothers with their horses and buggies. He watched them roll down the lane before returning to the horse barn to extinguish the lanterns. The house was dark when he returned, but Kirsten's silhouette against the window next to the front door nearly made him trip on the side stairs.

He gently eased the screen door shut and flipped the latch before closing the heavy, wooden door over it. When he turned to her, she was watching him.

"Was it okay that I showed them the ultrasound?" The worry was plain in her voice.

"*Jah*. It was fine," he reassured her.

"I'm sorry I didn't tell you that it's a girl before," she said, twisting her hands nervously.

"Most people don't find out until much later," he said with a grin. Kirsten smiled and sighed in relief.

He reached out to her, and she slipped her hand in his.

"Time for bed, I think," he murmured, stroking his thumb across her knuckles.

He stepped close and kissed her cheek tenderly, inhaling the smell of her skin, still caressing her knuckles.

"Good night, Kirsten."

"Good night, Silas."

It caused him near physical pain to watch her walk away from him.

— Chapter Twenty-Two —

Boxes of dry cereal were not what Kirsten expected to see on the table when she walked in the kitchen with a full bucket of eggs. Caleb was fast on her heels, his eyes lighting up as he spotted the items on the breakfast menu. Shelby and Anna were completely distracted with picking out which kind to try first. Kirsten waited patiently as the family clamored in and took their seats around the table.

Immediately after prayer, they began filling their bowls. Kirsten selected the Crispix, trying not to think about the hot breakfasts Mary and Amy had spoiled her with for a week now. A bowl of cold cereal didn't seem very satisfying compared to the French toast and sausages they had enjoyed just yesterday.

In record time, Silas and Caleb had finished their cereal and were refilling their bowls. Kirsten watched with wide eyes and noticed Daniel smiling at her expression. Embarrassed, she turned her attention back to the bowl in front of her. As hard as Silas worked, it really shouldn't be that surprising that it would take so much cereal to fill him. He and Caleb were both so thin; it was easy to see that they worked off huge meals in just a few short hours.

She was only halfway through her soggy Crispix when Daniel looked to Shelby and rattled off something in Pennsylvania Dutch. Kirsten listened carefully, hoping to catch a word here or there that sounded familiar or similar. It might have been possible if she'd heard one word at a time, but when the words all flowed together in one long sentence, it all sounded terribly foreign. It certainly wasn't the first time her new family had spoken in their first language, Pennsylvania Dutch, around her. But still, it felt odd to sit at a table where another language was being spoken. That was something that would take a long time to get used to.

Daniel turned his questions to Silas, still speaking in dialect. Kirsten stopped again to listen, hoping in vain to somehow get the gist of what they were saying. Silas's voice answered in words she didn't understand or recognize. It still sounded so strange to hear him speak in another language. As seldom as he spoke, she was desperate to understand every word he said. It was frustrating to be left out, though she knew none of them were intentionally excluding her. At least, she hoped that was true. There was always the possibility that some of the foreign phrases were about her. She wouldn't have a clue if they were.

Daniel cleared his throat, and Kirsten glanced up to see him watching her carefully. She had inadvertently stopped eating while the conversation continued. Her father-in-law considered her for a moment, and Silas turned his head to follow his father's gaze.

Perhaps they were talking about her.

"You asked what my plans were for tomorrow," Daniel began, sounding oddly formal. "After I bring yer mother to the store, I was hoping to come home and have Caleb's help in cleaning out the barn."

He was speaking for her benefit. Kirsten knew by his abrupt switch from Pennsylvania Dutch to English. Daniel missed nothing. Though his beard was graying, he seemed so strangely able to know when she was uncomfortable. It had been so long since she had lived with a man. Now she was not only sharing a home with her husband, but living under her father-in-law's roof. Having a father in her life, even if he was an in-law, was extraordinarily new.

She hadn't even known that she missed it. She'd mourned her daddy as a child, but life had gone on and she'd been forced to adapt, to grow up without one. Silas had promised to provide for her and care for her, but Kirsten had also gained a father's love. And this wasn't just any father. Daniel was tender and compassionate—much like Silas.

Looking at Daniel now, she could hardly imagine how different her life would have been if her dad had lived.

༺ༀༀ༻

Kirsten nearly skipped down the stairs and across the yard, past the garage to the workshop. It took several seconds for her eyes to adjust before she spotted him standing at a workbench beneath the long row of windows.

"Hello, husband," she chimed playfully, coming to stand beside him.

"Hullo, wife," he answered with a smile.

"I have brought you a snack," she announced, still holding her hands behind her back.

He glanced down at her, and then at his stain-covered hands.

"Close your eyes," she instructed.

Silas tossed the staining cloth on the workbench and obediently closed his eyes. Kirsten broke off a piece of a monster cookie she'd just finished making and reached up to push it past his lips. She watched as he chewed with his eyes still closed. He swallowed and opened his eyes.

"My favorite," he said, smiling at her.

"So I was told." Kirsten looked around and pointed at a wooden stool nearby. "May I sit here?"

"You may," he said, dazzling her with a gentle smile.

She pulled the stool close to the bench and sat, placing the pair of cookies on her apron and breaking off another bite.

"What are you working on?" she asked, offering the bite to him.

"Putting the finish on a chair," he answered before taking the cookie from her fingers. Kirsten tried not to shiver when his lips touched her fingertips.

"How long does it take to build a chair?" she asked conversationally.

"Depends on the type of chair," Silas said, swiping a streak of stain across the seat.

She fed him another piece.

"What kind of wood is it made out of?" Kirsten asked as she leaned in close to examine the perfectly turned leg.

"Maple."

"It's beautiful," she murmured. And it was. It reminded her of her bed, really.

"Is that what my bed is made out of?" she asked. Silas momentarily froze before nodding.

"Thank you, by the way." She beamed at him.

"Yer welcome," he said with a shrug.

Kirsten broke off another bite and held it out to him.

"How long have you been such an expert woodworker?"

Silas chewed while he thought. "About eleven years or so," he said with his mouth full.

"You started when you were ten?" she asked incredulously.

He nodded.

"Who taught you how to do all this?"

"Dad taught me some of it. Alvin Shrock taught me the rest."

"Wow."

Silas tossed the staining cloth on the bench and grabbed a stool, pulling it up close and sitting to face her.

"You ask a lot of questions, Mrs. Miller," he drawled, his tone teasing. Kirsten laughed and shrugged. "Are there any more?" he coaxed.

"Just one."

Silas waited, endlessly patient.

"I have a doctor appointment a week from Friday and was wondering if you would like to come with me."

Silas studied her for a long moment, his eyebrow raised in expectation. Her mind raced at his expression, and she suddenly realized her mistake.

"What I should have asked was, would you be able to take me to the clinic in town for my doctor appointment?" she clarified, a nervous blush tickling beneath her eyes.

"I can take ya," he answered with a grin, putting her back at ease. Kirsten fed him the last bite of cookie and stood to leave.

"Thank you," she said with a smile.

"Thank you," he echoed.

— Chapter Twenty-Three —

The next morning, Silas pulled the buggy to the side yard just after breakfast and helped Kirsten up. His hands on her waist felt strong and sure, and she was always disappointed when he let go. He landed in the seat next to her and handed her the reins. Kirsten shot him a panicked look, but he only smiled.

"Ya learn best by doin'," he reminded her.

Kirsten shook her head in silent protest.

"I'll be right beside ya," he reassured her, slipping his arm across the back of the seat.

"I don't know what to do," she whimpered as she stared at Titus's back end while he shifted.

Silas's long fingers curled around hers, and she felt the motion of his wrist as it snapped the reins lightly. Titus stepped into motion, but Silas pulled back on the reins with a low "whoa."

"Now you try," he said as he slid his hand off hers.

Chickens. Just think chickens, Kirsten thought to herself. She pinched her eyes shut and then opened them resolutely. With a deep breath, she flicked the reins, and Titus stepped forward. She looked excitedly up at Silas, hoping for some kind of praise.

"*Gut,*" he said with a nod, the smallest of smiles tugging at the corners of his mouth.

It took only fifteen minutes to get to Michael's place just down the road. Kirsten gently pulled on the reins, and Titus slowed to a stop by the white, two-story house with a wide front porch spanning the southern side. Behind the house and to the north rose a long, white barn, much bigger than the one at Daniel and Mary's farmstead. She could hear cattle bawling from the other side of the barn.

"I'll be back fer ya about five o'clock," Silas told her, swinging her down to the gravel driveway. Kirsten felt a small pulse of panic. She hadn't been away from him since they were married. He'd run a few errands to the market now and then, but this was the first time she had gone away from her new home and her new husband. What would she do if she needed him?

Judging by the concern on Silas's face, her fear was poorly disguised. Just as he opened his mouth to question her, Deborah stepped out onto the porch and waved at Kirsten with a wide, warm smile. Kirsten smiled back at her and felt the fear ease. She turned back to Silas and smiled sheepishly at him.

"Have fun," he murmured low, then he kissed her cheek and jumped back into the buggy.

Kirsten met Deborah on the porch but stopped to wave at her husband as he turned around and headed back home.

"Hullo, Kirsten," Deborah sang out as she hugged her tightly.

"Good morning, Deborah."

"Come in! Come in!" she said, pulling Kirsten inside.

Kirsten stopped just inside the door and stared around her.

"Is it okay for me to say you have a beautiful home?" Kirsten gasped.

Deborah beamed back at her. "It's fine to say that. And very kind of ya. My Michael built it just before we were married." Deborah's eyes sparkled at the memory. Kirsten took in the bright yellow kitchen and the white-painted cabinets. The floors were polished hardwood and stretched the length of the open floor plan. A large, spacious living room contained a leather couch, two matching wooden rockers, and an upholstered chair and ottoman, all gathered around a giant stone fireplace. It was a spectacular room in a simple and understated way.

There were no pictures hanging on the wall. Only one massive quilt draped down off an intricately carved, wooden quilt hanger on the wall behind the couch. Kirsten stepped close and examined the quilt. The tiny pieces were all carefully placed and sewn together in the most intricate pattern she had ever seen. The colors were bright and cheery and nearly sang in their beauty.

"Did you make this?" she breathed in awe.

"My mama made it for me," Deborah answered with a smile, gazing fondly at the quilt.

"It's…exquisite!"

"Of course, yer husband made the quilt hanger. And our dining set. And our bedroom set," Deborah explained and then laughed at Kirsten's wide eyes.

As she followed Deborah to the kitchen, Kirsten paused by the massive dining table with its ten chairs, four on each side and two on the ends. She could only imagine the countless hours he must have spent. Though she could picture him working on it—measuring, cutting, sanding, and finishing. Judging by its perfection, he had not hurried on any aspect of its construction. And that sounded exactly like her Silas.

Deborah set a basket of apples on the table, along with a few bowls and some knives.

"Silas brought these over yesterday," Deborah said as she picked up an apple and began peeling it.

Kirsten selected an apple and bit her lip. "I'm not very good at this yet," Kirsten admitted, sliding the knife ever so slowly beneath the peel, cutting first too deep and then too shallow.

"You'll get the hang of it soon enough," Deborah said with a smile, unfazed.

She was right. As the morning wore on, Kirsten got faster and more consistent. But her hands were soon too sore and her back ached from sitting. Deborah sent her into the kitchen with the first batch of apples to boil.

While they worked, Deborah told her more about her large family in Missouri, naming all eight of her brothers and sisters, their spouses, and their children. She told the story of how she met Michael when he came to visit Uncle Isaac for a few months one summer. She even shared the story of Johnny's labor and delivery.

As Deborah talked, Kirsten grew more and more comfortable, soon feeling completely at ease. Kirsten told Deborah of her own family, the hard times after her dad had died, and how hard her mom had worked to support them. She talked about the way she'd never really fit in at school, but skipped over anything that had to do with Logan. And she talked about meeting Silas, his kindness and concern. She even told Deborah of her adventures in the chicken coop, which brought a peal of laughter out of her new sister-in-law.

Kirsten laughed too. "If I ever bust open one of the feather pillows on my bed, I'll probably scream."

"I bet yer husband would love that," Deborah giggled.

"Oh…I don't…he doesn't…" she stammered. "I…have my own room. For now." She could feel her face flaming fiercely.

Deborah was surprised; that much was obvious. But her response was kind. "That's very considerate of Silas."

Kirsten nodded her agreement. It was a kindness that he'd been so very patient. And though her fondness for him grew each day, she was glad for the chance to love him first before being intimate. For a change.

Her day sped by and soon they were packing up a box of jars of applesauce that they'd canned for her to take home. Silas's footsteps sounded on the front porch, and Kirsten rushed like a giddy schoolgirl to let him in.

"Are ya ready to go?" he asked, grinning at her.

She nodded, her eyes dancing at the mere sight of him. He carried the box to the buggy while Kirsten hugged Deborah and thanked her for the wonderful day. She stepped into the buggy and waved excitedly back at the woman she truly considered a new friend.

Silas was waiting and handed her the reins. Without hesitating, Kirsten snapped the reins and Titus stepped forward.

"How was yer day?" he asked with a smile, leaning with his arm across the seat back, just barely brushing against her shoulder blades.

"Excellent."

"That's *gut*."

"Deborah is…wonderful," Kirsten said thickly. She was so profoundly glad for her sister-in-law's warmth and acceptance.

"So are you," he said, smiling softly.

"Must be those Miller men we married," she said as she grinned at him.

"No. The Miller men just know how to pick the wonderful women."

Kirsten giggled and bit her lip.

— CHAPTER TWENTY-FOUR —

Days later, Kirsten re-twisted her hair and slid the pins back into place. Downstairs, Mary was giving a long list of instructions to Amy. Kirsten came into the kitchen as Mary was looping her arm through a basket.

"You'll mind yer sisters," Mary said almost sternly, looking at Amy for a long time. Even Kirsten could hear the double meaning in her words. Amy glanced at Kirsten and nodded slowly.

Mary gave a satisfied nod and hurried out the door to where Daniel waited for her in the wagon. Kirsten watched as he helped her into the seat, sweetly smiling up at her. She'd caught them once in the backyard, hidden amongst the lines of laundry. Daniel's arms had been around his wife and he'd been kissing her tenderly. Kirsten had slowly and silently backed away, embarrassed but touched by the encounter.

It was different, this being part of a family. Though she knew he was far more stern and strict than her own father ever would have been, Kirsten could plainly see Daniel's love for his family. It was impossible to miss the delight he took in his children—young and old. He worked hard because he loved them. Her father had been a good man, a hard worker. But he had been rugged with a gruff exterior, seldom showing the softness or tenderness she'd seen in her short time in the Miller home.

There was no TV or radio in the Miller house. They had each other, and that was so much more than everything else in the world. Kirsten knew that better than most.

While she was standing at the window, Silas pulled up to the house with a buggy.

He lifted Shelby and Anna into the back and then turned to Kirsten with a sweet look in his eyes. She took his hand and climbed slowly up into her seat, holding on to his hand as long as she could. Amy swiftly sat down next to her in the front where Silas usually sat and picked up the reins.

"We won't be home until five, so yer own yer own for lunch," Amy said to Silas, who still stood on Kirsten's side of the buggy.

The buggy sprang forward long before Kirsten was ready, and they started on their way to Kirsten's first quilting frolic. She had woken up this morning feeling nervous, but convinced that if she was going to be the wife of Silas Miller, the *Amish* wife of Silas Miller, she had better start acting the part in social settings. Quilting frolics and work frolics were frequent gatherings according to Shelby. It was humbling to realize that a six-year-old knew more about being an Amish wife than she did.

The Lapps' house was a solid hour away by buggy, and the long ride did nothing to calm Kirsten's nerves. By the time Amy pulled into place in the long row of buggies in the yard, Kirsten was downright jittery. The house was full, and women had taken places all around an enormous quilt frame set up in the living room.

Rebecca Lapp stood in the kitchen, greeting the women as they arrived. This was to be her wedding quilt, and her eyes were already dancing with joy.

Amy abandoned Kirsten almost immediately for Emily, and Kirsten fought back the urge to hide. Just as she was about to seek out Shelby and Anna, who had gone outside to play, Deborah caught her eye and waved her to an open chair next to her.

Kirsten sank into the chair, her legs trembling.

"*Gut* morning, Kirsten." Deborah smiled as she pulled her needle through.

"Morning, Deborah," Kirsten's nervousness was easing, but she was still breathless.

"Did yer husband like the applesauce?" Deborah asked.

"Yes, he did," Kirsten laughed quietly, remembering how he'd taken a second helping after winking at her. "How about yours?"

"Michael says I should have ya over more often," Deborah giggled.

"I'd like that," Kirsten said sincerely.

Deborah smiled brightly. "You just watch me fer a while, and then I'll show ya what to do." Kirsten leaned over and peered closely at Deborah's needle moving in smooth, quick strokes through the fabric. Everything Deborah did looked so easy. But she also quietly explained what she was doing every step of the way. She had a calmness that made Kirsten believe she would be able to do anything asked of her.

"Ready to try?" Deborah asked after a few minutes of instruction. Kirsten took a deep breath and accepted the needle from Deborah with only slightly trembling fingers. Deborah watched closely but calmly as Kirsten pushed the needle through the fabric at a painfully slow pace. After several minutes of observation, Deborah simply turned to her basket, took out another needle and thread, and began stitching again. Kirsten had passed the unspoken test, and she felt a thrill of accomplishment at being trusted to continue on her own.

The ladies talked while they worked, even occasionally breaking out in song. Kirsten's neck began to ache after a time, but she stayed put.

Deborah seemed to hear all the things Kirsten never said and made sure to suggest breaks every now and then. With a warm smile, Deborah commented that Kirsten was doing very well and had a natural ability to learn quickly. Perhaps her high school transcript didn't matter so much anymore. Her dreams of college had dimmed significantly since the day she'd taken the pregnancy test. But she had always loved the academic side of school. She considered her new life a classroom of a different sort. Only now, lessons were hands-on.

Lunch was a picnic potluck, but it was sweltering outside and the humidity drove the women back indoors. Despite the absence of air conditioning or fans, the stone house was relatively cool and comfortable.

Much to her relief, the other women did not ask her hundreds of questions. She always feared that she would say the wrong thing and offend someone. She never worried about that with Silas. But there were plenty of other times when she chose to say as little as possible for fear her words would come out sounding far more English than she wanted them to.

Shortly before four o'clock, Amy motioned for Kirsten that it was time to go. After thanking Deborah for the lesson and saying goodbye to Rebecca, she hurried out to the buggy, where there was no Silas to help her up. She managed to get into the seat anyway and saw that Shelby and Anna were already seated and chatting behind her. Amy quickly got them on the road toward home.

"How often do you go to a quilting frolic?" Kirsten asked Amy after a few minutes of listening to Shelby and Anna's chatter.

"Oh…every time someone announces their wedding. Maybe a couple times a month."

Kirsten was silent as she processed this information.

"Was there one for me?" she asked after several minutes.

"*Jah*. It was at Deborah's."

They'd gathered for her too, then. The beautiful spread on her bed had been pieced together, surrounded by them, and sung over. It had been a reason for them to gather. Each woman had added her own touch to the fabric that would cover Kirsten's marriage bed. The bed where she would love her husband, conceive his children, grow round with life, and finally return emptied. The process to be repeated again and again as nature allowed. She wondered how they'd feel to know it covered her body alone—never his.

A loud crack of thunder jarred her. The sky behind them had turned black, and a high bank of clouds billowed tall in the sky. They were barely halfway home, and much of this road was oddly empty of Amish friends or neighbors. Amy's face tightened, and she pursed her lips. She flicked the reins, urging Molly on faster. Shelby and Anna grew quiet as the thunder growled long and loud overhead.

Only minutes later, the wind began to whoosh around them. The trees by the road bent and swayed heavily, then violently. They'd not yet reached their road, and there were conspicuously few farms along this back stretch of gravel. It was all cropland, with farmsteads on the opposite side of these fields lined up along the highway. Nowhere to stop and take shelter.

The first raindrops fell, making loud smacking sounds. Huge, heavy drops. Then more. Then heavy rain, a waterfall from the sky, drowned out only by the near constant cracks of thunder all around them.

If Kirsten had been driving in her car, she would have pulled over. This was a deluge beyond what windshield wipers could handle. Molly was still pushing hard down the road. The rain was whipped hard by the wind and fell nearly sideways. Kirsten could see almost nothing now, as even Molly's backside blurred from view. It was not a brief downpour, but a serious storm. The wind shook the buggy terribly and relentlessly. There was simply no escape, and for several long minutes they inched forward through the fierce torrent.

Before Kirsten even realized what was happening, Amy stopped the buggy while shapes moved beside and behind them. Amy abruptly vacated her seat next to Kirsten and moved to the back, where she wrapped her arms around Shelby and Anna. Kirsten glanced back at her briefly before the buggy suddenly shuddered and Silas's drenched body slammed down next to her. He grabbed the reins, snapped them brutally and shouted loud words in a language she did not know.

She could feel the tension in his body beside her, and she made no move to hold on to him, though she badly wanted to. He ruthlessly pushed Molly to move faster, and the buggy swayed heavily from the wind and the speed. Kirsten stared ahead, begging Silas's God for the lane to miraculously appear out of the deluge. Still her husband snapped the reins and shouted over the din. After many more tense minutes, he pulled the buggy sharply into the lane and slightly eased the pace. He must have covered the miles in half the time.

They rolled right into the horse barn where Caleb was waiting, rolling the door shut behind them.

Amy jumped down after Silas and took Anna on one hip and Shelby's hand with the other, pulling them quickly across the yard to the shelter of the house.

Silas rounded the front of the buggy, quietly and calmly murmuring in Pennsylvania Dutch to Molly, who drooped heavily from the hard ride. Slowly, he came around to Kirsten's side.

"Kirsten?" she heard her name as if through a fog, her wide eyes fixed straight ahead, unseeing. His hand was working gently to loosen her fingers from the seat. The sound of his breathing was hard and fast, as if he'd run every mile with the horses. It was that sound—the air pushing in and out of him—that snapped her out of her trance. Her tunnel vision receded and she could see him beside her.

He reached for her, and she slid her body out into his hands. He caught the sudden, falling weight of her, and she used the only strength she had left to grip his sopping-wet shirt in her fists. Kirsten's legs hung limply beneath her as Silas supported her against his body. She buried her face in the folds of his shirt and shook, finally sobbing into his chest. His shock registered for only a moment, and then his arms moved around her, holding her tightly as she fell apart.

For a long time, he simply held her while she cried. And then with a deep, shuddering breath, she unclenched her hands and slowed her gasps, her tears subsiding. His arms stayed locked around her, even as she leaned back to look up at him.

Silas's hair was dripping onto his shoulders. His eyes, weary from fear, peered anxiously down at her. She flattened her hands on his chest. It was still heaving, but he was breathing more slowly than before.

The rain was still beating against the barn, falling heavy and fast, drumming like the beating in his chest.

"Caleb, you see to the horses," Silas commanded, his eyes still staring into hers.

"*Jah*," came the quiet reply. Kirsten glanced over and saw him standing shyly behind the buggy, gently rubbing Titus's neck. The horse was still tethered to the back of the buggy, where he had made the terrifying trip home.

"Can ya make it to the house?" Silas asked, his voice so low it was gruff.

Kirsten nodded and felt his hand slide down her back and find her hand. There were massive puddles dotting the yard between the barn and the house. It wasn't more than fifty yards, but Kirsten knew she couldn't run on a perfect sunny day, much less in a monsoon while leaping puddles.

Silas pulled her quickly through the maze of small lakes and into the house. Amy stood, waiting in the kitchen.

"Get her into some dry clothes," he ordered Amy.

Amy took Kirsten's arm and helped her up the stairs and into her room. The rain smacked hard against the window pane while Amy pulled the dress, heavy with rain, from Kirsten's trembling body. She unwound Kirsten's hair and toweled it dry. Kirsten was shivering by the time Amy pulled her nightgown from its hook and slipped it over her head.

"Rest for a few minutes while I get ya some tea," Amy softly instructed.

Kirsten crawled beneath the wedding quilt and tried to stop the shivering. Slowly, the weight of the quilt pressed her body heat around her and the shaking stopped. The rain kept pounding against the window, and Kirsten dozed off.

A soft knock on her door woke her.

"Come in," she choked, hoping it was Amy with a cup of tea.

It wasn't. But it was better. Silas's face above the steaming mug in his big hands surprised her. She made no move to sit up.

"Are ya warmin' up?" he asked as he set the cup on her nightstand. Slowly, he lowered himself to sit on the bed next to her, and she felt the mattress slope under his weight.

She smiled and nodded, still curled up on her side beneath the quilt. He was wearing the jeans and sleeveless t-shirt again.

Tentatively he reached out and brushed a strand of damp hair away from her face.

"Have you ever seen our wedding quilt?" Kirsten asked, her hands running lightly over the fabric.

He shook his head. "Did ya have fun at the frolic?"

She nodded again, unsure of what to say.

"I missed you," she said quietly.

If his face wasn't so tan and the room wasn't so dim, she was fairly sure she'd see him blushing.

"Where do you get these clothes?" she asked, unable to bear her curiosity any longer.

"*Rumspringa*," he said with a shrug.

"I beg your pardon?"

He smiled. "*Rumspringa* is a time of running around for a teenager when the church sort of looks the other way. It's when we decide if we want to be baptized into the Amish church or leave."

"What does that have to do with these clothes?" she asked, running a finger inside the gaping armhole.

"My running around involved buying some modern clothes and learning to drive. Others go a little bit...further."

"Have you made your choice, then?" she asked, tracing the vein lines on the back of his tanned, weathered hands.

"I was baptized three years ago," he said, watching her finger on his hand.

"When you were eighteen?"

He nodded.

"You never really lost control?"

An unfathomable look flashed across his face and disappeared before Kirsten could even be sure she'd seen anything at all.

"No."

Kirsten whimpered suddenly and squeezed her eyes shut.

"What's wrong?" Silas asked worriedly.

"She's just stretching," Kirsten panted as she rubbed her hand in a circle over her quilt-covered stomach. She stopped when she felt Silas's enormous hand resting lightly on her abdomen. His face was furrowed in deep concentration. His patience was rewarded with a thump, then a roll, followed by a series of kicks. Silas's eyes grew wide, and a smile of wonder and amazement covered his face.

"Does it hurt?" he asked abruptly.

"Only every once in a while," Kirsten answered as she shook her head. She desperately searched for a way to keep him here, in her room, on her bed, his hand resting on her stomach. But Mary's footsteps in the hall jolted Silas upright, and he went wordlessly out the door as Mary entered and fussed over Kirsten.

Admittedly, Kirsten was exhausted from her day—the physical and emotional toll weighed heavily upon her. When Mary offered to bring supper to her, Kirsten gratefully accepted.

It grew dark quickly that night—the sky already darkened by the storm that had settled over them. Kirsten drifted off to sleep, dreaming of Silas's arms around her.

⚬⚭⚬

"Were ya not mindful of yer surroundings, Amy?" Daniel asked seriously over dessert.

"The storm came up awful fast," she quietly defended herself.

"Not as fast as Silas road Titus," Caleb mumbled.

"You shoulda seen how fast he drove the buggy!" Shelby exclaimed loudly. Mary frowned at her reproachfully.

"I didn't know they could go that fast," Amy muttered to her half-eaten piece of apple pie.

Silas hung his head in his hands and wordlessly endured the retelling of the afternoon's terror. As if he hadn't relived every agonizing second in his mind dozens of times already. The moment he and Caleb noticed the wall of clouds in the west. The worried phone call from the Lapps alerting him that Amy had started out for home at four and would most likely be only halfway there. Hearing the constant, low growl of thunder in the distance as he hurriedly threw a bridle on Titus. The panic he felt as he rode hard to intercept the buggy. The sheer determination to drive them safely home. The relief of pulling into the barn with all that precious cargo. All of that had been enough.

But then he'd seen how pale she was. She'd been so terrified that he wasn't sure he'd get her out. Eventually, she'd revived enough to fall into his arms, her body shaking with sobs and his with receding panic. He didn't know how many minutes he had held her. All he remembered was the way she had trembled against him. That had drained him.

It was too early to go to bed, but he was empty. His shoulders ached, and his head pounded. He'd wanted so badly to crawl under their wedding quilt and hold her in her warm bed. Any bed would do by now. Bidding his parents goodnight, he shuffled up to his room, stripped off his shirt and jeans, and fell heavily into his own bed. Sleep was immediate, but restless.

The dreams came like random thoughts. Her fingers brushing his lips as she fed him. Her body leaning against him as she slept in the buggy. The way she'd clutched his shirt and buried her face in his chest. The feel of her body in his arms as he held her tightly against him.

Then her finger trailing on his hand. Her hair slipping through his fingers as he brushed it off her face. Feeling life roll and kick within her. It was too much. The fire had been kindled and encouraged, and now it blazed inside him. Hot—much too hot.

He trembled as the heat slowly consumed his body. He couldn't stop the shivering—feeling cold and hot all at once. The ache in his shoulders spread down his back, and it slowly sank deep into his chest. The good dreams gave way to nonsensical and confusing images. He was deliriously unaware, locked in between consciousness and nightmares, when Caleb rose well before dawn to summon their mother.

Silas groaned in his feverish sleep when her hand wiped the sweat from his brow and rested coldly against his temple. As the drowning current of aches and chills swept over him, he concentrated on forcing a breath, a single breath, in. Then out.

When light finally spilled through the window, he woke to find Amy and Mary pulling him upright and forcing a glass of water down his throat. He was aware then that this was no longer a bad dream from which he would soon wake. His body was at war, and it would be a tiresome battle.

In between forced cups of hot herbal tea and frequent checks from his mother, the trembling left his limbs. But the ache remained. He struggled to take a deep, full breath, bringing on a coughing fit that nearly left him unconscious. He could feel the sweat roll in a river down his neck while his arms stayed tucked in warm layers of blankets.

"Must we take ya to a doctor?" Daniel asked, leaning over him.

Silas only shook his head and closed his eyes. Surely he was strong enough to fight this.

Hours later he woke to the sound of someone moving in his room. He cracked his eyes open just far enough to see his wife setting a tray on his nightstand. Through barely opened eyes, he watched her pull the wooden chair near his bed and lower herself onto it.

"You c-c-can't be here," he rasped. Speaking took more energy than he had to spare.

"Shhh," Kirsten shushed as she ran a cool cloth over his forehead. "Do you want some soup?"

"No," he growled through clenched teeth.

Her fingers trailed through his hair and his eyes snapped open.

"Kirsten...get away from me. You can't catch this." He heaved the words like they were boulders on his chest.

"I'll be okay—"

"Kirsten Miller, when yer husband gives you an order, you best obey," he barked. He had no strength to do any convincing. There was only a desperate need for her to listen and do as he asked. "I don't want ya here!" He nearly spat the words in an effort to punctuate his point.

She stared at him with wide eyes and then slowly rose and walked out of the room.

Moments later he heard a pair of hurried footsteps clomp across the porch.

"Kirsten? Kirsten!" Mary called loudly from the porch. Silas heard no reply. Only the normal sounds of the farmyard drifted through his open window.

"Yer brother is going to sleep downstairs on the couch tonight," Mary said in lieu of greeting when she checked on him later that evening. Silas lifted to his elbow and drank the glass of water she handed him.

"How was the soup?" she asked shortly.

Without looking at her he handed her the empty glass and fell against his pillow.

"Fine," he rasped.

"Yer wife spent the entire morning on it," Mary said through pursed lips.

She was getting at something, but he didn't know what. Why must his mother speak so cryptically? Silas didn't have the energy to figure out what any of her words or her tone meant. He fell asleep and woke to see Daniel peering down at him again. The fever was still running high, but Silas still refused to see a doctor. Amy brought him breakfast and lunch, explaining that Mary had gone to the market. Where Kirsten had gone, he didn't know. Perhaps to the market or to Deborah's. The house was extremely quiet.

By the time supper was delivered, he was beginning to feel a little bit better. Mary set the bowl of chicken noodle soup on his nightstand with a plate of bread and yet another cup of herbal tea. She paused awkwardly and sat.

"Silas, I won't tell ya how to be a husband. That's not my place," she began humbly. "But you should know that Kirsten was hurt by what ya said to her yesterday when ya sent her away. She's been right worried about ya and..." Mary stopped and sighed. "Yer father has often spoken truth to me—but it was always spoken in love. Even if you were right, you could still be wrong."

Satisfied she'd said her piece, Mary left the room. Silas stared out his window at the sun's last rays striking against the side of the barn.

Kirsten was hurt by what ya said to her.

The words seemed to echo off the walls of his room, and his stomach rolled uneasily with guilt and regret. The request that she leave had been right, but the delivery had been all wrong. Even though he hadn't meant to hurt her, there was no excuse for his harsh tone. Kirsten, of all people, had been wounded enough by the world. The last thing she needed was his callous words heaped on top of that pain.

When Caleb came in to get ready for bed, Silas asked him to send Kirsten in if she was still up.

He was sitting up against his pillow and reading in the low light of his lamp when her soft knock sounded on the door.

"Come in," he said, setting his Bible down on his nightstand.

She stood in the doorway but came no further.

"Are you feeling better?" she asked, looking down at her hands so that her eyelashes fell on her cheeks.

"A little," he answered. She wouldn't look at him. "Do ya want to sit down?" he asked, waving at the chair.

She hesitated. "Is that okay?"

He nodded, and she sat stiffly with her hands folded in her lap.

"I'm sorry I spoke harshly to you," he said after a pause. "I don't want ya to get sick."

She relaxed a bit and eventually nodded.

"Yer soup was *gut*," he said with a tentative grin.

Her mouth twitched. "Thank you."

"Are ya angry with me?"

She shook her head but said nothing.

"How are the chickens?" he asked, closing his eyes and leaning his head back against a dull throb of a headache.

He opened his eyes just in time to see a wry smile twist her mouth.

"Well…they weren't in the soup."

Even though it hurt, Silas laughed.

— Chapter Twenty-Five —

Though he was much better and the fever was gone, Silas spent a third day in bed, dozing and resting. He was asleep when Kirsten brought him his lunch.

She watched him. Even in his sleep, she could plainly see the well-defined muscles in his bare arms and chest. He had three days of dark blond stubble on his face. It would take him precious little time to grow a full Amish beard. Initially, she had thought it would detract from his looks, but now she could see he'd be just as handsome with one as he was without.

It was impossible not to see how attractive he was by Amish or English standards. She doubted anyone would be able to truthfully say Silas wasn't handsome. At his age, in the outside world, he'd most likely be in his last years of college. Put this man in a hoodie and jeans and the girls would be all over him. But they'd be missing out. They'd never get to see his long fingers gripping the reins or the way he could lift and pull wagons and machinery across the yard without a horse's assistance. How was it possible that he'd not settled down and married a nice Amish girl? It was inconceivable to her that none of the eligible ladies had noticed him. He didn't have to try. He was just that beautiful.

She stroked a curl back from his forehead and let her fingers sift slowly through his hair. His eyes opened then, revealing the sky blue framed by his dark lashes. Her hand trailed softly down his cheek and jaw, feeling the scrub of his whiskers, rough on the backs of her fingers.

He was watching her, his gaze piercing and intense. But she wouldn't rush this. Three days of not sitting by him for every meal, not watching him stride across the yard, and not hearing his beautiful, low voice was enough to make her stir-crazy. Now that she was here with him, so near to him, she wanted it to last as long as possible.

"How are you feeling?" she whispered, her fingers making another circuit along his jaw.

"*Gut*," he swallowed.

"I brought you some lunch," she said, nearly choking on the tenderness she felt for him.

His eyes flicked to the plate and back to her, still piercing and intense.

"Can I get you anything?"

He paused and shook his head.

"I'll come back to check on you in a little bit," she promised. It was bold. Borderline flirtatious. But he was her husband, and at their wedding one of the preachers said something about how Silas's body belonged to her and vice versa. She leaned over him and softly kissed his forehead, resting her hand on his cheek one more time.

It was entirely possible he could hear her heart pounding in her chest as she bent over him.

The whole family had chipped in to pick up the slack where Silas was concerned. Even Kirsten had tried to help, but most of the time she'd felt more in the way than helpful. She'd made some of the meals so that Amy could focus on helping Caleb in the orchard. And in her spare time, she'd cleaned the bathroom, dusted the living room, and swept out the kitchen. It reminded her a little of life in the trailer, except it was different in every possible way. Namely, she had a husband upstairs who needed her to at least take care of herself. As much as possible, she wanted to make sure she could take care of him as well.

Kirsten tried to shower quickly before supper, but when she stepped downstairs, Mary was already delivering Silas's supper. Her mother-in-law couldn't have known how much Kirsten was looking forward to seeing him again. And nothing was really stopping Kirsten from visiting him, except that now with the house full again she felt self-conscious about spending time in his room. Disappointment was heavy, and she sank low in her chair.

"You aren't takin' ill yerself are ya, Kirsten?" Daniel asked over dessert.

"No," she said sitting up straighter. "No, I feel fine."

"I wish Silas could play with us," Anna Mae said sadly.

"I'll play with you," Kirsten said with a smile.

Shelby and Anna grinned delightedly, and after supper Kirsten went out to play a challenging game of hide-and-seek. Caleb and Amy played too, making the game all the more fun. And playfully competitive. She loved hearing the laughter and screams of surprise echo off the barn.

At eight o'clock, Mary called the children in and Kirsten went with them, marching straight upstairs before hurrying back outside. She'd seen him sitting in the front porch swing. He was still there when she rounded the corner. His gaze swung to her, and a light grin crossed his features.

"Will you do something for me?" she asked.

He nodded. She moved to him and handed him his leather-bound Bible. He took it, his eyes searching her face.

"Read to me?"

He smiled then. "What would ya like to hear?"

"Your favorite parts," she answered, sitting next to him, close to him, on the swing.

He flipped expertly, almost as if the book would naturally fall open to that very page.

"Psalm 142.

"*I cry aloud to the Lord; I lift up my voice to the Lord for mercy. I pour out before him my complaint; before him I tell my trouble.*"

Silas paused, breathing deep.

"*When my spirit grows faint within me, it is you who watch over my way.*

"*In the path where I walk people have hidden a snare for me. Look and see, there is no one at my right hand; no one is concerned for me. I have no refuge; no one cares for my life.*"

"I cry to you, Lord; I say, 'You are my refuge, my
portion in the land of the living.' Listen to my cry for
I am in desperate need; rescue me from those who
pursue me, for they are too strong for me. Set me free
from my prison, that I may praise your name.
"Then the righteous will gather about me
because of your goodness to me."

Kirsten was silent for many long minutes. She'd just wanted to hear his voice, his lilting accent thrumming like a pulse in her soul. He could have said anything, read a phone book or a seed catalog, and she would have been satisfied. But he had chosen this passage. It was as if they were the words she'd felt deep inside and he'd just spoken them into the night.

"It's like...poetry," she choked.

"It is."

They sat, Silas gently pushing the swing into motion with his long legs. The cicadas buzzed their night-song into the dark.

"Will you read it again?" she whispered in the fading light.

He did and she closed her eyes, listening to him speak her heart. Darkness deepened and Silas closed the Bible in his lap. As he had read, she had leaned into him so that her head rested easily on his shoulder.

"We should do this every night," she whispered.

"I'd like that," he said, his breath warm on her forehead.

The night air blew cool around them, and a cricket mysteriously chirped close by. Kirsten's hand slid into Silas's and they kept swaying, even after the lamps downstairs were extinguished. She wished they could stay like this all night, basking in the perfect peace of the moment and the simple joy of being together, but her body betrayed her with a yawn that was immediately followed by a shiver.

"Time for bed," Silas murmured against her bonnet. She nodded and started to stand when he held on to her hand, locking her in place.

"Good night, Kirsten." His voice was rough and she wished she could see his eyes in the moonlight. She felt his warm lips against her cheek. The scratch of his whiskers gave her goose bumps.

— CHAPTER TWENTY-SIX —

"You know, you don't always have to wear shoes," Amy said with a grimace as she and Kirsten walked out to the garden just after breakfast. Kirsten looked down at her simple, black shoes, thinking of how good it would feel to take off her socks and get some air on her legs and feet.

"They'll get so dirty in the garden," Amy said with a small smile. "And feet wash up easier than shoes."

Kirsten nodded eagerly and set to work peeling off her shoes and socks while Amy took her place amongst the rows of green beans. Kirsten wiggled her toes in the air and stifled a giggle at how good it felt. She stepped into a row just behind Amy and felt the warm, soft earth sink beneath her. How had she never tried this before? She bent over and began plucking the long green beans from their vines, tossing each one into the bucket beside her. She still preferred being in the garden with Silas, but it was easy to see now in his absence how distracting he could be. She moved quickly and easily, filling the bucket and carrying it to the end of the row where she and Amy dumped their load into the larger five-gallon buckets.

"Kirsten!" Amy suddenly cried out and dropped to her knees in front of her. "What happened to your..."

Kirsten stared down, trying to peer around the slight bulge of her stomach to whatever it was that Amy was exclaiming over. She could see nothing to cause any alarm—just a pair of very dirty feet that would need a good scrubbing after her time in the garden.

"What?" Kirsten asked curiously.

"Your toes…are…" Amy stopped, still staring inquisitively at Kirsten's feet.

"Oh! It's just fingernail polish," Kirsten said, smiling down at the brilliant red peeking through the caked dirt. "I'm not bleeding or anything," she laughed, hoping to ease Amy's fear.

"Oh. You painted them," Amy said sheepishly.

"Yeah…about a month ago," Kirsten nodded. "Before the wedding."

"The paint lasts that long?" Amy questioned doubtfully.

Kirsten nodded, her eyes meeting Amy's as she stood to face her. She could see in her sister-in-law's face a mixture of jealousy and curiosity. And something else.

Disapproval. It was there, though Amy tried to hide it and pretend she didn't care. But it was clear that she did.

Kirsten followed her back into the garden, making sure to sink her toes deep in the soil where they wouldn't call attention to themselves or cause any more trouble. She'd gladly given up her makeup when she'd moved into the Millers' house. And honestly, with the gorgeous summer sun that she enjoyed each day, she never felt she needed it. There was no pretending here. Not with Silas or any of the Millers. But she had forgotten about her toes.

As she scrubbed the dirt off them with a hose by the house, an idea sparked in her head. It was possible, entirely possible, that she wouldn't have to wait to go to her Mom's for some fingernail polish remover. She quickly slipped her feet back into her shoes and hurried across the yard to the woodshop.

Silas was dry fitting a chair when she entered, pausing long enough to cast a smile across his workbench before finishing his task.

"Come to check on me?" he teased as he tested the fitting, inspecting it closely.

"Hmm…no. I came to ask for your help," she said, twisting her mouth to the side.

"What do ya need?" he asked as he clapped the dust off his hands.

"It's a bit of an odd request." Kirsten could feel her face blushing for no good reason.

"Oh." He was watching her now.

Kirsten rounded the workbench and pried her shoe off, dangling her foot above the dusty floor of the workshop.

"Do you have anything that could get this stuff off?" she asked, jiggling her foot slightly.

Silas bent down and looked closely at her toes. He stood and pulled a stool over to the bank of open windows.

"Sit over there," he said over his shoulder as he surveyed the containers lined up along one of the shelves on the wall. Kirsten sat and watched as he scanned the label on one of the cans. As with all men his age, he was most handsome when he wasn't trying to be. And Silas, her Silas, was never trying to be.

He grabbed a rag out of a box and knelt on the floor in front of her. She hadn't meant for him to do any more than hand her the materials she would need to do the job herself.

"Oh, I can do it," Kirsten said, suddenly breathless.

Silas shook his head. "The fumes aren't so good for ya. It's best if I do it."

Kirsten had no time for a response, as he was already pouring a small amount of the clear liquid on a clean rag. He screwed the lid back on tightly and turned to her. With one hand, he pulled her bare foot onto his thigh. His fingers gently curled around her foot, his one hand easily cradling the entire thing. The rag barely touched her foot, and Kirsten jerked it out of his grasp with a gasp.

Shyly, she looked up from her foot to see his eyes on her face.

"Sorry," she said with a grin. "My feet are horribly ticklish."

Silas looked to be fighting a smile as he nodded and reached for her foot again, this time holding it more firmly. Quickly, but gently, he worked at the remnants of the red paint, being careful to remove it all without rubbing the paint thinner on her skin. He finished with one foot, and before she knew what was happening, he had grabbed her shoe and slipped it on her. He tied the laces carefully and reached down for the next foot, working quickly to free it from her shoe. His touch was firm and strong, but his movements were not hurried. By the way he was working, Kirsten would have sworn this was either the only thing he had to do today, or at least the most important. His hands on her feet were warm, and she could feel the callouses on his palms that she normally only felt with her hands.

When he was satisfied, he scooped up her shoe and tugged it down over her foot.

"Now I won't scare Amy anymore," Kirsten said, smiling. "She thought my toes were bleeding."

Silas smiled as he put the rag and can of thinner on the workbench.

"I wondered what she would say," he laughed.

"Wait...you mean...you knew my nails were painted?"

"Kirsten Miller," he paused as he bent low over her. "Do you remember the day we met?" His eyes were soft, warm, and impossibly close.

Of course. He had saved her from tumbling down the staircase at the market, and she had blamed her clumsiness on her flip-flops. He'd known all along.

"You knew, but it didn't bother you?" Her eyes squinted up at him in confusion.

"I knew," he said with a shrug. "I figured it would either wear off or you'd ask for help, if you wanted it, whenever you were ready."

"Oh." Kirsten let him help her up. She turned to leave, but then she spun back to him and grabbed his hands.

"Thank you," she breathed and stood on tiptoe to kiss his cheekbone.

"*Yer wilkum*," he swallowed, looking instantly bashful.

Kirsten left him in the workshop and walked back to the house, pausing long enough to kick her shoes off in the grass and feel the blades tickle her feet. She looked down at her pale pink toenails and smiled. She wouldn't miss the paint either, she decided. It was only something she had done because all the other girls her age did it. Every time another worldly thing was removed from her life, she felt more and more free. And it was clear that Silas was not the one doing the removing—at least, not unless she asked. The things she gave up were by her choice, not his demand. And that made all the difference in the world.

⟡

"Will ya be helping at the Lapps' tomorrow?" Michael asked from across the picnic blanket after Sunday meeting.

"*Jah*, I can help for a while," Silas answered, nodding at his older brother.

"What's happening tomorrow?" Kirsten asked him, her expression confused.

"The day before the wedding is when we all help with setup," Silas explained to her.

"We're not leaving too early are we?" Caleb asked, wincing at Silas, who only stared at him.

Amy snorted. "You better just stay home and behave yerself. Get some sleep."

"Like you should talk! I'll beat ya home from Singing. Yer too busy lip-kissing to get home at a decent hour," Caleb laughed.

"Caleb," Silas warned. Caleb checked himself and sobered immediately.

Amy rolled her eyes. "The only one I wanna be lip-kissin' is my husband. Anything else would just be stupid." All of them froze as the impact of what she said sank in.

Amy's eyes flashed up to Kirsten in alarm. "I'm sorry," she gasped, glancing at Silas's stern expression.

"Don't be," Kirsten shook her head. "It's a good idea. The only one I wanna be lip-kissing is my husband." She grinned shyly, despite the blush that was painfully burning on her face.

Amy gave her a huge smile, and Michael tried to hide his laughter in a fit of coughing. Silas looked both amused and embarrassed. For the first time in his life, Caleb appeared to be at a complete loss for words.

◦⊚Ɛ Ǝ⊚◦

Kirsten woke from her afternoon nap to find the house eerily quiet. After smoothing her hair and putting on her cap, she went downstairs to find the house deserted. All except for the tall, handsome man sitting at the table reading a newspaper.

"Dad and Mom went visiting with Caleb, Shelby, and Anna. And Amy went to Singing," he said, spying her curious expression.

"What is this Singing?"

Silas sighed. "It's the Amish teenagers' social time."

"Did you ever go?" she asked, sitting next to him.

He nodded but didn't volunteer any more information. Kirsten wondered if she should ask him more, but he folded his paper shut and turned his attention completely to her.

"We're on our own for supper."

Kirsten twisted her mouth up as she thought about that. Cooking a few meals last week had gone well. But fixing a meal for anyone as hard-working as Silas was still a little daunting.

"How about a ham and cheese omelet?"

"Sounds *gut*."

Kirsten soon slid the finished omelets onto two plates, and Silas took her hand and prayed the Lord's Prayer.

"I'd like to learn that," she told him when he finished.

"I can teach ya," he offered.

"If you'll write it down, I'll work on memorizing it."

"I will."

Daniel and Mary came back with the girls just as they were washing the last dishes. Mary helped Kirsten dish up apple crisp and ice cream, a late-evening snack. Afterwards, Kirsten went upstairs to get ready for bed and was hanging up her good dress when a soft knock sounded on her door.

"Come in."

"Would ya like some more poetry?" Silas asked, hardly daring to look at her. His Bible was in his hand.

"Yes, I would." She beamed at him.

He sat down on her bed, tilting the book to catch the glow of the gas lamp on her nightstand. Kirsten scrambled up, sitting close to him, leaning her head against his shoulder.

"Psalm 103," he said, finding his place.

> *"Praise the Lord, my soul; all my inmost being,*
> *praise his holy name. Praise the Lord, my soul, and*
> *forget not all his benefits—who forgives all your sins*
> *and heals all your diseases, who redeems your life*
> *from the pit and crowns you with love and compas-*

sion, who satisfies your desires with gut things so
that your youth is renewed like the eagle's.

"The Lord works righteousness and justice for all
the oppressed.

"He made known his ways to Moses, his deeds
to the people of Israel: The Lord is compassionate
and gracious, slow to anger, abounding in love. He
will not always accuse, nor will he harbor his anger
forever; he does not treat us as our sins deserve or
repay us according to our iniquities.

"For as high as the heavens are above the earth,
so great is his love for those who fear him; as far as
the east is from the west, so far has he removed our
transgressions from us."

Silas paused.

"As a father has compassion on his children, so
the Lord has compassion on those who fear him; for
he knows how we are formed, he remembers that we
are dust.

"The life of mortals is like grass, they flourish
like a flower of the field; the wind blows over it and
it is gone, and its place remembers it no more.

"But from everlasting to everlasting the Lord's
love is with those who fear him, and his righteousness with their children's children—with those
who keep his covenant and remember to obey his
precepts.

"The Lord has established his throne in heaven,
and his kingdom rules over all. Praise the Lord, you
his angels, you mighty ones who do his bidding, who
obey his word. Praise the Lord, all his heavenly hosts,
you his servants who do his will. Praise the Lord, all
his works everywhere in his dominion.

"Praise the Lord, my soul."

"Thank you," Kirsten whispered when Silas softly closed the book.

"Yer welcome."

"What was that part about heaven?"

He made no move to open the Bible in his lap as he recited. "As high as the heavens are above the earth, so great is his love for those who fear him; as far as the east is from the west, so far has he removed our transgressions from us."

Kirsten mulled the words over in her mind, wondering at the poetic phrases and the vivid imagery.

"This is for you," Silas said, handing her a small, folded piece of paper.

"What is it?" Kirsten asked.

"Yer homework." He gave her a lopsided smile.

"The Lord's Prayer," she read. His handwriting was narrow and neat. Not at all fancy or particular, but very readable. There was not a mistake on the page.

"Good night, Kirsten." Silas kissed her forehead this time and stood tall, making her room suddenly seem very small.

His absence made it feel very empty.

— CHAPTER TWENTY-SEVEN —

"I'm wearing my wedding dress to a wedding," Kirsten observed with a chuckle.

"What are English wedding dresses like?" Amy asked from the back bench.

"White, puffy, elaborate, with long trains that drag on the ground. And expensive," Kirsten answered her.

"How much do they cost?" Amy questioned.

"It varies. I'd say most are about $1,000; some are less, some are more," Kirsten said with a shrug.

Amy gasped and Silas stared at her.

"What do they do with them then?" Amy persisted.

"Wear them once, put them in a box, and stick them in storage."

"They never wear them again?" Amy asked with a furrowed brow.

"Oh, no," Kirsten laughed. "English wedding dresses are highly impractical!"

The buggy moved down the road to the Lapps' house. Every Sunday, and for an occasional special outing like today, she got to wear her wedding dress and remember the day she became Kirsten Miller, wife of Silas Miller. Of course, seeing him in his wedding suit was an added bonus.

Amy chattered about the work frolic she'd gone to at the Lapps' on Thursday and how delighted Rebecca had been when presented with her wedding quilt.

"You didn't want to go the frolic?" Silas asked Kirsten.

"You were sick," she reminded him.

He hadn't truthfully expected tenderness and devotion so early in their relationship. But Kirsten had spent three long days making soup and sitting in the house, just in case he would need her. He wouldn't have faulted her if she had gone to the frolic. Still, she had chosen to stay near him, and it was impossible not to feel warmed and humbled by her kindness.

The yard was bustling with activity. Caleb and several of his friends were hostlers, assigned the important task of caring for the horses throughout the day. Amy climbed out and walked quickly down the lane to find Emily.

Kirsten waited beside the buggy while Silas unhitched Titus and handed him over to Caleb. She watched him intently as he worked.

"What's the matter?" he asked when he spotted the strange look on her face.

"When my cousin graduated from college, he used tape to make a big, white 'X' on his cap so we'd know which one of the hundreds of black caps was him," she paused, offering him her hand. He took it, his eyes showing his confusion. "I'm thinking I should do the same to your hat."

Silas laughed. "What if I take off my hat? You'd never find me," he teased.

"I'd have to resort to just searching for the handsomest man here," she said and smiled. Kirsten stopped and turned to him. "You look downright hot in that black suit, by the way."

"It is warm," he said, grimacing.

Kirsten giggled. "No. I was using an English term. 'Hot' means very, very good looking."

Silas considered that and then smiled at her and shook his head.

⁕

"*Gut* morning, Silas!" Michael called loudly as they neared the house. Kirsten felt his hand tighten on hers as they joined his brothers and their wives and children. She laced her fingers through his long ones as he talked with David and Michael and she talked with Deborah and Sarah.

"Time to go give our wishes to the bride and groom," Deborah said, smiling at her husband. Kirsten watched as David and Sarah walked over to a line of young ladies, Rebecca Lapp at the end, and a line of young men, where Eli Graber waited in his new wedding suit.

People were drifting through the lines, shaking hands, smiling, and laughing. Silas tugged her hand and made his way behind David.

"What are we doing?" she asked nervously.

"Givin' our wishes to the bride and groom," he answered, as if that explained everything.

"What do I say?" Her voice was already trembling.

"Something nice."

She had wanted more direction from him, but people had fallen in line behind them, and there was no way her questions would go unheard by others.

Think about chickens. Think about chickens. Kirsten chanted to herself, steeling against the tide of fear.

Silas began shaking hands with attendants, greeting each one by name for her benefit, she guessed.

"Hullo, Leah," he nodded to a girl roughly Kirsten's height. She had dark hair and dark brown eyes and perfect skin. She was beautiful. Really beautiful.

Leah nodded shyly back at Silas.

"Have ya met Kirsten?" his eyes warmly focused on Kirsten.

"We met at the quilt frolic," Leah said, more to Kirsten than Silas.

Kirsten nodded and smiled. "I remember. It's good to see you again."

Leah gave her a small smile and turned quickly to the people behind her. Kirsten wondered at her stiffness. She hadn't seemed uncomfortable until Silas had spoken to her. Kirsten turned again to glance at her and caught Leah looking longingly at Silas's turned back. Leah didn't know she was being watched, and her expression explained more than words could say.

Silas shook hands with Rebecca and offered his congratulations, which Kirsten echoed quietly. Then they moved through the line of young men, each of them smiling broadly at Silas and firmly shaking his hand.

"Yer comin' to play softball on Thursday, Silas?"

"*Jah*. I'll be there, Micah," Silas said and smiled at his friend.

"*Gut!*"

Eli appeared to be almost ready to explode with happiness. He was jubilant, the smile on his face never fading. He stole countless glances at Rebecca, who would smile back serenely.

Later, as the ceremony progressed, Kirsten could sense the joy permeating the people gathered around her. Rebecca was relaxed and peaceful, and Eli's eyes were bright as the preaching went on around them. The bride and groom held one another's hands tightly as they loudly and clearly said their vows. The smiles on the faces of the wedding guests were sincere and joyful.

Kirsten could feel Silas's eyes on her and found him looking intently at her as they heard their vows recited by the couple at the front. She hadn't forgotten a single word he'd said to her, and it was obvious by the look on his face that he still meant every one of them.

There was not a single person left unsmiling as the couple was introduced as husband and wife. She had never really realized that weddings were so life-altering before she'd gotten married. It had always seemed like just a nice ceremony. But getting married brought so many changes. Suddenly, this other person was in your life. And if you were Amish, marriage was for life. There were no divorces or separations. Choosing whom to marry was an extraordinarily important decision to the People because it was not something you could opt out of later. That Silas had known all this and still chosen her was almost beyond belief. Kirsten wondered at the new bride and groom. Of course, Rebecca would not need an entire year of supervised training like Kirsten. It was more than a little humiliating to think of all the many things Kirsten did not yet know how to do.

Deborah and Sarah rushed off to help with the meal as soon as the ceremony concluded. Kirsten drifted to Mary's side and ambled around with her, smiling at the ladies Mary talked to. But many of them were older, and Kirsten found she had little to add to the conversations.

The meal was inside on the main floor, where the tables and benches had been lined up. The men ate first, followed by the women and children. Kirsten swallowed the food almost without tasting it. A few young women her age sat with her and engaged her in polite conversation. But Kirsten got the feeling that they were nervous to ask her about anything. And she was still fearful of saying something non-Amish.

After the meal, people swirled around the yard. Kirsten briefly looked, but she could not spot Silas. Of course not. She sighed in frustration just as Deborah looped her arm through Kirsten's and wordlessly led her to a quilt laid out beneath a tree. Johnny quickly fell asleep, and Deborah turned her attention to Kirsten.

"Yer quiet today, Kirsten." It was a true statement, but Kirsten shrugged it off. Her eyes scanned the crowded yard, still not able to find him.

"Deborah, do you ever have trouble finding Michael in all these black coats and hats? They all look exactly the same."

Deborah laughed quietly. "Michael's right over there." She pointed to a group of men under a massive oak tree. "And Silas is right over there."

She was right. Kirsten recognized his frame standing amongst a cluster of young men. He was smiling and laughing, having shed his coat and hat.

"Thank you," Kirsten said sheepishly.

Deborah nodded and smiled wider. "You might have lost sight of him, but he never lost sight of you. Silas has been watching you all day."

"Oh." It was nice to know he'd not forgotten about her.

"There are more people here than there were at our wedding," Kirsten observed.

Deborah nodded uneasily. "This is a big wedding. Eli has a big family— lots of relations from Ohio are here."

Rebecca and Eli were wandering through the yard, holding hands and positively beaming at one another. They stopped to talk with friends and family, and their laughter sounded lightly through the crowd. As far as Kirsten could tell, they'd not been apart since they'd been pronounced husband and wife.

Her wedding had been downright somber compared with today's festive atmosphere. She'd been horribly awkward and nervous as a bride— not joyful and assured like Rebecca. She hadn't socialized, hadn't laughed, and hadn't exuded the serenity that oozed out of Rebecca. If only she had clung to her husband's hand, smiled more, and been the brilliant bride Silas deserved.

Kirsten offered to watch over Johnny when Michael and Deborah had to go help with supper. Shelby and Anna found her on the quilt, and they waited together for their turn at a table. Kirsten still had very little appetite and excused herself to go out with the girls when they finished. Once outside, Shelby and Anna sprinted off to find the other children, and Kirsten did a thorough scan for Silas…who was nowhere to be found.

.·ᴼᴾᴳᴼ·.

When the women began filtering out of the house, Silas watched for her. But she didn't come out with Mary, or Amy, or Deborah. Not even with Sarah. He knew where she was supposed to be, but she wasn't there.

For several minutes, he circled the yard, looking for her. After his second round, he felt a twinge of panic. How had she disappeared?

"So this is how she felt," he mumbled to himself. He stood, hands on his hips, surveying the circles of women that dotted the lawn. She was not there. Where else she could be, he simply couldn't fathom. He should have found her by now.

He held his body stiffly, belying the worry he felt inside. His chest tightened, and his eyes frantically darted around the yard. There was no way she would have started for home by herself. Surely not. She'd have to go on foot, and it was just too far to walk.

A walk. Maybe she'd gone for a walk.

He made his way quickly down the lane, and it was then that he saw the lone figure standing at the high plank fence that surrounded the pasture where the horses were grazing. Momentary relief flooded him. But as he considered her posture, he could tell something was wrong.

He quietly came up behind her, and she didn't move from her position leaning on the fence and gazing at the horses. Her chin rested on her forearms.

"I couldn't find you, so I came to find Titus," Kirsten said, somehow knowing he was there.

Silas stepped close behind her, placing a hand on the fence rail on either side of her. He was so relieved to find her that he wanted to hold her to him. Instead, he stood close, his chest nearly touching her back.

"And which one is Titus?" he quizzed in a low voice. The pasture was full of horses of every breed, size, and color.

Much to his amazement, she pointed directly at Titus.

"You can find my horse in a full paddock, but ya can't find me in a crowd," he sighed playfully.

She didn't respond.

With a low, distinct, practiced whistle, Silas called Titus to them. Kirsten's hand gently stroked the horse's neck until he sauntered slightly away. She was quiet for a long while, seemingly absorbed in watching the horses graze.

"It's supposed to be like this, isn't it?" she whispered finally.

"What do ya mean?" he asked when she didn't continue.

"Weddings. Weddings are supposed to be like this," she choked.

"Ours wasn't?"

He saw her shoulders droop. Her breath caught and she silently wiped her eyes with the back of her hand.

"You should've had all this…joy and celebration. Instead, you got stuck with a mistake you didn't make," she said thickly.

He was quiet for a long moment. He couldn't deny their wedding had been different. It was quieter and more subdued. There were many who came, but there were also some who didn't. After consulting with Daniel and Mary, they'd decided to keep things simple for Kirsten, hoping to avoid overwhelming her on the big day. And though she had handled it all remarkably well, at the end of the day, he had been glad that they had kept it as simple as they had.

Though not one of his friends or neighbors would have ever intentionally offended Kirsten, he could tell that they were still unsure how to treat her. So few outsiders ever became Amish. Kirsten's introduction into the Amish society was bound to be the most awkward part of her transition.

Still, it had been a happy day for him. It stung that she didn't remember it that way.

"I didn't get stuck," he said finally. Kirsten still stared silently into the pasture.

"Do ya feel yer baby is a mistake?" he asked by her ear.

She froze into absolute stillness. "I was so lonely and desperate. And Logan was...Logan. I should've realized he was only after one thing. But I was stupid and gave it all away in the backseat of his car. Such a stupid mistake." The pain dripped off every word she choked out.

Her words sank into Silas like knives. He'd never asked how it had happened, and she'd never told. Silas hadn't even known his name. But now the story burned in his mind. Images he didn't want flashed through his thoughts, and he futilely tried to push them away.

It was easy to hear the regret in her voice. And not a part of him doubted that if she could, she would go back and undo the events of that night. But no one gets to go back to fix mistakes. And despite the ache he felt as he reeled from the story, he could see a glimpse of goodness. There was redemption and hope flickering even now—a heartbeat that could only be brought about by divine purpose.

"Did ya tell him to stop?" Silas asked, sounding and feeling for all the world as though he had gravel lodged in his throat. He wasn't sure he wanted to hear her answer. And yet, he needed to know.

Kirsten swallowed loudly. "No. I don't understand why I didn't. I should have." She sniffed and wiped at her eyes. "Stupid mistake," she repeated.

"Just because ya made a mistake doesn't mean God did," he breathed quietly.

"Why, Silas?" she asked, straightening up but not turning to him. "Why subject yourself to the repercussions of my actions? I mean, surely there was someone else who wanted you, wanted to be your wife. Someone without so much baggage."

Silas said nothing. There may have been others. He'd seen girls look at him hopefully, smile at him shyly. But his feelings for them had never gone beyond friendship. He simply couldn't see them as anything other than sisters, even though they were clearly hoping for more. Much more. It had been the reason he'd stopped going to Singings. Enduring the longing in their faces had simply gotten old and...exhausting.

"No one?" his wife pressed.

"No." It was true.

"Not even Leah?"

Of course, Leah had made her interest the most evident. How Kirsten could possibly know that, he didn't know.

"No one ever made me feeling anything. And you made me feel... everything." He'd said as much to his parents that night he'd told them of his desire to marry Kirsten. For weeks, the pull had been a cruel torture. But when he'd finally given in and let himself love her, he'd instantly felt that he'd done the right thing. She was the one he was meant to love.

He shifted closer and she leaned back into him, her head falling back against his chest. She shuddered a sigh, and the muscles in her back relaxed.

"I could never see you or this baby as a burden, Kirsten. I know we started out differently, but that doesn't change how right it feels to be married to ya." He paused and listened as her breathing settled, the little, shuddered breaths slowing and softening. "Are ya unhappy?" he asked softly.

"No!" came her startled reply.

"Neither am I." His lips skimmed her temple.

"I'm happier than I've ever been." He didn't need to see her face to know the shy smile she was wearing.

"Me too."

— CHAPTER TWENTY-EIGHT —

"Silas! C'mon! We're gonna be late!" Caleb cried from the side porch.

Kirsten watched out the kitchen window as her husband ran across the yard from the stable. In one effortless leap, he cleared the steps, burst inside, and kicked off his boots. He sprinted past her and up the stairs in one-two-three-four bounds. Less than two minutes later, he and Caleb clamored into the kitchen, ball gloves in hand.

"Don't forget to pick up yer father at the market," Mary reminded them.

"Don't be late," Silas said as he bent over Kirsten and kissed her cheek.

Mary's eyes twinkled, and Kirsten felt her face flame. The women set about packing two large picnic baskets, which were loaded into the buggy with a stack of quilts. Mary got in and handed Kirsten the reins.

"I'm to let ya drive," she stated.

Kirsten sighed and shook her head. Silas was persistent. That much was obvious.

They rolled into the softball diamond at the schoolhouse. Kirsten had never been here before and was fascinated by the charm of the simple, one-room structure. Try as she might, she could not imagine Silas as a little boy, sitting in one of the desks. The yard around the school was cluttered with buggies. Mary pointed to a spot and Kirsten pulled in, seeing that Titus was calmly hitched next to them at the rail.

Amy ran to sit by Emily on a quilt along the chain-link fence. Other spectators were arriving and choosing spots to spread their quilts or set up their lawn chairs.

"It's marrieds versus unmarrieds," Mary told Kirsten as they approached the diamond. "You'll want to sit on yer husband's side." Kirsten helped Mary spread the quilt in an empty space several feet behind the marrieds' dugout.

The game was about to begin, and Kirsten quickly spotted Silas and waved. He grinned and she blushed all over again, remembering his kiss on her cheek. The players finished warming up, and soon he strode into the dugout with all the other bearded men, many of them a decade or two older.

"He looks so young," Kirsten whispered without thinking.

Mary laughed. "I used to say the same thing about my Daniel!"

The opposing dugout near Amy and Emily's quilt was intimidating to say the least. Kirsten recognized several of them as the groom's attendants from the wedding yesterday.

"*Ach*, Silas! Why'd ya have to go and get married?!" one of the single men called loudly as Silas took his seat on the bench. There was laughter on all sides, and Silas just shook his head. Kirsten was sure he was smiling, even though his back was turned to her.

The unmarrieds were up to bat first, and Silas took his place at third base. A hefty single man stepped up to the plate with a bat in his hands.

"Micah Zook," Mary told her. He was the one who had asked Silas about the game in the receiving line at the wedding. He was not lean like Silas, but Kirsten doubted there was an ounce of fat on him. He looked dangerous as he whipped the bat through the air. He took a few practice swings as Daniel stepped onto the pitcher's plate and tossed the ball lightly.

"Dad pitches?" Kirsten asked in surprise.

"*Jah*. Ever since he was about Caleb's age.

Daniel lobbed the ball high into the air, and Micah's bat whipped around fast. The ball pinged loudly off his bat and sailed over the outfield fence into the hayfield beyond the schoolyard. Everyone laughed and cheered as Micah slowly rounded the bases. Silas shoved him playfully as he tagged third. Kirsten noticed that both teams were clapping and smiling. There was a friendly competitiveness between them—perfectly balanced to make it challenging and fun.

"Do the marrieds ever win?" Kirsten asked Mary as Micah stomped on home plate.

"Kirsten Miller! Have a little faith in yer husband and his team!" Mary scolded.

Kirsten shook her head and smiled, doubting very much that a little faith from her would make any difference.

Two more batters struck out before Caleb stepped up to bat. He looked small, though he was tall enough. In a few years' time, he'd surely be as tall as Silas. He was wiry and looked more like a little brother to one of the unmarrieds than a member of the team. Of course, until a few weeks ago, he *had* been a little brother to one of the unmarrieds. Kirsten bit her lip nervously. Hopefully Caleb would at least make contact and not strike out in front of all these people.

Caleb dug his foot into the dirt and brought the bat back high behind him. Daniel lobbed the ball high and Caleb waited. Finally swinging the bat through the air, he made good contact with the pitch, and it zipped past Daniel's knees. The shortstop snapped it up and whipped it through the air to first base. Caleb sprinted and beat the throw, arriving safely and winning applause from the players. Kirsten was surprised at his quickness and clapped enthusiastically for her brother-in-law.

"Caleb is fast," Mary said with a smile, "but Silas is faster."

Silas made a diving catch for a line drive to get the third out. Kirsten clapped for him as the married men came in from their places in the field.

When the first two batters got on base, Kirsten tried to hide her shock. The married men played smarter, placing the ball precisely in gaps in the outfield instead of swinging for the fence. The third batter was thrown out at first base, but the runners advanced to second and third. It was then that Kirsten noticed Silas's arm and the red gash on his elbow.

"Silas, you're bleeding," she said loud enough for him to hear. He turned around and curled his long fingers into the chain-link fence between them.

"Are ya enjoying the game, Mrs. Miller?" he asked much louder than necessary. The way he was looking at her warmed her from her head to her toes. He'd said he was happier than he had ever been. The look on his face made her believe him even more.

"Silas! Yer up to bat, my boy!" Daniel boomed.

Silas spun around and made his way out of the dugout.

"Ach! We finally get some young blood, but he's too smitten to be any good!" Daniel shouted to his teammates while Silas grabbed a bat and jogged to home plate. The men groaned and laughed, and Kirsten blushed.

Silas took his place at the plate and flashed her a brilliant smile before raising the bat high above his shoulder. The pitch was lobbed, and Silas stood to let it sail past, getting the ball. Daniel burst into laughter and Silas just shook his head.

The next pitch sailed higher, and Silas braced himself to swing. Whereas Micah's swing had been fast, Silas's was hard and more powerful, as if every muscle in his body strained to bring the bat around as hard as he could. With a deafening crack, the bat crushed the ball and sent it flying.

Kirsten had been unconsciously holding her breath, but it whooshed out now as his body twisted in a backswing. People stood to see it soar impossibly high and long, sailing far over the fence and disappearing into the hayfield. Silas stood straight as he watched it fall from the sky. It seemed to take forever for it to come down. The married men gave a loud whoop of a cheer and came out of the dugout while Silas began leisurely jogging around the bases. Kirsten joined the others in their cheering and stopped only when he rounded third based and she could see his face, a shy smile firmly in place. How desperately she wanted him to keep running until he was close enough to hold. She knew how strong those arms were from personal experience, and she'd just been reminded of that fact. She didn't ever want to forget it. Her heart pounded as Silas's teammates and opponents clapped him on his back and shoulders. He calmly accepted their exuberance and led the way back to the dugout. Before he sat, he stepped up to the chain-link fence, looked up at her, and winked. If she hadn't been sitting down, she would have had to.

.෨෬ ৩৯.

"I cannot believe we lost," Caleb moaned and slumped into his chair.

"It was a good effort," Mary soothed. Caleb rolled his eyes.

"We would have won if we still had Silas," he pouted, nearly glaring across the table at his older brother.

Silas was trying, but only half succeeding, to bite back a smile.

"Kirsten, will ya get the dessert?" Mary asked.

Kirsten took her time at the counter, carefully slicing and sliding each piece of cherry pie onto a plate and placing a mound of ice cream on the side. She carried one plate to the table and set it down in front of Silas, her hand resting on his shoulder. He stopped mid-sentence, either at her touch or at the sight of cherry pie—she wasn't sure which.

Kirsten served the rest of them, and when she sat down, Daniel nodded and they all ate.

"Mmmm," Silas moaned. Kirsten got goose bumps.

"Kirsten, yer a fine cook!" Daniel praised. His kind smile nearly brought tears to her eyes. She was only able to nod her thanks.

Silas's eyes snapped up to her. "You made this?"

She nodded and smiled. "Think of it as your welcome-to-the-marrieds-team and congrats-on-your-big-win dessert."

Caleb snorted in disgust and Silas gave her a wide smile.

"What would you have given me if we'd lost?" he asked with dancing eyes.

Kirsten sighed dramatically. "Oh Silas, I'd never think such a thing was possible."

Mary threw her head back and laughed loudly.

"Dad, I'm curious…" Kirsten paused. She'd never called him that to his face before. It was clear that he noticed by his huge smile. "Why did you laugh when Silas didn't swing at the first pitch?"

Daniel laughed again. "Because he could have hit it."

"But it was a ball," Kirsten argued, glancing at Silas, who was chewing and trying not to smile.

"Silas can hit anything," Daniel explained. "He chose not to because he couldn't have hit it as far."

Kirsten considered this for a minute.

"Yeah, okay, that sounds like something Silas would do."

They all laughed then. Even Caleb.

CHAPTER TWENTY-NINE

"Our Father in heaven," Kirsten began from her seat in the buggy.

"Our Father which art in heaven," Silas corrected.

"Our Father which art in heaven, hallowed be thy name. Thy kingdom come. Thy will be done..."

"On earth," he prompted.

"On earth as it is in heaven. Give us today—"

"Give us this day."

"Give us this day our daily bread and forgive us our debts as we forgive our debtors..."

"Lead us."

"Lead us not into temptation, but deliver us from evil. For thine is the kingdom and the glory and the power forever. Amen!"

"*Gut*," Silas said, smiling. "Now let's say it together."

They recited the prayer three more times as Titus clopped along the road.

"I haven't prayed this much in a buggy since the day of the quilting frolic and that bad storm," he chuckled.

"Hmm. That was the one and only time I did not want to be in a buggy with you. I wanted to be with you. But not in the buggy," she said, pursing her lips.

"That's funny, I remember having trouble gettin' ya out," he said, his face furrowed in mock confusion.

Kirsten smiled and shook her head. "You got so sick after that storm," she said, growing suddenly serious. "That was almost as scary."

"It's a beautiful day today," he reassured her.

"Will you come in to see the doctor with me, or would you rather sit in the waiting room?"

Silas thought for a moment. "What would ya like me to do?"

"Come with me." She sounded decisive.

He nodded in agreement.

"You don't have to stay if he does an exam," she allowed.

Silas had no idea what she meant by that, but he hoped it would be obvious.

The clinic sat far back from the road, with a large parking lot in front and the hospital right next door. There was a long rail along the far side of the lot where Amish patients could tie up their horses. Silas looped the reins around the rail, and at Kirsten's request, he explained the simple process. The lot was mostly empty as they walked across it and through the automatic doors.

He hadn't been to the clinic in years, but Kirsten was obviously familiar with the process. He followed her to a large reception desk.

"Kirsten Miller. I have a 7:30 with Dr. Burke."

The receptionist clicked the keys on her computer.

"What did you say your name was, hon?"

"Oh...um...well, it used to be Kirsten Walker," she glanced over at him. "I got married."

"Congratulations," the woman said unemotionally. "Is your address and phone number still the same."

"No," Kirsten answered, biting her lip.

"I'll need you to fill out this change of information form," the woman said as she slid a clipboard across the counter. Silas followed his wife to a corner of the empty waiting room. He watched her write her name across the top line, feeling a lightness fill his chest.

"What's your...I mean our address?" she asked as she turned to him.

"14598 152nd Avenue," he answered with a grin. She'd only moved just down the road, and only one number needed to be changed.

"Should I just put my mom's phone number on here?"

"You can if you want. Or you can put down our cell number," he said, leaning close to her. The urge to kiss her was almost overpowering. Obviously, this wasn't the place for that kind of thing, but if she kept biting her lip he was going to have to divert his attention.

She blinked up at him, her pen poised over the paper. "We have a cell phone?"

He nodded.

"Where on earth is it?" she asked.

"In the barn," he stated, finding her shocked expression amusing and alluring all at the same time.

"Why is it in the barn?"

"It's against the rules to have one in the house," he said, shrugging his shoulders.

"But having one in the barn is perfectly okay," she clarified.

He nodded.

"Right. Okay. What's our phone number?"

After she wrote it down, Silas delivered the finished form to the reception desk, and a scrub-clad nurse rounded the corner almost immediately.

"Kirsten," she said, smiling directly past Silas to his wife. "How are you, honey?" the nurse asked as they stood to follow her.

"Good, thank you," Kirsten tipped her head. "This is my husband, Silas," she said, turning to smile at him. It was entirely possible that he could hit a thousand homeruns at that moment.

"Oh! How nice! Congratulations!" the nurse cried enthusiastically.

She led them back to a small exam room, took Kirsten's blood pressure, and then ushered her down the hall to be weighed. Silas tried to relax in the vinyl-covered chair, but the room and its unfamiliar instruments and posters made him nervous. Not to mention it smelled funny.

Kirsten shortly came back in the room, sat beside him, and squeezed his hand. She didn't seem nervous, and the gesture was probably more for his comfort than her own.

"Dr. Burke will be in in just a moment," the nurse said and smiled Kirsten.

"Bev, could I have a sheet to cover my legs?" Kirsten asked abruptly.

"Oh! Of course! I'll bring one right in," the nurse answered, pulling the door shut with a heavy thud.

Silas was curious about the sheet, but he was too unsettled to ask.

"She's really nice," Kirsten sighed. Silas could only nod.

Five minutes later, a tall, blue-scrub-wearing man with a receding hairline strode through the door, making Silas's stomach flop.

"Kirsten, good to see you!" he said, extending his hand.

"Hi, Dr. Burke," she greeted him with a smile. "Um, so I got married a couple weeks ago, and this is my husband, Silas Miller."

Silas shook the Doctor's extended hand.

"Nice to meet you, Silas." It was impossible to miss Dr. Burke's surprise.

"So...you're Amish now?" Dr. Burke asked, turning his attention back to Kirsten.

"I am," she answered, grinning as she turned her smile to Silas. He'd wanted so badly to see her satisfied and content with living a plain life. But to see her happy in it, joyfully participating in his life and seemingly very much at peace was beyond all he could have dared to ask. Her bright smile now sucked the air right out of the room.

Dr. Burke flipped open a file folder and reviewed Kirsten's information. "You finally gained some weight, which is good to see!"

"I've been spoiled," Kirsten admitted shyly. "Silas's mother and sister are excellent cooks."

Dr. Burke nodded. "The Amish are very hard-working people," he said looking at Silas. "I don't want you to overdo anything."

"I'm being careful to get enough rest and to take it easy when I get tired," Kirsten reassured him.

"You're into your third trimester now—thirty-one weeks. Any swelling?" the doctor looked down at Kirsten's ankles.

"Sometimes in the evenings," Kirsten admitted. She was swelling in the evenings? Silas mentally castigated himself for not noticing.

"Why don't you hop on up here and we'll take a listen," Dr. Burke stood and waved at the exam table.

Kirsten climbed up and draped the white sheet down over her legs. Silas wondered if he should step out, but he couldn't seem to make his legs move. He stared down at his boots, vaguely aware that Kirsten was lying back on the table and pulling up the skirt of her dress. Dr. Burke stood between them, slightly blocking Silas's view. Silas chanced a glance up to see his wife reclining, with only the pregnant bulge of her stomach exposed and a long, white sheet over her bare legs. He'd touched her belly only once and felt the baby's movement. But he'd never seen her bare skin where it was stretched tight by the child she carried. Dr. Burke moved a small instrument over her that crackled loudly in the tiny room. There were some loud thumps and then a steady thrumming sound—the same steady but rapid pace of a horse's trot.

"That's the baby's heartbeat," Dr. Burke announced and glanced down at his watch. Silas sat transfixed, the sound interrupted by an occasional thump. Kirsten turned to meet his eyes and smiled softly. He grinned back and shook his head slightly in amazement.

"Good, strong heartbeat. And some good kicks," Dr. Burke said as he helped Kirsten sit up. "Got yourself a soccer player," he joked.

"I think she'll be more of a softball or volleyball player. Or maybe a tree-climber," Kirsten said, grinning. Her message was clear only to him. No matter this child's beginnings, Kirsten wanted her future to be Silas's to shape and mold. The heartbeat they'd just heard wasn't of his making, but it would be the one he held tight against his own as he rocked her to sleep. This was their child. Her daughter. His daughter.

"I'll see you back in a few weeks," Dr. Burke said, scribbling on a piece of paper and handing it to Kirsten. She stood and slid off the table when the doctor walked out of the room, careful to pull her skirt down past her knees before she slipped the sheet off. Silas stepped close and offered her his hand as she stepped off the exam table.

"Pretty painless," she said, tossing the sheet onto the table.

They retraced their steps down the long hallway and back to the reception desk.

"How 'bout a 7:30 on September 10?" the receptionist asked.

"Would that be okay?" Kirsten asked, turning to Silas. He nodded his approval and tried to keep the surprise off his face. It startled him that she had asked his opinion so easily. The world saw the idea of submission to a husband as some abusive type of control. He knew that much from his parents' interactions with outsiders at the market. But to him it seemed so loving—a consideration for each other. If there was love and trust, how could a wife ever fear that her husband would withhold his consent to anything out of spite? To him, it wasn't about control. It was about unity.

"You're pretty quiet, Silas Miller," Kirsten said quietly when he pulled up to the market. Her eyes were in her lap. "Everything okay?" Even though she was talking to him, her gaze was resolutely fixed downward.

Silas waited for her to look at him. When she didn't, he gently took her chin in his long fingers and turned her face to his.

"I am very blessed," he said slowly, emphasizing each word.

She smiled. "It didn't scare you off then?"

He shook his head. "It was…" He couldn't find the words.

"Pretty cool, huh?"

"*Jah*," he said, grinning.

"At least it wasn't so…invasive this time. That's not so fun." She grimaced. Silas didn't want to think about another man's hands on her or in her, even if that man was her doctor.

"So a softball player or a tree-climber?" he chuckled, desperate to think about something else.

Kirsten laughed, then suddenly got serious. "Just don't you teach her to play hide-and-seek! I don't think I could handle that."

Silas laughed and kissed her cheek, promising nothing.

— CHAPTER THIRTY —

On Monday morning, Deborah was waiting on her wide front porch when Kirsten and Amy pulled up to the house.

"Let's see what we have here," Deborah murmured to herself as Kirsten unpacked her basket. Deborah ran her fingers over the bundles of snowy-white fabric.

"This will give us a *gut* start!" she announced. "First, we'll cut the pieces, and then I'll show ya how to sew it together."

Kirsten helped Deborah lay out the yards across the table. Silas had stopped to check on the inventory at the market on their way home from the clinic. Mary had promptly taken Kirsten over to the shelves of fabric bolts.

The market was more than just a tourist stop along the highway. It was also where almost all of the Amish families in the district shopped for basic necessities. Those aisles of fabric, bulk supplies, and dry goods had looked quaint and old-fashioned to Kirsten before. Now they looked like an Amish Wal-Mart. Mary had helped her select the right fabrics and materials she would need to make clothes and diapers for the baby.

She'd nearly danced all the way out to the buggy when Silas was ready to go, her arms wrapped tightly around the string-tied bundle in her arms. She'd hugged it all the way home, much to her husband's amusement. The package had sat on her bureau like an unopened gift for three days. The thought of cutting the cloth into pieces that would be assembled into a dress both thrilled and terrified her.

Deborah laid out the pattern and expertly snipped the cloth, freeing one piece. She handed the scissors to Kirsten and smiled at her panicked expression.

"It's always better to do it yerself," she said cheerily. She sounded an awful lot like a certain blond-haired man who frequently tossed a similar phrase her way. Deborah stood right at her elbow as Kirsten slowly worked the scissors through the material. Not once had the Millers' close supervision seemed overbearing. Whenever any member of the family offered to introduce her to anything new, they stood close by, offering encouragement, helpful correction, and praise. All of them had been careful not to crush her spirit and seemed to genuinely want for her to be able to do things herself.

Kirsten slowly, carefully freed the remaining pieces from the lengths of fabric and took her place behind Deborah, watching over her shoulder as she ran the pieces through her peddle-operated sewing machine. With one pass finished, it was Kirsten's turn to try. She sat and watched as the needle moved in and out of the fabric.

"What's yer husband doing today?" Deborah asked Kirsten, leaning over her shoulder and watching her progress.

"He's actually helping my mom move to an apartment in town."

"You didn't want to go along?"

"Oh, I did," Kirsten sighed. "But Silas thought I might overdo it or do too much lifting. Don't tell him I said this, but he was probably right," she said as she twisted her mouth slightly.

Deborah laughed at Kirsten's perturbed tone.

"Caleb went along, so they'll probably get done early." Kirsten cheered herself with the comment.

The truth was Kirsten ached to be there. She could barely imagine Silas interacting with her mom. And it made her more than a little nervous that she would not be there to deflect or interpret anything her mother might say. Silas didn't need her interference, but it was unnerving to be so out-of-the-loop.

Deborah was a very patient and gentle teacher, just as Mary had promised. It was a daunting task to make all of her daughter's clothing by hand, but as the tiny dress began to take shape before her eyes, and in her very own hands, Kirsten got more and more excited.

By three o'clock, she had finished the dress. Deborah inspected it, gently testing the seams and snipping away a loose thread here and there. Finally, she stopped, placed the dress in Kirsten's lap, and looked in her eyes.

"Kirsten Miller, you made yer daughter a fine dress," she said softly, with a gentle smile.

Kirsten stared down at the tiny gown. It wasn't perfect. Surely Deborah or Sarah or any other Amish woman would have done a better job. But she had made the effort to learn, had faced yet another fear, and then had simply done it with her own two hands.

It was the first tangible item she had in preparation for her daughter's arrival. And she had made it herself. The satisfaction and joy was overwhelming. The tears spilled down her cheeks, and her breath caught in a sob.

"Kirsten! Whatever is the matter?" Deborah exclaimed worriedly.

Kirsten shook her head and threw her arms around Deborah's shoulders, hugging her fiercely.

"I don't know how I can ever thank you," she choked through her tears.

"You don't need to," Deborah laughed lightly, gently hugging her back. "Yer my sister and I'd do anything for you."

Kirsten packed up her things, delicately placing the dress on top. She hugged Deborah goodbye, thinking that, second only to Silas, she might be Kirsten's most favorite person in the world. How very happy she was to know such a gentle soul.

⚬ᴥ⚬

When Silas pulled into the yard early that evening, he could see her standing at the window, waiting. He worried a little when he came into the house and she watched him take off his boots and wash his hands with an undisguised and uncharacteristic impatience.

"Yer mom is all settled in her new place," he said easily, hoping to calm her nervousness. Still, she wrung her hands and bit her lip. Something else had her troubled.

"What's wrong?" he asked as he dried his hands.

"Come with me?" she pleaded, taking one of his hands in hers.

Much faster than he expected, she pulled him through the kitchen and up the stairs and turned the corner to her room. When they entered, she released his hand and spun to latch the door closed. She slowed as she moved past him to the bureau and slowly, so slowly, pulled something from the top drawer and turned to face him. She held it out to him like a gift, her face suddenly, radiantly lit by a smile. Silas forced his eyes away from her face to the tiny gown as he took it in his large hands.

"Did ya make this yerself?" he asked as he smiled at her.

Kirsten nodded, bit her lip, and stared into his face.

He could see the weight of the moment for her. Plain women frequently made clothing for their children. But to Kirsten, this was obviously a distinct accomplishment. It was sweet to see the joy and pleasure she was feeling at this common task.

"Our daughter has a fine dress to wear home from the hospital," he said, cradling it in his hands.

Kirsten giggled then and stood on tiptoe to kiss his cheek. Silas laid the gown gently on her bureau and reached for her. She visibly hesitated, but she recovered quickly and stepped close to him. He pulled her wrists up around his neck and slid his hands down her arms to her shoulders, placing them finally on the back of her waist. He rested his forehead on hers and slid his hands on either side of her stomach.

It was not lost on him that from that very first day at the market when he'd helped her to her car, this life had been within her. Impossibly, they'd lived less than a mile apart and God had not orchestrated their meeting until this baby's heart had already started beating. This tiny heart, this tiny life—their daughter.

"Supper's ready," Mary called. Silas sighed in frustration; Kirsten giggled. He dropped his hands, but she caught one and held it as he led her back downstairs. He sat at the table, and her hand trailed across his shoulder while she went to help set the food on the table.

When Daniel bowed his head and began the Lord's Prayer, Kirsten softly joined, her voice lifting and flowing through the phrases in her English accent. So much the same and yet gently different. The "Amen" was spoken, but no one moved to fill their plates.

Daniel smiled gently, warmly at the newest member of his family. Kirsten caught his gaze.

"Silas taught me," she said softly. Daniel nodded and the meal began.

"How did yer sewing lesson go with Deborah?" Mary inquired.

Kirsten beamed. "Can I show you instead?"

Mary nodded and Kirsten jumped from the table, returning and presenting the gown to Mary, who inspected it thoroughly.

"Very *gut*, Kirsten!" she finally said with a smile.

"Deborah is an excellent teacher." Kirsten said, smiling sincerely as she laid the gown on the table behind Daniel's chair. "Mom taught me how to cook. Amy taught me how to bake. Caleb taught me how to put a bridle on a horse. Shelby taught me how to sing 'Loblied,' and Anna Mae showed me the best hiding spot. Which I will not reveal to anyone."

Silas sighed dramatically. "And all I could do was teach you to pray."

"Oh no, you've taught me much more!" Kirsten argued. It was an honest statement, but both of them blushed horribly.

"*Ach.* It seems I have been lacking in my role as head of this house! I've taught ya nothin'!" Daniel said in mock disgust.

"Not true!" Kirsten said, shaking her head vigorously. "You've taught me the joy of having a family and how to enjoy each precious day with them."

She couldn't have known the impact of her words. Simply allowing her to become part of this family had put them in danger of losing it altogether. Daniel knew to value each precious day because he'd lain those days on the altar, just as Abraham had given Isaac. Kirsten didn't know, but Daniel, Mary, and Silas did. Daniel looked at her with such warmth that Silas had to look away. He could hear his mother choking back her tears.

In only three short weeks, Kirsten had found a place in all their hearts.

Nearly every night for the past week, Kirsten had woken up shortly after midnight to use the bathroom. As silently as possible, she padded down the hall in her bare feet. There were certain spots on the floor that squeaked, and she was getting better at avoiding them. She was just on her way back to her room when she heard the click of the door downstairs. Her blood ran cold. All the doors were closed upstairs—everyone seemed to be sleeping. She tiptoed down the stairs to see Amy's silhouette in the kitchen room. She was sitting in one of the chairs at the table, bent over, her head in her hands. Kirsten could hear her soft sniffles.

"Amy, are you okay?" Kirsten whispered, coming into the kitchen.

Amy's head snapped up and she quickly wiped the tears from her cheeks.

"I'm fine," she mumbled thickly.

"Are you sure?" Kirsten laid a hand on her shoulder. Amy didn't say anything but looked abruptly away. Kirsten was no stranger to middle-of-the-night tears. But why had Amy been outside? For some reason, she felt as if she had to find out the reason.

"Is there anything I can do?" Kirsten asked, sitting in the chair across from Amy. Instead of ignoring her, Amy turned her angry glare on Kirsten.

"I think you've done enough already," came the biting response.

"I'm sorry?"

Amy said nothing.

"Were you just outside? Is something wrong?" Kirsten craned her neck to see out the window.

Amy stared at her for a long moment. "Lucas Beiler told me he couldn't see me anymore."

"Who's Lucas Beiler?" Kirsten asked, her mind spinning, trying to grab hold of something that made sense.

"Doesn't matter anymore."

"Why can't he see you anymore?" Kirsten asked numbly, certain this was not going to be good.

"His father said the Millers were fence-jumpers, and no son of his would marry a fence-jumper." The words were unmistakably bitter.

"What's a fence-jumper?" Kirsten asked, her head beginning to ache.

"People who leave the church for an English life."

"Well, that's just ridiculous," Kirsten nearly snorted. "No one here would do that."

"Wouldn't they? "

"No!" Kirsten insisted.

"What about Silas?"

"What about him?" Kirsten said through numb lips.

"He's pushed the limits with you already. Seems his marrying you has caused some problems worse than you having to learn how to sew and cook."

Kirsten had worried to Silas that she would bring shame to his family. He'd said he would never be ashamed to have her in his family. But that didn't change how others would see her. Worse, how others would see the Millers as a whole. It was impossible for them to shield her without bearing her burden—her mistake. Even Amy was now suffering consequences of Kirsten's actions.

"I'm sorry, Amy. I never wanted you to be hurt," Kirsten whispered. "Maybe I could talk to Silas. Or your dad."

"No!" Amy protested desperately. "Don't! That will only make it worse."

Kirsten looked at her helplessly.

"There's nothing you can do," Amy sighed in resignation. She left Kirsten sitting at the table in the dark, where she stayed for several long minutes. The worst thing she could do would be to go against Amy's wishes and tell Silas or Daniel.

.ₑℰ ℊₐ.

Silas had heard the footsteps on the porch and their voices whispering in the dark. He'd stood at the top of the stairs, out of sight, but able to hear them. He'd intended to go down when he heard Kirsten's voice, but he'd stopped at Amy's mention of Lucas. The Beilers were a notoriously strict family. Silas had certainly felt a few people who used to be friendly politely distancing themselves since his marriage to Kirsten. It was petty that they take out their fears and worries on Amy. But some people were bound to place blame on the whole family.

A small part of him couldn't blame them. What he had done was crazy—*ferhoodled*. He hadn't just married an English girl—he'd married a pregnant English girl. Sweet as Kirsten was, if someone didn't know her, he could understand their suspicion and uncertainty. He couldn't necessarily say that he'd do the same thing in their shoes. But their behavior was not surprising to him.

Still, it wasn't a price Amy should be asked to pay. And because of this midnight confession, it was another burden Kirsten had to bear. He crawled back in bed and lay awake for a long time wondering just how much more she could take.

⚬⚬⚬

Days later the encounter with Amy was still running through Kirsten's mind. With a vigorous snap, Kirsten shook the wet pillowcase, sending a gentle spray wafting through the air. Mondays were wash days now that Kirsten was here to help. It kept her busy—with eight people in the house, the bedding alone would be a significant chore. But as Kirsten was learning, living on a farm, caring for animals, working in the garden, having a furniture-making business, meant hours of washing the piles of dirty, homespun clothes that had accumulated over the past week and weekend.

She'd made sure to start the wash first thing after breakfast so that it had plenty of time to hang out in the hot, humid summer air. After lunch, she'd taken a nap, though it hadn't been very refreshing. She loved sleeping at night with the windows open and the cool summer breeze blowing into her room. Most of all, she loved the quiet sounds of the farm, the crickets chirping, the occasional hoots of an owl, and the sound of the wind rustling through the leaves of the trees all around the yard. But naps in the daytime were not as peaceful. The farmyard was noisier, the livestock bellowed, the birds sang brightly, the cicadas droned loudly, and it was much, much warmer. Kirsten had finally escaped the warm upstairs and made her way out onto the porch, taking a few minutes to soak in the breeze, even though it was a warm one.

By the sound of it, Silas and Caleb were busy in the woodshop. Caleb had been spending more and more time learning the basics of woodworking with his older brother. When Kirsten brought a cold glass of lemonade to the shop, many times she'd find Caleb peering eagerly over a workbench while Silas worked. Not only had Kirsten not had a father, she hadn't had any siblings either. She could hardly imagine what it would be like to have such a patient and enduring older brother as Silas. It was easy to see that Caleb and Silas had a close relationship, in spite of their extraordinarily different temperaments. She'd make sure to bring two glasses of lemonade today.

But first, she surveyed her laundry and checked for items ready to come off the line. She plucked the clothespins off the undershirts and work shirts and aprons. The slacks weren't dry yet, nor were the socks or the dresses. She turned to the long line of bedding behind her and began pulling the summer-fresh sheets from the line. Just as she was about to reach up and pluck the pins off the long, blue sheets from Caleb and Silas's bed, she noticed a pair of boots showing beneath them. A second before she could process what was happening, a set of arms on the other side of the sheet came around and grabbed her tightly, wrapping her in the blue fabric.

Kirsten screamed in fear, but the arms didn't let go. In fact, they tightened. With a jerk, Kirsten pulled the sheet off the line, sending the fabric falling over her head. She yanked it down to find Silas's face only inches from hers, his arms still tightly wound around her and the sheet. He had a wicked grin on his face, and his eyes were bright as he looked down at her. All the while, he held her steady.

"Silas Miller!" she scolded. "You'll scare this baby right outta me!"

He laughed loudly and carefully released her.

Kirsten tossed the sheet into the basket and pulled the bonnet off her head. It had gotten tugged askew in her struggle under the sheet, and she could feel strands of her auburn hair blowing in the breeze.

"Since when are you such a troublemaker?" she teased, shaking her bonnet at him.

"Am I in trouble?" His smile was slow, crooked, and downright dangerous. Try as she might, Kirsten could not keep herself from laughing.

Silas stepped close again, sweeping the strands of her hair behind her ears. Instantly, she stopped laughing and looked up at him. He was still smiling, though his eyes burned with an intensity she did not recognize.

His fingers trailed down her jaw, holding it lightly between his fingers. She stared into his eyes, surprised by his sudden closeness and tenderness.

"You, Kirsten Miller, are so beautiful," he breathed. With a sigh, he dropped his hand and stepped back, breaking the spell. "If I help ya get these in, will ya come have a cool drink with me?"

"Sure," Kirsten squeaked. But it was going to take several very cold drinks to quench the fire he'd just set.

— Chapter Thirty-One —

"Happy Birthday, Kirsten!" Shelby said, bouncing up and down when Kirsten came down to help with breakfast.

"Thank you!" Kirsten smiled as she wrapped her arms around Shelby and Anna.

"How old are ya, Kirsten?" Anna Mae questioned.

"I am *nineteen!*" Kirsten said with dramatic emphasis. They giggled and ran to help set the table. Kirsten started the coffee, and soon Amy and Mary came in with their own birthday greetings. These past several days, Amy had been polite, but distant, much as Kirsten had expected after their encounter that late Sunday night.

In short order, there were stacks of pancakes and a full plate of crisp bacon waiting on the table between the orange juice and the oatmeal.

Daniel came in and enthusiastically wished Kirsten a happy birthday. Finally, Silas strode across the porch and through the screen door. He washed his hands, kicked off his boots, and crossed the room to her.

His arm slid around her waist, and he kissed her tenderly on the cheek.

"Happy Birthday, Kirsten Miller." His voice was low and intimate in her ear, his breath warm on her neck. Kirsten felt her knees weaken and goose bumps creep across her skin.

The entire family was sitting at the table when Caleb came slamming through the screen door slightly out of breath.

"Sorry Dad...Mom," he huffed as he fell into his chair. Daniel bowed his head and led the family in silent prayer.

"What were ya up to that made ya late fer breakfast?" Mary asked her youngest son.

Caleb smiled. "I got the eggs." His smile twisted in embarrassment. "Happy Birthday, Kirsten."

Silas snorted loudly, and Kirsten elbowed him.

"That was a very thoughtful birthday gift, Caleb," she said with a smile. Silas went into a coughing fit in an effort to hide his laughter.

When breakfast was over, Mary announced that David and Sarah and Michael and Deborah would be coming over for a special birthday supper. Kirsten had hoped to see Deborah today but was a little surprised David and Sarah would be there, too. They'd been very careful in her presence, and Sarah almost never spoke directly to Kirsten. Certainly any time they had talked, they had kept to safe topics, which did not include Kirsten's pregnancy. In fact, Deborah was the only Amish woman Kirsten had really discussed pregnancy with. Though Kirsten suspected that Deborah was equally as thrilled to have a confidant since they were both expecting.

Later that afternoon, Kirsten pondered the connections and friendships she had made while she sat at the sewing table, piecing together yet another baby gown. She was so absorbed in her own thoughts that when Silas bent over her chair and whispered a greeting in her ear, she nearly fell over.

"How about a birthday picnic?" he murmured.

Kirsten looked around, but the room was empty.

"Just us?" she tried not to sound too hopeful, but judging by the look on his face, she failed miserably.

"Just us," he promised with a smile. He led her out to the buggy and helped her in. Wordlessly, he drove down the lane and turned toward Michael's farm, which he passed. They continued on past David's until Silas pulled into the little abandoned farmyard.

"You proposed here." Kirsten smiled at him. It seemed like a lifetime ago, not mere months.

"I did," he confirmed. As he helped her down, he pulled her close against him in a way he never did at home. She looked up at him in surprise, but he just smiled. He spread the quilt on the ground under one of the trees, opened up the basket, and set out sandwiches, chips, apples, caramel dip, cookies, and cans of soda.

"A feast!" Kirsten proclaimed.

"Amy put it together," he admitted.

"It's wonderful."

They ate and watched the squirrels chase each other, jumping from branch to branch.

"You never talk about yer father," Silas observed.

"I don't really remember him that well. I was only eight when he died, and my memories aren't that clear," she said with a shrug.

"It was ten years ago," he agreed.

"I remember him working a lot and watching baseball on TV at night," Kirsten said, squinting into the sunlit sky.

"*Jah*. He told me about the baseball," Silas laughed.

"He *told* you?"

Silas nodded, crunching a massive bite of apple.

"How? When?"

"Michael broke his arm when he was thirteen. It was Sunday, and my parents were out visitin'. I ran to yer place and yer Dad took me and Michael to the hospital. Stayed with us the whole time. Bought us a candy bar out of a...machine. Brought us back home and drove us right up to the door. He told Dad what had happened."

Kirsten gaped at him.

"He was kind to us," Silas said finally.

"I don't remember any of this," Kirsten said quietly, sitting perfectly still.

"You were only six," he reasoned.

She nodded woodenly as she tried to imagine her dad sitting in a hospital waiting room with a nine-year-old Silas. Her Silas. Kirsten shook her head.

"And now here we are," she said quietly, not even sure he could hear her.

"The Lord works in mysterious ways."

"How come I never saw you before that day at the market?"

Silas smiled. "Wasn't meant to happen until then." Then he laughed. "It's not really all that surprising, is it? That ya didn't see me before. You have trouble finding me now!"

Deborah turned the dresses over and over, examining each one and pointing out Kirsten's successes.

"Yer doin' *gut* work, Kirsten!" she praised.

Mary, Amy, and Sarah were busy preparing yet another feast. The men came in from caring for the horses, their voices loud and boisterous. Chairs were added, and Kirsten soon found herself pressed close to her husband's side at the crowded table.

The food was tremendous. Mary had prepared all of Kirsten's favorites, even though she had many. After supper, she helped dry and stack the plates as Amy washed. The flash of headlights in the yard caught her attention, and Kirsten turned to see Elizabeth climbing out of the van with a package in her hand.

"Mom!" Kirsten called cheerfully, meeting her on the porch.

"Happy Birthday, honey."

"I didn't know you were coming!" Kirsten smiled. She knew it must be somewhat strange and awkward for her mom to come visit as often as she would like. Most often, Elizabeth's visits happened during the day when Kirsten happened to be outside.

"Mary called to invite me to your party. I just got off work or I would have tried to make it for supper."

"I'm so glad you're here," Kirsten said, beaming at her. "Come inside!"

Elizabeth let her daughter eagerly pull her inside where Daniel and Mary and Silas all greeted her warmly.

"Yer just in time for cake!" Mary cheered.

Silas steered Kirsten into a chair, his hand staying on her shoulder as everyone gathered around. Kirsten felt tears stinging in her eyes as they sang what had to be the most spectacularly buoyant round of "Happy Birthday" she'd ever heard.

"Thank you," she choked as Silas's thumb rubbed a small, soothing circle on her shoulder blade.

After ten years of quiet birthdays, being sung to only by her mother and perhaps her grandparents, having a room full of people all gathered around her was overwhelmingly sweet. This is what birthdays were supposed to feel like. This is what she had missed for ten years. But the Millers had just changed all that. Silas had changed all that.

They gathered in the living room, which was easily big enough to fit all of them, though they had to bring in some of the chairs from the kitchen. Elizabeth handed a gift-wrapped package to her.

"It's heavy!" Kirsten laughed as she took the small, flat rectangle and tore the paper off. "A Bible," she breathed.

"I asked Silas what he thought you might like, and he suggested this," Elizabeth explained with a slightly doubtful look on her face. Silas was staring down at his boots.

"I know you like to read," Elizabeth allowed.

"Not as much as she likes Silas to read to her!" Caleb laughed, bringing on quiet snickering from his family and a blush from Kirsten.

"Thank you, Mom," Kirsten said meeting her eyes.

Michael stood and brought a brown paper package to her, setting it carefully in her disappearing lap. Kirsten stared up at him in surprise, and then quickly looked to Deborah to find her smiling gently. Kirsten hadn't expected gifts, at least not from anyone except her mom.

Slowly and carefully, she loosened the tape and pulled the paper back to reveal a pink and white baby quilt in the same intricate pattern as the one hanging on Deborah's wall. Kirsten gasped and pulled it out, spreading it across her lap. Her hands wandered over the fabric, feeling its soft perfection.

"The white is fabric I had left over from Silas's wedding shirt," Deborah said, smiling at Kirsten.

"You made Silas's shirt?"

"Mom asked me to make his wedding suit. She was busy making yer dresses."

Kirsten stared down at the quilt with all its tiny pieces of Silas's wedding shirt. Somehow, that extra touch was intensely moving.

"Deborah it's...it's exquisite," Kirsten choked. Carefully, she passed the quilt to Elizabeth, who was also clearly moved by the beautiful gift.

"I'll be right back," Silas whispered in her ear before walking quickly out of the room. It was only minutes later that his footsteps sounded on the porch. He came in and set a beautifully carved wooden cradle in front of her.

"Happy Birthday, Mrs. Miller." He smiled up at her shyly.

Kirsten's jaw dropped. It was maple, just like her bed. She stood and slowly dropped to her knees beside it. She trailed her fingers over each side, where he'd carved an intricate apple tree. With a gentle push, it slowly swung back and forth in a perfectly smooth motion. It was sturdy. Strong. Beautifully handcrafted.

"Oh, Silas," she breathed, watching it sway. No one spoke. Kirsten looked up to where he stood watching her. She bit her lip and swallowed back her tears. "Thank you." Her lip quivered, but she willed herself not to cry. She stood, took his hands in hers, stared up into his face, and kissed his cheek.

⊷⊶⊷

Kirsten returned from the shower to find the cradle had mysteriously appeared in her room, nestled in the corner between the southern and western windows. Quickly, she changed into her nightgown and brushed through her hair.

She took the pink and white quilt and placed it gently in the bottom of the cradle. Then, turning to the bureau, she pulled out one of the tiny gowns she had made and set it on the quilt. With the slightest touch, she rocked the cradle back and forth.

The cradle was empty, the quilt was empty, the tiny dress was empty. But she was full—growing rounder with child with every passing day. And her heart was nearly bursting with happiness.

The smallest sound behind her made her turn to find Silas in her doorway, his Bible in hand, his eyes focused on her. She smiled shyly in the dim light. He came in and shut the door.

"You're still going to read to me?" she asked hopefully.

"If ya want me to." His voice was so low and quiet.

"I thought maybe you suggested a Bible for me so you wouldn't have to."

"I don't have to. I want to," he said, his finger trailing along her jaw. Kirsten was frozen at his touch. She stared into his warm, dark eyes. He dropped his hand, and Kirsten followed him to the bed, where he sat.

"Psalm 121," he said so only she could hear.

> *"I lift up my eyes to the mountains—where does*
> *my help come from? My help comes from the Lord,*
> *the Maker of heaven and earth. He will not let your*
> *foot slip—he who watches over you will not slumber;*
> *indeed, he who watches over Israel will neither*
> *slumber nor sleep."*

He paused and Kirsten wondered if he was done. Silas looked up from the page open in his lap to her face, studying her. He reached out and brushed her hair back, his fingers lingering on her cheek. Without looking away, he continued.

> *"The Lord watches over you—the Lord is your*
> *shade at your right hand; the sun will not harm you*
> *by day, nor the moon by night. The Lord will keep*
> *you from all harm—he will watch over your life; the*
> *Lord will watch over your coming and going both*
> *now and forevermore."*

Silas leaned down and softly pressed his lips to her forehead, then her cheek—slow, soft kisses. Kirsten closed her eyes and heard him leave. She didn't want to open them and see that he was gone. She imagined him still sitting beside her, his voice still falling and rising in its Pennsylvania Dutch drawl, his lips still pressed against her face, his eyes still soft and dark, watching over her.

Never had she had a birthday where she felt this loved and celebrated. And no one had ever given her a gift as meaningful as the three she'd received tonight.

But all good things come to an end, and tomorrow things would go back to normal. No more Caleb doing her chores. No more leisurely picnic lunches with her husband. No more festive parties with gifts. But the memories of this day would never, never leave her.

— Chapter Thirty-Two —

Kirsten giggled as Silas shook his head. Caleb came bounding around the front of the truck and wrenched the passenger door open. Kirsten slid over to the middle of the long bench seat and found herself tucked pleasantly close to her husband's side. Silas carefully looped the lap belt across her legs and fastened it in the latch next to his.

"Ready to go?" Silas asked Caleb, who merely smiled widely and nodded.

Kirsten felt as if she'd stepped into another world as she watched Silas slip on a pair of very stylish-looking sunglasses. He looked ridiculously handsome. And surprisingly, he was perfectly at ease as he drove down the highway. He casually looped his fingers over the steering wheel and reached his other arm across the back of the seat behind her. For Caleb's sake, she fought the urge to move closer to him.

Not that he would have noticed. Caleb leaned forward on the seat, nearly hanging his head out the window, intently watching the scenery whizzing by. She suspected that he'd begged to come along simply because of the special trip into town, a place Caleb rarely got to go. But now, watching him, she wondered if it wasn't more about the ride in the truck and less about the destination.

Kirsten needed no enticing. Any invitation to spend time with Silas was something she jumped at. Normally, they would use a horse and buggy. But since a stop at the building supply store was on the day's agenda, Silas had decided to use the truck for its extra hauling space. In the past few weeks, several custom furniture orders had come in. A set of kitchen cabinets for a neighboring Amish family, a dining set for a local English family, and a set of rocking chairs for David and Sarah. Judging by the amount of time Silas had spent sketching his plans, it was definitely going to be a lot of work. She wasn't sure how many of her daily visits to the workshop he'd tolerate, but she hoped an extra couple wouldn't bother him too much.

The parking lot was reasonably occupied for a weekday morning. Silas slid out of the truck and turned to help her gently ease off the bench seat to the pavement. They trailed behind Caleb's eager gait, holding hands and strolling in no particular hurry.

When the automatic doors slid open, Kirsten could hardly hear Silas's suggestion that she and Caleb look around for a few minutes while he ordered the lumber. Her heart was hammering as she nervously glanced around at the other customers. She'd expected curious stares and pointing, which she shamefully had to admit to doing herself not so long ago. But much to her relief, not a single person in the store seemed to notice them at all. They were customers—nothing more, nothing less.

Silas purposefully strode away, and she and Caleb selected a cart and moved slowly down the aisles. It was a small store, but Caleb seemed utterly overwhelmed by the contents of the racks and shelves surrounding them. He frequently stopped to stare at one thing or another while Kirsten patiently followed behind with the cart.

They moved into the animal care section and stopped to survey a saddle on display.

"Someday, when I get my own horse, I'm going to buy a saddle from Mark Schwartz," Caleb sighed longingly.

"Oh? When will you get your own horse?"

"Silas got his when he was fourteen," Caleb said, a hint of jealousy in his voice.

"Oh." Kirsten nodded seriously under Caleb's equally serious gaze.

"I could always buy my own, I guess," Caleb smirked. "Silas said if he bought a new horse, he'd give me Midnight," he chirped hopefully.

"How many horses does Silas have?" Kirsten asked curiously. She'd never realized that he might actually own several of the horses in the stable himself. In an Amish family, much of their worldly possessions became community property. Sharing with other plain neighbors was encouraged. Sharing with your own family was pretty much a given.

"Three. Titus, Midnight, and Star," Caleb answered, bending to inspect the factory-made saddle more closely.

"Kirsten?" It was a male voice. And oddly familiar.

Her eyes darted up to the man standing at the opposite end of the short aisle. He was medium height, slightly overweight, and his hair was somewhere in between gray and brown. She knew him. Or she recognized him anyway. And the mere sight of him sent her heart racing.

Richard Webb. Logan's dad.

His cart contained a large bag of expensive dog food and some doggy toys. His face wore a shocked expression as he took in the sight of her dress, apron, and bonnet. Kirsten said nothing in response to his questioning greeting. Caleb seemed to sense Kirsten's discomfort, and when he stood, he moved closer to her, placing his body strategically between Kirsten and the man.

"I...I...uh...didn't realize you were...are..." Logan's father stumbled over his words, still staring open-mouthed at Kirsten.

Kirsten stared back at him, unsure of what to say.

Richard's eyes flicked to Caleb, who still stood in an imperceptibly protective position. If Richard moved, Caleb would undoubtedly also move, keeping himself in the middle.

"How are you doing?" Richard asked, taking the briefest glance at her stomach.

"Very well, thank you." Her voice was strong, but polite.

The dimmest of shadows hovered behind her, and she could see Richard's eyes look past her. But more than anything, Kirsten could simply sense her husband's presence.

"This is my husband, Silas Miller," Kirsten said, turning slightly. "Silas, this is Richard Webb. Logan's father."

Silas's eyes were focused on Richard in a blank-faced stare. He nodded his greeting to Logan's father, who had to look up to see Silas's face, even from several feet away.

"It's nice to meet you," Richard mumbled.

Silas only offered another nod.

"How long have you been married?" Richard asked, clearly stunned.

"Since August," Silas answered.

"Congratulations," Richard mumbled again.

"Thank you." Silas's voice was perfectly calm and clear. Kirsten kept her body turned at such an angle that she could easily see him.

"Well, I, uh, better get going," Richard said, pushing his cart past them. "It was good to see you, Kirsten."

She nodded stiffly in acknowledgment and turned to face Silas. His eyes were now fixed intently on her face. Richard moved out of sight, and Kirsten took a deep, cleansing breath and swallowed audibly.

"Are ya all right?" His voice was close, concerned.

"I'm fine," she said calmly. His gaze lingered on her, and she held his eyes, feeling a new strength nearly pulsing through her.

"Who was that?" Caleb asked, still curiously looking after the inquisitive stranger.

"Richard Webb," Kirsten answered matter-of-factly.

"Oh. So what else do ya need?" Caleb asked, blissfully unaware of who Richard Webb was or why the encounter was so tense.

They moved slowly through the aisles. Silas was careful to keep her close to his side. It was a slightly unnecessary measure, but appreciated nonetheless. In fact, Kirsten felt a great peace simply because of the unexpected meeting. The secret was out now—officially. It wouldn't be long before Logan knew. In fact, Richard had probably dialed his son's cell to pass along the new information before he'd left the store. Really, it made no difference to her. Kirsten's life had changed so dramatically that it felt like a literal lifetime ago when even hearing Logan's name had caused her heartache. His vehement rejection of and revulsion toward her and the baby they'd created had been a twisting knife, perpetually imbedded in her chest.

Until Silas. His tender kindness had suddenly redefined her as someone worthy of love. The opinions of the outside world no longer mattered. Whether Logan loathed her or regretted his actions was of no consequence to Kirsten. As long as he left her and the baby alone—that was all she wanted. That, and her Silas, who was intently reading the label on the container of varnish nestled in his large hands. The urge to wrap her arms around him was practically unbearable.

"I think I might get somethin' in the candy aisle," Caleb stated.

"How about I make you and your handsome brother some fudge when we get home?" Kirsten asked him.

Caleb's eyes opened wide. *"Jah! Jah,* that'd be *gut!"*

Silas grinned and set the can in the cart.

"We'd better get some lunch and get home, then." He smiled at her. Kirsten felt heat rush up her spine at the sound of his voice.

Kirsten hid her surprise at the checkout when Silas swiped a debit card to pay for the lumber and supplies. She wasn't sure what she was expecting, but a shiny plastic bank card wasn't it.

He helped her up into the truck and then backed it up to the loading dock. Less than ten minutes later, he eased into a back spot at McDonald's and Caleb beamed his approval.

It was 11:30 and they'd mostly beaten the lunch crowd. But in this place there were plenty of curious stares and whispered comments. Kirsten merely tucked her hand in her husband's, lacing her fingers through his. He gently squeezed her hand as they waited in line. Caleb volunteered to wait at the counter for their order while they found a table.

Silas slid into the booth next to Kirsten and turned to face her.

"Yer sure yer all right?" he asked.

Kirsten smiled slightly and nodded. "For a long time, I was angry and afraid," she said with a shrug. "But today, I didn't feel that way. He doesn't matter to me anymore." She said the last while looking into Silas's eyes.

He smiled. "So you've forgiven him, then?" he asked quietly.

"What exactly does that mean?" She furrowed her brow as she considered the word.

"That ya release him to God's judgment and hold no anger in yer heart."

"Yeah," Kirsten said, nodding. "That's how I feel."

Silas smiled widely at her just as Caleb rounded the corner and slid the heaping tray onto the table. Kirsten watched him reverently unwrap his burger and give it a long look before picking it up and taking a huge bite, sighing audibly as he chewed.

"I'm savin' room for the fudge," Caleb reassured her, his mouth completely full.

"*Gut*," Kirsten said with a nod. Silas choked on his soda and Caleb gave her a broad smile before taking another enormous bite.

— CHAPTER THIRTY-THREE —

Surely it was just Kirsten's imagination, but even the sky seemed mournful this Sunday morning. Amy nearly dragged herself out to the buggy, plopping heavily in the seat behind Silas and Kirsten. When they pulled into the Beilers' driveway, Kirsten was certain she heard Amy sigh.

It was terribly unfortunate for Amy that it was the Beilers' turn to host the Sunday meeting this particular week.

As soon as they stopped, a young man approached the buggy to help Silas unhitch Titus. The boy looked past Kirsten to peer in at Amy. His face was so sad and apologetic. Not that Amy noticed. She refused to look at him, escaping out the opposite side of the buggy and quickly walking down the lane to the house. Kirsten watched the wordless exchange with wide eyes, finally turning to see that Silas had been doing the same. The boy walked away dejectedly, leading Titus to the pasture gate.

Kirsten stared after him for a few minutes and then slid out into Silas's steadying arms.

"Who was that?" she asked.

"Lucas Beiler." Silas's voice was flat.

"Oh," Kirsten mouthed. That explained a lot. Clearly, Lucas regretted hurting Amy.

They walked further into the farmyard. The house was fantastically huge and set far back from the road. To allow for as much privacy as possible, she guessed.

"How many children do the Beilers have?" Kirsten asked, staring at the giant house.

"Ten," Silas said with an amused grin.

"That's a lot," Kirsten commented.

Silas only grinned wider. "Big families are common for our people. Of course, it makes a difference if ya get an early start."

Kirsten suddenly understood his expression, and her eyes widened at him.

"How many children do you want, Silas?" she asked nervously.

He shook his head, still grinning like a fool. "As many as the *gut* Lord sees fit to give us."

Kirsten took a deep gulp of air.

"They also have a good-sized herd of cattle," Silas said, looking up at the barn. Kirsten followed his gaze. The white barn towered far overhead.

"That is extraordinarily high," she said.

"You should see the view from the top," he replied with a grin.

"Why on earth were you on the top of the Beilers' barn?" she asked, horrified.

"I helped build it. The barn raisin' was four years ago."

"You helped build it," she repeated.

"I worked mostly on the roof," he said with a nod.

"Well, of course you did." She shook her head. It wasn't shocking really. The way he could climb trees, well, Silas had no fear of heights. Something she couldn't necessarily say for herself.

Kirsten was afraid of a lot of things.

❦

Moving around was getting more difficult all the time, and as part of her daily routine, Kirsten had taken to walking up and down the lane to get the mail. Every day, just before lunch, she'd wander past the garden and bring the contents of the white mailbox to the house. These days, the garden was mostly empty. Fall was coming, and the leaves on the trees were beginning to turn. Kirsten particularly loved the walk back to the house. To see her home surrounded by the yellow, red, and orange foliage made her feel like she lived in a postcard.

The cooler air outside was refreshing as she made her way back with the small bundle of mail. She scanned the contents and found there were several bills, a newspaper, and two letters. One of which was address to Silas Miller. Kirsten's fingers smoothed the envelope along his name, which was written in a particularly blocky scrawl.

He was already sitting at the table when she came through the screen door. Kirsten handed the pile of mail to Daniel, who thanked her with a kind smile. Then she handed the single small envelope to Silas, who took it without surprise or pause. He sliced it open with his knife and read it. She watched his face as she helped finish setting the table, but she could discern nothing by his blank expression. To say she was curious about who sent the letter or what it was about would be an understatement.

Everyone clamored around the table and fell silent as Daniel bowed his head. After the "Amen," they made work of filling their plates. Silas's arm smelled of sawdust as he reached for the bread. She wanted to breathe the smell in, but there were too many pairs of eyes that would notice.

"Uncle Isaac has written asking for Caleb and me to come to the barn raisin'," Silas announced.

Caleb's head rose in surprise, a happy grin already stretched across his face. Of course, Kirsten might look equally as happy at the prospect of a day spent with Silas, but that was for a very different reason. In a way, she envied Caleb. She'd often wondered if Silas and his little brother spent the minutes before falling asleep talking together in their room.

"When will that be?" Daniel asked.

"Tuesday through Friday."

"Will ya be able to get a car to drive ya by then?" Daniel inquired.

"I think so. I'll call today," Silas answered in between bites.

"Call a car to drive you where?" Kirsten asked in confusion.

"Missouri," Silas answered.

"Missouri?" she repeated.

"Ya best go down on Monday then," Mary commented.

Kirsten's head swung around in shock to see Silas nod.

"When will you come back?" Even Kirsten could hear the panicky edge in her voice.

"Thursday or Friday sometime," Silas said with his eyes focused on his plate, not perceiving her tone.

"Five days. You're going to be gone for five days?"

Now he raised his head, hearing the hysteria in her words. He glanced at her and nodded, quickly turning back to his food.

"But...but...I have a doctor appointment on Friday," Kirsten protested.

"I could take ya, Kirsten," Mary offered with a sweet smile.

Kirsten stared at her and then abruptly back at Silas, who was still focused on eating.

"But I'll be almost thirty-six weeks!"

He looked squarely at her then.

"You can't leave for five days when I'm thirty-six weeks! " Kirsten argued, the alarm making her voice high. Her breathing was shallow and quick with desperation to make him understand.

The atmosphere around the table changed. Movements slowed and eyes focused on Kirsten, then Silas. But Kirsten barely noticed. She was staring intently, beseechingly at his face. She could see the muscles in his jaw clench.

"You won't really go, right? You'll write back and say you can't make it?" she begged.

He considered her seriously. "No," he answered, his tone determined.

"Kirsten, it will likely be a while before yer baby comes," Mary said, trying to calm her.

But Kirsten ignored her. She stared desperately at Silas as he resumed eating. He was deliberately ignoring her now. Silas, who had never let his attention to her waiver, was blatantly disregarding her. Kirsten's jaw moved, desperate for words but finding none. She bit her trembling lip as the tears stung her eyes. He was determined to go. Even though she'd asked him not to, he still wanted to leave. And somewhere in Missouri, he would be perched on top of an impossibly high barn roof where one wrong step could mean a disaster she could not even begin to fathom.

What could happen to him? What could happen to her?

It was several minutes before she picked up her fork to eat, swallowing each bite without tasting it.

Perhaps he can be reasoned with yet, she thought, trying to calm herself. She'd find a way to convince him to stay. Silas had never truly, harshly refused her anything she'd asked of him. If he understood her fears, her concerns, he wouldn't consider going. She just had to make him understand.

.୶ୡ ୨ୡ.

Silas had no desire to ever endure such an embarrassing and uncomfortable meal as long as he lived. He couldn't for the life of him figure out why Kirsten had gotten so upset. The scene she had caused was even more of a mystery.

He'd resisted the urge to rebuke her in front of everyone, even though she felt free to argue with him in front of his family. He had never seen his mother or sisters-in-law act in a similar manner. Though disagreements between husband and wife came up, they were always handled in private.

Her anxiety over the nearing of the birth was rather unfounded. It would likely be several weeks before her time came. And it wasn't as if he were leaving her at home alone. She'd be surrounded by people totally capable of helping her with whatever she would need in his absence. Truthfully, both his mother and his brothers' wives were far more capable of watching over her, teaching her, and assisting her than he could be.

Besides, this was not a trip without a purpose. When the time came for him to build his own house, he'd need all the help he could get. The more he helped others, the more help he would receive in return.

Her disrespectful arguing smacked of selfishness, which was certainly not an Amish trait. He'd wanted a wife partly for companionship, but any other Amish woman would have understood, accepted, and even rejoiced in opportunities to help neighbors and friends. This clinginess was becoming stifling. It would be nice if Kirsten could just toughen up a bit and not be so needy.

Kirsten Miller still has much to learn about being a gut Amish wife, he thought to himself as he picked up the surface planer and ran it swiftly over the wood.

.ஒ ஓ.

"Silas?" she was careful not to startle him whenever he was in his workshop, lest he be injured. "Can I talk to you?"

He stopped his work, breathing heavily from the effort and *thunked* the planer down onto the bench between them.

"I'm nervous about you being gone so long when I'm this far along," she said after waiting for a response she didn't get.

"You won't be alone," he said without looking at her. He selected a sanding block and started smoothing it briskly over the piece in front of him.

This wasn't what she wanted to hear. He hadn't acknowledged her feelings or concerns. And she already knew she wouldn't be alone. That was obvious every single day of her life. In fact, she could count on one hand how many times she'd been truly alone since she'd married him. Really, the only alone time she had was at night when she went to bed.

"It's just...if something happened and I went early—"

"I'd come home, then." His words came fast. Too fast.

"But you might be too late," she said, her voice barely above a whisper.

"It would be the Lord's will," he answered with a shrug.

He didn't sound the least bit concerned about missing the birth of her baby. The worry in the back of her mind came whispering quietly through the silence between them. Maybe he would feel differently if the child she carried was truly his. If it was Miller blood thrumming through this baby girl's tiny heart, would Silas understand and feel a stronger need to be there the first time she drew a breath or opened her eyes or squealed a cry? What then? Was this just a baby in the way of his future children?

Kirsten tried to listen to the voice of reason above the fearful worry pulsing through her.

"What if something happened to you?" she pleaded.

"It would be the Lord's will," he repeated, not looking at her.

"How many people will be there?" Kirsten asked, hoping a different approach might help him see things her way.

Silas shrugged. "Probably forty or so."

"So you and Caleb wouldn't really be missed if you couldn't..." she stopped, as he was already shaking his head.

"Silas," she choked, "I'm begging you."

"My answer is no," he said without looking at her. She might as well be invisible. He'd barely glanced at her once, and he'd soundly rejected every request, every plea for him to change his mind. He wouldn't change it. She could tell that by the way he stood. In stunned silence, Kirsten turned and shuffled out of the workshop.

◦᧞ℰ 𝟡ℛ◦

At Mary's request, Daniel, Caleb, and Silas were all slated for haircuts in the backyard in the fading light on Saturday evening. Kirsten watched as Mary trimmed the hair first on her husband and then her youngest son. When Silas came out, Mary handed Kirsten the scissors as though she were passing the torch to her successor. Silas lowered himself onto the stool, and Mary fastened the sheet over his shoulders. He heard Kirsten draw a long, deep breath and then felt her fingers deep in his hair, combing through it before she began cutting. Soon he could hear the blades working while her hands pinched sections of his hair between her fingers. Thankfully, Mary stood behind him, watching his wife work. The feeling of her hands in his hair, against his scalp, even sweeping past the back of his neck was ridiculously pleasurable. His eyes involuntarily fluttered closed several times as she worked. By the time she finished with the back, his arms were covered in goose bumps. She came around to face him, and if he peered up through his eyelashes he could watch her work. Kirsten's face was a mask of serious concentration; her eyes narrowed and her lips pressed tightly together. When she was finished cutting, she took her hand and ran it roughly back and forth through his hair, shaking loose the extra strands. He nearly fell off the chair. She undid the sheet and swept it against the back of his neck.

"Well done, Kirsten!" Mary praised. "You have a natural talent for cutting hair, that's fer sure. I should have ya cut Daniel's and Caleb's, too."

Kirsten nodded solemnly. Silas waited for her to meet his eyes so he could smile his thanks, but she busily began cleaning up.

He eventually gave up and walked back to the barn.

She'd made no more attempts to persuade him to stay home. For that, he was thankful. He'd been able to arrange a ride for Monday after lunch. Apart from that, he'd spent long hours in the workshop, attempting to finish a dining room table before he had to leave.

Despite the longer hours in the workshop, Kirsten's visits had almost come to a complete stop. She still brought out an occasional cup of coffee or glass of lemonade, but she didn't stay, and he'd had to bring the mug with him into the house when he came in for lunch. Her world seemed to revolve around the sewing machine, where she was spending countless hours working on those tiny dresses of hers for the baby.

The baby. Kirsten was growing in size, though she still appeared much smaller than other expectant women he'd known. When he'd married her, her pregnancy had hardly been noticeable. Now, only months later, she was showing more, but her shape was still fairly well-concealed by her dress and apron.

The progressing pregnancy was taking its toll on her, slight though she seemed. She had retired to her room earlier than usual these past several days. There had been a distinct weariness on her face when he'd knocked on her door to read to her. She hadn't cuddled next to him as she used to. Instead, she had sat with a careful space between them, her hands folded in her lap.

He was sure that she didn't want him to go. She hadn't changed her mind. But he had not changed his. A little space would be the best thing for her.

— Chapter Thirty-Four —

For once, the preaching seemed to be over in the blink of an eye. But then again, everything seemed to be speeding toward Monday afternoon and Silas's departure. She'd not dared to confront him again, lest he get angry and avoid her even more.

He'd spent so much time in the workshop that she'd come to think of it as his new hiding spot. All day he worked steadily on his projects. Even in the evenings he would escape to the shop for a few more hours of work after supper and before bed. She'd tried to bury herself in her own work. Simple, tiny dresses took her long hours to make, but she was persistent and dogged in her preparation. While other English women would be decorating a nursery, buying jogging strollers, and registering for baby gifts, this was virtually the only thing Kirsten could do for the impending arrival of her daughter.

Of course, her every thought seemed to drift to when that might be. Mary had even started slipping the uncertainties into her sentences, saying things like, "After yer baby comes, we'll get ya started on some new trousers for Silas," or, "Those screens have to come out before the baby does." Kirsten was sure Mary didn't mean to make her nervous, but those little asides were like being hit in the face with an icy snowball.

Silas made his way across the grassy yard to where the Millers had spread out their quilts after lunch. Kirsten watched as he laughed loudly at something Michael had said. Danny broke free from Sarah's arms and ran to Silas with his arms outstretched. Silas smiled broadly and caught him in his run, tossing him high in the air and catching him. Danny squealed with joy, and Silas placed his hat on Danny's little head. A sob caught in Kirsten's throat and she tried to cover it with a forced cough.

Her pleading with him to stay had only driven him further away from her. She could think of a hundred reasons for him to stay; good excuses that anyone would accept without hesitation. But if the baby wasn't enough to keep him here, then nothing would be. So to see him lovingly embrace his nephew was touching, but painful. What was important to her was so much less so to him.

She straightened up as the men approached. Deborah was watching her with a quizzical expression. Kirsten did her best to smile at her, but given how hollow she felt, she doubted it was very convincing.

.୬ℰℐ୭.

On Monday, Caleb was nearly bouncing out of his chair, and it took a stern look from Daniel to calm him down.

"Maybe Uncle Isaac will tell some of his stories again!" Caleb bubbled as he waited for lunch to begin.

Silas looked at the empty chair beside him at the table. Kirsten was late for dinner, which was unusual. She came down a minute later with a flushed face and red eyes.

"I'm so sorry I'm late," she apologized to Daniel. He nodded and began the prayer. Silas pulled her hand into his, but her fingers were cold and her palm was clammy.

Caleb's chatter was temporarily interrupted by his eating.

"You best be careful doin' all yer work," Mary reminded her sons, casting a long look at Caleb. "*Ach*, but it'll be fun for ya, too, seeing yer cousins again."

Silas ate quickly, shoving massive bites into his mouth, knowing the car would be there soon to pick them up.

"Caleb, you listen to yer brother now. Don't be doin' nothing foolish or reckless," Mary chided.

Silas reached past Kirsten to the pitcher of water and noticed she was sitting back. She had a fork in her hand, but the food on her plate was untouched. Her face was paler than he'd ever seen it.

Suddenly, she jumped up and ran from the table, her footsteps loud and hurried on the stairs. A door slammed shut and everyone around the table froze uncomfortably.

Mary stared after her with worry. "She's takin' this mighty hard." She shook her head. Even Silas's father stared at the foot of the stairs, his brow creased with worry.

"She's been sick several times this morning," Amy agreed quietly.

Sick? Why had no one told him? Silas pushed his chair back to follow her just as he heard car tires crunching their way down the lane. He hurried up the stairs and saw the closed bathroom door.

"Kirsten?" he called as he knocked lightly.

No response.

"Kirsten, are ya all right?"

"I'm fine." Her voice was weak, muffled.

"The car is here. I have to go," he said, hoping she'd come out.

"Have a good trip," she said through the door.

Silas stared at the door for several long seconds before reluctantly turning away and thumping down the stairs. Caleb was already sitting in the front passenger seat. Silas dropped his bag in the trunk and slumped into the backseat. Just as he was about to close the door, Kirsten appeared on the porch where the rest of the family had gathered. Silas jumped out of the car and ran up the steps to her.

Her arms were wrapped tightly around one of the posts. He slipped an arm around her back and felt her body trembling. He pressed his lips to her cheek, which smelled strongly of soap.

"I'll be back in a few days," he reminded her, his voice low in her ear. She swallowed hard and stared at the floorboards. Silas forced himself away from her and got into the car. He watched out the back window as his mother wrapped an arm around Kirsten's waist to support her.

He hadn't known she hadn't been feeling well. No one had said. And he'd been too busy, too preoccupied with the upcoming trip and the work to be done in his shop, to notice. With a sick feeling in his stomach, Silas realized he still had much to learn about being a *gut* Amish husband.

.⊛⊛.

There would be no call from him to say that he'd gotten there safely. She'd only find out if there was a problem. And then...well...Kirsten couldn't imagine what would happen to her life.

She lay down on her bed, weary from the goodbye and exhausted from the sudden return of morning sickness. Stress always made her queasy. Even as a young child, she'd frequently missed school due to an upset stomach. This had been especially true in the months after her dad died.

The first trimester of her pregnancy had been hellish. Dr. Burke had considered expensive prescription medications to control the vomiting and help her gain weight. But then school had let out, and the nausea had left. Living at the Millers' under Silas's care had brought her great relief and the ability to enjoy Mary's outstanding cooking. She'd thought she'd kicked the queasiness for good—until this morning when she'd spotted the packed bags waiting in the kitchen.

In her condition, four days without him was scary enough. But that he seemed utterly unconcerned about her feelings or fears and had basically ignored her appeals stung painfully.

Exhaustion overtook her, and she jerked awake to find it was nearly supper time. She shuffled to the stairs but stopped when she saw the open door to his room. She tiptoed down the hall, past the stairs, and stepped in. The bed was perfectly made. It smelled like him. The suspenders normally tossed on his bedpost were gone—probably on his body. His Sunday suit coat hung on its peg along the wall. Kirsten trailed her fingers over it. His arm had been so steady and strong that evening of their wedding day. He'd seen her fear then and taken her aside to calm her. Kirsten's eyes drifted around the room and spied the empty nightstand. He'd taken his Bible with him then. There'd be no one to read to her tonight.

Quickly, she turned and rushed from the room and down to the table. Mary gave her a small, hopeful smile. Daniel prayed and Kirsten sat at the bustling table, surrounded by dear, sweet people, feeling utterly alone.

⚬⚬⚬

Kirsten would hate this, Silas wryly thought to himself as he and Caleb ate breakfast with the other men gathered for the barn raisin'. Straw hats, blue shirts, black trousers. Nearly all of them in identical homespun clothing. *I'd be utterly invisible to her*, he thought, fighting a smile. He pictured that first day—their wedding day—when he'd raised his head to see her searching for him, the frantic, almost panicked, look in her eyes when he'd spotted her.

And then it hit him. That was the look he'd seen on her face yesterday when he'd left. She'd been afraid. Desperately afraid. But of what? There wasn't anything left for her to fear. She'd faced every fear that she'd had—doing chores, driving a buggy, sewing a baby gown, going to Sunday meetings. She'd soundly faced them all. In fact, the one that he'd thought would undo her had proved to do just the opposite. She'd faced Richard Webb with a calm strength not even Silas had felt at that moment. The only thing left to get through was the birth of the baby she carried. Perhaps thinking of the birth made her nervous. He could understand if it did. Truthfully, it made him nervous.

But he'd watched her carefully as she'd faced each one of those other obstacles, realizing she was stronger than she understood. He'd been right there by her side, and she'd never cracked under pressure. He had been careful not to do it for her—not to fight her battles—but he'd been there in case she couldn't handle it.

Of course, now he was a long way from her side. All his promises that she wouldn't be alone hadn't helped to comfort her. She'd been desperate for him to stay. It was the one thing she had ever asked him for. And he'd denied her.

He'd tried to soften it by telling her that whatever happened would be the Lord's will. That was calming to him. The Most High God was in control. Nothing would happen without the will of his Father in Heaven. But to Kirsten, who did not know God, it must have seemed like he was brushing her off. She had no faith to cling to as he did, so instead she clung to him. And he'd shaken her off.

Why couldn't he have given her some reassurance? Promised her that he would come running to her side if she needed him? Told her how deeply he wanted to be there whenever she needed him. Because truly, he did. Being close to him was important to her. And it was to him as well. If he'd only taken her aside, listened to her, calmed her, held her... but he'd left. Left and told her the future was in God's hands—a God she didn't yet know, love, or trust.

Silas nearly choked on the realization of what she must feel. She hadn't been so utterly busy with dress-making. She had withdrawn, retreated, recoiled; she had pulled back into her own world, where the only person she could depend on was herself. It hadn't worked so well for her before.

Kirsten's history was full of people who had left her for one reason or another. Now he was among them.

Silas pinched his eyes shut and shook his head. He hoped Kirsten Miller was a patient woman, because as clumsy as he'd just been with her tender heart, he doubted he knew the very first thing about being a *gut* Amish husband.

With a steady eye on Caleb, Silas handled his frustration the only way he knew how—by working hard. Just months ago, his ruthless toiling had been an attempt to rid himself of thoughts of her. Now it was to punish himself for not thinking enough of her.

It worked, in a way. By suppertime, he was nearly hanging over his plate in exhaustion.

"Silas, I've never seen anyone work like you do," Uncle Isaac announced in a voice much like Daniel's. "You run instead of walk, lift more than ya should, and ya practically run up the beams to get to the roof."

Silas shrugged off the compliment, if that's what it was. As far as he was concerned, he didn't deserve one ounce of praise for the way he had behaved.

"Yer still awfully quiet though. I thought maybe a wife would get ya talkin'." Isaac's eyes twinkled at him.

"Oh, he talks to his wife!" Caleb quipped. This won him a round of laughter from his uncle, aunt, and cousins. And a healthy glare from Silas.

"How is she adjusting to the plain life?" Isaac asked with undisguised curiosity. It was a question Silas had gotten more times than he could count. Nearly every encounter with any of his friends and neighbors had led to similar inquiries.

"Very well," he answered honestly.

"What does she miss of the English life?" his uncle prodded.

Silas considered the question for a long moment. David had once asked the same thing, and Silas had made a joke. But Kirsten had never told him or anyone what, if anything, she missed from her former life. She'd always seemed so...content. Even grateful for the goodness of living simply.

"She seems very happy," he said finally, wincing slightly as a vision of her face on the porch just yesterday haunted him.

"It had to be tough though," his cousin said suddenly, "to go from English to Amish. It's one thing to give up what ya don't even know is there, it's another to give up all the comforts of the outside for less."

Uncle Isaac nodded. "Plenty of Amish go English, but very few English go Amish. I've only known one other person who's done it."

Silas sat, quietly absorbing the thought. Kirsten had left her former life without looking back. She'd given up a great deal for him and never once complained. In fact, she had melded into the family almost effortlessly.

Before, she'd spent her evenings alone, watching television or reading a book. Now she sat in a dimly lit house, playing board games and listening to stories. Before, she'd driven into town or wherever she wanted to go on a whim. Now she enjoyed buggy rides. She'd been alone for much of the last ten years. Now she was nearly constantly surrounded by people—a family.

It was amazing, astounding. She had never complained, even when she had a right to. And he suddenly saw it for what it was—an act of her love for him.

— CHAPTER THIRTY-FIVE —

Kirsten woke early and saw the others off. Daniel, Mary, Anna, and Amy were to spend the day at the market, and Shelby was off to school. Kirsten would be alone at the farm, but only until Michael finished with milking. Then he was coming to pick her up to spend the day with Deborah. As glum as Kirsten felt, the idea of a whole day with her sister-in-law, her friend, cheered her.

In the hushed quiet of the empty farm, Kirsten slowly wandered around in the crisp, late September air. Almost involuntarily, her feet wandered to Silas's workshop. The sawdust still hung in the air and lazily drifted in the streaks of morning sunlight that poured in through the bank of east-facing windows. The smell of wood was rich and warm—like Silas after an afternoon of work.

She stepped through the aisle of workbenches, his tools looking as though he'd just put them down and stepped out for a moment. Past the workbenches, in a large open area with a sliding door, sat the in-progress trestle dining table. It was unfinished, the raw oak waiting for the touch of his skilled hands to bring out the richness of the color and the variations in the wood. She smoothed her hand over the surface, as if she were wiping it clean after a meal. It was smooth, butter-soft to the touch. At nearly eight feet long without the three additional twelve-inch leaves, it would be an impressive set when he finished. In fact, she rather hated to see it go.

The sound of a buggy brought her scurrying outside to see Michael pulling up.

"Silas ask ya to get started on the chairs for the dining set?" Michael joked.

"No," Kirsten laughed, surprising herself. "I'm quite sure I'm not even remotely qualified for such a thing."

Michael helped her up and they started down the road.

"Do you know who owns that little abandoned farmyard down the road?" Kirsten asked as they rattled toward Michael and Deborah's house.

Michael's eyes widened. "You mean the kissin' corner?"

"The what?" Kirsten gasped.

"Silas didn't tell ya it was called the kissin' corner?" Michael laughed.

"No!" Kirsten was sure she was blushing.

"*Jah*, I know who owns it. They're a *gut* family." Michael smiled to himself. "Have ya been there often?" he teased. Kirsten had only ever been teased in school, and then it had been painful. But Michael's gentle ribbing was different, and somehow she knew he'd sooner shoot his own horse than hurt her feelings.

"Oh, all the time. Silas proposed there," she stated matter-of-factly.

Michael's laughter echoed loudly inside the buggy.

"That Silas is full of surprises," he said finally.

Deborah was delighted, as usual, to see her. And though the light-hearted conversation with Michael had momentarily made Kirsten forget the ache in her chest, Deborah's gentleness and warmth brought it sweeping back in like a cold draft.

"What's the matter with ya lately, Kirsten? Yer not yerself," Deborah prodded as Kirsten watched Deborah's knitting needles closely.

Kirsten tried to swallow them back, but she felt the tears rising. "I begged him not to go," she finally choked.

Deborah looked at her sympathetically. "And he went anyway," she finished what Kirsten couldn't even say.

Kirsten only nodded.

"I don't imagine he wanted to leave ya. In fact, I suspect yer the reason he went," Deborah soothed Kirsten as her knitting needles clacked together.

"What do you mean?"

"I think that Silas is fixing to build a house for ya one day. If he helps his friends and relatives, they'll be more inclined to help him when the time comes."

A house. Silas was going to build her a house. This was something Kirsten had never once considered. On some level, it made sense. They couldn't really stay at Daniel and Mary's forever. If they had more children, well, they'd have to have more room. She'd been so totally focused on simply delivering the baby that she'd almost forgotten Silas's comments about having as many children as the Lord would give him.

"He doesn't ever leave ya, and I'm thinking he's probably half out of his head for ya about now." Deborah smiled, her eyes focused on her knitting.

Kirsten suddenly felt foolish and extremely selfish.

"I argued with him in front of...everyone," she confessed.

"We all have our...disagreements," Deborah said with a shrug. "Maybe next time you just talk it out in private."

"So you don't think I'm a horrible wife?" Kirsten asked desperately.

Deborah sternly looked her in the eye. "Now Kirsten Miller, ya miss yer husband when he's gone. Ya had a little disagreement. You'll make it right when he gets home. Ya have nothing to be ashamed of."

Kirsten's mind spun. "You really think he wants to build me a house?" she squeaked. It was just too fantastic to believe.

"I think Silas wants a home with a wife and lots of children. That day gets nearer all the time." Deborah knew, of course, that Kirsten was a wife in only certain respects, and her comments were a direct attempt to make Kirsten see that things would change one day.

"Ah, Kirsten, the Miller men had a great example of a *gut* marriage. Silas will make things right."

"I wish our story was more like Daniel and Mary's, or yours and Michael's," Kirsten sighed.

Deborah dropped her knitting and grabbed Kirsten's hands. "There is nothing wrong with yer story. One day you'll see that. It's just not yers to write." Her voice was soft and sincere, and Kirsten couldn't help but believe her.

That evening, on the way home, Kirsten turned to Michael.

"I want you to know that I think your wife is the kindest, most sincere and wonderful woman that I have ever known. I know it hasn't been... easy to welcome me into the family. But thank you for allowing her to see me. Her friendship means the world to me."

Michael was clearly surprised by her speech, and for a long while he was quiet. Finally, he shook his head. "She loves you too, ya know."

Kirsten was slightly more cheerful at supper, but the empty chair next to her still made her ache for Silas's company. She was busy washing dishes when she heard the distant ring of the phone in the barn.

"Kirsten! Kirsten! It's Silas!" Amy cried, bursting through the door.

Kirsten felt her knees go weak. She couldn't move or think. Amy stared at her and then lightly shook her shoulders.

"Well, are ya going to take his call or not?"

Kirsten forced her legs to move across the yard to the barn.

"Hello?" her voice was shaky and breathless in the receiver.

"Kirsten Miller?"

"Y-yes."

"It's *gut* to hear yer voice." It was him. Her Silas.

"Yours, too."

"So how are ya?" His words were low and quiet.

"I'm good. I miss you."

He paused. "I miss you, too."

There was an awkward pause, and Kirsten waited for him to say something. She didn't know where to begin. And poor Silas was completely unaccustomed to talking conversationally on the phone.

"You found a phone?" she said finally.

"*Jah.* It's Ezekiel's. My cousin."

"A cell phone?"

"*Jah,*" he answered.

"*Rumspringa?*"

"Yup," he laughed. She drank in the sound.

"Hurry and finish that barn, Silas Miller," she commanded gently.

"I'll be home Thursday night." His voice was even lower now.

"Promise?" she begged.

"*Jah*. I promise."

"Silas...I...I miss you," she stuttered.

She could almost hear him smile. "Good night, Kirsten."

"Good night," she choked, clutching the receiver in a white-knuckled grip.

Slowly, she hung up the phone and pried her fingers from the receiver. She leaned her forehead against the barn wall.

He had cared enough to do something she was sure he'd never done before. Perhaps he'd wanted to hear her voice as much as she had his. It had been a little awkward, but then they had never required a lot of words. Quiet togetherness was often enough. Even now, after such a precious gift as a phone call, she ached to snuggle into him and listen to his breathing, always so slow and steady. He cared. As much as she had felt him withdrawing, he'd reached across hundreds of miles to let her know that he really did care. Her throat burned, and a trail of hot tears blazed down her face as she hid against the wall.

"Kirsten? Is Silas all right?" Daniel was close behind her. She whirled around and wiped at her eyes until she was able to see the fatherly concern in his.

"Oh...um...yes. He's fine." She sniffled and wiped her eyes on her apron. "I'm just...I'm just..." She gave up on words and shrugged.

"You miss him." Daniel's expression relaxed into a gentle smile on his bearded face.

Kirsten nodded and stared at her feet, feeling very young and foolish.

"Come sit," he said, waving to a bench in the corner. "Did ya ever hear of the time I went to help my brother—Uncle Isaac—with his barn raisin'?"

Kirsten shook her head.

"David was only three months old, and Mary asked me not to go. But I did. While I was gone, David got sick. Don't remember what it was, but Mary spent five days and nights with that screamin' boy. Wasn't much left of her when I came home. She was angry with me for a while, but we talked it out."

"So you don't think I'm a bad wife for asking Silas to stay?" Kirsten had asked the same question of Deborah, but somehow Daniel's opinion mattered just as much to her.

"No, no. I think yer a young wife with a young husband. It takes some time to figure things out."

It made sense. And Daniel was nothing if not sensible. It seemed no one thought she was a failure for the way she'd handled things. Now all she wanted was for her husband to come home so she could tell him she was sorry for causing such a fuss.

"Dad?"

"Jah?" He had moved to get up, but he sat back down.

"What does 'if it's the Lord's will' mean?" she asked. She had tried desperately to unwrap that phrase, but she still didn't understand it.

"Did Silas say that to ya?"

She nodded.

"I imagine Silas was putting you in the best possible hands—the only ones that could truly care for you and protect you when he couldn't. God is in control. Silas knows that and trusts Him to watch over ya."

So it hadn't been just a little phrase he'd thrown out to dismiss her. According to his faith, this was the greatest thing he could do—place her in God's hands. She didn't know what that meant or who this God really was. Why God seemed so ambivalent to the world around her was a mystery. She'd prayed plenty of times and been disappointed. Then again, she'd asked for him—for Silas—and against all odds, she'd been granted that one request.

Kirsten paused to stare up at the star-filled sky as she walked back across the yard to the house.

As far as the heavens are above the earth, so great is His love for those who fear Him. Silas feared Him. Kirsten was sure that meant God loved Silas in a fairly limitless way. That, at least, was something she could identify with.

⋆⊚⊚⋆

"I bet it's nice to have a wife," Ezekiel said, leaning back on his lawn chair and taking a drag off his cigarette.

Silas smiled, knowing what his cousin meant but mindful of young Caleb sitting next to him.

"You should try it someday, Zeke," Silas said, dodging a subject he was not fully qualified to speak on.

"I suppose I should," Ezekiel sighed. Then, sucking long on his cigarette, he laughed. "One of these days."

Ezekiel was only nine months younger than Silas, but still very much in the middle of his *Rumspringa*—his running-around years. Judging by the pack of cigarettes and cell phone he always carried, he wasn't in any hurry to run home and get baptized.

"You ever meet the guy who got her pregnant?" Ezekiel asked as a cloud of smoke billowed above his head.

Silas shook his head, desperate to avoid this discussion.

"And he doesn't want the baby?" Zeke asked.

Silas shook his head again.

"But you do?" Zeke asked with a raised eyebrow.

"*Jah.* I want both of them."

"What'll ya do if she doesn't ask for baptism?" Zeke's question was a good one, one Silas didn't even want to consider.

Silas shrugged. "It's in God's hands."

Zeke didn't press the question, but that night in bed, Caleb pushed him further.

"Why don't ya just tell her what she needs to do, Silas?" he whispered into the dark.

Silas was quiet for a long time. "I don't want her to just go through the motions. I want for her to really, truly find faith in God and seek baptism out of love for Him. To believe in her heart and not just her head."

"But what if she never does? She'd be shunned," Caleb said after several quiet moments.

"I have to believe that God gave me this...love for her and opened these doors for a reason," Silas answered.

"David said maybe God was testing you..." Caleb dared.

"Maybe He was or is. That doesn't mean I wasn't supposed to marry her. Maybe my test was if I trusted him enough to marry her, knowing what could happen." David's doubt didn't surprise him. He'd expected more of it at first. Michael and Deborah's unconditional acceptance of Kirsten had, quite frankly, shocked Silas. Amy was no longer angry, but nor was she loving. Caleb, Shelby, and Anna had, on the other hand, been completely taken with her. Daniel and Mary, too, had a tremendous fondness for this new daughter that had forsaken her life to live theirs.

"What will ya do if Kirsten is shunned?" Caleb's whisper hung in the dark.

Silas squeezed his eyes shut at the thought. "I'll go."

"But you would be…" Caleb croaked.

"I know," Silas said, cutting him off.

It had been Silas's decision alone not to tell her—something he didn't regret. If she knew that she had a limited amount of time to learn not just the Amish ways, but to come to faith and request baptism, she'd do it just for him—just to give him what he wanted. That he was absolutely certain of.

Instead, he had chosen and was still choosing to allow God to work out His will in Kirsten's life in His perfect timing. If she came to accept Jesus as her Savior, then it would be because God had brought her there and not because she wanted to make her husband happy.

That Kirsten find a real, true, and personal faith in the Lord was more important to him than whether or not their earthly life would be Amish.

— CHAPTER THIRTY-SIX —

She was standing on the porch in the fading daylight, her dress blowing gently on her legs.

"She's waitin' for ya." Caleb grinned as they pulled into the lane.

Silas nodded and grinned back as they pulled closer, suddenly nervous and remembering the way they'd left things. But then, she hadn't sounded angry on the phone. Hopefully, he'd soon have a chance to apologize for his part in the mess.

Despite his nerves, or because of them, he was nearly out of the car before it had stopped moving. His long strides quickly covered the distance between them. Very quickly. He leapt onto the porch and slid his arms gently around Kirsten while she reached hers up to wrap around his neck. She buried her face in his chest and he simply held her.

Neither of them spoke. He could feel the tension in her arms as she held him tightly. He tightened his hold on her but tried not to hurt her.

Caleb wandered inside with the rest of the family, but still Silas stayed on the porch and held Kirsten to him.

"I won't leave ya again," he murmured.

"I understand why you did," Kirsten said, tipping her head back to look up at him.

He looked down into her face and brushed his thumb along her jaw, curling his long fingers behind her neck. Sometimes at night, he'd had trouble remembering what she looked like. Tonight, he drank in the sight of her. Her long eyelashes, her deep brown eyes, her pale skin dotted with a few freckles, and her full lips. How many times had he dreamed of kissing her? It would be impossible to count.

"Let's have some dessert," Mary announced to the family loudly enough that Silas could hear her.

He reluctantly dropped his arms and followed Kirsten inside. Chocolate brownies, still warm from the oven and covered in vanilla ice cream and homemade caramel sauce, were placed in front of everyone. Caleb excitedly told of all their barn-raising adventures. Silas smiled at his enthusiasm and added a comment every now and again. Kirsten sat much closer than necessary, and he had to be careful not to elbow her. Not that he minded. He'd been away from her for too long, and he felt a dangerous need to be close to her.

She was washing the dessert dishes when he came downstairs from unpacking. He rested his hands on her shoulders and leaned close.

"Come with me," he whispered into her ear.

He led her to the porch and eased his weary body onto the swing. Kirsten curled up next to him, her legs resting against his. He wrapped an arm around her, and she pressed her face into his neck.

For a long time, neither of them spoke. Silas gently pushed the swing into motion, and they listened to the voices and laughter coming from the house. Eventually, the bedtime commotion quieted and grew silent. He was tired, but he was not ready to leave her. He had never been, would never be, ready to leave her.

"I'm sorry I worried you," he finally murmured. "I shoulda been more compassionate."

"I'm sorry I argued with you in front of your family and that I was so selfish," she said, her breath soft against his throat.

"I missed you," he sighed.

"I missed you, too." She was smiling; he could hear it in her voice.

"You're tired," Kirsten whispered after a while.

"Mmmm."

"You should go to bed," she said, turning her head to whisper in his ear. Silas got goose bumps. Bed was precisely where he wanted to go. Though not without her.

He moved to look at her soft, brown eyes, wishing that, at least for tonight, he could allow himself to be a real husband to her. He blinked too long, and Kirsten stood, pulling him to his feet. She tugged on his hand to follow her inside, but he stood his ground, pulling her close to him instead.

He stroked the side of her face with one hand and kissed her jaw, then beneath her ear, her temple, her forehead, and between her eyes.

"Good night, Kirsten," he whispered in her ear.

Before he could change his mind, he pulled her quickly into the house and up the stairs. With one last kiss on the cheek, she went to her room. Alone.

⚬⚬⚬

"Abraham was a little...crazy. Don't you think?" Kirsten asked.

Silas smiled but kept his attention on Titus as the horse pulled them toward home and a welcome Sunday nap.

"I mean, who would do something like that? Sacrifice your only child? These days, he'd be committed to a mental institution," she trailed off.

She glanced over and saw a strange look pass over his face.

"The Bible is full of people of great faith who did seemingly...crazy things out of obedience to God. In the end, their faith was rewarded."

Kirsten nodded. "Like Noah. I can only imagine the flack he must've gotten for building a huge boat in the middle of nowhere."

Silas appeared to be momentarily frozen, and his eyes widened. "Where did you hear about Noah? That wasn't in the preachin'."

"Silas Miller, you were gone for four days and three nights, and there was no one to read to me. I took matters into my own hands."

It was several minutes before he could overcome his shock.

"*Jah*, Noah is a *gut* example. Also Moses, Joshua, Gideon, Daniel, Elisha. And others."

"Okay, I don't know about those. You're going to have to tell me where those stories are."

Silas smiled broadly and bobbed his head.

Kirsten had tried to find the parts he'd read to her and succeeded in locating a few of them. But then she'd wandered through other portions of her new Bible, wondering if it was all so poetic. It wasn't, of course. But the stories she'd read in Genesis had truly fascinated her all the same.

"You believe it? I mean you believe that all that stuff in the Bible happened?" she asked him.

"Every word," he said gently, but firmly.

"Why?" She couldn't help but ask.

"I believe Scripture is the very word of God."

"Is there a God?" she asked, unsure.

"I believe there is," he began, then paused to look at her seriously. "I have a great peace and assurance that a loving God fashioned and formed the earth. I believe He loves us, cares for us, and provides for us. And I believe that He sent His only son to die for my sin."

"But where's your proof?" Kirsten asked, hoping her skepticism wouldn't upset him.

Silas shook his head and smiled. "God doesn't need to prove anything to me. But I do see evidence of His existence everywhere, all the time."

The words were nice and heartfelt. But Kirsten was hoping for something more solid, something she couldn't deny. She wanted to push further, question him until he said something that helped her see things his way, but she didn't know what else to ask.

"Do you read your Bible often, Silas?" she finally inquired.

"Every night," he answered with a grin and a wink. "And then I read some in bed before I fall asleep."

"And does that...help you understand God...or believe in Him?"

"Yes." He smiled to himself now. "Very much."

If she was ever going to fully know and understand Silas, she'd have to become much better acquainted with this God of his.

— CHAPTER THIRTY-SEVEN —

The weather had turned much cooler, and the fall produce was ready for harvest. David had invited them all over for a pumpkin-harvesting party. It would take many hours, but the work was almost always fun and lighthearted. Today, it would be especially so, given the golden sunshine that was almost unseasonably warming the air. Still, Silas tossed an extra lap robe in the buggy before he pulled it up to the house. By nightfall, the temperature would quickly drop, and even though it was a very short ride to David and Sarah's farm, Silas would take no chances with Kirsten in this stage of her pregnancy. She'd offered to walk with the rest of the family, but he'd insisted that the two of them take the buggy, just in case.

She stepped up into the buggy with his assistance and got settled in the seat next to him. He'd ridden in buggies all his life, but not until he'd taken her for that first ride had he realized how enjoyable buggy rides were. A basket of freshly baked rolls sat on Kirsten's lap. The feast wouldn't take place until after the pumpkins had all been gathered into the wagons. They always sold well at the market, where they would be lined up outside the store.

"Ya won't try to lift anything too heavy, will ya?" he asked, smiling at her as they neared the farm where the family had already gathered.

"Hmm...no. I've learned that lesson a time or two." She twisted her mouth in embarrassment. "I'll make sure to take it easy," she reassured him with a smile.

Silas nodded, satisfied. His warning was only partly necessary. There would not be a minute when he wasn't watching her. If she tried to do anything remotely difficult, he'd intervene.

All of them were soon out in the pumpkin patch. Even Johnny was toddling around, picking up tiny pumpkins and carefully setting them in five-gallon buckets. Shelby and Anna, too, were busy finding smaller pumpkins to carry to the wagons David had parked along the edge of the field. Caleb was determined to find the biggest pumpkin and carry it himself. Silas was greatly relieved to see that Kirsten only selected pumpkins that Shelby or Anna could carry.

The work was not easy, but they had a marvelous time, laughing and working together as they always had. Even stern Sarah was smiling and laughing as Michael tossed a large pumpkin to Caleb and he struggled to catch it before toppling over.

The meal was a potluck of sorts. Everyone contributed something. Kirsten's homemade bread rolls sat in a small basket on the table. When it came time for dessert, Silas's mother set out a large bowl amongst the pies and plates of cookies.

"Oh dear," Kirsten sighed as she spied the bowl.

Mary patted Kirsten's arm and smiled.

"What's the matter, Kirsten?" Deborah asked curiously.

"That," Kirsten said, pointing to the bowl, "was supposed to be a pumpkin layer cake. But I did something wrong because the layers wouldn't stack and it all just fell apart." Kirsten nervously bit her lip.

"Happens to all of us," Deborah laughed, and soon Kirsten smiled widely, enjoying her own flop and laughing as she shook her head.

Silas wisely chose a piece of cherry pie and a large scoop of Kirsten's pumpkin-cake dessert. He carried his plate to the picnic table outside, where his brothers had gone with the children in the fading light of the day.

Soon the women came out with knit caps for the children. Kirsten appeared behind him and began collecting the dessert plates.

"You know, it was the funniest thing. I had just spotted a large pumpkin, but when I turned around to go get it, it was gone," Michael said mysteriously. "I strongly suspect Kirsten smuggled it out of the field." Silas shook his head as his brother smiled mischievously.

Kirsten rounded the table, snatched Michael's fork and plate, and said, "Oh no you don't, Michael Miller! You must be mistaken. See, it was your wife, innocent though she may seem, who smuggled the pumpkin. I was duly warned that I had enough to carry already."

Michael threw his head back and laughed loudly. David smirked, and Silas could only grin at his wife as she winked at him.

"Might need some help re-roofing my workshop before it snows," David said after a while.

"I thought you were going to hire the Beilers to do that," Michael said quizzically.

David kicked uneasily at the rocks on the driveway. "Seems they don't really want the job. Said they're too busy." David turned suddenly and looked directly at Silas. "Actually, I think it's more than that. Word has it that Lucas Beiler was courting our sister until Silas here got married to an *Englischer*."

While everything he said might have been true, David wasn't supposed to talk about such things. Who courted whom was considered a secret. Even if a family knew or suspected, they never spoke of a beau until the couple had decided to marry. Silas averted his gaze, feeling the heated remarks from his brother.

"Have ya talked to yer wife, Silas?" David asked pointedly.

"I talk to her every day," Silas answered levelly.

"About fixing the mess our family is in, I mean," David argued, apparently unwilling to let the subject go.

Silas shook his head.

"You know, you set a dangerous precedent. You not only interacted with an English girl, but ya fell for her and then married her! How long before the other young people see what you were allowed to do and our community is harmed by more outsiders?" David railed.

"This was different," Silas said quietly.

"Different, maybe. But not wise. There were plenty of nice Amish girls you could have chosen. But you chose a pregnant English woman who can't cook, can't keep a home, and doesn't know a thing about our ways. You were suddenly so eager to be a husband that ya made a hasty decision. Hasty decisions make messy mistakes. And now our whole family is paying for it."

Anger rolled inside of Silas, and he swallowed hard, shaking his head while David spoke. Michael silently sat by, his face a mask of serious concern. Whether he agreed or not, Silas couldn't say. The silence lingered oppressively for several long minutes until Caleb strolled over and sat beside Silas. The brothers' heated discussion had gone unnoticed, and his little brother was oblivious to the tension at the picnic table.

"I'm going to sleep *gut* tonight." Caleb stretched his long arms high over his head. "Unless Silas starts snoring again," he teased lightheartedly.

"How would ya know if Silas is snoring?" David snorted.

Caleb instantly fell silent and shot a panicked look at Silas.

David caught the look and his mouth fell open. Michael was quiet, but he seemed unsurprised.

"You don't share a room with yer wife?" David asked incredulously.

Silas could feel the skin on his face burning. He made no response to David's bold question. This wasn't his business. None of it was. It was true that his marriage had impacted the family, but that did not mean the details of it were public information.

Silas quickly stood and walked inside the empty house. He filled a glass with water and chugged it down, desperate to calm the fury that boiled inside him. As his anger settled, he realized he could hear Caleb clearly through the open kitchen window. Looking down, he noticed that only half the dishes had been washed—the dirty ones were still piled on the counter next to the sink.

Kirsten. Where was she? Last he'd seen her, she'd been collecting plates to wash them. No. No, no, no. Had she overheard David's harsh words? He prayed not.

Silas quickly turned and went to find her. He was about to go upstairs when he saw her standing quietly, statue-still at the window on the opposite side of the house.

"Kirsten?"

She did not speak or turn around, but she looked down at her shoes.

Silas struggled for words, desperate to say something. The silence stretched between them. David had accused him of harming their community, setting a dangerous precedent, hurting the family, making a mistake, and marrying a woman only because he wanted someone in his bed. Silas did not know how much she had heard, and his mind swam with thoughts on what he could say to ease her pain.

Kirsten drew a deep, silent breath. "I'd like to go home." Her voice was thick, muddled. Silas's stomach dropped.

"Please?" came her quiet plea.

"I'll get the buggy," he said, taking a step to her, but stopping. She needed comfort, but more than that, she needed to leave—to get away.

Minutes later, he pulled the buggy up to the yard. Kirsten was already walking to meet him. Deborah moved to catch her before she left, but she stopped awkwardly when she saw Kirsten's face. Before Silas could get out to help her in, Kirsten had climbed clumsily into the seat next to him, handing him an empty bowl and basket. He quickly tucked the lap blanket around her and wordlessly drove them off the yard.

They were silent all the way home. He stole a few glances at her, but she was stone-faced and withdrawn.

He stopped the buggy by the house. Kirsten peeled the blanket off and carefully stepped out, accepting his hand but not looking at him. She quickly walked up the steps and disappeared into the house. He stared after her for a few minutes and then flicked the reins, urging Titus to the horse barn. Before he went inside, he grabbed the empty bowl and basket. There had been some pumpkin dessert left. Had she thrown it away? He hoped not. It was a mess of frosting and pumpkin cake crumbled together, but it had tasted good. Had she heard the comment about her not being able to cook? How many insults had she endured, alone in the shadows of the kitchen?

He set the bowl and basket on the table and sighed. He'd wanted to shield her from pain. But it seemed that pain just followed Kirsten. He slowly climbed the steps, finding that her door was firmly shut. He moved down the hall to his room, stripped off his shirt to his undershirt, and dropped his suspenders off his shoulders.

Noiselessly, he crept down the hall and stood at her door, waiting to hear if she was moving about. He thought he heard a sniffle.

"Kirsten?" he called softly through the door. "May I come in?"

It was deathly quiet for several long moments, and then the door creaked open. He couldn't see her face clearly in the unlit doorway. She was wearing her nightgown, her hair in a long, uncharacteristic braid. Most Amish women wore braids at night. His own mother and sisters braided their hair before bed every night. But Kirsten never had.

Until now. Why now?

He followed her into her room and watched as she wordlessly climbed beneath the covers, her back to the door. What could he say to her? What words would heal her? His legs moved to her side of the bed so he could see her face. He lowered himself to the floorboards, kneeling beside her bed in the same position he had been in when he had received baptism. The water had poured down over his head and face and neck that day. But tonight, tears trailed down the face of his wife. She did not sob or make any sound at all. But tear after tear spilled down her nose, dripping onto the quilt clenched in her fist.

"You heard?" he finally asked, his voice raspy.

She stared at his chest and slowly blinked once, sending another tear spilling down her face.

Silas reached up and brushed the tears from the corner of her eye.

"I'm sorry," she whispered, her lip trembling.

"No. You have nothing to be sorry about," he gently argued. "I'm the one who's sorry. I'm sorry you were hurt...by my own brother."

"He was right," she said, closing her eyes.

Silas waited until he felt like he could breathe without choking. "No. He wasn't." Silas slowly stroked the side of her face. "Kirsten I didn't marry you because ya were pregnant, or because ya needed to be rescued, or because I was in a hurry to be a husband. I married you because in my heart I knew you were the one God meant for me. I cared about you then, and you can only imagine how much more I care about ya now."

Kirsten finally met his eyes. She reached up and took his hand from her face, lacing their fingers together. He held her hand gently and watched as the tears continued to fall, even as her eyes closed and her breathing deepened. After a deep, shuddering breath, the tears stopped and she fell asleep. He watched her for a long time, not releasing her hand until he was sure she was asleep.

How could things have gone so quickly from their laughter and joy in the pumpkin patch to the brokenhearted girl who slept soundly before him? She'd gone from laughing at her dessert to feeling such shame that she threw it away. Silas stared at her for several long moments before he stood and untied the band on the end of her braid. Slowly, without waking her, he untwisted her hair until it lay in loose waves over her pillow. Kirsten was anything but a mistake to him. In fact, he was reasonably sure that marrying her was one of the wisest things he had ever done.

⋆ை☙⋆

Sunday morning dawned dim and overcast. It looked like it might rain, but the sky simply hung heavily all day. Since it was a no-preaching Sunday, Kirsten went for a morning walk with Silas. They meandered down the road, stopping at the top of Michael and Deborah's driveway.

"Should we go say hello?" he asked, turning to her with genuine concern.

Kirsten nodded and gripped his hand tighter as they very slowly made their way down the driveway toward the house.

They weren't halfway there before Deborah and Michael came out of the house to the yard to meet them.

"Hello, brother," Michael said with a gentle smile. Kirsten could hear the concern in his voice and saw it matched in his expression. Silas shook Michael's outstretched hand.

"Kirsten, *wilkum*," Michael said, turning to her. Deborah shifted nervously beside him, peering anxiously at Kirsten's face.

"Did ya walk all the way here?" Deborah asked Kirsten, wrapping an arm around her shoulder.

"Yeah, it was slow-going. I had to stop a few times," Kirsten admitted shyly. How Silas had made his long legs go so slowly to match her pace, she could hardly understand.

"How are you?" Deborah asked. Kirsten knew it was more than a polite question.

She shrugged, still not feeling very emotionally stable.

"Michael told me David said some harsh words to Silas," Deborah said as she pulled Kirsten into the house well ahead of the men, who lingered outside.

Kirsten could only nod. She couldn't help replaying the words over and over in her head, even though she so badly wanted to forget them.

"Oh, Kirsten, did you overhear him?" Deborah gasped, spying the look on Kirsten's face.

"Yeah. Most of it, I think."

"We don't all feel that way. I want ya to know that," Deborah said sincerely, her voice thick with emotion.

"I know," Kirsten said with a nod.

Silas and Michael stepped into the house and hung their hats on the pegs on the wall.

"Shall we sit in the front room?" Michael asked his wife. Deborah nodded and smiled, and the men turned to lead the way. Just before she reached Silas, Kirsten abruptly stopped, her stomach tightening as it had on the walk over. But this time, it was painful and she clutched her stomach, gasping. Instantly, Silas stopped and fixed his gaze on her, and Deborah moved quickly to her side.

"No, no. I'm fine," Kirsten breathlessly assured them all. She caught the look that passed between the three of them, who were all staring fixedly at her. Despite her repeated assurances, Michael and Silas insisted that she make the return trip home in the buggy. Deborah and Johnny rode along with them, arriving just in time for lunch. The day had not brightened much at all, and the air was much cooler than the sun-warmed day they had enjoyed just yesterday. Kirsten found herself hurried inside by Silas and Deborah and then placed firmly in a rocking chair near the blazing fireplace.

Kirsten went upstairs to lie down after Michael and Deborah left, waking to find Silas lowering himself next to her bed, where he'd stayed so long last night. He stroked a strand of hair away from her face, and her cheeks warmed, remembering how she'd woken up to find her long hair unwound from the braid.

But now, his eyes were serious and worried.

"David and Sarah are here," he announced.

Kirsten hoped he would tell her that she could simply sleep through this visit. She wouldn't, of course, be able to sleep a wink. But neither did she want to make an appearance.

"David asked if he could speak with both of us." Silas swallowed.

Kirsten wanted to find a way to refuse, but she knew she shouldn't. Minutes later, she followed her husband back downstairs to find David sitting alone at the kitchen table while the others stayed in the living room.

Kirsten carefully lowered herself into a chair across from him, and Silas sat next to her, quickly claiming her small hand in his large one.

"I wanted to apologize for my words yesterday," David said, swallowing. Kirsten had never seen him so nervous. "I should not have spoken so harshly with ya, Silas, and neither should I have…made those remarks about you, Kirsten."

David stopped, apparently finished. Kirsten wanted to hear him recant all his claims from yesterday, even though she herself believed some of them to be true. Specifically, she wasn't a great cook, despite Silas and Daniel's encouragement. And she knew precious little about how to keep house all by herself—at least in the Amish way. Furthermore, there was no denying her marriage to Silas had caused pain to the Millers. Amy especially. But David said nothing more, and Kirsten knew this was the best she could hope for at this point. David was not Michael, and Sarah was not Deborah. They had not spent time with Kirsten and had hardly gotten to know her at all.

With a glance at Silas, Kirsten took a deep breath. "I accept your apology."

"We forgive you, David," Silas added quietly.

David nodded, looking relieved and embarrassed all at once.

"My Sarah brought over a cheesecake. Heard it was yer favorite, Kirsten," he said with unmistakable hope in his eyes.

Kirsten could see how badly he wanted to move past this awful rift. And she had nothing to gain by holding a grudge. But even as she smiled and nodded, she could tell David was a long way from really accepting her into their family, much less the Amish community.

— CHAPTER THIRTY-EIGHT —

Kirsten slowly wound the yarn around her needle and moved the hooks together, connecting loops one through another. She shifted uncomfortably on the rocking chair, silently blaming Dr. Burke for the discomfort she'd felt since Friday morning. She'd known he was going to do an internal check. He'd said as much two weeks prior.

At least Kirsten had been able to warn Silas. He had very respectfully ducked out of the room before she'd changed into the revealing, open-backed hospital gown. When the exam was over, Kirsten quickly dressed and opened the door to see him leaning against the opposite wall, handsome as ever.

She'd tried to tell herself that the gentle, concerned smile he'd given her made all the lingering discomfort from the exam worth it, but three days had passed and she was still uncomfortable. It was going to take a lot of her husband's gentle smiles to push the pain from her mind.

Though her body was changing all the time these days, there was something distinctly different lately. She hadn't been walking normally. Kirsten knew that, though she hoped no one else had noticed. But Mary had given her some curious looks, so it was possible she had noticed.

Kirsten had tried to politely ignore the way her mother-in-law had been watching her. She hoped fervently that Mary would keep her thoughts to herself and not mention Kirsten's worsening waddle. It was a small relief that Daniel had taken her and Amy to the market while Shelby was at school. Only little Anna Mae was in the house, busy drawing a picture at the kitchen table. The fewer people she had observing her, the less self-conscious she was.

Kirsten had only been sitting for thirty minutes, but the rocking chair was horribly unforgiving this morning. She shifted again, and this time the ball of yarn went skittering off her lap and across the wooden-plank floor. Kirsten sighed and stared at it. She kicked at it with her foot and it got closer. Placing the needles across her lap she carefully leaned forward so as not to upset her balance. Just when she pinched it in her fingers, she felt a pop and an odd sensation.

"Anna Mae?" Kirsten called in a shaky voice.

Anna bounced into the living room, paper and pencil in hand.

"Will you please go get Silas? Tell him I need to see him about something." Kirsten wanted very much not to frighten the little girl. "I think he's in the workshop."

Anna Mae nodded and put her paper and pencil ever so carefully on the table, then skipped out the door. Kirsten desperately hoped that her tiny sister-in-law wouldn't get distracted by a butterfly or a horse and forget about her errand.

Several agonizing minutes later, Anna Mae's light footsteps sounded and her small frame rounded the corner.

"He said he'd be in pretty soon for some coffee," Anna relayed.

"No. No, he needs to come in right now," Kirsten said, shaking her head. "Go back and tell him I said he needs to come in now."

Anna Mae's eyes widened. Kirsten knew the little girl had never been asked to be the carrier of such a demanding message, and she wondered briefly if Anna would refuse. She didn't refuse, but her pace was much slower. She'd picked up on Kirsten's tension.

Footsteps sounded again, though this time they were loud, thumping ones. He was in the house before she had time to think.

"What do ya need?" he drawled. Anna Mae hid behind his legs, peeking around at Kirsten.

"Anna, why don't you go show Caleb that pretty picture that you were working on?" Kirsten said, trying very hard to smile as though nothing was out of the ordinary. Anna hesitated and then turned to obey.

Once the door closed, Kirsten stood slowly. Very, very slowly. "My water broke."

Silas blinked at her once, then again, realization finally hitting him and making his head snap up and his eyes go wide.

"I'm going to change, and then we should go," Kirsten quietly coaxed him.

He nodded, hands still on his hips, shock still written on his face. Abruptly, he spun on his heels and strode out of the house. Kirsten heard him call for Caleb in a voice that didn't sound like his.

She made her way upstairs and stripped off her dress. She'd just managed to pull on a clean one when the pain hit. Her hands gripped the carved foot rail of her bed, and she gasped for breath. The pain washed over her in waves, taking all her thoughts with it.

She never heard his approach and started at his touch on her back. The contraction slowly faded away and allowed her senses to function again. Silas was beyond concerned; his eyes were pinched in worry.

"I'm okay," she panted. "Just help me get my apron." He snagged it off the bed, slipped it over her head, and gently tied it in back. She let him help her down the stairs, where he directed her to a kitchen chair. Silas knelt down in front of her and looked intently into her eyes.

"Can I get ya anything?"

"Just my bag...upstairs." She'd just finished packing it a few days ago at her doctor's urging.

Silas looked to Caleb, who was silently standing next to Anna. Caleb ran up the stairs and returned with her bag mere seconds later.

"Yer mom should be here soon," Silas said, peering pensively out the window. "She's going to drive us."

Kirsten nodded, thankful for only the second time in her life to be spared a buggy ride.

The van came to a skidding halt just minutes later. Dimly, Kirsten noticed Mary climbing out of the passenger seat of Elizabeth's van. Silas helped Kirsten to her feet as another contraction struck, pulling her under its tide. She clutched his hand and whimpered as it overtook her. Silas stood very still while she buried her face in his chest. His arms were wrapped around her, though she couldn't really register them. If they weren't holding her up, she would have collapsed to the ground. When the dull ache melted away, she was aware of Mary rubbing her back and Elizabeth anxiously standing nearby. Silas eased his grip on her slightly, not sure if he should let go.

"Okay, I'm ready," Kirsten said to Silas, who had wordlessly endured her grip on his forearm. He helped her into the van and jumped in beside her, taking her hand in his.

Mary calmly and quickly climbed into the passenger seat, and Elizabeth could hardly put the car in gear for her shaking hands.

Kirsten watched them all as if from afar. She looked at Silas. He was nervous, but steady. She squeezed his hand and smiled. She wasn't scared like she'd thought she would be. He was with her, by her side. And with him there, she could do absolutely anything.

⚜

The ride to the hospital was sickeningly fast. Silas gently eased Kirsten into a wheelchair and then briskly pushed her down the hall. Kirsten wondered if Mary and Elizabeth had to run to keep up with them.

The labor and delivery nurse smiled warmly when they burst through the doors of the O.B. Department. She showed them to a room and waited while Silas helped Kirsten out of the chair.

"You can keep your bonnet on, but all the rest comes off and you put this on," she said, handing Kirsten a flimsy cloth hospital gown with more openings than closings. Kirsten nodded but didn't look up from the material in her hands.

Silas moved to follow Mary out the door, but first he stopped at Kirsten's side and tenderly kissed her temple. They left Elizabeth to help her undress and slip into the gown. Her mother helped her into the bed and adjusted the pillows, sheets, and blankets to Kirsten's liking. When she stepped out the door to fill out paperwork at the nurse's station, only Mary came back in.

"Where's Silas?" Kirsten asked after a few moments.

Mary glanced at the door and then smiled sadly at Kirsten.

"He c-c-can't be here?" Kirsten could hear the hysteria creeping into her own voice.

Mary sat on the edge of her bed and faced her. "He can be, but he's choosing to protect your honor," she answered calmly.

"But I need him," Kirsten choked as a tear burned down her cheek.

"He'll not leave ya. He's just down the hall," Mary reassured her, taking Kirsten's trembling hand.

Kirsten tried to process this new development, but another contraction hit and it was all she could do not to crush Mary's hand.

"Will you stay with me?" Kirsten panted as the pain ebbed.

Mary nodded.

⋅⊙⧉⊙⋅

For the next fourteen hours, it was Mary to whom she clung. Elizabeth was there, nervously fluttering in the background, giving words of encouragement, but anxiously hanging back. If Kirsten needed something, Elizabeth volunteered to go get it. But it was Mary who held her hand through every contraction, cuddled her head to her chest when they administered the spinal anesthesia, and walked countless laps up and down the hallway at her side. Mary rubbed Kirsten's back, wiped her brow, and fed her ice chips.

It was Mary's eyes that bore into Kirsten with steady reassurance—a belief that not only *could* Kirsten deliver this baby, but that she *would*. Seven babies had given Mary invaluable experience in the birthing process. And when Mary assured Kirsten that she was doing well, Kirsten believed her.

When Dr. Burke came in and said it was time to push, Mary held Kirsten's leg and counted loudly. When the pain was too much and Kirsten cried out in agony, Mary called her name. Kirsten looked deep into her eyes and found compassion, empathy, and strength. She felt determination flow into her, and with one last cry, baby girl Miller came into the world.

⋅⊙⧉⊙⋅

The waiting room was small and mostly private; for that, Silas was grateful. He was even more grateful when the other occupants of the room left and he could turn off the TV. All that constant noise and chatter gave him a headache. Of course, that could partly be blamed on the stress of waiting.

Elizabeth's periodic updates were appreciated, but never-ending. It was torturous to be apart from Kirsten now, but it was best. He'd spent all these months trying so hard to respect her and protect her dignity. It wouldn't be fair to either of them for him to see her now for the first time. Not like this.

At first, he'd been afraid to leave the waiting room to eat. But he was far too accustomed to eating large meals three times a day, and he finally escaped to the cafeteria late in the evening. He ate quickly and hurried back upstairs, only to wait another impossibly long stretch. It was eleven o'clock when his mother calmly came into the waiting room. Silas jumped to his feet, waiting.

"Ya have a fine daughter." Mary's eyes shone.

Silas's mind raced. She was here. Finally here.

"And her mama is doing just fine," Mary added.

Kirsten. He had to see her. To see them both.

"We'll sit here for a bit, and then ya can go on back and see them." Mary waved at the chairs that Silas had grown to hate.

"They're really all right?" he asked.

"*Jah.* Healthy and strong. Six pounds, one ounce, eighteen inches long. Early, but *gut*," Mary relayed.

Silas nodded.

Elizabeth soon came bursting through the door and hugged him enthusiastically.

"She wants to see you," Elizabeth breathed in relief.

Silas slowly made his way down the hall, feeling his heart beating in his throat. He nudged the heavy door open and stepped into the dimly lit room.

Kirsten sat in the raised bed, an impossibly tiny bundle in her arms. He could see the tears shimmering in her eyes when she looked up at him. He stepped closer and lowered himself ever so gently onto the bed, facing his wife.

"Oh, Silas," she choked as she peered down at the little one in her arms. "I didn't know it would be like this." He smiled and leaned close, peeking past the blankets to see a tiny face with a tiny nose and pinched-shut eyes.

"Do you want her?" He could hear the question in her question. The tears were silently streaming down her flushed face.

"*Jah.* I want her," he managed.

Kirsten moved to put the baby in his hands, but she paused.

"This...is your daddy," she crooned to the tiny girl in the crook of her arm. Silas beamed and then carefully received the sleeping baby in his hands. So tiny. So light. So new and amazing.

"She needs a name, Dad," Kirsten said, leaning close to run her finger across the baby's forehead.

"Grace," Silas murmured. "Unexpected. A gift from God. And so wonderful."

"Grace Miller," Kirsten echoed with a smile.

Silas settled the baby close to his chest and ran a calloused finger down her impossibly soft cheek.

"How are you?" he asked, turning his attention to Kirsten.

"I'm better than I've ever been," she answered, smiling.

For a long time, Silas held Grace in his arms, wondering how any man ever felt really ready to be a father. His heart was nearly exploding with happiness and joy. And love. He hadn't truly expected to feel love just yet. Protectiveness, relief, nurturing, yes. But as Grace lay snuggled against him, he could hardly breathe. His world had utterly shifted—not as if his focus moved, but more like all the other pieces seemed to fall perfectly into place.

"She looks so tiny and cozy in your arms." Kirsten grinned. "But your arms are a pretty great place to be."

Silas laughed quietly.

A nurse knocked softly on the door and stepped in.

"Mind if we take her to the nursery to check her vitals?" she asked with a smile. Silas stood slowly and brought Grace to the bassinette. He laid her down gently, and she whimpered slightly as he slid his hands out from underneath her. Carefully, he adjusted her little knit cap and watched as the nurse rolled a piece of his heart right out the door.

He returned to Kirsten's bedside, sitting very close to her. He brushed a strand of hair off her face and tucked it behind her ear. She sighed and gazed at him.

"Kirsten Miller," he murmured, "yer the best thing that's ever happened in my life." He paused. "And I love you," he said quietly, but clearly.

He'd felt those words for so long, but he hadn't been able or ready to say them. She stared into his eyes, and a slow, sweet smile spread across her face.

Silas leaned closer still and ever so lightly touched his lips to hers. Her mouth was soft and warm. He didn't want to pull away, but he eased back, running his finger along her jaw.

"You won't leave, will you?" she whispered, her breath on his lips.

"I'll never leave you," he answered before kissing her again.

He held her hand until she fell asleep, and then he settled himself in the recliner. For the first time, Silas Miller shared a room with his wife.

— CHAPTER THIRTY-NINE —

It wasn't much of a restful night. Kirsten was visited twice by her little Grace. It was surreal when the nurse lightly knocked on the door and pushed in a small, clear plastic bed containing a baby who wanted her mom. Despite her exhaustion, Kirsten loved snuggling and nursing her very own baby girl. Silas was asleep in the recliner in the corner, rarely stirring and never waking.

Early morning light was just beginning to filter in through the window when Kirsten heard a tiny, squeaky cry warble in the quiet followed by a quiet shushing sound. There in the shadows was Silas, and in his arms was their Grace. He was pacing quietly, his head bent low. Kirsten watched him for several minutes. He had always been so gentle, kind, and caring with her. She'd never really doubted that he would be a good daddy. Still, it was nice to see him in action with Grace. Knowing him, he'd gotten up at five o'clock and had been keeping her quiet while Kirsten slept.

"Yer mama is awake, Grace. She's watching us," Silas whispered loudly enough for Kirsten to hear. He looked up and met her eyes, both of them smiling. "Did ya get any rest?" he asked, sitting down on the side of her bed, cradling Grace in his long arms.

Kirsten reached out to touch his stubble-covered face. Her eyes lingered on his lips. He'd kissed her. It had been so gentle and slow and sweet. Not the kind of kiss that erupted in sudden passion, but the kind that lingered and left you waiting for more. She hoped, fervently, that there would be more. Many, many more.

Silas was watching her intently, his eyes fixed on her face.

"I'm fine. Better than fine," she said, still stroking his face. Grace let out a tiny, shaky cry.

"Is she hungry?" Kirsten asked, sitting upright and peering at Grace's tiny face.

"*Jah*, I think so." Silas smiled down at the fussing baby in his arms.

"I'll go get some breakfast," he said, handing Grace to Kirsten.

"That's a good idea," Kirsten said, nodding and taking Grace's tiny body in her arms.

Silas slipped out of the room and Kirsten nursed Grace, marveling over her miniature fingers, perfectly formed ears, and wrinkled feet. She had just finished feeding her when Elizabeth and a nurse with a breakfast tray came in. Kirsten handed Grace to her mom.

"Grace is a beautiful name for a beautiful baby," Elizabeth crooned.

Kirsten ate while Elizabeth snuggled her granddaughter.

"I felt so guilty," her mom began abruptly. "Like I had no other choices to offer you, and your best option was to become Amish. I felt that I had failed you somehow. Even with all my extra hours, I couldn't afford to support both of you. I even called your grandparents to see if you could live with them for a while," Elizabeth choked. "I never thought you would be this...happy."

Her mom paused as she looked at Silas's hat on the table by the window. "He's such a good young man. I've always liked the Millers, but he's just..."

"Wonderful," Kirsten finished for her. "He's wonderful."

Elizabeth nodded in agreement.

"I'm so glad. For you and for Grace," Elizabeth said as she smoothed Kirsten's cheek.

⚬৩৫৯৯⚬

It was well after lunch when Kirsten showered, dressed, and pulled her hair up. Silas had changed into a fresh shirt and washed his face. Kirsten sat in the recliner, her body sore, but healing. Silas sat in the wooden rocking chair with Grace snuggled peacefully in his arms.

There was a light knock on the door.

"Come in," Silas called.

They knew who it would be. They'd made a call earlier in the morning after a long, serious talk.

Kirsten's attorney entered, followed by Richard and Logan Webb. She watched them, their nervousness evident. But she and Silas were relaxed, calm.

Logan curiously looked her over, his eyes wide in shock at her Amish dress. His gaze darted to Silas sitting beside her and then flicked down at the baby in his arms.

"Congratulations, Kirsten. We hear the baby is healthy," Richard stuttered awkwardly.

Kirsten nodded once and turned her attention to Grace, still nestled safely in Silas's embrace. He was gazing down at Grace with a look of utter peace and adoration—as if there was no one but the three of them in the room.

Richard cleared his throat. "We have a proposal for you," he began. "We don't dispute that Logan is Grace's father."

Silas's eyes snapped up and fixed on Richard.

"Biologically speaking," Richard quickly clarified. "In exchange for our payment of all legal and medical expenses, Logan wishes to sign away his rights to Grace." Logan stared at the floor, unmoving. "We'd also cover any cost of Mr. Miller's adoption of the ch—of Grace," he stumbled.

Kirsten's attorney looked at her and explained that she would never receive any financial assistance from Logan. Kirsten looked to Silas, who met her eyes. He nodded slightly.

"We'll agree to those terms," her voice was quiet, but clear—no trace of nervousness. "Logan, this will be your one chance to see her," Kirsten stated.

He started to shake his head, but Richard pushed him forward. With a reluctant shuffle, he crept near Silas and peered down at the tiny, beautiful face of Grace Miller. Silas, too, peered down at her, and when Grace opened her eyes, it was Silas who was close enough for her to see. Logan stepped back and Richard made arrangements to stop by Kirsten's attorney's office to sign the paperwork.

Without a backward glance, Richard and Logan left the room. Kirsten thanked her lawyer and sighed when the door closed behind them all, leaving just her and Silas and their baby girl in the dimly lit room. He was watching her again, as he so often did. As glad as she was for the arrangements they'd just made, a part of her ached for Grace and the way Logan could walk away. Every part of this experience would have been excruciating if it weren't for the gentle man mere feet away from her.

"We'll tell her the truth, Kirsten, but we won't burden her with more than she can bear," Silas murmured. "Her biological father wasn't ready to be a father. That's all she really needs to know."

Kirsten could only nod.

⋅⊙℘ ℊℴ⋅

Only hours later, Elizabeth tiptoed in the door and placed an infant carrier on Kirsten's empty bed.

"I know you don't have cars, but I thought if you ever needed one that you should have one. Just in case," she explained with a shrug.

"That's a good idea, Mom. We'll need one to get Grace home, anyway," Kirsten said, smiling.

"It's gender neutral. So if you have more babies..."

Silas had to bite his lip to keep from smiling. He secretly hoped that one day Elizabeth would have more grandchildren than she knew what to do with.

"Thank you, Mrs. Walker," he said with a nod.

"Oh, it's the least I can do." She waved dismissively. "This grandma wants to shop, but Kirsten made all those darling dresses."

One of those darling dresses was now fastened carefully around Grace's little body.

"Are we almost ready to go? Should I bring the car around?" Elizabeth asked.

"I think we're ready." Kirsten smiled at Grace. "Silas, would you put Grace in the car seat wile I finish packing up?"

Silas warmed every time she trusted him to hold Grace, burp her, swaddle her, or even carry her across the room. He nodded and scooped her up in his hands. With a gentle kiss on Grace's forehead, he lowered her down into the seat. He fastened all the belts closed and looked down at the little person that he now called his. This little girl would always be a picture of grace to him—God's goodness bestowed.

Kirsten tucked a hat over their daughter's head and then placed the quilt Deborah had made over Grace's body. Only her face was visible—a small dot amongst the layers of fabric covering her.

"She's so tiny," he breathed.

Kirsten wrapped her arms around one of his and leaned her head against his shoulder. Together, they stared in wonder at Grace as she slept in her car seat.

"Are ya ready to go home, Mrs. Miller?" he asked, looking down as her face tilted up to his.

She nodded and he lowered his face to hers, his lips finding hers again. He'd never lip-kissed anyone before, and he knew he had no idea what he was doing. But he loved being so close to Kirsten, feeling her breath on his face and her lips pressed to his. He pulled back and smiled at her. She sighed contentedly and laced her fingers through his.

Silas picked up the baby seat in one hand, squeezed his wife's hand in the other, and left for home.

— CHAPTER FORTY —

Anna Mae and Shelby Jo were bouncing impatiently at the screen door when they pulled up. Silas got out and immediately turned to help Kirsten out of the car. It hurt some when she moved, but for the most part, Kirsten felt better than she'd expected to. Her stomach had flattened quickly, and the nurses had said she'd have to eat a lot so she wouldn't lose too much weight while nursing. Silas easily lifted the carrier out of the van and followed Kirsten up the stairs to the house.

It was past suppertime, but the whole family was waiting inside. Even David and Sarah and Michael and Deborah were there.

They were all gathered in the kitchen, eager and quiet. Deborah hugged Kirsten tightly as Silas gently set the carrier on the table, his long fingers making quick work of the restraints. With extreme care, he lifted Grace from her seat, his big hands easily cupping her tiny body. The look on his face was one Kirsten never wanted to forget. Joy. Peace. Contentment. He handed Grace to Mary, who cradled her so that Daniel could inspect his new granddaughter. Daniel tugged the blanket back and smiled widely, his eyes dancing with delight.

"*Ach,* Silas, a wonderful little daughter ya have," Daniel said quietly.

Silas's eyes shone and he could only nod. Kirsten went to him and wrapped her arms around his waist. He held her tightly to his side, and she could feel his chest rising and falling in deep breaths.

Grace was passed around, and Kirsten watched as each of them treated the newest Miller with a love and tenderness Kirsten had never expected. Silas disappeared upstairs with their things, and by the time he came back down, Grace was fussing.

"I better feed her," Kirsten said to him.

"There's a chair in yer room," he told her with a nod.

Kirsten carefully climbed the stairs and stood in stunned silence at her door. There was, indeed, a chair in her room. A rocking chair just like the ones in the living room was perched facing the cradle. Silas had made it, no doubt. It was made from a perfectly matched piece of maple.

Only after she sat down and began nursing Grace did Kirsten notice his clothes hanging alongside hers, his boots lined up along the wall, his Bible on the nightstand opposite hers.

In one short stretch of time, they'd shared a kiss and a child. They'd made a leap, and now they were going to share a room, a bed even. It could have easily made her nervous for any number of reasons, but it didn't. It was calming, just as being near him always was.

When Kirsten came back down, Elizabeth was gone, though she'd promised to stop by in a day or two for a visit. Silas timidly met her eyes, and Kirsten beamed at him. He smiled shyly back. Grace was settled in her car seat and placed directly behind them while they sat down to a fantastic supper with the family. Frequently, Kirsten or Silas would turn around to check on Grace like typical, nervous new parents. When Grace cried her tiny infant squeak, Amy jumped up and offered to take her.

Amy gently lifted Grace into her arms and began pacing, staring sweetly down into her face. Kirsten was more than a little surprised. Grace was, in a way, the reason for Amy's recent problems with Lucas. Kirsten had expected her to be distant, resentful, and even angry. But there was no evidence of hard feelings now on Amy's glowing face as she bounced Grace lightly in her arms.

Kirsten turned back to the table, but she had trouble focusing on anything or anyone other than Silas. His face was scruffy, the shadow of a beard darkening his jaw. He was quiet, as usual. And though she was sure he knew that she was watching him, he simply let her look.

It was late and very dark when Kirsten nursed Grace and laid her gently in the cradle. She'd changed into her nightgown and was brushing her hair when Silas stepped in.

"She's asleep?" he whispered as he craned his neck to look in the cradle.

Kirsten nodded and peeked in at Grace's bundled body. Silas winced as the door latched, and Kirsten smiled at him reassuringly.

"Will she wake up if we read?" he asked, his voice low and quiet but not a whisper.

"I don't think so," Kirsten replied.

He sat on the bed, and she eased down next to him.

"I've been saving this one," he smiled wryly, the Bible in his lap.

"Psalm 139.

> "You have searched me, Lord, and you know
> me. You know when I sit and when I rise; you
> perceive my thoughts from afar. You discern my
> going out and my lying down; you are familiar with
> all my ways. Before a word is on my tongue you,
> Lord, know it completely. You hem me in behind
> and before, and you lay your hand upon me. Such
> knowledge is too wonderful for me, too lofty for me
> to attain.
>
> "Where can I go from your Spirit? Where can I
> flee from your presence? If I go up to the heavens,
> you are there; if I make my bed in the depths, you
> are there. If I rise on the wings of the dawn, if I settle
> on the far side of the sea, even there your hand will
> guide me, your right hand will hold me fast. If I
> say, 'Surely the darkness will hide me and the light
> become night around me,' even the darkness will not
> be dark to you; the night will shine like the day, for
> darkness is as light to you."

Silas paused and looked at the cradle where Grace slept.

*"For you created my inmost being; you knit me
together in my mother's womb. I praise you because
I am fearfully and wonderfully made; your works
are wonderful, I know that full well. My frame was
not hidden from you when I was made in the secret
place, when I was woven together in the depths of
the earth. Your eyes saw my unformed body; all the
days ordained for me were written in your book
before one of them came to be.*

*"How precious to me are your thoughts, God!
How vast the sum of them! Were I to count them,
they would outnumber the grains of sand—when I
awake, I am still with you."*

He paused and slipped an arm around Kirsten's waist, pulling her close.

*"Search me, God, and know my heart; test me
and know my anxious thoughts. See if there is
any offensive way in me, and lead me in the way
everlasting."*

Silas quietly closed his Bible and held it on his knee. Kirsten traced his hand where it covered the Bible, easily as large as the hefty book.

"I'm going to take a shower," Silas whispered and left the room.

Kirsten checked on Grace once more before crawling beneath the wedding quilt that she was about to share with her husband for the first time. There was no reason to be nervous given her recovering state and the speech she'd gotten from the labor and delivery nurse. Silas's closeness now was a welcome presence. She'd be nervous if she was alone in the room with Grace, solely responsible for her care.

The door opened and Silas came in, hanging his clothes on the wooden pegs. Kirsten watched his form move through the darkness, only able to make out his dark silhouette. He made his way to the right side of the bed, and the mattress lowered slightly under his weight. The covers shifted as he slipped beneath them, the smell of soap filling the air as he settled between the sheets. For a long time, Kirsten listened to his breathing.

She couldn't tell if he was sleeping, but she could see his chest rising and falling at a slow, steady pace.

Lulled by the sound of Silas's breathing, Kirsten began to drift off to sleep, but she started awake with sudden fear. She couldn't hear Grace stirring or breathing—the cradle in the corner was silent. In the darkness, she tried to focus her listening, but still nothing.

"Silas?" she whispered into the dark.

"*Jah?*" As quickly as his answer came, he must have been awake.

"Can you hear Grace breathing?"

He was quiet for a short while.

"Should I check on her?" he asked after a few long moments.

"Yes, please," Kirsten whispered.

The mattress sloped as he eased out of bed. In the dim moonlight, she could make out his figure leaning over the cradle. He was soon back in bed.

"She's sleeping *gut*," he whispered.

"Thank you," Kirsten said.

Silas shifted and she felt his hand stroking her face, then his lips against hers.

"Get some rest, Kirsten," he murmured.

༺ ༅ ༻

It was only a few hours later when Grace's cries sounded from her cradle. Kirsten sat up in a mixture of relief and exhaustion. She slipped out of bed and went quickly to lift Grace from her sweet bed.

Kirsten sank into the rocker and held her daughter to her. Silas stirred but didn't wake, just as he had slept in the hospital. Kirsten pulled a cover over her chest, undid her nightgown, and nursed Grace. She turned slightly so she could see Grace in the moonlight. She stared at her tiny ear, perfectly formed. How had Silas said it? *Fearfully and wonderfully made.* Yes, that made sense. More sense than believing something as incredible as Grace coming out of nothing or happening by chance.

As she marveled over Grace's features, Kirsten could see the words Silas had read living and breathing in her arms. He had called her wonderful when he'd named her. Kirsten finished nursing and pulled her baby up high on her chest, nestling Grace's fuzzy little head into her neck. Grace's squirming settled as Kirsten ever so lightly patted her back and slowly rocked. She could feel Grace's heart beating and her steady, slow breathing.

It hadn't been that long ago that Kirsten had mourned over this little life. But now, it all seemed so right. Silas had told her that even if she'd made a mistake, that didn't mean God had. Could it be that God, if He truly existed, had brought Grace into Kirsten's story on purpose? That this sweet little baby had been designed and planned by the God that her husband prayed to and believed in so deeply?

Grace was so unexpected—at least as far as the human participants were concerned. But to God, Grace wasn't a surprise. That's what Silas had read. And there was no doubt this healthy little baby was a gift. Kirsten knew she could never earn something or someone as wonderful as Grace.

After all those nights when Kirsten had cried asking why this had to happen to her, she now sat in an Amish farmhouse, rocking her precious baby while her husband slept in her bed. Tears streamed down her face once again. Only this time, she didn't ask why out of pain and anger. Instead, the question came out of wonder. Why had she been given this child? Why was all this now hers?

Silas was right. Grace was an unexpected gift from God. Truly wonderful.

With the warmth of her baby against her chest, Kirsten whispered the only two words she had left for the God who was still such a mystery to her.

"Thank you."

— Chapter Forty-One —

For most of his life, Silas had been waking up at five o'clock. Evidently, sharing a room with a newborn baby and his wife was not going to change his body's internal clock. Silas stared across the pillow at Kirsten, who was sleeping peacefully. Much like Grace who was snug in her cradle. He'd often imagined what it would be like to see her lying in the tiny bed as he'd so carefully constructed it. But his daydreams had been nothing like this. He'd never pictured such an amazing new person with tiny lips and impossibly small clenched fists.

He dressed quietly, making extra effort not to wake either of them, and went outside to find the rest of his family already busy with their chores. By the time he walked back to the house, the air was just beginning to warm with the sunlight spilling over the top of the barn.

Mary and Amy had prepared a hearty breakfast of pancakes, bacon, eggs, and cinnamon rolls. Everyone moved differently this morning, much more quietly than normal. Even little Anna Mae was whispering, though that was going a little far.

Silas scooped her up and asked her if she'd helped with breakfast. She smiled and nodded. Her little face had been so concerned when Kirsten had sent her back to his workshop to get him. That she'd returned a second time would have been enough to warrant a trip inside. But her trembling voice had sent him hurrying. He smiled at her now and set her down.

"Did ya get some sleep?" Mary asked him.

"*Jah*. I slept fine," Silas answered without looking at her. Even though it was an innocent question, Silas could still feel his face warming.

"I only heard her once," Mary commented as she set the table.

Silas hadn't heard her at all. Kirsten wasn't in the kitchen, and he hoped she hadn't had a rough night.

"We should let her sleep," Mary told him as he stared up the empty staircase.

When she still hadn't appeared by the end of breakfast, Silas went up to check on both of them. With a quick check on the small occupant of the cradle, he rounded the foot of the bed to where his wife still slept in their bed. He bent over her to study her face. The urge to kiss her was almost overpowering, but instead he brushed her hair off her forehead. Kirsten's eyes snapped open and she struggled to sit up.

"W-w-what time is it?" she stammered.

"About 7:30," he answered, still leaning over her.

"I missed breakfast," she blurted as she swung her legs over the edge of the bed and stood up.

"We saved ya some," he reassured her with a smile.

Kirsten rubbed her forehead. "I'm sorry. I got up around six and fed Grace. I thought I'd just rest for a minute before breakfast...but I guess it was more like an hour."

Silas put his hands on her shoulders and turned her to face him. "Kirsten, ya just had a baby. You need yer rest."

Her body eased slightly under his light grip.

"Did you sleep okay?" she asked him worriedly.

"*Jah*, I slept fine." The blush was back on his face. It didn't help that she was so distractingly beautiful in the morning, with her hair falling in loose waves over her shoulders. And though it was a modest nightgown, it was still a nightgown.

"Was she up a lot?" he asked, his voice sounding husky even to him.

"Only a few times," Kirsten whispered, glancing at Grace.

"No one expects you to work today," he said seriously. "I want ya to rest," he added with a gentle but authoritative tone.

She nodded. "Do you think I have time for a shower?" she asked, eyeing the cradle doubtfully.

"*Jah.* I'll tell Amy to listen for her," he assured her.

Instantly snapping into action, Kirsten grabbed her things and hurried out the door and down the hall. Silas went out to his workshop. He tried to work with attention and focus on the remaining dining chairs, but his mind wandered fast and far. First to his daughter, sleeping in the cradle he'd made. It was almost too much to comprehend. He wondered if he'd get a chance to hold her if he took a break this morning. And then his thoughts turned to Kirsten. He'd always intended to move into her room when the baby was born, though he hadn't exactly planned on doing so for several weeks yet. He'd hoped to sleep lightly enough to help once in a while, but so far that hadn't worked out.

The transition was easy for such a big move. There was no pressure or expectation that he'd prove his love for her. He had no intention of violating the nurse's embarrassing orders that they abstain for six weeks. He truly couldn't imagine how wounded her body was. She seemed to be feeling well and only moved slowly at certain times. There were so many new adjustments for her. Kirsten had confessed her ignorance when it came to caring for a baby. She'd never changed a diaper, swaddled a baby, or soothed an infant to sleep. But after a crash course in the basics at the hospital, her intuition had kicked in. He could see how tired she was at times, but her tired eyes still gleamed when she looked at her sweet Grace. Kirsten never once complained, but then again, Kirsten really wasn't the complaining type.

◦ගඓ ඉ෧◦

Standing at the kitchen window with Grace on her shoulder, Kirsten watched as Silas crossed the yard and neared the house for supper. He lifted his head, the brim of his hat rising so she could see his eyes. He smiled and she waved with her free arm. He strode into the house and quickly washed his hands.

"Hullo, Mrs. Miller," he rumbled into her ear as his lips skimmed her jaw; her whole body tingled at his nearness. "How's my little Grace?" he asked, his hand touching the tiny head resting on Kirsten's arm.

"Wonderful," Kirsten answered with a smile.

"And how are you?" Silas asked, his eyes warm.

"I'm good. Amy watched Grace for me so I could take a nap this afternoon."

"That's *gut*."

Truthfully, Amy had been extraordinarily helpful. She'd taken Grace countless times so that Kirsten could have a few minutes to take care of herself. And Amy's tender ways with Grace were nothing short of shocking.

They sat down to supper and then gathered in the living room afterward. Daniel held Grace for the first time, marveling over her and rocking her in the chair. When she fussed, Silas took her. He paced a slow circuit back and forth past the doorway, singing softly to her, the gentle motion of his steps swaying her back to sleep.

"I think he's quite taken with her," Mary said, smiling at Kirsten. Kirsten could only nod.

The family retired to bed, and Kirsten excused herself to use the bathroom while Silas looked after Grace. When she came out of the shower, Silas was in their room, leaning over Grace, who was awake and squirming on the bed. He'd lit the lamp and was watching her kick and clutch his finger. He wore only his trousers slung low on his hips, his chest bare. Silas was all sculpted, lean muscle. She could see that now. The several days of stubble on his face completely overtook her thoughts for a moment.

"What's wrong?" he asked worriedly, and Kirsten realized she was staring at him.

"Oh...um...nothing. Nothing's wrong."

He was still looking at her.

"It's just that that stubble on your face is highly distracting." She blushed at the honesty of her statement.

Silas rubbed his jaw. "I didn't have time to shave last night. I meant to do it this morning, but I forgot," he admitted. "I'll go do it now."

"No!" Kirsten said it too loudly and Grace startled. She sat on the bed and picked her up, soothing her. Silas stood in obvious confusion at the door. "It's distracting in a very good way," Kirsten said as she bit her lip.

He considered that for a moment. "Do ya want me to grow a beard?"

"No. I'd like for you to forget to shave every other day or so," Kirsten admitted, so embarrassed she couldn't look at him.

Silas rounded the bed, pulled Grace from Kirsten's arms, and laid her down in the cradle. He turned back, leaned over Kirsten, and kissed her. Kirsten curled her fingers through his hair. Her lips moved on his and he froze momentarily in surprise, then followed her lead. Grace protested at being set aside, and Silas pulled away, smiling. Kirsten could still feel the scrub of his face on hers when the door closed behind him. He obviously had no idea what he was doing...to her.

— CHAPTER FORTY-TWO —

Late autumn, as Kirsten discovered, was an extraordinarily busy time for an Amish farming family like the Millers. It was even truer for Silas. In the weeks after Grace's birth, he spent long hours in the workshop. Then came the days when Silas and Caleb were gone nearly all day helping friends and neighbors harvest their crops.

Soon David came to ask for their help with his many acres. Silas had once explained to her that David depended heavily on the help of his friends and family to handle as many acres as he farmed. Michael helped when he could, but he also had to tend to his dairy. Daniel even took a few days away from the market to lend a hand. Every morning, Silas left immediately after breakfast and worked until dark.

Amy spent longer hours outside, tending to the horses and sometimes handling the milking with just Mary's help. But every time Amy came in, her attention focused on Grace.

The yard was terribly quiet and empty when the men went to work elsewhere during the day. The windows were empty of the familiar scenes. Silas wasn't striding across the yard. Caleb wasn't mucking out the barn. Daniel and Mary were down the road at the market, often taking Anna with them for the day. It was nice to have the house quiet, with only Amy's company. But Kirsten missed her husband, even though her days were full in their own new way.

Between feeding Grace, changing diapers, and making sure they both of them got enough sleep, Kirsten only had limited time to help cook meals and keep up with laundry. Still, it was hard not to feel a little resentful that Silas was called away from home so often. Kirsten knew, could plainly see, how hard it was for him to leave her and Grace. His hugs were long. And every morning, just before walking out the door, he'd press a kiss to Grace's fuzz-covered head. On the one hand, she admired him for the selfless way he was giving his time to his brothers and their neighbors. But when he came home at night, Kirsten had to bit her tongue to keep from begging him to take a day off. His clothes and hands showed the evidence of a day working in the field. It was absolutely all she could do to get his clothes clean. However, the heaviest weight she bore was seeing his weariness. Silas was only twenty-one, soon to be twenty-two, and she'd seen him work hard almost every single day of their married life. But there was something about these endless harvest days that left him spent. And quiet. Even for Silas.

It was a relief, in a way, that Grace had been born so early. Kirsten had healed significantly since the birth and had gotten the hang of nursing. She just couldn't imagine juggling the immediate physical toll of the birth with a husband as work-worn as Silas was.

The first few weeks with Grace, he'd been so attentive, so devoted to caring for them both. He still wanted to be—that much she could see. But his time at home was in short supply; his time with her was even less. Instead of long, leisurely evenings, he came home, ate supper, showered, and fell asleep wherever he landed. Kirsten ached to help him somehow, but the best she had to offer was a healthy daughter and a warm smile.

It was weeks into harvest and the golden, warm days of early fall were descending into the dark, dreary cold that preceded winter. She woke with a start as the wind blew hard, sending the few remaining leaves scraping against her window. She reached for Silas, but the bed beside her was cold and empty. She sat up quickly and strained to see in the pitch-black darkness.

"I'm here, Kirsten." His voice came from the rocker by the window. Kirsten's eyes cleared and she could see him then, a little baby snuggled on his bare chest.

"Does she need me?"

"She's okay. You can go back to sleep," he murmured quietly. The wind swished around the house, and then the rain hit hard against the window, sounding more like pebbles than drops of water. But then came the sound of Silas's low voice singing quietly in Pennsylvania Dutch. It was several minutes before he stopped singing and several more before he slowly stood and gently placed Grace in the cradle. Grace grunted, but he swayed the cradle soothingly and she quieted. Kirsten felt his body return to the bed. She reached out and found his shoulder.

"Did I wake ya?" he whispered.

"No," she answered. Her hand slid over his bare chest and up his neck. She found the hard stubble of his face and pressed her palm to it. His fingers wrapped around her wrist and they lay still for a long time. It was enough to simply be together.

"I miss you, Silas," she whispered finally.

He sighed. "I know. I'm sorry I haven't been around more for you and Grace."

"No. I understand, and it's okay. I just miss you," she reassured him.

"I miss you, too," he said as his thumb rubbed circles on the back of her hand.

"This is one way to make me look forward to winter," Kirsten said with a light smile. "You'll be inside more."

"Yeah. Then you'll get sick of me," he joked.

"I seriously doubt that could happen," she answered, and Silas laughed quietly.

Kirsten could feel her heart beating hard in her chest. She'd waited for the right moment and then struggled to find any moment at all. He was so quiet. Had he fallen asleep? If not, then he soon would be.

"Silas Miller," she whispered into the dark, "I love you."

— CHAPTER FORTY-THREE —

Silas snapped the reins and urged Titus toward home. Caleb bounced lightly in the seat next to him. Silas's back ached and his head throbbed, but he felt relieved. The harvest was done, in for another year despite the rain storm of the night before. This far into November, they were fortunate that it had been only rain. Some years, they had battled freezing rain, sleet, or snow. This had been David's biggest year—the most acres and the best yield that he'd ever had. There was no mistaking David's relief and happiness. He was so pleased, in fact, he had invited the whole family over for supper the following evening.

Caleb offered to put up Titus, and Silas walked into the house, his footsteps weary but satisfied.

"Did ya finish today?" Mary asked as he stepped into the washroom and shed his coat and hat.

"Yeah. Done. Finally done," he sighed.

"Praise the Lord!" she proclaimed

He walked through the kitchen and found Kirsten in the living room. His wife, who loved him. She'd said the words, though at first he'd thought he'd imagined or dreamt it. But he'd pulled her to him, kissed her, and held her as they'd fallen asleep.

She smiled up at him and glanced down at Grace, sound asleep in her arms. Silas leaned down and kissed Kirsten's cheeks, then Grace's forehead.

"How was your day?" Kirsten asked as he kneeled close, watching Grace.

"We got done."

She looked up and beamed. "Good," she said, nodding.

He watched them a while and then left to shower. When he stepped into their room, Kirsten was alone and waiting for him beside the bed. She motioned for him to sit and he lowered his body to sit in front of her. Her hands worked their way across his shoulders, kneading his sore muscles until they tingled. He moaned as her fingers loosened the knots in his neck. She finger-combed his wet hair, and Silas's eyes slid closed.

"You need some supper," Kirsten murmured quietly. Silas nodded, though he was perfectly content to remain right where he was. She held his shirt for him, and he eased his arms into the sleeves. She pulled it up on his shoulders, and he let her fasten the buttons. By the time she turned to the door, he wanted to refuse to follow her. But he was powerless to stay away from her, so he plodded heavily after her.

Everyone seemed to be in good spirits. Daniel was especially pleased and jovial to learn of the completion of harvest. Silas sat at the table for a long time, listening to his father's stories. Kirsten lingered for a while, then carried Grace upstairs to put her to bed. Silas followed after a while and found her standing near the cradle, watching Grace sleep.

Silas stepped in the room and closed the door. He moved close behind Kirsten and slipped his arms around her slim waist. Resting his chin on her shoulder, he followed her gaze down to Grace, sleeping soundly beneath her quilt. Kirsten sighed and leaned her back into his chest.

She turned her head slightly, as if she could hear his thoughts, and Silas brought his lips down to hers. For a long while, it was enough to simply cover her mouth with his and hold her against him. But then, it wasn't. She twisted around in his arms and turned to face him, winding her fingers in his hair. Hunger overcame him, and he gasped as her tongue met his. His hands slid from her waist to her shoulder blades and down again. She was meeting his kisses and matching his intensity, their embrace taking on passion he'd never known.

Gradually, she eased back and he loosened his grip, feeling her fall away from her tiptoed stance. His breathing was ragged and quick; Kirsten's was softer, but deep.

"You need some sleep, Silas," she whispered, her fingers still stroking through his hair. He felt her hands smooth down his shirt and undo the buttons she'd fastened just hours earlier. His knees were weak by the time she slipped it off his broad shoulders.

It wasn't time yet. She needed more time. He'd spent months waiting, and he absolutely refused to rush.

They crawled into bed and Silas quickly fell asleep, Kirsten's head on his chest and her hair falling in waves across his shoulder.

⋅ତ୧ତ⋅

David and Sarah's home was different than Michael and Deborah's. It was oddly darker, the walls paneled wood. There was less furniture, and what was there was all very simple wooden pieces. There were no quilts hanging on the wall or vast windows allowing in the natural light. The rooms were not painted in bright, cheerful colors, but in darker tones. It was hard for Kirsten to feel comfortable. But then again, other than Silas, no one had shown her as much love and acceptance as Deborah. Sarah had very deliberately and politely kept her distance, especially after the pumpkin harvest. Kirsten could only hope this night would be different.

The women gathered in Sarah's country kitchen. Sarah cooked with a woodstove and had no electric or gas-powered appliances. Kirsten had always been secretly grateful for the semi-modern Amish home in which she lived. Daniel and Mary had taken steps over the years to modernize their house in accordance with the permissions and allowances of the church ordinances. A generator ran their refrigerator, the deep freeze, the gas stove, and the furnace. Michael and Deborah's house was much the same in terms of conveniences. But David and Sarah had elected to be more restrictive with their lives, choosing only to install a furnace.

Grace had been bundled up warmly for the buggy ride, wrapped in layers. Riding in a buggy in the winter was going to take some definite getting used to. If it was only her and Silas, she'd probably appreciate and enjoy the excuse to snuggle close to him on the bench. As it was, she was worried to the point of distraction about protecting her infant daughter from even a hint of cold air.

Deborah protested when Kirsten started setting the table, telling her she would do it. But Kirsten handed Grace to her instead and waved her to a chair nearby. Deborah took the bundle in her arms and immediately began talking to her in her own Pennsylvania Dutch drawl. Grace would grow up bilingual.

There was simply no denying that Sarah was an excellent cook. Every dish was prepared to perfection, and Kirsten could not help but take seconds. After a knockout dessert of chocolate cheesecake, the men retired into the front room, taking the children with them.

Just seeing Silas in his clean blue shirt, black suspenders, and dark-gray trousers was distracting enough. Watching him cuddle Grace to his chest was nearly too much. Kirsten felt as if her heart might explode out of her body. Much as she'd felt the night before when he'd kissed her—really, really kissed her. In high school, she would have called it "making out." But she wasn't sure that was something that applied to a married couple. His kiss had been so passionate, and she'd melted into him almost involuntarily. It was as if some part of her had taken over and reacted in a way beyond her control. Still, it had been Silas who had set the pace of their physical relationship all along, and she'd not upset that, even though she badly wanted to.

"How old is Grace now?" Deborah asked thoughtfully.

"She'll be six weeks in a few days," Kirsten answered with a smile, shaking her head in disbelief. Even with all the sleep-deprived nights and endless caretaking, the time had gone so fast.

Deborah nodded. "And yer healin' well?"

"Yeah, I think so. I feel good anyway," Kirsten said as she sat in the chair next to Deborah in the corner of the dining room, where their words wouldn't be overheard.

"I hear Daniel and Mary and the kids are going to Missouri to visit Uncle Isaac," Deborah continued. It seemed an abrupt turn in the conversation.

"Yeah, I guess so," Kirsten agreed. She'd heard of the plans for the three-day trip.

"But you and Silas are staying home?" It didn't sound as much like a question as it did an observation. Deborah seemed to be hinting at something.

"Silas thought it was a little soon to be traveling with Grace," Kirsten said, once again grateful for his decision. She was in no hurry to travel overnight with an infant.

Deborah nodded and then leaned closer. "So you'll be alone with yer husband for a whole weekend."

"Well, Grace will be there, but yes," Kirsten said, shrugging.

Deborah looked fixedly at Kirsten, lifted a brow in expectation, and waited. Kirsten stared back in confusion and then suddenly understood. They would be alone. *Alone* alone. Grace would be six weeks old by then. All of the doctor's restrictions on Kirsten's physical condition would be lifted.

Her mind raced back to last night's kiss. It had started sweet and innocent, but it had rapidly accelerated in passion. She couldn't possibly expect to kiss Silas like that and not awaken need for her. Certainly not when they were married and they shared a bed.

It wasn't that she didn't want to be intimate with her husband. Truth be told, she very much did. But it had seemed like something to put off until later. But later was now.

Of course, Silas must have thought it out—even had a hand in planning it. The timing made logical sense. She could only hope that this was not the sole reason for Daniel and Mary's trip. Even though they all lived under the same roof, Kirsten liked to at least pretend she had some level of personal privacy. Though it was probably more of an illusion than she wanted to admit.

Her eyes rested on her husband sitting in the other room. It had been such an awful mistake—a foolish, desperate thing to do—the first and only time she'd given herself away. But this would be so drastically different. She knew it already. This man, her husband, her Silas, loved her. She believed it with every fiber of her being. She had trusted him with everything, and though there had been a few moments of miscommunication, he had never once intentionally hurt her. He'd even made Grace's birth an event to anticipate and celebrate when it could have been much different. He had rescued her in a way, but he had also given her the firm ground on which she'd found her footing. Kirsten had stepped out of her world into his and found more peace, joy, fulfillment, and love than she'd ever known. And through it all, he'd been so uncommonly patient.

No, there was nothing to be anxious about. A little nervous maybe. But definitely not scared.

୶ଈ ୨ଈ୶

"Yer wife is makin' eyes at ya again," Michael observed with a grin. Silas's gaze flicked up to find Kirsten watching him. "She seems to be doin' that a lot lately," Michael teased, his grin widening.

Silas made no reply.

"She's more fond of ya than I ever thought she'd be," David admitted.

"And yer more fond of that little baby than I thought you'd be," Michael said, smiling warmly.

"Grace is my daughter," Silas stated matter-of-factly.

"In practice, anyway." David nodded in agreement.

"In every way that counts," Silas retorted calmly, but firmly. "The adoption will be finalized next month."

"Yer adopting her?" David gasped in disbelief. Michael glanced nervously between his brothers.

"*Jah.*" Silas paused. "Is there something wrong with that?" he asked with a slight edge in his voice.

David swallowed visibly and shifted uncomfortably in his seat. "I just thought you'd wait. Until later."

David didn't elaborate, but Silas knew precisely what he meant.

"I don't see why I should," Silas answered, the edge in his voice sharper.

"If yer wife doesn't seek baptism," David began in a hushed tone. Silas began shaking his head in silent protest even as David spoke. "She would be shunned." Silas already knew all of this.

"Would ya leave with her, Silas?" Michael finally asked. This was the brother Silas had needed so badly in his life these past few months. Michael had been more of a friend than ever before, seeming to understand and sympathize with him. If there was a brother to lean on, confide in, and imitate, it was Michael. More than ever, it was Michael.

Silas nodded his response. David frowned, but Michael considered him seriously.

It was a possibility that Kirsten would not seek baptism, would not find a saving faith in God. But Silas didn't let his thoughts travel down that path. He'd put not only his own life in God's hands, but also that of his wife and his daughter. And until he was led to act differently, Silas felt peace that that was precisely where they were meant to be. Baptism or not.

.⋅οℚ ℊℴ.⋅

It was early, but still dark. Kirsten quietly eased into bed, trying not to disturb Silas. She was tired, but awake after a middle-of-the-night feeding session. Kirsten watched Silas sleep in the dark, his chest slowly rising and falling. One arm tucked up beneath his pillow. Dark lashes resting on his high cheekbones. Lips barely open. Hair tousled and curling lightly on his forehead and temples.

Deborah's comments had made Kirsten even more conscious of Silas. He'd been terribly quiet on the way home—even for Silas. But she hadn't tried to draw him out of whatever world he was lost in. Kirsten had enough thoughts of her own occupying the extra space in her mind. The quiet helped. Considering all she'd been through over the past year, the idea of being intimate with someone deserved some serious thought.

Watching him sleep now, she felt a familiar ache of tenderness. She loved this man with the tan face and work-calloused hands. Softly, she brushed a finger across his lips. Silas shuddered with a sigh in his sleep, but he breathed deeply and didn't wake. Grace often did the same thing when she slept. Kirsten touched his hair and lightly brushed it off his forehead, feeling it gently curl around her fingers.

His eyes opened suddenly, narrow, sleepy slits that immediately focused on her. Kirsten pulled her hand away shyly.

"Sorry," she whispered, wincing.

His eyes closed, but he slid closer to her and pulled her to his side, where her head rested on his bare chest. His heartbeat pulsed beneath her cheek, and Kirsten felt his lips brush her forehead. His warmth felt almost hot against her, the heat of his hand on her back blazing through her nightgown. How she loved the scrub of his unshaven face on her skin and the feeling of his breath on her hair.

"Can't ya sleep?" he mumbled.

"No," she whispered. She probably could have slept if she had tried. There was no hope of that now.

"Did Grace keep ya up?" His hand was gently stroking her back.

"No." At least she was honest.

Silas was quiet then, and she wondered briefly if he'd drifted back to sleep. But his arm pulled from beneath the pillow and his fingers curled under her chin, pulling her face up to his. His lips were soft on hers, moving slowly. Kirsten reached up and curled her fingers in his hair again, pulling his kiss deeper. He responded and held her tightly. She couldn't help but sigh when he gently pulled away.

"Time for chores," he rasped, his breathing fast. Before she could protest, he had thrown back their wedding quilt and swung his legs over the edge of the bed.

"Get some more rest," he whispered, leaning over her and kissing her cheekbone just beneath her eye. The door closed softly behind him. Kirsten buried her face in his pillow and snuggled into the warm spot he'd left beside her.

She shivered—not from cold, but from the absence of his heat. There was no doubt in her mind that she'd follow him anywhere. He'd practically walked her straight out of hell. Trusting Silas wasn't hard. He loved her. It wasn't only something she felt for him; it was something she believed in with every fiber of her being. He was her present and her future, despite the ugliness of the past, with all its mistakes and brokenness. It was a past that really didn't seem to matter anymore. Whatever he asked of her, Kirsten couldn't withhold.

— Chapter Forty-Four —

There was an odd, hurried silence that morning. Silas wondered at first if it was just his imagination. But even the pace and demeanor in the barn during milking seemed off. Caleb seemed confused, thrown off by the urgency of Daniel's actions and instructions.

For the past several days, the entire family had taken on extra work to prepare for their long weekend away. Friday and Saturday's work had been sprinkled in bits across the preceding days. Barns were cleaned. Stalls were mucked out. Feed bins were filled. The same was true inside. Laundry was done. Sheets were changed. The house was cleaned. Baking was done.

It was unnecessary. Silas could easily handle the farm on his own. He'd done so countless times. And though Kirsten was a busy new mother, she'd have plenty of time to bake or clean the bathroom.

But they'd all worked steadily, and Silas had wondered more than once why his parents were pushing to get so much accomplished. He and Kirsten would be home for nearly three whole days together. Even though he didn't want to believe it, he knew they were doing their best to give them as much time alone as possible. There were very few secrets in the Miller family. His mother had most likely calculated the timing and planned this trip accordingly.

He'd taken an unconventional wife, become a father in a rather unordinary way, and only recently started kissing his wife with any amount of passion. It almost stood to reason, as preposterous as it was, that he and Kirsten would have a honeymoon of sorts...now.

It wasn't as if he'd tried to hide his intentions, but he'd certainly never uttered a word of them to anyone. Not even Kirsten. Though she seemed strangely, instinctually aware—even expectant of their increasing closeness.

For several mornings now, he'd woken up to find her tucked in close against him, sometimes her arm draped across his chest. Whether this was a conscious move on her part or simply a new sleeping habit, he had no way of knowing. But he liked it. He more than liked it.

He'd tried so hard to be discreet, nearly always keeping their kisses behind closed doors. There had been a few exceptions, especially lately. If he'd failed to keep his affection for her respectfully hidden in any manner, it could only be in the way he looked at her. He often frustrated himself with his inability to simply look away. He'd stared at her intently through Sunday meeting, gazed at her in the living room in the evenings after supper, and tracked her movements in the kitchen during mealtimes. It had become almost reflexive, his watching her. If she was nearby, he was highly distracted. Most likely, anyone who was paying the slightest bit of attention had noticed.

Daniel and Caleb made some final preparations and then went swiftly back to the house to clean up before the hired driver arrived to take them down to Missouri. By the time Silas finished the work in the barn, they were loading their bags in the minivan. Shelby and Anna were nearly trembling with excitement, climbing in and out of their seats in the back of the van.

With quick goodbyes, Daniel and Mary hugged Silas before stepping into the van. They were well down the lane before any of his previous embarrassment came back to haunt him. But then again, he no longer really cared what they knew or suspected. Living in a big house surrounded by family had mostly desensitized him toward infringements on his personal privacy. And really, there wasn't any shame—no matter the unconventional nature of his marriage.

With a final wave, he turned to see Kirsten standing at the window, the interior of the house glowing golden-warm and yellow behind her.

He ducked his head shyly beneath his hat and climbed the steps up to the screen door. He hung his hat on a peg and shrugged out of his coat as the warm air in the washroom swept over him.

"Coffee or hot chocolate with your breakfast?" she asked from the doorway.

"Hot chocolate sounds *gut*," he answered, smiling without looking away from his fingers as they worked to loosen the laces on his boots.

Silas settled into Daniel's place at the head of the table, and soon Kirsten set a plate of pancakes and bacon in front of him, along with a generous mug of homemade hot chocolate.

Kirsten had made a little nest on the floor for Grace, who lay on her back on top of a thick quilt, busily exercising her legs. Silas took Kirsten's hand and prayed over their breakfast.

"Your hands are like ice," Kirsten said, keeping one of his hands in hers. He felt her warm, soft hands clasp tightly around his and suppressed a shudder. "Here. Hold your mug. That should warm you up." She fastened his hands around the ceramic mug. He liked this—this way she took care of him. He hadn't known he was missing it—this personal attention—all those years before her. Of course, his mother had taken care of and nurtured him in her own motherly way. But that had been years ago. She'd long since pulled back in certain ways to give him his space—perhaps to encourage him to find a wife who would, in fact, notice or care if his hands were cold.

"I'm not much of a cook yet, I'm afraid," Kirsten apologized.

Silas stuffed a forkful of pancakes into his mouth. "Pancakes are my favorite," he said as he chewed.

"Well, that's good because they're very easy," she laughed. "Although I thought Mom's homemade cinnamon rolls were your favorite."

"*Jah*. I like those too, I 'spose."

"You must. I think you ate three on Sunday morning." She shook her head incredulously.

"Did I?"

"Yes," she laughed again. "Evidently, you didn't notice me staring at you in awe and wonder." He loved the sound of her laughter, the way her eyes sparked in the low lantern light.

"I noticed," he disagreed, spearing another stacked wedge of pancakes and lifting it, stopping just before putting it in his mouth. "I just figured you were staring 'cuz ya thought I was so handsome." He shoved the bite into his mouth, deliberately not meeting her eyes and fighting a grin.

Laughter bubbled up and spilled out of Kirsten. Silas surrendered to the smile.

"Well…there was that, too," she laughed and then blushed.

The air shifted almost tangibly, taking on a subtly charged quality.

Grace squawked loudly, jolting them from the awkward silence. Her fists were balled up into tiny, frustrated fists.

"Are you hungry too, Grace?" Kirsten cooed as she folded her slender body over their daughter and scooped her up. Grace calmed immediately.

Silas finished his breakfast and cleared the table. He filled the sink with water and set to work washing the dishes while Kirsten fed Grace around the corner in the living room.

"I can do the dishes, Silas," she called over her shoulder.

"It's all right. I don't mind," he answered. Had his voice quivered? A plate slipped in his hands and splashed into the sink, sending a spray of soapy bubbles up and soaking his arms. He stopped to roll up his sleeves to just below his elbows. His long fingers were unfamiliar with this work, and he wiped clumsily at the plates, taking much longer, he was certain, than it would have taken Kirsten. He didn't put up a fight when she gently pushed him aside. Instead, he picked up a towel and dried as she finished the washing. The last plate clinked loudly on the stack, and for a moment neither of them moved. Silas felt almost nauseous with anxiety, but he turned to her. Gently, he took her warm, water-softened hands and pulled her to face him.

He felt as though his heart must be visibly beating in his throat.

"Is she sleeping?" He might as well have gravel in his throat for how raspy he sounded.

Kirsten nodded, glancing at the pack-n-play in the corner of the living room where Grace napped from time to time during the day.

For another long moment, he felt frozen, unsure of how or when to pull Kirsten's attention away from their daughter. He shyly stared at their hands, rubbing circles on the backs of hers with his thumb. He took one slow, deliberate step toward her, closing the slight gap between them, and her gaze swung abruptly to his face. He slipped an arm around her waist and kissed her. Kirsten didn't hesitate to wrap her arms around his neck, and he pulled her closer to him, his lips never leaving hers.

His hands reached up and pulled her arms down as he broke from the kiss. The confusion in her eyes was impossible to miss. He didn't smile, but he looked down at her longingly. He pulled her hand back into his and led her quietly past the living room to the stairs and up to their room.

.ஒஐ ஓஉ.

Kirsten pulled the two crusty, brown loaves of honey wheat bread out of the oven just as the van pulled up to the house. Through the window in the twilight, she could see Daniel and Mary unloading the family, frosty wisps of breath floating suspended in the bitter air. Shelby and Anna bounced in, full of extra energy after being cooped up in the car for hours on end.

"Ah, it smells *gut* in here!" Mary exclaimed, unwinding her scarf. "It's nice to come home to a warm house on such a cold evening," she breathed as she hugged Kirsten.

"Are you hungry? Shall I fix some supper?" Kirsten asked, feeling an odd role reversal.

"*Ach!* No. But the children might like a little snack?" Mary said, her eyebrows raised at Shelby and Anna, who nodded vigorously.

"Honey wheat bread?" Kirsten asked. The vigorous nodding continued. She sliced it, though it was almost too hot to touch, as Daniel and Caleb came in with the bags.

"Where is Silas?" Daniel asked after he pulled up his chair at the table.

It was totally unreasonable, the blush that burned on her cheeks at such an innocuous question.

"He went to Michael's to help with a sick cow," Kirsten answered, turning quickly away from the family gathered at the table. Almost on cue, a horse and buggy galloped by the house to the stable.

"He wanted to be here to welcome you home," Kirsten murmured, watching him guide Titus into the horse barn. She turned back to the steaming slices of bread, covering each one with a generous coat of butter that melted almost instantly. After a plate was slid in front of each person at the table, she fixed up a plate for Silas.

When his boots stomped across the porch and into the house, she turned to greet him. He strode directly to her, his arm sliding easily around her waist. His face was cold, but his lips were warm as he gently kissed her.

"Hi." His breath was warm on her cheek.

Kirsten smiled at him and bit her lip as his hand lingered on the small of her back. There was a whole new catalog of expressions he wore for her now. And only her. Slowly, he turned his smile to his family, greeting them warmly. No trace of the self-consciousness in him that she felt. His demeanor was easy and comfortable as he sat at the table, talking with his family.

"So everything went smoothly here, then?" Mary asked later as she washed the dishes. Kirsten knew the question was meant in a casual manner and was not probative, but it took a beat for her to steer her thoughts away from blush-worthy memories.

"I did have one mishap with a pan of cookie bars," Kirsten grimaced, remembering how she'd dropped the topping-loaded bar pan just as she'd moved to slide it into the oven. She had screamed and Silas had come rushing to her side, making sure she was okay and then patiently helping her clean out the oven. He hadn't scolded her, though she'd been careless and clumsy.

Silas. Always patient.

"Ah, yer a *gut* wife, Kirsten," Mary said, shaking her head. "You took *gut* care of yer family all on yer own."

Kirsten glowed with the praise. Of course, she felt different now. She was Silas's wife in every sense of the word. The change in their relationship was anything but subtle, as far as she was concerned. To feel so connected to this man that she loved was overwhelming at times. The past few days had been filled with secret smiles that needed no explanation and lingering looks that said more than words could communicate. She'd wondered how much of it would continue when the others returned. Perhaps he'd tone it down a bit. Silas would most certainly not pull her down into his lap when she served supper to the family, as he had this past weekend when it was just the three of them. He'd probably save the long, lingering kisses for their alone time and not march into the kitchen for a passionate embrace. That, of course, made sense. She preferred it that way, if the family was home.

But his kiss when he came in told her that he had absolutely no intention of reverting all the way back to their former ways. Even now he was looking at her in a knowing way that gave her goose bumps.

It seemed almost unnatural, how gentle and tender he could be. It wasn't typical behavior for most twenty-one-year-old males. Silas had patience well beyond his years, something she could hardly understand. She knew the wait for her had not been easy for him. It hadn't been for her either. But still, he'd shown a respect and a reverence for her that Kirsten hadn't known existed. With Logan, things had been so awkward, desperate, and painful. But being with Silas had been so contrary to her expectations and limited past experience that she'd been affected on an unbelievably emotional level. There was not a single, solitary doubt in her mind that he loved her as much as he claimed.

Crawling into bed and into his arms felt so intensely natural. As if this was where she was meant to be; that they belonged to one another in some predestined way. When the house quieted and the rest of the family lay tucked in their beds, Silas turned her face up to meet his kiss, and Kirsten knew she was home.

.ෙ𝒢ა.

It wasn't yet dawn, but Silas was awake. Kirsten lay next to him, her head on his chest. They'd fallen into an entirely new rhythm—one he loved but that overtook so many of his thoughts he often found it difficult to work. Absentmindedly, he curled a tendril of Kirsten's hair around his fingers, listening to and feeling her slow, deep breathing.

On the surface, life was much the same as it had been only a week ago. And yet, he felt permanently altered. Going through the motions of getting married but not actually taking her as a wife had been far more difficult than he'd anticipated. Truthfully, if he had known how tested he would be, he may have made a different decision about their living arrangements those first months. At times, it had seemed a cruel form of self-punishment. It had been his idea for her to have her own room. Of course, then Grace was born and all three of their lives had been changed entirely.

Sharing a room with his wife while still abstaining had been nothing short of an exercise in extreme self-discipline. She'd needed him for his reassurance and for occasional late-night baby duty. But now, they were everything they'd vowed to be all those months ago. How was it only months? The changes had seemed extreme, life events that take years to walk through. Yet they'd been on the fast track and only had months to process and adjust to each step.

In a legal sense, nothing had changed since Grace's birth. But in every other way, everything had changed. So much so that it almost felt as though he'd been physically altered. He felt oddly taller, broader, and even stronger. The knowledge that two people depended on him for his provision, protection, and love weighed on him, but not in an unpleasant way. There was a weight to his work—to his very existence—that hadn't been there before. It was suddenly as if the normal, everyday things that he did mattered because they mattered to Kirsten and Grace. He even walked differently. The eyes staring back at him in the mirror held a new knowledge, a subtle, humble assurance about himself. Gone was the boyish shyness that he'd worn and felt for so long; it had been replaced by a quiet strength.

Something quite different had happened with Kirsten, he'd noted with silent satisfaction. It certainly wasn't that she'd been humbled or brought down. No. Instead, she'd softened and yielded to him. And her work, too, had taken on its own light. She cared for him by her actions, doing things that he needed, not because he needed the help, but because she loved him. She wasn't the same timid girl he'd married. Yesterday morning, he'd laughed loudly when he'd overheard her greeting the chickens with a "Hullo there, ladies!" Anymore, when there were new things—things she didn't know how to do—she simply asked to be taught how to do it. They'd spent an hour in the horse barn on a lesson on how to hitch and unhitch a horse to a buggy. Kirsten had an additional learning curve that he'd never had to overcome. He had grown up this way. His way of life had stayed intact while her entire world had been turned upside down.

She shuddered in her sleep, and her arm wrapped around his waist. Finally, they seemed to be on the same page. There was only one hurdle left, and it was not his to clear. He could not run her race without getting in the way. In fact, he was trying very hard to stay out of the way. If there were questions she needed answered, he'd certainly help. But she had to be the one to ask them.

He sighed. Until then, this room in this house was their only private retreat.

— Chapter Forty-Five —

Few things in Kirsten's life could compare to the festive atmosphere in the Amish community over the holidays. Kirsten knew she should feel exhausted by the endless work frolics scattered amongst their neighbors and friends, but they were so much fun that instead, she'd felt energized by the mini-celebrations. Somehow, even with the added busyness at the market, Mary and Amy managed to prepare fantastic meals, even heartier in the winter months than they'd been in the summer.

Silas, on the other hand, spent little time anywhere other than the workshop. Holiday shoppers had ordered two huge dining sets. And there were three requests for kitchen cabinets. In addition, he had endless smaller pieces that he needed to keep in stock at the market, like rocking chairs, quilt racks, and corner cupboards. He spent long hours in the shop, even working long after supper. By the time he'd finally come inside, he would nearly collapse into bed.

Though, Kirsten thought with a warm flush of embarrassment, *his tiredness is only evident when he actually sleeps.*

Elizabeth came one Saturday afternoon to pick up Mary, Kirsten, Shelby, and Anna and take them all to do some Christmas shopping in the nearest city. But soon, inside the third store, Grace began crying in earnest. They all took turns trying to soothe the little one, but no one, not even Kirsten, could calm her. By the time Kirsten slid out of the van and yanked open the sliding door, her head was pounding. Silas suddenly appeared at her side and lifted the car seat from the van, bringing them both inside.

"I can't make her stop," Kirsten choked, tears brimming in her eyes and blurring Silas's face from her vision. "I don't know what's wrong with her."

He unfastened the seatbelts and lifted Grace out. With her head tucked under his chin, her scrunched, angry face buried in his neck, he began to murmur quietly in Pennsylvania Dutch. Grace settled momentarily, listening, then shuddered a sigh. Her arched back curled and snuggled into Silas's chest, and her tightly balled fists relaxed. Her tiny fingers stretched and took a loose fistful of his shirt in her hands. It was silent but for Silas's low, quiet voice and his slow, pacing footsteps.

Mary shook her head. Elizabeth stared in astonishment. Kirsten sank into a chair.

"Wow. That's just...incredible," Elizabeth whispered.

"He was *gut* with Anna Mae, too," Mary said with a smile.

"I think you're going to have to learn to speak Pennsylvania Dutch," Elizabeth said to Kirsten.

"Maybe," Kirsten laughed weakly, "but I think it's more than that." It was his voice. She knew because it did the same thing to her. "Sorry, Mom. About today," Kirsten sighed.

"We can try again another time." Elizabeth shook her head.

"I'm not going anywhere without him," Kirsten said, her eyes following Silas's slow pacing.

"I wouldn't either if I were you," Elizabeth laughed quietly.

Night fell and Grace sank into a deep sleep after all her fussing wore her out.

"Did you know that the only thing people stare at more than an Amish woman Christmas shopping in Target is an Amish woman Christmas shopping in Target with a screaming baby?" Kirsten whispered across the pillow. She could feel Silas's chest shake with silent laughter.

"Silas, I would have lost my mind if you hadn't been here for us tonight," Kirsten sighed, rolling to his side.

"I'll always be here for you and Grace." He smiled into her hair.

Kirsten sighed, deeply contented. She had absolutely no reason to doubt him.

❦

Daniel held the family Bible on his knee while the family gathered in the living room for devotions.

"Silas, would you read Matthew 1:18-25?" his father asked, holding the book out to him.

Silas flipped open to the passage, though he knew what he'd find there. Kirsten settled in next to him on the couch while Amy and the girls sat on the floor to entertain Grace.

> "This is how the birth of Jesus the Messiah came about: His mother Mary was pledged to be married to Joseph, but before they came together, she was found to be pregnant through the Holy Spirit. Because Joseph was a righteous man and did not want to expose her to public disgrace, he had in mind to divorce her quietly.
>
> "But after he had considered this, an angel of the Lord appeared to him in a dream and said, 'Joseph, son of David, do not be afraid to take Mary home as your wife, because what is conceived in her is from the Holy Spirit. She will give birth to a son, and you are to give him the name Jesus, because he will save his people from their sins.'
>
> "All this took place to fulfill what the Lord had said through the prophet: 'The virgin will be with child and will give birth to a son, and they will call him Immanuel—which means, "God with us."'
>
> "When Joseph woke up, he did what the angel of the Lord had commanded him and took Mary home as his wife. But he did not consummate their marriage her until she gave birth to a son. And he gave him the name Jesus."

Kirsten was motionless at his side, and he could nearly feel her surprise. They knelt side by side for prayers, and Kirsten's hand slipped easily into his. Her "good nights" to his parents were distracted and quiet. Amy offered to take Grace up to bed, cradling her and talking softly as she carried her up the stairs. Kirsten's questioning expression came as no great shock when she looked at him as they sat alone in the living room. For a long while, she was silent, and he could almost hear the thoughts racing through her mind.

"Joseph sounds a lot like...you," she finally murmured.

"There are some similarities," Silas allowed with a crooked smile.

"He married a woman who was carrying a baby that wasn't his," Kirsten observed.

Silas nodded.

"And he waited until later," she said, her voice barely above a whisper. "*Jah.*"

"I hadn't realized...it started out like that...exactly."

Messy. Unconventional. Out of order. Not according to plan. Yes, it had been all that way for Mary and Joseph then, just as it had been that way for them. Silas suddenly noticed how very real this Bible story was. Even though it was filled with angels talking in dreams about an impossible circumstance, it connected with him.

"God works in mysterious ways," he murmured the almost cliché phrase. Most of the time, it came off sounding like a verbal shrug. As if you had just given up on making sense of anything and blamed consequences on a mysterious God who spent his time thinking of ways to confuse people. But tonight, Silas meant it with a profound sense of wonder and awe. This was certainly not how he would have written the story of Christ's conception and birth. He'd thought the same thing about Kirsten once—that had it been in his hand to write her story, he would have ordained her days much differently. And yet, it all had happened just as God had intended. Who was he to complain? Kirsten's story would have been blissfully pain-free, but then she wouldn't really be Kirsten Miller, his beloved wife, mother of their little Grace. These roads of pain and suffering so often led to blessing. He'd seen it a hundred times in the lives of his church family. Now he'd witnessed it in a very personal way. It was only the smallest glimpse of God's goodness, but it was real, tangible, and entirely overwhelming.

— Chapter Forty-Six —

Kirsten had expected a long church service on Christmas morning, but she was surprised to find the pace slow and leisurely. No one was in a hurry to go to any church meetings. Silas didn't stir until nearly six o'clock. He opened his eyes and smiled sleepily at her. He rolled to his side and pulled her close to him, sending a ripple of pleasure through her.

His lips brushed hers, and she sighed deeply.

"I should go do the chores," he said in a gruff voice. Kirsten's only response was a quiet groan of protest. She watched him roll out of bed and stretch his arms high over his head. Was it Amish-approved behavior to interfere with a husband's chores? She didn't really need an answer, though she doubted even the most sensible Amish wife would feel any differently if they were married to Silas Miller.

It wasn't until breakfast time that he came bursting into the utility room, stamping the snow off his boots and removing his hat.

Silas smiled when he saw her peeking around the doorframe. He shook out of his coat and spun and grabbed her, pulling her all the way into the utility room and into his arms. She felt his lips at her ear.

"Merry Christmas, Mrs. Miller," he murmured, holding her tightly against him. Before she had a chance to respond, his mouth covered hers. He kissed her deeply as they hid just around the corner, out of sight of the family gathering around the table. The door yanked open, and Caleb stomped in, awkwardly stopping when he spied his brother kissing his wife. Kirsten blushed and struggled out of Silas's arms—an exercise in futility. But he let her go, smiling broadly and without the slightest hint of embarrassment at poor, red-faced Caleb. Kirsten rushed into the kitchen, sure she looked as frazzled as she felt.

Breakfast was loud, lively, and festive, full of Daniel's childhood Christmas memories. Though he must have heard them dozens of times, Silas smiled and laughed just as much as Kirsten, who was hearing it all for the first time.

Slowly, the breakfast dishes were cleared away until only the mugs remained on the table, waiting for yet another refill of hot chocolate. No one rushed off to work on anything. They all sat by the table and laughed until it was time to begin lunch preparations. David and Michael and their families would be arriving soon for the feast and for more celebrating.

Kirsten soon found herself locked in the joyful embrace of Deborah, then Michael, both of them wishing her a "Merry Christmas." The children congregated around Grace, shaking her rattles and tickling her tummy. Kirsten could see the appeal in a large family—children to play with their siblings and cousins. She often wondered how many she and Silas would have. Though she was in no hurry to revisit the experience of labor and delivery, she'd gladly have as many babies as they could feasibly make. The joy of Christmas with children and a large family was almost more than she could process.

There was near constant eating, a display of cakes and treats on the kitchen table the likes of which Kirsten had never seen. There was singing. Some of the songs she recognized, though they were almost all in Pennsylvania Dutch. The gifts exchanged were simple and inexpensive, but also sweet and meaningful—each one chosen specifically with the recipient in mind.

"Come with me." His voice was at her ear, his hands on her waist. She followed Silas wordlessly up to their room, not at all sure what he intended to do there. He opened the door and stepped aside. At the foot of the bed sat a hope chest—maple, of course. How he had managed to sneak it in here during the course of the day, she had no idea. Kirsten knelt by it and lifted the lid. It smelled of its cedar lining. She ran her hands along the front, perfect in its smoothness. It was simple—no carving or ornate scrolling—but it was breathtakingly beautiful.

"Most Amish women get their hope chest years before they get married. I didn't have time to make it before our wedding."

She could hear the smile on his face. Kirsten closed the lid and smoothed her hands along the top. The wood-grain markings were flawless; Silas must have spent extra time selecting the boards.

"You made this for me."

It was perhaps the most blatant statement-of-the obvious ever uttered. But that he had spent precious workshop time handcrafting a gift for her—not a bed or a chair, which were practical necessities—was touching. For her. Just for her. She could picture him measuring, cutting, fitting, assembling, gluing, sanding, and finishing. She'd watched him many times, sometimes holding a lantern so he could work for another hour after supper.

"You can't imagine how much this means to me," Kirsten whispered in the dim bedroom. She stood then and looked at Silas where he leaned on the wall. She stepped close and kissed him. It was several minutes before she pulled away.

"We have to go back downstairs, don't we?" she sighed dramatically.

Silas laughed lightly, but it ended in his own sigh of regret. She smoothed his shirt while he finger-combed his hair. Downstairs, the party continued with games. Elizabeth arrived just before supper, and Kirsten was warmed to see how the Millers welcomed her into their lively conversation.

With nothing short of happy exhaustion, Kirsten slipped beneath the wedding quilt late Christmas night. Grace snoozed soundly in her cradle after being worn out by the attention of her extended family. Kirsten longed to sleep, but she forced herself to stay awake until Silas came to bed. He soon slipped quietly in the room, shed his clothes, and eased into bed.

"Silas?"

"Yeah?"

"Thank you. For the hope chest."

"Yer welcome."

"This was the very best Christmas of my entire life," she whispered.

"Mine, too." He was smiling again.

The hope chest was a treasure. But equally wonderful was the way he'd given her a family. She had never had a Christmas filled with so much joy and love and so little commercialism or holiday stress. To have shared it with her husband and her daughter—this was more than she'd ever dared to dream.

Silas leaned over her and kissed her deeply. This, right here, was heaven. Paradise.

— Chapter Forty-Seven —

Midwest winters are bleak and excruciatingly long. On certain days, with a healthy dose of sunshine and a fresh dusting of snow or frost, the beauty almost made Kirsten forget how bitterly cold it was. The scene outside the window looked picturesque—like the glitter-encrusted Christmas cards that she'd loved as a child. With a horse and buggy easily tugging down the lane through the snow drifts, it almost felt like she was living in a painting.

But Silas's ice-cold hands when he came in from outside were evidence enough that the beauty was brutal. She spent several minutes rubbing his hands to warm them and get his circulation going each time he came inside. He had very gently, but firmly, instructed her to stay in with Grace. The subzero temperatures were dangerous. The woodstove in his workshop helped to take most of the bite out of the air as he worked, but it was still too cold for him to spend as much time as he wanted working on his many projects.

She watched the porch swing sway in the biting wind, its chains coated in a solid layer of ice. It was hard to believe they'd spent so many summer evenings out there, just the two of them. She doubted if it would ever be so humid and sultry again. Silas stepped behind her, his arm circling her waist.

"I miss Deborah," Kirsten sighed. "It's been weeks since I saw her." Kirsten and Grace had missed Sunday meetings because of the cold. Her social outings had come to a screeching halt, and she was feeling the pangs of cabin fever.

"Give it a few more days. This cold snap should break soon. If it does… when it does, I'll take ya over there."

He was faithful to his word. Three days later, the wind stopped and the icicles dripped slowly, lazily into the snow. Silas hitched up the buggy, and Kirsten bundled herself and Grace into multiple layers. The three of them would spend the day at Michael and Deborah's—the men in the barn repairing a broken buggy and the women in the house for a quilting lesson while the children slept or played at their sides.

"It's really good to see you again," Kirsten said as they snipped pieces of fabric from the chosen bundles.

Deborah smiled. "It's been a long winter already."

"Has it made you extra anxious to have your baby?"

"Oh, not anxious really. Just ready. But I have another month to go," Deborah laughed.

"Caleb is desperately hoping to share his birthday with a new niece or nephew," Kirsten said, smiling.

"That would be a week early or so. That'd be okay," Deborah said, craning her neck and staring at the ceiling as if there were a calendar on it.

"Did you go early with Johnny?"

"Only a few days early. But very, very fast." She emphasized the last words.

"Oh?"

"Four hours. Start to finish. Michael had a hard time getting me to the hospital in time."

"Wow." Kirsten shook her head. "That must have been…intense."

"*Jah*, it was," Deborah agreed with a light laugh. "The doctor warned me that the next one would probably come quickly, too."

Kirsten was momentarily lost in the memory of Grace's birth. They were, without question, the hardest fourteen hours of Kirsten's life. But also the most rewarding. Maybe next time Silas would stay with her. That would surely make things better. Not fun. But better.

Lunch was fried chicken, mashed potatoes, green beans, fresh whole-wheat bread rolls, homemade applesauce, and mocha brownies for dessert. Deborah, like most other Amish women, was an amazing cook. The only thing better than the food was the friendly conversation amongst the four of them. Michael was very funny. Kirsten already knew that. But she'd never seen Silas so relaxed and at ease, never heard him laugh so much.

"You get along well with Michael," Kirsten observed as they made their way home.

"*Jah.* It's better now…than it used to be."

"He's a lot like your father. Has his…cheerful disposition. Caleb, too."

"David was that way when we were growing up," Silas told her, nodding.

"I cannot picture that." Kirsten paused. "What about you? Were you a jovial child?"

"No." Silas grinned almost sadly. "I was quiet and reserved. Nothing like my father or my brothers."

"I happen to think you are a lot like Dad," Kirsten said thoughtfully.

"How so?" His eyes narrowed in curiosity.

"You have his strength, his peace, and his calm. This solid, unwavering conviction in everything you do. Yet somehow, you pull it all off with humility, warmth, and kindness. You might be more quiet, but you're also far more intuitive."

She could feel his gaze on her face.

"Also…more handsome," she added.

Silas laughed and pulled her close. One of the best things about riding in a buggy was that her husband could drive and kiss her at the same time.

.୧ଛ ୭ବ.

It was a highly unfair price to pay for a single day away, but little Grace came down with a cold. She was terribly congested and frequently irritated that she couldn't breathe through her nose. Kirsten felt guilty at first when Grace woke Silas several times throughout the night. But after only two hours of sleep, she was numbed to the point of inability to function, and who was up when didn't even register in her sleep-deprived brain. She wasn't even able to mumble her thanks when Silas took Grace and carried her downstairs. Kirsten merely melted into a state of unconsciousness, alone in their bed. Silas woke her two blessed hours later so she could nurse Grace. Neither of them were remotely coherent at breakfast.

It was Amy who shuttled Kirsten upstairs for a midday nap. When Kirsten came downstairs, she found Amy gently rocking Grace in the living room. Grace's tiny fingers were curled around one of Amy's. Amy was softly singing a hymn Kirsten had heard many times at church, her beautiful voice pure and sweet. Kirsten felt a swell of thankfulness that Grace would learn these hymns from her Aunt Amy, whose voice was as lovely as any Kirsten had ever heard.

For a few minutes, Kirsten simply watched them. The look on Amy's face was the only thing more stunning than Grace's quiet. She'd seen the look on the faces of other women—other mothers adoring their own sweet babies when they didn't know others were watching. But seventeen-year-old Amy was most likely several years from having her own babies, especially if Lucas was as out of the picture as he seemed to be.

And yet, here she was, adoring this little baby that had been the source of the problems between her and the boy she loved. There had never been even a hint of resentment in Amy's treatment of Grace. And now there was an undeniable love and adoration. Amy could not possibly love Grace more if she had truly been born to Deborah and Michael or to Sarah and David. Or to Silas.

Kirsten stepped further into the room and Amy glanced up.

"You're good with her." Kirsten smiled softly.

"She's such a sweet little girl," Amy said, smiling down at Grace.

For the next several nights, Amy would knock gently on the door to their room and offer to take Grace for a while when she fussed. Kirsten knew it was an act of love for Grace more than anything else. And it was with no small amount of relief that Kirsten and Silas slept soundly in their bed. If it hadn't been for Silas's help or Amy's nurturing, Kirsten didn't know how she ever would have made it as a single mother. Which is exactly what she would have been if Silas hadn't offered her a home and a family.

There was little she wouldn't do to pay them back.

CHAPTER FORTY-EIGHT

"Happy Birthday, dear Caleb. Happy Birthday to you!" The voices of his family rang loudly in the small kitchen, and Caleb's chest puffed out confidently. Silas quietly laughed to himself at the sight. His little brother rather loved being the center of attention and had been talking nonstop about his birthday dinner for most of the last week.

He had not gotten his birthday wish of a new niece or nephew born on his birthday. At least, not yet. Kirsten and Deborah sat in rockers near the fireplace, their heads bent close together as usual. Deborah, still pregnant, looked with concern at Kirsten, who was obviously trying to convince her expectant friend and sister-in-law of something or other.

Grace babbled loudly just then, her hand flailing just beneath his chin. He smiled down at her and was rewarded with a gummy smile that lit up her whole face and made her look as if she'd burst into a fit of giggles. She was definitely feeling better and had slept well for the last week. A relief for everyone.

"So, ya got yerself an open-air buggy?" Michael asked Caleb.

"*Jah*. Silas seemed to think his courtin' days were done, so he passed it down." Caleb grinned at Silas.

"Somehow I 'spect we'll see ya out driving it around in the dead of winter," David laughed.

"Naw. He didn't give me a horse." Caleb's face fell and everyone laughed. "Of course, if he ends up being shunned, then I might get Titus!" Caleb joked.

All movement and conversation froze. Silas felt as though his heart had fallen out of his body.

"Caleb!" Daniel's rebuke sounded miles away, so loud was the thrumming pulse in Silas's ears.

"Why would Silas be shunned?" Kirsten's voice came from behind him. Caleb shot Silas a panicked, apologetic look. Silas hadn't wanted her to know what hung in the balance—he hadn't wanted her to feel as though there were expectations hanging over her head. He surely hadn't wanted her to find out like this. Silas slowly stood and turned to face Kirsten.

"If you would fail take baptismal instruction within your first year, we would be...shunned," he said, meeting her eyes.

Her brow furrowed in confusion. "Meaning?"

"We would be cut off from the church and my family. I'd leave." The truth. Finally, the whole truth.

"Leave?" she asked, her voice hard and incredulous.

"Take you and Grace and leave my family."

No one breathed. Kirsten processed that seriously for a moment. A brief moment.

"Okay...well...just tell me what to do then," she said with a shrug.

Silas could only shake his head.

"Silas...just tell me what I need to say or do so that we can stay. You said something about classes. I'll start them this week," she persisted.

"No."

"No?" she demanded.

"No."

"Why not?"

"You're not ready," he said simply, knowing by her very words that she wasn't.

"Sure I am," she insisted.

"No. Yer not."

He could see the panic rising in her.

"This is ridiculous," her voice shook, still attempting to lighten the mood. "I would never do anything to come between you and your family. In fact, I should have done...something...these baptism classes... months ago."

She'd just spoken his greatest fear. She was treating it as merely an item on a to-do list. A formality. She'd go through the motions if he so much as told her what they were.

"Can't you just tell me what to say to the bishop?" she pleaded.

"I could." Yes, he could. So easily. With some coaching and key phrases she could so easily be taught exactly how to gain admittance into the church. "But I won't," he said quietly and gently.

"You won't," she repeated. "What happens if I go to the bishop on my own?"

"I won't stand to witness for ya." The silence in the packed kitchen was deafening. "And if I don't witness for you, no one will."

"I don't understand," she gasped as she stared at him.

"I will only stand and witness for ya when ya would choose faith over all else—even me."

She shook her head and frantically began searching the faces of his family. They avoided her eyes. Finally, her shoulders sagged in defeat. Wordlessly, and with tears brimming in her eyes, she took Grace from him and went quietly up the stairs.

He ached to follow her, to wipe away her tears and make empty promises about how it would be okay. Instead, he turned and grabbed his coat off the wall. It was early to do chores, but he did them anyway. She needed time. He'd hurt her—he knew that. So many times, he had thought about telling her, always deciding the last thing Kirsten needed was another expectation hanging over her head. She was so determined to adjust that she would have studied faith like a school lesson, locking it all in her mind but never really believing with her heart. He wouldn't stand by and listen to his wife make a dishonest vow—wouldn't help her fabricate a life of faith. Unless he could be sure she'd chosen to accept Jesus out of love and devotion to Him, he would not allow her to choose baptism because of their marriage. It seemed harsh and extreme to others—some of his own family had questioned his request to not speak of the consequences. But it was necessary. In fact, it was essential.

David and Sarah soon left and the party dissolved away. When he came back inside the house, Deborah and Michael were still there, sitting at the table.

"She wants to see you," Deborah said without looking at him.

Silas quickly crossed to the stairs and made his way to their room, fervently hoping that she somehow understood his position.

She was sitting on her side of the bed, staring out the window, her back to him.

"Kirsten?"

She didn't turn, but she spoke with her back stiff and straight.

"I'm going to Deborah's to be there when the baby is born. Amy needs to stay so that she can help at the market. It makes the most sense for me to go." It was then that he noticed the bag packed and ready to go on the bed next to Grace's car seat. "If you'll allow it."

The last words were unmistakably bitter.

No! He wanted to scream it. He wanted to take her by the shoulders, make her look at him, and tell her he absolutely forbade it. Somehow, he had to explain to her that running away wouldn't help. He needed to beg her not to take Grace. He'd put his foot down if she insisted.

All the arguments swirled in his mind and died in this throat. Forcing his will any further would only hurt her and drive her further away.

"Is that yer choice then?" His voice sounded dead, lifeless, just as he felt.

She nodded once, still not looking at him.

Numbly, he turned from the room and shuffled down the hall. Michael had pulled his buggy up to the porch and was inside, helping Deborah into her coat. They fell silent when Silas came into the room and crossed to Grace's cradle in the living room. He picked her up and felt a wave of panic wash over him. Kirsten walked briskly into the kitchen, setting the car seat on the table. With trembling lips, Silas pressed a kiss on Grace's fuzzy head and handed her to Kirsten. She buckled Grace in and covered her in hats and blankets, then slung the handle over her arm and walked out to the waiting buggy. Silas followed to the porch in a daze, not even pulling on his coat. Without a backward wave or glance—not even a glare—Kirsten climbed into the buggy with Grace, and they were gone.

Gone.

"She'll see past the anger, Silas," Mary said quietly. She sounded more as though she hoped it was true than that she believed it.

"She's not angry," he said, watching the buggy turn onto the road. "She's hurt and terrified." And that was much worse.

He abruptly turned and went back inside, walking briskly to the stairs and up to their room. His room. It was frighteningly void of any and all traces of his wife and daughter. She'd taken all of her dresses and all of Grace's things with her. Almost as if she'd not be coming back. The only trace of her was the wedding quilt spread on their bed. His bed.

He was shaking now—violently—whether from cold or fear or pain, he didn't know and didn't care. He collapsed onto the bed, fully dressed, pressing the side of his face to the quilt. For a long time, he lay still, listening for a buggy on the lane, her footsteps on the stairs, Grace's warbling cry. Anything. But there was nothing. Nothing. Just as there had been before he'd met her. No wife, no baby, no…joy.

He had never envisioned this, not since the day he'd married her. The risk of being shunned carried the risk of losing his family. That he'd attempted to imagine a time or two. But not her and not his daughter. Never them. He had made a choice full of hope and faith. But it was one Kirsten couldn't understand or agree with. If she would ever see his reasoning, he didn't know. All she saw now was how much he'd hurt her by refusing to help her do the only thing she knew to do. Her lip had trembled as she'd buckled Grace into the car seat. And all the words he'd wanted to say had stuck on the lump in his throat.

He curled himself into a ball, clutching fistfuls of the quilt to cover his face and muffle the sob that he felt building in him almost of their own volition—like a hiccup or a reflex.

His breath broke the overwhelming silence, catching hard in his chest, tearing at the lump in his throat.

"No," he moaned as tears blurred his vision. He squeezed his eyes shut and gritted his teeth, his breath coming in short, sobbing pants. When the pain ebbed to a dull ache and he was nearly empty, he had only one thing left—prayer. Wrapped in the only thing left of her, he let his whispered prayers carry him to sleep.

⁖⊕⊙⊛⁖

Kirsten was sure of two things. First, that she had a thousand thoughts about what had happened. And second, that she couldn't think of any of them. The only things that her mind could access were images—Silas shaking his head, Silas's quivering lips as he kissed Grace goodbye, Silas's hands balled into fists as he stared at her in the buggy. Those three images replayed on an endless loop, even infiltrating her dreams.

She went through the motions of daily life, helping Deborah with laundry and baking and cleaning. Much of it she did robotically and in silence. Supper was brutally quiet, though she hardly cared.

Michael read a story from the Bible about a man who went out and sold everything he had to buy a field. Ridiculous. Why can't anyone ever leave well enough alone? Kirsten sniffed a laugh.

"Do ya have something to say, Kirsten?" Michael asked her.

She could tell by his Daniel-esque tone of voice that not answering was not an option. Not wanting to be kicked out of his home, she decided to just answer him honestly.

"Smacks of discontent and greed," she said with a shrug. "The grass is always greener on the other side of the fence."

Michael considered that and studied her closely before responding. "But what if it was worth it?"

Kirsten's eyes flashed to his face. "You think it's worth it to risk everything you have on a slim chance?" There was underlying anger in her voice, though none of it was directed at Michael.

"Sometimes." His answer was simple, honest, and totally unaffected by her tone.

"So you think he was right, then?" They both knew Kirsten was referring to Silas.

"I believe Silas would rather suffer any consequence than get in the way of yer salvation," Michael said levelly.

"Salvation."

"Eternal life in the kingdom of God," he explained.

"Even if it costs him everything?"

Michael looked at Deborah for a long moment and then nodded.

"Why?" Kirsten persisted.

"Because he loves you," Michael said, looking back at her.

"But…it's not just his…loss. They are my family, too. And Daniel and Mary would…" The tears coursed hot down her face as her voice trailed off.

"I don't want to lose any of you," Kirsten choked, looking at Deborah.

"No one wants anything bad to happen," Deborah said, squeezing Kirsten's hand.

"Then tell me how to stop it," Kirsten whispered hoarsely.

"Did ya bring yer Bible with you?" Deborah asked suddenly.

"Yes," Kirsten mumbled as she wiped her eyes.

"Maybe you'd like to read one of the gospels," Deborah said.

"What's a gospel?"

Michael showed her how to find the book of Mark.

"Oh. I'd only gotten up to Esther, I guess," Kirsten admitted.

"That's *gut*," Michael reassured her. "But this is *gut*, too." He smiled.

Kirsten sat in the guestroom, the gas lamp burning while Grace slept in the pack-n-play in the corner. She read of the birth of Jesus, which was familiar from the Christmas season she'd just enjoyed. And then came the miracles. The healings. The feedings. The exorcisms. And then the stories of his teaching—the life lessons on how to spend money, how to give to the less fortunate, and how to love. Love. This man was so humble, kind, compassionate, sincere, gentle, and loving. So much like Silas. It was easy to see who her husband had modeled his life after.

The next night at supper, Kirsten brought her Bible to the table with her.

"Do you really believe all this happened?" she asked Michael a bit incredulously.

"Every word."

"Even the supposed miracles? I mean, how could he have fed five thousand people or walked on water or cured all those people?"

Michael spread his hands. "He is the Son of the Most High God."

Kirsten couldn't tell if that was a statement or a wonder to him.

"So…why? Why do you believe it?" she said finally.

Michael furrowed his brow and thought seriously, though with a slight grin on his face. "Let me put it this way: do ya believe Silas loves you?"

"Yes," Kirsten dropped her head and whispered to her plate.

"Why?"

She hadn't expected the follow-up question.

"He tells me," she blushed. "And he shows me by his actions—things he does for me. He takes care of me. And he took a huge risk for me."

Michael's grin spread across his face into an earsplitting smile. It wasn't mocking, but understanding—as if every word she'd said he had already known. And as if she had answered her own question.

"So you believe God exists because you feel His love for you?" Kirsten asked.

"I believe God has revealed Himself to me in His word and in His goodness to me," Michael answered.

"Oh." Kirsten nodded, though she would need hours to absorb and unpack this conversation.

That evening, she continued on with her reading. Jesus's triumphal entry, his sudden betrayal, his abandonment by his friends and family, his joke of a trial, and then his cruel punishment. His death. Still, she read on, remembering her own grief when her father had died. Her many trips to his grave, just as these women went to Jesus's tomb. Would they curl into a ball at the foot of his grave the way she had at her father's? Would they gasp for breath between their sobs? Would their tears soak their clothing?

Kirsten sat up slowly as she read the angel's words.

Risen? Like alive? This is where her story had taken a drastically different, more realistic path. Her father had not risen. No. Not at all. God hadn't done that for her or her mother. He had not revealed himself to her with that goodness, even though he was supposedly capable of it. No. Instead, they had grieved for years, struggled to survive on not nearly enough money, lived in near poverty, and barely scraped by. He hadn't shown his goodness then. With her mom working long hours, she'd been so lonely and desperate for someone's attention. And then Logan had used her and left her. Left her with a baby. Where was God then? He had not only not revealed Himself; He had outright hidden from her.

She slapped her Bible shut and turned out the light. It would take a lot to believe in His goodness. In fact, lately He seemed downright mean and distant.

— CHAPTER FORTY-NINE —

Kirsten woke with a jolt from a nightmare that had her running through a cemetery looking for her dad's grave, unable to find it. Then, she'd stumbled on a small stone with one name engraved across it.

Silas Miller.

She'd screamed then, though evidently not out loud. Grace was still slumbering peacefully in her bed.

But in the hall, Kirsten heard footsteps quickly running down the stairs. She got up and peered down the hall—Michael and Deborah's door stood open. She tiptoed to it and listened for movement or voices, but she heard neither. Deborah's pregnant silhouette moved in front of the moonlit window, her hands pressed to the small of her back.

"Deborah?" Kirsten whispered then.

"Michael went to call our driver," she panted. "Help me into my dress?"

Kirsten pulled the dress over Deborah's head and fastened the apron strings. She twisted Deborah's fantastically long, thick hair up and pinned it into place. By the time she had tied Deborah's shoes, Michael was back to help her down the stairs. Kirsten knew he was completely capable of helping his wife to the car, could probably carry her there if need be, but she took Deborah's elbow and offered her own strength as they went down the long flight of stairs and out to the porch, where the car had just arrived. Despite the obvious contractions, Deborah was calm, even smiling serenely at Michael when he looked at her worriedly.

With one last squeeze of Kirsten's hand, Deborah eased into the car. The driver pulled away quickly, leaving Kirsten in the yard. Johnny and Grace were sleeping soundly in the house, but Kirsten could not rest. Her mind and heart were with Deborah all those miles down the road. There was nothing to do but wait. Though really, what was she waiting for? There would be no phone call. Most likely, Michael would find a way to get word to her. He must know how desperately she would want to know.

It was a long, dark night. And after not sleeping at all, Kirsten was ready and waiting when Johnny woke up at six o'clock wanting breakfast. Juggling two little ones was not easy, but she found it surprisingly calming. It felt good to be busy—to be doing something. And something helpful at that. Deborah and Michael need not worry a moment about Johnny. He was in his home, being watched over. At least that should give them some comfort. It did her.

For now, Michael was the one who would coach Deborah through her labor. Kirsten thought back to her delivery of Grace with a pang. Mary had been there, and her presence had been a gift. But even then, a part of her had longed for Silas to be the one to bear her steady grip and whisper his own words of encouragement. Would he ever coach her and help her through the delivery of a baby of their own making? What was she going to do when she was no longer needed at Michael and Deborah's and there was no excuse to stay away? How long would this break be? Why hadn't he come after her and begged her to come home—offered to help her talk to the bishop? So little made sense any more.

She'd fed both of the children and had just sat down to play with Johnny when a horse and buggy clattered into the yard. Amy and Mary were on the porch by the time Kirsten had made her way to the front door.

Amy immediately went to Grace, scooped her up, and kissed her soundly on the forehead. Mary looked at Kirsten for a long moment. There was no condemnation or judgment in her expression. No disapproval. Just concern. And sadness. As if she was bearing the pain in her own way.

"Would ya like a ride to the hospital? Amy can watch the children for a few hours if you'd like to see Deborah," Mary offered with a small smile.

Kirsten only nodded.

"How are ya, Kirsten?" Mary asked as they made their way down the road.

"Worried," she answered. About Deborah. About Silas. About every single tomorrow that stretched in front of her.

"Michael is with her, and she's walked this road before," Mary soothed. "You'll see someday when ya have another. The second comes a bit easier."

Kirsten had no response for that, though she desperately hoped every word was true.

"You're not mad at me?" Kirsten finally asked as she blinked back sudden tears.

"No. No, I'm not mad at ya," Mary said quietly.

"Why not?"

Mary sighed. "I can't say that I agree with ya leaving yer husband the way ya did. But I don't know what all this must be like for ya, either. I grew up Amish and I never had to face the struggle you have. I miss ya though. I love ya as my own daughter, and the house isn't the same without you and Grace." Mary's voice was choked with emotion.

Here was yet another reason Silas was wrong not to help her—to show her what she needed to do so that they could hang on to their family. Mary was, had become, the mother to Kirsten that Elizabeth never could be. As much as Kirsten loved her mom, she'd recognized long ago that the hand life had dealt them demanded a sacrifice. Elizabeth had sacrificed time with Kirsten, leaving her alone for long stretches while she worked to provide for them. It wasn't her fault really, just her price to pay.

But Mary was the opposite—able and willing to sacrifice time at work any time her family needed her. Time was the currency in which the Amish dealt. And by those standards, they were ridiculously wealthy. How Silas could ever think of sacrificing Mary's presence in their life was totally beyond Kirsten. His refusal to witness for her felt very much like him taking away some of the most important people in the world to her. All so she would somehow put her trust in a God who had consistently disappointed her.

They walked down the long hallway to the obstetrics department. The sights, smells, and sounds were all vividly familiar. The nurse went down the hall, and soon Michael was rushing toward them.

"A girl! Six pounds, twelve ounces. *Gut* and healthy. We named her Katie," he said with a wild joy dancing in his eyes. He was positively beaming, and Kirsten had to choke back a sob before she could smile. "Deborah's *gut*, too. Come see!"

They followed his fast pace down the hall and into the dimly lit room. Deborah sat up in bed, cradling her own tiny bundle. Her face broke into a glorious smile when she spotted them.

Mary held Katie and praised her fine features, *oohing* and *aahing* as any grandma would. Soon, she passed Katie to Kirsten and told Michael they should go make a few phone calls. Kirsten barely noticed them leave, so taken was she with this new one.

Katie was beautiful, her face scrunched up, soft down on her body, perfectly formed fingers with tiny, pink fingernails. Fearfully and wonderfully made. Kirsten was totally unprepared for the flood of emotions that pulsed through her. Deborah was so dear to her, and to hold this beautiful new baby—her niece—was extraordinarily precious. She tried to imagine never seeing Katie again, not living just down the road, not celebrating birthdays or Christmases or a simple Tuesday night supper. Katie would grow up fast, and Kirsten wanted so badly to see it all. The tears spilled over her cheeks and ran down her neck.

"Kirsten?"

"She's just so wonderful, Deborah!" Kirsten breathed, keeping her sadness to herself.

Kirsten sat on the bed, and Deborah ran her hand over the fuzz on Katie's head.

"All that pain for something as wonderful as this," Deborah said, smiling.

Kirsten looked at her suddenly. Deborah met her eyes with curiosity.

Pieces of thoughts swirled and started to come together in Kirsten's mind.

"Pain gives birth to…" Kirsten didn't know how to finish.

"Life." Deborah smiled. "Just as night gives birth to morning and winter gives birth to spring."

Kirsten nodded slowly, her mind still spinning.

"God has a way of redeeming what was broken by the world and restoring it to fullness in Him," Deborah whispered. "I'm not glad that it hurts, but I take joy in the fact that we have a loving Heavenly Father who can bring goodness and life in spite of the pain."

Kirsten stared at Deborah.

"A Heavenly Father," she echoed. She'd heard it before at Sunday meetings, in Daniel's prayers, and even in family conversations.

"*Jah.* He loves you. As Daniel loves his children. As Michael loves Jonathan and Katie. As yer dad must have loved you. And as Silas loves Grace. God doesn't wish for you to have pain—only to hold on through it."

Kirsten's mind reeled. A good, gracious, and loving God who loved his children enough to redeem their pain? This was Silas Miller's God—the One in whom he put his trust? She passed Katie back to Deborah just as Michael reentered the room.

"I'm going to go get some coffee," Kirsten said, excusing herself. She walked woodenly down the hallway, Deborah's words echoing in her mind.

She didn't even see her until it was too late.

"Kirsten Walker." It was a statement, not a question.

"Hello, Deb," Kirsten said, seeing her old classmate standing in the hall, staring at her.

"Well...I heard you went Amish, but I could hardly believe it," Deb stated, crossing her arms. "Guess it's true," she laughed shortly. "You married that Amish guy?"

Kirsten nodded, the lump in her throat swelling rapidly. "Silas Miller." She didn't know why she said his name. In fact, she didn't really even want Deb to know it. But it felt good to say it, like she'd been holding her breath for too long.

"And you had the kid?"

"My daughter. Grace," Kirsten said evenly, terribly glad Grace was not with her at that moment.

"So you live together—one happy little family?" Deb was more incredulous than sarcastic or critical.

Kirsten nodded.

"No electricity?"

"No."

"What's that like?" Deb pressed.

"It's very peaceful," Kirsten answered honestly.

"And no cars?"

"No." Kirsten could hardly keep from smiling.

"Do you have to work anywhere?"

"Just at home." Kirsten shook her head.

"Hmm. So you screw my jerk of a boyfriend, get knocked up, have his baby, meet some other guy, get married, and live happily ever after."

"Something like that," Kirsten allowed.

"Wow," Deb said quietly. "Well, you probably heard Logan dumped me the day after he moved in at college." Deb shrugged.

"No. I hadn't heard."

"Yeah. He's an idiot. But I got my CNA license, and I really like my job." Kirsten noticed her scrubs for the first time. "I'm going on for my LPN."

"That's nice." Kirsten smiled politely. "I'm glad you're doing well." Was she really? It surprised her, but yes, she was glad. This Deb was by far preferable to the old one.

Deb shook her head. "I wasn't very nice to you. Okay—I was awful to you," she admitted. "But I am sorry."

Kirsten nodded. "I forgive you," she said quietly.

"It's good to see things turned out so well for you, Kirsten," Deb said as she moved past her.

"Thank you," Kirsten murmured.

Things had turned out so well? She'd had a rough childhood – much of it shadowed by her father's death. But he had loved her.

Her mother had struggled to provide and had worked long hours. But she had sacrificed so that Kirsten could live in her childhood home.

Kirsten had made a bad decision and wound up pregnant and broken-hearted. But Grace was alive and well, and there was a wonderful man who loved both of them and had given them a home and a family.

Silas. Grace. The Millers. All of them a precious gift. Goodness given beyond her deserving. Could it be that God had redeemed all that pain and brokenness, given her all these blessings, simply because He loved her? It's what Silas would do—give when she hadn't earned it. Love was not something received, measured, and then distributed accordingly. In all her love for Silas and Grace, she'd never felt as though they had to somehow earn her love for them. She gave it unconditionally and received theirs in return.

God hadn't turned His back. She could see that now. He'd waited, just as she'd wait for Silas and Grace to accept her love. He'd taken all those days of pain and brought her through them to these days of mercy.

Did He really love her that much? She didn't know, but there was one person who did. She ran down the hall to the pay phone and dialed a number she knew by heart.

"Mom? I need a ride."

— Chapter Fifity —

The yard was a muddy mess due to the unseasonably warm weather of the last two days, but Silas still felt cold inside. He'd made himself go through the motions. He'd worked relentlessly in the workshop, finishing all his orders and starting on inventory for the market.

It wasn't enough to fill the void. Nothing could. He missed his daughter and longed to hold her, to listen to her cooing and watch her sleep. His ache for Kirsten was deeper and almost impossible to tolerate. The evenings were hard. The nights were excruciating. He was always the first one up, as though he couldn't stand to be alone in the silence of their room. Used to be that he loved being alone, almost craved solitary moments. Now they stretched on interminably.

He slogged across the yard, having just heard Michael and Deborah's good news of a daughter. The pain in his chest throbbed. *A daughter*. He tromped back out to the workshop, not even bothering to skirt the mud puddles. The sound of a vehicle on the road followed by the distant slam of a car door caught his attention. He turned and watched a lone woman wave at the van and walk down the lane, her skirt and apron blowing in the warm wind.

Kirsten.

Without thinking, he changed direction, walking quickly to her. She could be angry. He supposed she had a right to be. She was probably still hurt. He didn't blame her. But he needed to be near her.

He met her halfway down the lane, where she stopped just steps short of him. There were tears in her eyes. He could see them now. She looked at him almost desperately and then slowly sank to her knees in a muddy patch of grass. With her head bowed she drew in a deep, shaky breath.

"Silas, can you forgive me for the pain I caused you, the disrespect I showed you, and the anger I felt towards you?"

Felt? It was...gone? He dropped to his knees in front of her, the icy-cold wetness seeping through his trousers and onto his skin.

"I forgive you," he rasped.

She looked up into his face through tears that hadn't yet fallen.

"I'm so sorry," she choked.

"I am, too," he whispered, nodding.

"I need to know something," she said, her eyes already pleading.

It would be the one thing he simply could not tell her. He was sure of it.

"What?" he asked, hearing the surrender in his voice.

"How can God, a good Heavenly Father who redeems our mistakes, love someone as messed up as me?" The tears fell now, spilling silently down her face.

Silas's heart hammered in his chest and throat.

"Does He love me that much?" she choked.

How? How had God brought her here—to this point—to these questions? It didn't matter, he supposed.

"*Jah*. He loves you even more than I do—more than I ever could." Silas swallowed, wiping away her tears with his calloused thumb. "Let's go talk about it."

⋅ೋ❀ೋ⋅

Silas led her to the workshop, which was quiet and empty. He pulled two stools close together, and they sat. He listened as she told him of her time away and the questions she'd asked herself, the passages she'd read and the conversations she'd had. Michael. Deborah. Even Deb.

God had orchestrated every single event—the time alone to think and read and process and question on her own, the seemingly random conversations that were exactly what she needed to hear at exactly the right time.

While Silas had been aching and questioning, God had been working and using nearly every opportunity to reach Kirsten. Silas's presence would have been an impediment.

"It was never so much about belief as it was trust," Kirsten said quietly, her hands folded in her lap. "And I couldn't love Him until I trusted Him."

Silas nodded.

"But I see now. I...trust His goodness. That He used all these bad things to bring me blessings. Grace. Your family. This life I've grown to love. And you," she finished quietly.

"Do you love Him now?"

"How could I not?" she answered, blinking.

He smiled into her eyes and felt a place open inside his chest.

"Have ya told Him?"

"I don't really know...how," she admitted.

Silas took her hands in his and bowed his head and prayed out loud, pouring out his heart, his thankfulness, love, and joy. Then Kirsten prayed her own informal, but heartfelt prayer, asking Jesus to live in her heart and show her more and more what it meant to live for Him.

Silas felt like laughing for joy when she said "Amen."

"Silas? Will you take me back to Michael's?"

The question suddenly froze him.

"To get my things. And our daughter." She smiled.

He nearly collapsed in relief. In record time, he had Titus hitched to the buggy. He lifted his wife inside, stopping only to kiss her soundly before snapping the reins.

꧁ ꧂

"If there ever was a time not to be sick..." Kirsten murmured to herself as she gripped the sides of the bathroom sink. "Stupid nerves. It's just a normal Sunday," she breathed. Evidently, she wasn't convincing herself. As her stomach rolled, she could hear him downstairs, waiting for her. She shoved away from the sink and forced herself upright.

"Are ya all right?" Silas asked in his familiar drawl when she reached the kitchen.

"Fine," she said a little too breathlessly. The truth was she was a mess of nerves. She hadn't felt this nervous since their wedding day.

"We should get going," he calmly observed, as though the meeting would start once they arrived.

How could he be so calm, so unaffected? This was the day—the day that could change absolutely everything or blissfully leave it as it had been for the past several months. Wordlessly, she followed him out to the buggy and got settled in the front seat with Grace in her lap. Silas tossed his black suit coat in the back and bounded up next to her.

"Not wearing your suit coat?" she asked, desperate for a distraction.

"I wouldn't want to get too hot," he smirked, driving the buggy down the lane.

"Too late," she replied dryly, which only made him laugh. Laugh! She couldn't even crack a smile.

Sensing her discomfort, Silas slid an arm around her and gently pulled her to his side. They'd made this trip so many times since the day Katie had been born. The first time Kirsten had met with the bishop for instruction, she'd been intimated. But Silas had stayed with her the whole time while she'd studied, and after the first few meetings, she found she genuinely liked the bishop. He had a kind, gentle way about him and never seemed to tire of her questions.

Silas, too, had been most patient. All the way home from instruction classes, she would grill him on what she'd learned. All of it in preparation for today.

"Shortest buggy ride ever," Kirsten sighed as Silas pulled into the bishop's lane. He huffed a laugh and threw on his jacket.

They were nearly late, and the benches lined up in the bright May sun were mostly full. Kirsten sank, gratefully but shakily, to a spot next to Amy. She spent the next two hours wishing the preacher would hurry up, only to panic when he sat down and the congregation sang a closing song.

The bishop stood then and smiled at Kirsten. She couldn't hear his words over the drumming pulse in her head, but she stood when Amy took Grace from her.

Robotically, she walked to the center where the bishop stood, still smiling. Just where she'd stood when she'd married the handsome young man sitting in the front row. She met Silas's eyes for only a brief moment; he was still calm, but serious.

Kirsten made herself focus on the bishop's words and answer his questions honestly and clearly. But the nerve-wracking part came after she had passed examination, when the bishop turned to the congregation and asked if anyone would witness for her. She watched Silas then, completely unable to look away. He stared into her eyes and then stood slowly—as though he had all the confidence in the world—never looking away from her. For a moment, they stood, eyes locked. Then in her peripheral, she saw Daniel stand, and Michael, and David. She turned to see Mary and Deborah with tiny Katie. Even Sarah. All standing.

Tears welled up in Kirsten's eyes and their faces blurred, though she'd caught their tender smiles. Her eyes swung back to Silas, whose own eyes were brimming with joy.

"What say you, congregation?" the bishop called loudly.

Kirsten could hear and see them rise from their benches, all standing in her favor. This was their vote then—that Kirsten Miller be welcomed into the fold of the Amish people. Her tears were still streaming when the baptismal water ran down her head and neck. Silas was there to steady her when she stood. The look on his face was one she'd never forget. Perfect peace.

⟿ ⟾

Daniels' laughter boomed loudly, bouncing off the walls of the big kitchen. It seemed all of the Millers felt a giddy lightness. Kirsten had thought the burden was all hers, but now she could see how they'd all carried a weight of not knowing what the future would hold. They'd always trusted God to work out His will for them, and now there was a joy in seeing His provision.

Silas, to her knowledge, had not stopped smiling since the water had rained down on her. Even now, several hours later, he was still jubilant.

"So. Are ya goin' to build a house now, brother?" Michael asked, smiling at Silas.

"*Jah*," Silas said with a nod. "We'll start in a couple of weeks, I hope."

"Wait...what?" Kirsten said, shaking her head.

"We love havin' ya here, but I think yer husband would like a home of yer own." Mary smiled as she moved past Kirsten, who was standing motionless in the center of the kitchen.

"Where? Where will it be?" Her words came out hysterical and high-pitched. Part of her wanted that house to call her own and another part of her didn't want to be separated from them. And it was nearly incomprehensible that they were discussing building a new house for her. She could almost count on one hand how many new things she'd ever had. And now this. She felt as though they must be talking about someone else—some new Amish bride—not her. Surely not her. There had to be some limit to the goodness of this life. She lifted her blurry gaze from the floorboards to find everyone watching her, their faces worried over her panic-stricken face.

"I have some land," Silas said quietly, crossing the room and standing in front of her.

"You do?"

He nodded.

"It's a *gut* spot." Michael smiled mischievously.

"The abandoned farmstead west of David's place," Silas said, the grin faintly returning.

"Where you proposed?" Kirsten said, stunned.

He nodded, smiling broadly now.

"The kissing corner?" she pressed incredulously.

More nodding.

Kirsten spun to look at Michael. "But you said—" she accused him.

"I said a *gut* family owned it," Michael argued with a laugh.

"Oh!" she paused to let it all sink further in. Silas was still studying her. "It's the perfect spot." She finally smiled, a winning, brilliant smile for her husband.

"Can you have it finished by February?"

She watched his brow furrow briefly in confusion.

"*Jah*. We'll be in by this fall, I think," he answered.

"How many bedrooms?"

"How many do ya want?" he asked with a crooked smile.

"Many. But definitely a pale pink room for Grace and a sunny, yellow room for the baby."

"The baby," he whispered as his eyes searched her face.

Kirsten nodded, smiling softly.

"A baby!" He smiled and slid his arms around her waist, pulling her against his hard chest.

"God has blessed us again," she said with a smile. The joy on his face made tears sting past her eyes and fall on her cheeks. She'd taken the test in her mom's apartment while visiting few days prior. Of course she'd cried, just like the last time. But this time, she'd cried with a smile on her face. And last time, the father of the life within her hadn't picked her up and gently swung her around, as the father of this baby did now.

Her laughter bubbled up through her with her joy. She'd found her place—not just here in Silas's arms, but in this love that was beyond her heart's comprehension. She could see now so clearly how God had loved her all along—always there in all the dark days and every happy smile. He always would be. And now, when she looked for evidence of Him, she could see He was everywhere, revealing Himself in every gift of His goodness. Strangely, even painful times bore His gentle leading and preparation. God had worked through it and in spite of it all.

These people surrounding her were proof, as was this man still beaming at her, the little girl tugging on her Grandpa Daniel's beard, and the life within her.

Her life had changed drastically when her father died, even more drastically when Grace came to life inside her. All of it—every hill and valley—had brought her to know Him. Silas had been the one to point her in the right direction, though he'd never pushed. Silas, ever patient, had waited for her to find her way home, to his heart and to God's.

Though by the look on his face now, she was sure that waiting to meet this new one in February would test that steady patience.

"Grace, yer gonna be a big sister!" Silas smiled, scooping her up and bouncing her in his strong arms. Grace squealed and grabbed fistfuls of Silas's shirt. He smiled down at her and then at Kirsten.

Kirsten wrapped a hand around Silas's bicep. Grace reached out for her and Kirsten lifted her into her arms, feeling Silas's arms sliding around them both. She sighed and pressed her cheek against Grace's forehead.

God's grace surrounded her, just as surely as Silas's arms were wrapped tightly around her and their children. Kirsten was suddenly glad she couldn't go back and undo past mistakes. If given the chance, she would have written her story differently. But then she would have missed so much. The Lord's ways were certainly better, and His grace knew no peak or valley too great.

Grace had surely changed everything.

— Epilogue —

The early evening breeze blew through the budding trees, swirling her skirt against her bare legs. Kirsten inhaled deeply. The pungent smell of freshly turned soil was thick in the air. Silas had spent the afternoon turning the soil in the small garden across the driveway. Kirsten could see David off to the east in the field, busy with planting. Sarah was due to have another baby any day now.

The life of Kirsten's children would differ starkly from her own. Whereas she'd grown up an only child with no close family other than her mother, Grace and Benjamin would have a childhood full of cousins, aunts, uncles, and grandparents—not to mention a community of plain people. Most notably of course, they would have a fantastic father.

Grace giggled as little Benjamin attempted to eat the rubber ball that she had rolled across the soft green grass to her baby brother. Kirsten smoothed out the old quilt where she and her son sat in the fading sunlight while Grace danced around the yard.

The sound of an approaching horse and buggy made Kirsten lift her head, a knowing smile already on her face. As the rig neared, she could see him sitting tall, but relaxed, his straw hat low on his head to shield against the setting sun.

Grace and Benjamin snapped to attention as the buggy pulled into their short driveway. Kirsten beamed when she saw Silas's brilliant smile at seeing his little ones. He waved at Grace but pulled right into the barn to unhitch Titus and close up the barn for the night.

At the sound of the door rolling shut, Kirsten looked up to see Silas crossing the side yard. How was it possible that he was even more handsome now than he'd been when they'd met? He still took her breath away.

Grace squealed and ran across the grass with her arms lifted high over her head. Silas bent low to catch her, tossing her high over his head but never releasing his grasp on her.

Lifting Benjamin to her hip, Kirsten stood by the steps leading up to the wrap-around porch. Silas came near and laid his large hand on Benjamin's beautiful blond curls—so like each other, those two. After a tender smile at his son, he turned his warm eyes on Kirsten. He bent and placed a lingering kiss on her cheek. She blushed and didn't even attempt to fight it.

"Mom said yer pie was *gut*." He grinned at her.

"Is she feeling better?" Kirsten asked, concern etching her face.

"*Jah*. She's much better today. Just needed some rest," he reassured her with a nod.

They went into the house and spent an hour tucking in their little ones. Kirsten showered quickly while Silas listened for the children. She came downstairs to find him staring out the large bank of windows by the enormous dining table he'd made just weeks after Benjamin was born.

He turned when he heard her behind him, and Kirsten could see his Bible tucked under his arm. There was no need to speak. For months, they'd been enjoying the evenings on the wide porch, snuggled together on the swing Silas had built and installed when they'd moved in just a month and a half before Benjamin had arrived. How he'd found the time to make it, she still didn't know.

The summer had been so busy with the normal activities of managing the garden and the occasional furniture project, not to mention his near constant need to oversee the construction of their home. Of course, the whole Miller family had stepped up to help, but the burden had largely fallen on Silas's broad shoulders. True to form, he'd never complained and rarely seemed weary. After a long week of work and swarms of visiting Amish friends and family, their home had risen on the very spot where

Silas had proposed. Slowly, over the long winter months, furniture pieces handcrafted in the back of the old barn had made their way into their house.

Of course, when Benjamin was born, all of Silas's attention was focused on his family. He'd been with her through the labor and delivery this time. When that familiar, squeaky wail had filled the room and the doctor had announced that they had a son, they had both cried.

Kirsten had wondered if Silas would feel differently toward this child—his flesh and blood. Though she never doubted his love for Grace or questioned his attentive care and affection for his adopted daughter, part of her could understand if this time would be different. And perhaps it was different—but not in the way she'd worried. It was clear he did not love Benjamin any more or any less than Grace.

Silas followed Kirsten to the swing and they sat close, the quilt nearby in case of a cool breeze. Kirsten drew her feet up and tucked herself beneath his arm, sitting snugly against his side. Silas's long legs gently pushed against the floor, setting the swing in motion.

On the cold winter nights, they'd spent these quiet times in the front room on the brown leather couch. But they had been eager for the warmer weather of spring and had missed very few evenings together on the swing. Kirsten was sure this would always be their own special tradition of sorts—a part of their daily routine.

For a long while, they simply sat and enjoyed the sounds of their farm, Silas's Bible on his lap and his arm pulling her tight against him. Kirsten closed her eyes and focused on the rise and fall of his slow breathing. He had become so familiar, and yet there was a part of her that always marveled at their union. It was as unlikely as any she'd ever heard, but it had taken shape and meaning in God's own perfect handwriting. What had at times seemed like a marred and painfully chipped-away life, she could now see as a wonderfully carved piece of craftsmanship. Surely Silas had always trusted the Master Carpenter, and his quiet faithfulness had shown Kirsten that the painful etching was necessary to see the glory beneath the surface.

She sighed deeply, pushing harder into his side.

"Are ya cold?" His voice still captivated her.

"No," she answered. "Just thinking how very glad I am to be a part of your story." She tilted her face up to his and lingeringly brushed her lips on his.

"I should read before it gets too dark." He smiled softly, eventually pulling away. Kirsten smiled and nodded. He flipped his Bible open, and she wondered briefly how he'd ever be able to make out the words.

"Psalm 23," he said.

She smiled, knowing he knew this one by heart.

> "The Lord is my shepherd, I lack nothing. He makes me lie down in green pastures, he leads me beside quiet waters, he refreshes my soul. He guides me along the right paths for his name's sake. Even though I walk through the valley of the shadow of death, I will fear no evil, for you are with me; your rod and your staff, they comfort me. You prepare a table before me in the presence of my enemies. You anoint my head with oil; my cup overflows. Surely goodness and love will follow me all the days of my life, and I will dwell in the house of the Lord. Forever."

CPSIA information can be obtained
at www.ICGtesting.com
Printed in the USA
FFOW04n1104140117
31220FF